"In this absorbing, bighearted novel, Holly Robinson explores sibling bonds, love in middle age, and the intricate dance of a blended family. The painful past is everywhere in *Beach Plum Island*, but the present moment shines through." —Elizabeth Graver, author of *The End of the Point*

"In *Beach Plum Island*, Holly Robinson's rich details transport you to picturesque New England and right into the core of the conflicted Barrett family. Robinson tugs at your emotions from the viewpoint of the three complex and very different Barrett sisters, through whom the author deftly explores grief, secrets, and shunned family ties. This story reveals the way people become stronger when they are together rather than apart, and proves that it is never too late to become a family. *Beach Plum Island* is a triumphant family saga filled with heart and hope. I couldn't put it down!" —Amy Sue Nathan, author of *The Glass Wives*

"Holly Robinson is a natural-born storyteller and her tale of three mismatched sisters and the lost brother they search for will keep you turning those pages as she quietly but deftly breaks your heart. I loved every single one of her characters and you will too; here is a novel to savor and share." —Yona Zeldis McDonough, author of *Two of a Kind*

*continued . . .*

Written by today's freshest new talents and selected by New American Library, NAL Accent novels touch on subjects close to a woman's heart, from friendship to family to finding our place in the world. The Conversation Guides included in each book are intended to enrich the individual reading experience, as well as encourage us to explore these topics together—because books, and life, are meant for sharing.

Visit us online at www.penguin.com.

"Robinson masterfully paints the portrait of a damaged family in the quake of a tragedy, struggling to put the pieces back together again. Each sister is sensitively drawn, their individual dramas meticulously rendered. This novel is a thoughtful exploration of the fragility, and the tenacity, of the ties that bind."          —T. Greenwood, author of *Bodies of Water*

# The Wishing Hill

"One of the deep pleasures of *The Wishing Hill* is Holly Robinson's keen sense of story. Another is her willingness to give all her characters, young and old, second chances. I loved reading about Juliet and how she and her family invent and reinvent themselves as they struggle to reconcile past and present. Many readers will surely glimpse themselves in this vivid, compassionate novel."

—Margot Livesey, author of *The Flight of Gemma Hardy*

"Who and what makes us who we really are? In Robinson's luminous novel of buried secrets, she explores how the past can jump-start the future, how motherhood can be more than genetics, and why finding yourself sometimes depends on discovering the truth in others."

—Caroline Leavitt, *New York Times* bestselling author of
*Is This Tomorrow*

"A novel that sings: of love for a child, loss and regret for a life, and the quiet triumphs of survival and finding each other again."
—Susan Straight, National Book Award nominee for *Highwire Moon*
and author of *Between Heaven and Here*

"A story about love, loss, secrets, and finding out where we're really supposed to be in our lives. As Juliet navigates the terrain of divorce, pregnancy, and exploring new love, her greatest gift comes from a place she never expected to find it: revisiting her unsettled past. I loved this book."          —Maddie Dawson, author of *The Stuff That Never Happened*

ALSO BY HOLLY ROBINSON

*The Wishing Hill*

# BEACH PLUM ISLAND

## HOLLY ROBINSON

NAL Accent
Published by the Penguin Group
Penguin Group (USA) LLC, 375 Hudson Street,
New York, New York 10014

USA | Canada | UK | Ireland | Australia /|New Zealand | India | South Africa | China
penguin.com
A Penguin Random House Company

First published by NAL Accent, an imprint of New American Library,
a division of Penguin Group (USA) LLC

First Printing, April 2014

 REGISTERED TRADEMARK—MARCA REGISTRADA

LIBRARY OF CONGRESS CATALOGING-IN-PUBLICATION DATA:
Robinson, Holly, 1955–
Beach Plum island/Holly Robinson.
p. cm.
ISBN 978-0-451-24102-3 (pbk.)
1. Family secrets—Fiction. 2. Fathers and daughters—Fiction.
3. Brothers and sisters—Fiction. 4. Domestic fiction. I. Title.
PS3618.O3258B43 2014
813'.6—dc23          2013037398

Printed in the United States of America
1   3   5   7   9   10   8   6   4   2

Set in Adobe Caslon Pro
Designed by Elke Sigal

*For my husband, Dan, and for our children,*
*Drew, Blaise, Taylor, Maya, and Aidan.*
*You are my everything.*

*And for my mother,*
*who tells better stories than anyone else I know.*

# PHANTOM

*Plum Island, a wild and fantastical sand beach, is thrown up
by the joint power of winds and waves into the thousand
wanton figures of a snow drift.*

—JOSHUA COFFIN, 1845

Black backed gulls stare wall-eyed
    at a place
        where beach plums once crowned dunes, part
    river's bottom,
part sea's.
Here, time
  elapses tide by tide, the Atlantic
part Arctic, part appetite. This is what's left: ice age
 water, winds that curl
        ghost dunes until they crest into waves atop
    which teeter—
dining rooms, a chaise lounge.
So you thought you could stay?
     A barrier island's function is change;
        the sea—the current's yeoman, the
    implacable sculptor—
ferries sand north to south.
Twleve thousand years, you think, is tide enough for art.
    But the moon—part light, part
        master—summons its shore and leaves

the sand pockmarked by filter feeders,
    sets the gulls aloft.
In this world, part wind, part waves, the fanciful
        is hope, phantom-like
the insistence
of your own ornamentations.


—CARLA PANCIERA,
    ORIGINALLY PUBLISHED IN *The Carolina Quarterly*

# BEACH PLUM ISLAND

# CHAPTER ONE

A walk, first, to clear her head. Then she'd call her sister again. She wasn't going to give up until she'd convinced Elaine to do the right thing.

Ava Barrett stepped outside her pottery studio and saw that last night's wind had scoured the beach clean. The June sky was a day-dreamer's blue and a pair of white egrets picked their way along the water's edge. School had only been out a week and the tourists hadn't yet descended; the beach was blissfully empty. She headed south, walking fast on the hard, cold-packed sand. It felt good to move after working all morning. Summers, she liked to put in a few hours in her pottery studio before the boys woke up and shattered her concentration.

By the time she returned to the cottage it was noon, the best time of day to call Elaine, who typically spent lunch hours holed up in her Boston office with a salad. At thirty-six, her sister was still single and a workaholic, the sort of woman who texted even on the beach.

Elaine answered on the first ring, as breathless and abrupt as always. "Yes?"

"Please don't hang up," Ava said.

"Then don't tempt me. I've already told you three times! I'm not coming to Dad's service."

"You don't have a choice."

"Of course I have a choice," Elaine said. "You've given me your reasons. I've listened to them. And now I'm making my choice."

The wind had picked up and it was difficult to hear Elaine over the surf; Ava retreated back into the studio. "But it's the wrong choice. Even if I forgive you for not going, you'll never forgive yourself."

"What's the point?" Elaine said. "Dad didn't even know who we were at the end, and it's not even him they're putting in the ground. Just a box of ashes, most of which probably aren't his. You know what they say about cremations. Besides, the best thing about Dad dying is that we're done pretending. We never have to see those people again."

By "those people," Ava knew Elaine meant their father's second wife, Katy, and their half sister, Gigi. "We should both be there. Who else will show up from Dad's side, if not us? Everyone else in his family is gone. And you know he didn't have any friends."

"Gosh, I'm sorry, but whose fault was that? Anyway, I certainly don't have the time or patience to stand around watching Katy fake-cry."

"What makes you think she'd be faking?"

"Oh, come on, Ava! You can't honestly still believe Katy was really in love with Dad. That makes no sense. She's younger than I am."

"Since when did love ever make sense?"

"I am not getting into this with you now," Elaine said, "and I'm certainly not showing up at some trumped-up service."

"I really think you'll regret not being there."

"God! You're relentless! Why is this so important to you?" Elaine demanded.

"Does it matter why? It's important to me. Can't that be enough?" By the brief hesitation on the phone, Ava sensed her sister wavering. She quickly pressed her advantage. "And what will the boys think, if you're not there? What would I tell Evan and Sam about their aunt skipping their grandfather's funeral?"

"Goddamn it." Elaine sighed. "All right. *Fine.* I'll be there. Just don't expect me to wear black." She hung up.

Ava slid the phone into the pocket of her overalls, sat down at her pottery wheel, and smacked a ball of clay onto the metal head. If only relationships were like clay. Even if you made something out of clay that dried out and shattered into crumbs, you could always, with the right amount of water and heat and wedging, recycle the scraps and re-form the clay into something new.

She braced both elbows on her knees to center the clay on the wheel. She had ten more pitchers to make this morning if she was going to fill the order for that new client in Portsmouth on time.

Ordinarily, she loved making pitchers. Some stood straight, while others curved outward from a tapered waist. She liked to think of her pitchers as women in long, flowing skirts. But now her focus was fractured by thoughts of her father. Every pot collapsed, the cylinders folding in on themselves as she thinned the walls. Her clay bucket filled with scraps.

*I want your brother to know the truth.* Those were her father's cryptic last words before he died.

Katy had left the hospital to pick Gigi up from camp, so Ava was the only one with him at the time. Her father—a big man with a strong jaw, protruding ears, and hands like mitts—had shrunk to doll size, his husk of a body deflated on the hospital bed beneath the white sheet. His death was peaceful. No evident pain, just a fluttering of papery lavender eyelids and then a sigh that went on so long, it was as if her father were exhaling every last atom of his being into the atmosphere as he moved on to mingle with the dust motes and water droplets.

Now Ava was left puzzling over his last words: *I want your brother to know the truth.* She didn't even *have* a brother, so how could she tell him anything?

And what was the truth?

Gigi hadn't meant to say yes. It had just happened.

Justin went to her prep school and lived in Ipswich, two towns over. When she posted that thing on Facebook about her dad dying, he'd texted *what a fn drag.*

Surprised, she'd texted back to say thanks, and he'd replied, *hey, we're tying our boat up in Nbt Fri, big ass boat, come see.* Then he'd sent another text saying his parents were going out for breakfast. *Come early to miss em.*

Justin wasn't hot or anything, with his skinny goose neck and zits. But he'd graduated this spring, and that automatically made him cooler than she was; she'd just finished freshman year. Plus, he had a nice car and was MVP on the varsity baseball team.

So Gigi rode her bike from her house on Newburyport's High Street down to the docks along the city's waterfront park and found *The Last Hurrah.* The boat was ginormous. Justin had a tan already and was friendlier than at school, maybe because nobody else was around. "Sucks about your dad," he said once she'd climbed into the boat.

Her eyes brimmed, but Gigi pretended to admire the brass steering wheel. "Yeah. Totally."

Justin gave her some kind of iced tea his mom always drank.

Then they sat not looking at each other, watching the seagulls wheel around over their heads while they talked about the weirdness of being in a prep school where everybody knew your name and had this idea of you. At least going to college meant you could finally leave all that stuff behind.

"I'm going to reinvent myself," Justin said.

"As what?" Gigi honestly wanted to know.

"As a guy who makes things happen."

She had no idea what this meant, but Justin seemed ready to make things happen right now, before his parents returned from their eggs Benedict and Bloody Marys. He took her downstairs into a cabin with a kitchen and a bathroom so narrow she practically had to stand up to pee. When she came out, he kissed her and ran his hands over her breasts, tugging on her nipples before unzipping her jeans. Once he'd yanked her jeans down to her ankles, he stopped to politely ask Gigi "permission to enter," as if he were a lowly peasant and she were guarding a castle or something.

She was both too flattered and too embarrassed to say no. After all, she wasn't a virgin. There had been a boy after the winter semiformal, at a party where she had been drinking and made the woozy decision to eliminate virginity from the long, boring list of things she felt anxious about.

"Sure, I guess," she said.

Justin sat on one of the bench seats, pulled her down on top of him, and raised her shirt, prodding his way inside her at the same time even though her ankles were still trapped in her jeans. At that point, Gigi realized she didn't want to be here at all, doing this.

She became acutely aware of the dappled shadows of the water reflecting on the round cabin windows, the stink of fuel mixed with fishy air, and the screams of the seagulls outside. More than anything, she wanted Justin to finish his damp heavy breathing. He sounded like her grandmother's dying cairn terrier. That dog was like ninety-six in people years.

When it was over, they did that A-frame kind of hug and Justin said, "You're a sweet kid. Have a great summer. Text me if you're ever in Amherst and want a tour of campus."

Then she'd ridden off on her bike, pedaling fast to make it to camp before the instructor called her mother to ask where she was.

It took her twenty minutes to ride from Newburyport's waterfront to the stables. She followed Route 1A, the winding shore road that paralleled Route 1 between Newburyport and Boston, forty miles south of here. She hugged the shoulder now that the commuter cars were zooming by with their hoods and bumpers gleaming in the sun, the drivers already fierce looking as they woke up and began their days, mouths pursed around travel mugs or moving as they talked into headsets, getting work done as they drove, or who knows, maybe fighting already with their lovers, wives, husbands, kids. Their oversized sunglasses made the commuters look like a race of insects, drone bees or maybe worker ants on wheels.

It was hot and humid, too hot to be biking. Gigi felt sick to her stomach, but forced herself to pump hard on the pedals, wondering if the drivers in those cars could tell what she'd done by looking at her. She could still smell boat fuel and fish; she hoped that wouldn't be what she thought of from now on, if she ever did have sex for real. Sex that mattered.

Gigi went through the rest of the day in a coma. She hated riding camp, where her stupid instructor was always yelling things like "Heels down, back straight, post on the diagonal!" in that nasal voice of hers.

The only decent part about camp was being alone with the horses in the barn. Gigi loved the way the animals flickered their ears in some secret horse Morse code, and how their muzzles felt like velvet, the nostrils coin-sized and damp against her palm as they searched for carrot nubs. The horses sought out her company, snorting when they saw her and hanging their heads over the stalls to nod hello when she called their names.

When she rode in the riding ring during lessons, though, Gigi lost her connection to them. She hated forcing the metal bit into their soft trusting mouths, imagining how that steel bar would feel tugging at the corners of her own mouth while some moron slapped her with a crop to make her jump over a stupid striped piece of wood, when she'd rather roll in a dusty paddock or nibble on grass.

At least Mom wasn't teaching here this summer. Before Dad got sick, Mom was a royal pain, practically living at the barn and always checking in with the other instructors to find out how Gigi's posting trot was coming along or whatever. Such a drag, having a mom who was hotter than you, as too many boys had told Gigi, and a former Junior Olympian, too, one of those fearless riders who could command show jumpers to hurdle seven-foot brick walls like they were wading through puddles.

Mom wanted to turn her into a "real" horsewoman, but all Gigi wanted was to watch the horses cantering in the pastures, tails high and flowing like fountains. She enjoyed riding the trails, too, and discovering hidden groves of ferns deep in the woods, or tall trees with violets making bruised carpets around the trunks.

Dad had understood this. He had loved the same things about horses she did. He'd tried to argue with her mother, saying, "The girl just wants to bop around on a horse. Why force her into the show ring if she doesn't want to be there, Katherine?" But Mom always won. Dad had trouble saying no to anything she wanted.

Thinking about Dad now made Gigi huddle in the tack room, where she pretended to be searching for a currycomb in one of the boxes. She was crying and her nose was running; she wiped her face with one hand and then rubbed her hand on her jeans. She was supposed to curry her horse after each ride; this was another part of camp she enjoyed, unlike the other girls, who were always ready to rush out of the barn and go to the beach or whatever. She wasn't like them, these country-club girls with the swinging hair, the girls who magically knew which phone apps were cool and what jeans to wear.

Her father hadn't ever really belonged here at the club, either. Not because Dad was too old—lots of women at the club were married to men older than they were, just like her mom—but because of more mysterious reasons. Gigi hadn't completely worked these out yet, but she thought they might have something to do with Dad not being Ivy League or having "real money," as Gramma Dawn called it.

Whatever. It didn't matter what anybody else thought of Dad. Gigi had adored him. They went trail riding together. They had fierce checkers matches and tennis games, and she had loved going into her father's study after dinner while he read the paper and Gigi did her homework. She loved to lie on the sofa in his office with her head on his knee, comforted by the sound of her father's ticking watch near her ear.

Her father told her things even Mom didn't know. "Your mother is a delicate flower," Dad always said. "You and me, we're tough as weeds. People can cut us down, but we'll always come back stronger."

At the end, he hadn't acted like a father. He was more like a friend. Dad listened to her talk instead of always telling her what to do. He gave her books he'd loved as a kid and they shared a secret obsession: rock music. Sometimes he'd get out his old CDs and they'd sing to the Rolling Stones and Aerosmith, the Who and Pink Floyd. "Timeless classics," he called them. "Like us."

Gigi found the currycomb but stayed bent over, her hand in the tack box, rummaging for nothing, while the other girls passed, giggling on their way out of the barn. Her father had been her best friend, and now he was gone. But she knew some of his secrets, secrets so big that it felt like her skin might split wide open trying to keep them inside.

It was a simple graveside ceremony. The polished wooden box containing the ashes was supported on a wrought iron stand that to Ava looked suspiciously like one of the plant stands from her father's office at the bank. The Episcopalian minister was a pudding-faced man whose belly strained his black shirt. He spoke about their father's devotion to his work; to his daughters Ava and Elaine; and to his second family, Katy and Gigi.

"Robert Barrett was a man who clearly loved his community and the women in his life," the minister said. "He had found a way to be happy in a world where happiness is a choice, not a guarantee. His illness may have defeated his body, but his spirit was whole and joyful."

There was more, of course, but Ava stopped paying attention. She was distracted by a cardinal, a scarlet teardrop caught on a branch of the pine tree shading the grave, and by the minister's implication that it was a good idea for Dad to divorce their mother, Suzanne, and start his life over with Katy.

Was it? Was her father's spirit "whole and joyful" at the end of his life? She hoped so.

Truthfully, she had expected her parents to splinter sooner than they did. As a teenager, she had even pleaded with them to separate; she was so sick of the constant bickering. But they'd stayed locked in a well-choreographed battle that alternated periods of icy silence with fiery arguments.

Then Bob had done the impossible: he had set himself free of his scripted, methodical life by taking horseback-riding lessons, something he later told Ava he'd always wanted to try as a boy. Six months later, he was living with Katy, his young blond riding instructor.

As the minister said the final prayer, Ava bowed her head and tried to take her mind off the hot fist of sun on her neck. Her sons towered on either side of her, both wearing cast-off suits from her ex-husband that didn't quite fit, reminding her of knobby-kneed giraffes itching to nose through trees or canter through the cemetery. Anything but stand still.

Evan and Sam were blonder than she was, but both had their father's dark eyes. They were sixteen and seventeen years old, nearly inseparable. Most people thought they were twins until Sam shot up a good two inches last year. Her sons shared clothes, video games, food, and even, once, disastrously, a girlfriend. Their easy camaraderie always surprised Ava, since she and Elaine had such a contentious relationship despite being five years apart.

Ava glanced over at her sister. She half expected Elaine to be texting during the ceremony, but her head was bowed and her eyes were squeezed shut. Elaine was as dark-haired and angular as their mother had been. Like their mother, too, Elaine was the sort of woman who looked elegant even in sweats and a T-shirt because of her sharply planed features, long legs, and creamy complexion. As promised, she hadn't worn black to the service, but a broad-brimmed straw hat and a teal sleeveless sheath that showed off her toned arms. She looked like the First Lady of some small European country.

Katy stood next to the minister, dressed in a severe black dress and short black veil, her straight blond hair done up in a French twist that only made her look younger and more vulnerable. The rest of the crowd was made up of Katy's friends and family. They were amiable, horsey-looking people with strong chins and good manners. It still amazed Ava that Dad had considered these people his family. But here it was, yet more evidence that she'd hardly known him toward the end of his life.

The only person who looked as out of place here as she and Elaine did was her half sister. Ava wouldn't have guessed who it was if Gigi hadn't been standing next to Katy. The last time she'd seen her, Gigi was a blond, doughy middle schooler with a precocious vocabulary. Now she was skinny and sullen-looking, taller than her mother. She looked like a punk superhero, with her short hair dyed marine blue, heavy black eyeliner, and defiant piercings in her nose, lip, and eyebrow. Her earrings looked like fish lures, bright blue feathers that dangled to her shoulders, and Gigi wore black in her own way: combat boots, ripped fishnets, and a sleeveless black dress that hung from her narrow shoulders like a cape.

Ava was startled out of her reverie by the sudden movements of her sons, who abruptly began jogging toward the car. The service was over. She hurried to catch up, wishing she'd worn a different pair of shoes. She wasn't used to heels and she was so wobbly from the heat that the sidewalk felt like it was wriggling beneath her.

Evan and Sam played a Red Hot Chili Peppers CD in the car, arguing over whether the old guitarist or the new one was better. Ava was so used to their heated debates that she knew this wasn't fighting, just the way boys talked.

She loved listening to her sons because they were insatiably curious about subjects that might never cross her mind: "Mom, did you know that more people die every year from having vending machines fall on them than from shark attacks?" "Did you know that lobsters pee out of their heads?" She just wished they didn't always devolve into farting and belching when she was trapped in the car with them.

The circular driveway of Katy's house was jammed with gleaming Mercedes sedans in various colors and styles. Some member of Katy's family must own a dealership. Elaine had parked her red BMW right in the middle of them, where it stuck out like a clown's nose. Ava chose to leave her green Honda on the street and walk up the driveway instead.

As always, it was odd to approach the house that had once been their childhood home, an elegant three-story white Federalist, square-shouldered and stern looking with its flat roof and rows of tiny windows, up the formal front walk instead of just letting herself in through the side porch as she had done throughout her childhood.

At the front door, Ava had to force herself to ring the bell, because her impulse was to fling it open as if she might surprise her own mother inside. This thought made her so queasy with grief, she had to steady herself on the wrought iron railing.

Katy's mother greeted her. Dawn Talbot was in her sixties, a delicate woman with Katy's gray eyes and fine, even features. The few times they'd met at awkward family parties, Ava had always thought she was beautiful, but now Dawn's fair skin was lined and papery, her features startlingly asymmetrical. Her quizzical expression seemed permanently stitched into place, like a scarecrow someone had put together in a hurry.

As they lightly embraced, Ava remembered that Dawn had suffered a stroke last year and was still recovering. This didn't seem like the right time to say anything about it; Dawn was exclaiming over how much Sam and Evan had grown and how handsome they were. Ava was relieved to see that the boys shook hands gracefully and weren't horsing around in the hallway. She wondered, not for the first time, what Dawn had thought about her daughter marrying a man so much older. It must have been a horrible shock. As a mother, she must have imagined this very scene: Katy nursing a sick old man and ending up a widow and single mother in her thirties.

"I'm so very sorry for your loss, dear," Dawn said. "Such a tragedy for everyone."

"Thank you," Ava said. "Please accept my condolences as well. I know my father loved being part of your family."

"He will certainly be missed," Dawn said, bowing her head.

Dawn sounded sincere. On the other hand, this woman was clearly accustomed to navigating social situations—she was already ushering the waiter toward Ava with his tray of wineglasses—so sincerity would be a natural stance for her to assume.

Above Dawn's shoulder, Ava caught a glimpse of her own reflection in the gilt-edged mirror hanging over the hall table. Her face was pale, her green eyes enormous, her lipstick too dark. Her hair was an afterthought, carelessly arranged around her shoulders like a shawl in loose tawny curls. She was a mess. Everything about her was coming undone.

She declined the wine and walked down the hallway with her sons so close behind her that one of them stepped on her heel. The hall had been redecorated since she was last here. The bird wallpaper her mother had put up was gone; now the walls were pale blue and the trim was stark white.

Ava swallowed past a hard lump in her throat and continued down the hall. Most of the family was gathered out back. Katy had created an impressive garden here, separated by stone knee walls and crushed gravel paths. There were perennial beds, a cutting garden, and several elaborate twig arbors; everything had been obsessively trimmed and pruned, with bark mulch raked up to the neck of every stem. Not a weed or wandering border in sight.

Evan and Sam darted ahead, probably intent on finding food to fill their hollow legs. Most of the crowd had retreated to the shady corners of the lawn. Ava didn't have the stomach to smile and min-gle. She looked for Elaine and found her with a glass of white wine in her hand and a defiant look in her eyes. Her sister was standing alone in the hot sun next to a Japanese garden with a little stone footbridge.

"So. Was it as good for you as it was for me?" Elaine asked.

Ava laughed, then swallowed the laughter as a few people glanced their way. Of course they would; Katy's family and friends must all be wondering about them, these two daughters of Bob's, both older than their own stepmother. It wouldn't do to create a scene, but she could see in Elaine's eyes that her sister had every in-tention of making one.

"Don't," Ava said.

"Don't what?" Elaine widened her brown eyes and signaled to a waiter to bring her another glass of wine.

When the waiter, hardly older than Sam, scurried across the hot stone patio to her, Elaine grabbed two glasses. She downed one of them fast enough to tap the retreating boy on his bony shoulder and return the glass to him. With her sweetest smile, she quickly plucked another glass off the tray and said, "Come back soon. I'll be waiting for you right here."

The boy smiled at her, dazzled, then retreated to the kitchen.

"Please don't," Ava repeated.

"Don't what?"

"Don't do whatever it is you're thinking of doing or saying!"

Elaine swirled the wine in her glass. "Katy should have at least bought something better for us to imbibe on this somber occasion than such a pedestrian chardonnay, don't you think?"

"I'm guessing her mother planned the party," Ava said, fasci-nated but alarmed by the shifting emotions passing like shadows across her sister's pale face.

"Me, too." Elaine took another swallow. "Wow, coming back to this house is a shock, isn't it? I was thinking about our last Christmas here with Mom, before she freaked out and hoofed it back to Maine. I remember I was stressed about some online class I was taking."

Ava smiled. "You were always stressed. You still are."

"So true. Type A plus, that's *moi*. Anyway, *that* sorry little Christmas, I remember getting royally pissed off because Mom gave us clothes she'd bought at Salvation Army."

Ava squinted into the sunlight. The heat was making it difficult to think. "That's right. Mom gave me this awful pink sweatshirt with kittens on it. It didn't make any sense. Mom must have gotten half of everything. I always wondered what she did with it all."

"Who knows?" Elaine waved a hand. "Mom never was a details person. Anyway, the other thing I remember about that Christmas was our leftover tree."

Ava laughed. "God, that's right. The man at the gas station felt so sorry for us when you told him our mom couldn't afford a tree, he just gave you one, right?"

"Yes," Elaine said. "And we spent hours collecting seashells on the beach and making ornaments out of them with paint and glitter, remember? Then we drilled holes in them and hung them all over the tree with bread ties. Mom always saved those stupid bread ties."

"She was kind of a hoarder. Especially at the end."

"Because Dad drove her crazy," Elaine said, and swallowed the rest of her wine. She signaled to another waiter, a girl this time, and plucked a fresh glass of wine off the tray. "These people probably don't have any idea what sort of man he really was."

"Stop it," Ava said. "Mom was the way she was. So was Dad. Lots of marriages don't make it. Mom and Dad did the best they could. Don't torture yourself about the past. Or Katy," she added, following Elaine's dark gaze, focused now on Katy's slight figure in the shade. "Let's say our good-byes and go. We've done what we came to do."

"Maybe you have, but I haven't." Elaine crossed the patio to the buffet table and picked up a fork. She clinked the fork on the wineglass so hard that Ava was afraid it might shatter. When everyone was staring at her, she said, "I'd like to propose a toast to my dear old dad."

"Elaine, no," Ava hissed, wishing she could disappear behind one of the pine trees.

"Our father was a mystery man," Elaine said loudly, raising her glass. "He married our mother right out of high school and worked hard all his life, climbing the ladder of success so fast, we never really knew which rung he was on until he'd reached the top. He was so high up we couldn't see him anymore. Meanwhile, our mother kept house and tried to keep up with us, sometimes successfully, sometimes not."

Elaine was swaying a little. "You must truly be something special, Katy, to coax our father home every night. You must have cast some kind of magic spell to make him take off weekends and go riding with you, to get him to Gigi's birthday parties and all those holiday dinners. So I propose a toast not only to our father, the mystery man, but also to you, Katy. May you prosper now in what was once our family's *almost* happy home."

Elaine lifted her empty glass. "*Salud!*" she cried, and then she was crying for real, her face splotched with red. She dropped the wineglass, shattering it on the patio, and ran for the garden gate, her straw hat flying off behind her.

Ava ran after her, but Elaine was through the gate before she got there, then spinning away in her red BMW, charging straight across the lawn, her car tires carving deep grooves in the grass. Ava heard the scrape of the car's underbelly as her sister hurtled over the sidewalk and down the curb, then a screech of tires as she sped away.

"Was that Aunt Elaine?" Sam and Evan had followed and were standing on either side of her again. It occurred to Ava that her sons had been following her around all day and trying to protect her like a pair of loyal guard dogs, bless them.

"Yes," she said, "I'm afraid so."

"Wow. That was so fucking cool," Sam said. "She almost took out that bush."

"And did you hear those tires?" Evan said. "She must have been doing, like, sixty miles an hour when she hit the street. That was fucking epic!"

"Don't say 'like,'" Ava said automatically. "And please don't swear around your mother."

"So are we staying here or going after her?" Evan asked.

"I don't think there's much point in going after her now," Ava said. "Do you?"

Sam shook his head. "No. We'd never catch her."

"Right. And I'd better go apologize to Katy."

"Good luck with that, Mom," the boys said nearly in unison, then turned to escort her back into the yard, where they made a sudden sharp turn toward the food.

The party was buzzing. More people had arrived and Elaine's performance had electrified the crowd. People turned their heads to stare as Ava threaded her way through the knots of people.

She found Katy in the gazebo, sitting with her mother. Katy's veil was lifted and her face was puffy, nearly unrecognizable, her gray eyes as flat as cement.

"Katy, I'm so sorry," Ava said. "Elaine's not herself."

Dawn, stone-faced, took her daughter's hand. Katy twisted a white lace handkerchief between her delicate fingers. "Oh, I think Elaine was being very much herself," Dawn said.

She was right, of course. Ava touched Katy's cool, bony shoulder. "I am sorry," she repeated, then turned away, humiliated and furious, her churning emotions nearly blinding her as she prepared to leave.

The boys were nowhere in sight. Ava entered the kitchen. It, too, was newly renovated, a chef's dream with stainless steel appliances and enough counter space to skate on. The caterers milled around, barking orders and filling trays. Ava passed through them unnoticed and stopped in the front hall, wondering where to look next for the boys.

A soft rustling sound caused her to glance into the room to her left, now a formal parlor done up in flowered Victorian furniture and hunting scenes framed in gold. Hats and purses were piled on one of the sofas; the noise was coming from a figure hunched over them.

As the figure straightened, Ava recognized Gigi's blue hair. The girl was dressed in jeans and a tank top now, rather than the black dress she'd worn to the service, and she had her hand deep in someone's pocketbook.

"Hey," Ava said. "What are you doing? That's not your purse!"

Gigi glanced up, startled, her blue hair standing straight up like the feathers of some exotic bird. "How the fuck do you know?"

Inwardly, Ava sighed. She couldn't blame the girl for being hostile, especially now. "Because it doesn't match your shoes."

Gigi glanced down at her filthy bare feet, then back up at Ava, locking eyes. To Ava's relief, the girl started laughing, making Ava laugh, too, until tears were running down both their faces.

"Shit," Gigi said. "I wasn't stealing. I was only looking for a smoke."

"Why? Because our dad died of lung cancer and that was so cool?"

"Oh, shut up," Gigi said, and fled the room.

Ava headed for the front door, hoping the boys would miraculously meet her by the car so she could avoid taking another Walk of Shame through the crowd to find them, but she didn't see them anywhere in the house. They must still be in the yard. She ducked into her father's office and dug the phone out of her purse.

*Where are you?* she texted Sam, who never went anywhere without his phone, even sleeping with it under his pillow, a fact he probably thought Ava had missed. *Meet me at the front door in 5 min.*

She slipped the phone back into her purse and glanced up, longing for one last look at her father's life. She'd probably never be invited back into this house again after Elaine's little spectacle.

Dad's office looked exactly the same as it always had: cream walls, a tan carpet topped by a beautiful blue Oriental rug, a massive cherry desk, a leather sofa, Audubon bird prints framed in black. A neat stack of papers was centered on the desk, the pens arranged in two leather containers that resembled small whiskey barrels.

Then Ava spotted one of her own pots on the far corner of his desk, holding Dad's favorite gold fountain pen. It was a small green stoneware vase, one of her very first pieces. She'd given it to him the Christmas before he met Katy and moved out.

Her knees buckled. She found her way to the leather couch across the room and collapsed onto it, undone by the memory of her father sitting here in his office, his silver head gleaming in the lamplight, absorbed in paperwork but always looking up to smile when he saw her.

She was crying now, the tears dripping off her chin and cheeks. She was searching frantically in her purse for a tissue when someone pressed a handkerchief into her hand.

"Here," he said. "Keep it."

Ava pressed the cloth to her face, smelling mint and something musky, then looked up at the man standing in front of her. He was blond and blue-eyed, probably in his early forties. The man was tall and rangy; he wore a charcoal suit with a white shirt and a narrow tie in a surprising deep gold. His eyes were so sympathetic that she started sobbing again, all of her grief leaking out, a profound damp sadness rising out of her very pores. Even the skin on her bare arms and legs felt damp.

The man went away, then returned with a whiskey. He put the crystal glass in her hand. "This should help."

"After that scene in the garden, I'd think you'd be afraid to give any woman alcohol," Ava said.

"You're not your sister. Drink."

God, so he knew who she was. This was awful. She needed to leave, the sooner the better. Ava tossed the drink into her mouth and was immediately sorry. The whiskey made her throat burn and her eyes tear. She started coughing.

The stranger sat down beside her and rubbed her back, but that only made things worse. His touch set her off again. She wept into the damp handkerchief, wishing it were a blanket she could throw over her head. Her grief felt enormous, like the chilly shadow of a cliff too big to go around.

The man put an arm around her shoulders and drew her close. Ava leaned into him as the grief continued to come in waves, buffeting her like a storm she couldn't control. She missed her mother and father, this house and being a child in it with Elaine. Most of all, she missed being young enough to think that life wouldn't come with such terrible losses as you grew up.

Finally, she sniffed and pulled away, embarrassed now by the fact that, on top of Elaine making a scene in the garden, she was making one here and drenching this man's suit in the process.

"I'm so sorry," she said. "This is all very hard. I'm afraid I'm not coping very well."

"Don't apologize," the man said, smoothing a damp lock of hair out of her eyes. "Of course it's hard. You'll have plenty of time to cope later. Right now, you need to grieve. You and my sister get to be the queens of grief today. Nobody should tell you what to do or how to feel."

*My sister.* "Oh, God," Ava moaned.

The man narrowed his eyes in concern. "What is it? Do you need water? Another whiskey?"

Ava managed a shaky laugh. "Definitely not another whiskey. No, it's just that I've only now realized you're Katy's brother. Have we met before?"

"No. I was overseas for the past five years, working in Hong Kong. I'm Simon Talbot." He stood up, giving her shoulder an awkward pat. "See? No need to be apologetic. We're all family here, and families should help each other through hard times like these."

She stood up and straightened her skirt. "How is Katy doing, really? I feel guilty that I didn't do more to help her take care of Dad. I tried, but she never seemed to want me there until the very end."

"Katy's an extremely private person," Simon said. "She didn't let any of us help, either. You were generous to offer. Now, are these gentlemen with you?" He gestured toward the doorway.

Ava turned and saw Evan and Sam, hovering uncertainly. "Mom? Are you okay?" They looked, amazingly, like they were ready to take on even this tall, confident man in a suit on her behalf.

"I'm fine now. I think it's probably time to go, though, don't you?"

She turned back to Simon, who pressed her hand between his, warming it. When he released her, Ava felt instantly bereft again.

"Thank you, Simon. You're very kind," she said, then went to her waiting sons.

There was a quick and dirty cure to fix the way Elaine was feeling after an afternoon as horrible as this one: a hookup.

She sped back to her condo from her father's house, playing a discordant jazz track on Pandora and pounding the horn a couple of times at people who insisted on driving the speed limit in the fast lane, pulling out her phone to check her e-mails at the lights. No matter what she did, though, she couldn't shake the image of her stepmother lifting her veil and putting a hand to her mouth, defeated and helpless looking.

All right. *Fine.* Maybe Ava was right and Katy *had* loved her father. So what? That didn't change the fact that when Dad left them for Katy, he'd shattered their mother.

Back in her condo, Elaine showered and slipped into a clingy sleeveless dress in a pleasing deep plum color. She blew her glossy chestnut hair straight and painted on a shout of red lipstick, trying to avoid looking at the photograph of her mother tucked into the corner of her mirror, the last one Elaine had taken of her. She had forced her mother to get dressed and stand in the yard in front of a hydrangea bush in full bloom, the flowers like lacy blue handkerchiefs. Mom hadn't even noticed the flowers. She just stood there blinking in the sun like some tunneling frightened rodent, obeying Elaine only because Elaine had hidden her pills and wouldn't give them back until she was outside for twenty minutes.

Elaine shuddered and spun away from the mirror to grab her favorite wedge sandals out of the closet. When her father left, she'd been a senior at Tufts, twenty-two years old, and living at home, doing an internship in the local courthouse. She'd assumed that she and her mother would stay in the Newburyport house after Dad went to live with Katy, but her mother lasted only a month.

"These halls might as well be haunted," Mom said. "I see your father everywhere. I need to go home."

"Home" was a small town in northwestern Maine two hours from any highway, a place with moose in the woods and loons on the lake. Elaine hoped to never hear another loon again. That strange cry was the sound of a loneliness so ancient and terrible, you would sooner die than suffer it yourself.

She didn't think much of moose, either. The tourists paid big bucks to be taken on moose safaris, but all you had to do was drive along one particular road the townies called "Moose Alley" to see the animals grazing in swamps. Moose were about as magnificent as donkeys, with their hairy chins and knobby knees.

The town itself was nothing more than a cluster of rickety stores on a deep lake where floatplanes landed to carry people even deeper into the wilderness. The year-round residents wore hunting camouflage and, depending on the season, rode ATVs or snowmobiles to the bars because gas prices were high and the roads were mostly dirt.

Elaine found work as a waitress in the only year-round restaurant. The tips weren't bad. She was cute, she had good legs, and she was smart enough to read the bartender's handbook and mix drinks in a pinch if the bartender was too smashed. She took online college classes and contemplated buying a rifle but never did.

Pills and alcohol were even more of a problem for Suzanne in Maine than they'd been at home. The only person they ever saw was her mother's aunt Finley, a thickset, mannish woman with three cats and a passion for mystery novels too gory for Elaine to read. The rest of the family had either died or sensibly stayed in Canada.

Elaine had lived with her mother on this forgotten edge of the world for nine months. Then, when the owner of the cabin said he wanted to rent it to summer people, Suzanne had insisted on moving into Aunt Finley's upstairs apartment and banished Elaine back to Boston. She was dead of a heart attack a year later. Elaine knew there was no such thing as dying of a broken heart, but that's exactly how it had seemed.

Elaine strapped on her shoes and jammed a handful of condoms into her purse. She had to get out of here *right now*.

She hurtled across the Charles River on the BU Bridge. After years of trial and error, she had learned where to go for safe, pleasurable hookups. She steered clear of the pounding downtown clubs—too many swingers in their twenties ready to blow their wallets up their noses—and headed instead to Cambridge. The bars around MIT were tricky; she needed someone older and more experienced than a graduate student. But there was one particular jazz club in Kendall Square that suited her needs. It was frequented by foreign scientists and engineers easily enticed by American women who they correctly perceived were leading freer lifestyles than women from their own countries.

She was lucky it was a Saturday night. There was a live jazz band and the place was packed. Elaine liked to think she gave as much as she got out of these encounters. She even, occasionally, bought men drinks to get things going.

Tonight, she stuck with seltzer water and cranberry juice, asking for a lime so it would look like she was enjoying a cocktail instead of sobering up from a disastrous afternoon. She moved slowly through the crowded bar, focusing on the throbbing bass line of the music to stop feeling like she was at the wrong end of a telescope.

Whenever anyone at work asked Elaine how she was feeling about her father's death, she said, "Numb." People assumed she meant numb with grief, but Elaine wasn't sure that was accurate. She was just numb. Ava had confessed that the day after Dad died, she had gone to a midday movie and wept silently in the empty theater, nauseated by the stink of bad popcorn and her own grief.

Elaine envied Ava's easy relationship with her emotions. Ava laughed and cried easily, at the least provocation: movies, a friend weeping in front of her, even certain television commercials. Elaine was always on guard against her own emotions, keeping them stoppered tightly because they were such a nuisance. However, this meant her feelings sometimes came to a boil under the surface and then exploded out of control, typically beyond whatever a particular moment warranted. It made her furious that she'd erupted at Dad's funeral.

Everyone in the bar seemed to be with someone but her. Never mind. She was probably more contented with her life overall than most of the couples in here. A lot of them were probably together despite already having realized they'd made bad choices. Elaine took a sip of her drink and tried not to sneeze as the fizz went up her nose.

Finally, after one more tour of the room, she selected her prey: a man considerably younger than she was. He had olive skin, sleek black hair, and fine features. He wore his button-down plaid shirt tucked into his blue jeans, a look that he doubtless thought made him seem more American.

She made a point of standing directly in front of his table. He was seated with three other men in similar outfits. They were clearly friends; she imagined them working long hours in adjoining cubicles, probably in one of those mazelike Cambridge industrial complexes. She swayed to the music with her back to the man, almost close enough to touch, knowing he and his companions would be admiring her shining dark hair, tiny belted waist, and long legs. Then she summoned the waiter over and bought the man a drink.

His companions hooted, urging him to speak to her. Elaine could hear this going on behind her but didn't rush things. She didn't even turn around as he approached.

Standing next to him at last, Elaine was pleased to see that the man was half a head taller than she was despite her heels. He smelled of cinnamon and had eyes like melting chocolates in the flickering light.

He asked her to dance and guided her to the crowded floor with one hand touching the small of her back, making her shiver in anticipation. When the band broke between sets, she suggested going somewhere quiet to talk. Elaine would have preferred leaving for his place right away, but she had learned through the years that the stereotype was true: men desired you more if you pretended to be hard to get. You didn't want to spook them.

They went to the bar upstairs, where the man told her about his job as a software engineer and his family in India. Elaine mentioned only that she worked in marketing. She never let anyone know the name of her company or that she was its vice president. She didn't have a Facebook page and her Twitter account was under a different name; she made quite sure to be impossible to track.

As the bartender announced closing time, the man invited her to his place for a brandy. He offered to drive her there, but she said she preferred to take her own car: "I'm sure you understand. It's a new BMW, and I hate leaving it unattended in this part of Cambridge. Besides, this way you won't have to drive me home."

These statements had the desired effect. The man was clearly impressed by her new car and now he was acting nervous, probably worrying that she wouldn't be as easy as he'd thought.

His condo was exactly what she had expected, a tidy one-bedroom, third-floor walk-up in Cambridge with Ikea furniture. This told her that the man was probably a newly minted PhD, spent most of his waking hours at work, and most likely sent half his earnings home to India, where his mother was tirelessly, devotedly scouring the countryside for a suitable bride to join him.

Elaine sipped the brandy politely, complimenting everything from his kitchen cupboards to his sofa pillows, then slipped off her heels and crossed her legs. Her bare feet usually sealed the deal. She was always careful about pedicures, and this week her nails were a pearly, girly pink.

She bounced her foot and laughed at something the man said, then ducked her head a little, letting her hair partly cover her face, playing it shy. "I should probably go," she said. "It's getting awfully late."

This gave him the impetus to make his move. Elaine wasn't disappointed. Her new lover was eager and delicious, his hairless bronze skin as smooth as a succulent plant, his hands gentle and pleasing as he leaned over to kiss her, whispering, "Stay with me."

It was just the thing to take Elaine's mind off sorrow, and loss, and how badly she had hurt Katy. She had meant to do it. Of course she had. She just hadn't expected to feel so miserable afterward.

# CHAPTER TWO

The Monday after the service, Ava drove her sons to their jobs—Evan to the local supermarket, where he was a bagger, and Sam to the landscaping company in Newburyport where he loaded mulch and gravel into trucks all day, making her tease him and call him "the Incredible Hulk."

Both boys were saving money to pay their father back for the new instruments he'd bought them at the end of the school year. Evan, quieter and less confident, played bass, and Sam had a bright blue electric guitar. They had formed a band with their friend Les, a drummer, and Ava had recently given them permission to turn her living room into a music studio, God help her.

Back home, she ate her usual breakfast of oatmeal washed down by strong Darjeeling tea, then worked for several hours in the studio. When she'd thrown the last piece, she sat up and stretched her back. She wasn't used to spending this many hours at the wheel. During the school year, she taught art at the local high school, which meant she was often too busy to pursue her own pottery projects at home. Ava tried to make up for this in the summer months by producing enough pottery to sell throughout the year through local galleries and craft shows.

She decided to take a walk before glazing the pots she'd fired over the weekend. She started south toward the wildlife sanctuary, then headed inland. Here the beach grasses grew in thick tufts beneath twisting shadows of the gnarled miniature plum trees that gave Beach Plum Island its name.

*Poverty grass*: that's what some islanders called the beach heather that grew in thick carpets and seemed to need little more than air to thrive. Without it, there would be no Beach Plum Island, because the shoreline would be eroded by storms and tides. And without Beach Plum Island acting as a barrier, the northern Massachusetts coastline would be carved away by hurricanes and snowstorms.

Ava turned around after half an hour, driven by thoughts of Elaine. She would have been even more furious at her sister if she didn't also feel guilty. Ava had spent practically every minute of her last two years of high school with Mark, her ex-husband; he was a skinny track star so besotted with her that he had spent an entire summer's wages to buy her an engagement ring with a diamond chip the fall after they graduated. They had married at twenty, and by the time Dad left, she was too busy with the boys to help Elaine with their mother.

At least that was the way Ava had always tried to rationalize the events of that horrible year. In reality, in the fierce cold light of hindsight, she could have done more. She wasn't teaching then. She had time on her hands. She never went to see them after they moved to Maine, despite several frantic phone calls from Elaine about Mom's increasingly bizarre behavior. If she had been around, would things have turned out differently? Maybe. At the very least, Elaine wouldn't be so angry and hurt now.

Ava continued down the beach, lifting the soft sand with her toes and watching it spray in front of her. As always, thinking about the past made her feel as if a crowd of people were in her head, all shouting at once in languages she didn't understand. It didn't help that she was feeling so emotionally wrung out by her wakeful night. She'd been having a recurring nightmare for years. Now, given her father's last words, she had begun to wonder if it wasn't a dream at all, but an actual memory. Whatever it was, she was always left shaken by it.

She slowed her pace, concentrating hard, gathering the few fragments she remembered. She saw herself as a small child walking down a dim hallway. She opened the door to a dark room, a room she knew she was never supposed to enter because her mother had forbidden it.

As Ava opened the door, a little boy not much bigger than she was dashed out, grabbing her around the waist and pressing his face against her neck, making strange, snuffling animal noises and saying, "Who you? Who you?" She was paralyzed with fear as the little boy kept clawing at her arms and touching her face, laughing at her until she cried and pushed him away. Only then did her mother come running, soothing her and shutting the other child back in the bedroom, this time locking the door with a hook too high up for a child to reach.

Her friend Olivia would probably say this recurring nightmare was all about her inner child. But Ava woke every time drenched in sweat, her heart pounding. The dream felt as real as her life.

She forced herself to walk faster to shake her ragged mood, then stopped to pick up a mussel shell, admiring its swirling sheen of violet and pink. She wondered if she should glaze her new pitchers that way. She pocketed the shell and continued walking, surprised to see a figure standing on tiptoe near her studio, face pressed to one of the windows.

"Hey!" she yelled. "Can I help you?"

It wasn't until the figure spun around, climbed onto a bicycle in the driveway, and rode away that Ava realized it was Gigi. What was she doing here?

Gigi wasn't going back to camp again. Not after seeing Lydia beat the crap out of that poor horse. She winced just thinking about the way the crop had sounded, almost like gunshots, Lydia red-faced and slapping it against the flank of her sweet-tempered bay gelding.

Lydia said she was punishing the horse for not clearing the brick wall, and only laughed when Gigi said, "But he's a horse, Lydia. He doesn't know why you're hitting him now. He's already forgotten the jump. They have the brains of three-year-olds."

"Yeah, like you're such a friggin' expert," Lydia had huffed. "You can hardly even *ride*. It must suck to suck."

It used to be fun, going to the club for riding lessons, or for tennis camp and dinner with her parents afterward. Gigi didn't mind the club when she was younger, though she was grateful her parents never made her take golf lessons. She'd rather pluck her eyes out with tweezers than waste hours trying to hit stupid little white balls into holes.

Then things started changing, or maybe Gigi did, when Dad got cancer. The other girls acted like she was the one who got sick and it might be catching. They were always polite, except for Lydia, but never invited her to their houses anymore.

That was mostly fine with her. Gigi didn't want to be like any of them. She wanted to be an artist, or maybe the lead singer in a band. She didn't have any burning desire to troll the mall or Instagram people. What a freakin' waste of time and money.

Not that money was a problem. All Gigi had to say at home was that there was another club fund-raiser for Haiti or abused women, and her mother practically emptied her wallet into Gigi's hands.

Mom didn't need money now, since she never left the house. This worried Gigi. She'd told Gramma Dawn that Mom wasn't eating or taking showers, but her grandmother seemed to think this was normal, saying, "She'll snap out of it, dear, you'll see."

Gigi wasn't so sure, but what could she do about it? Meanwhile, it was easy to write a note to the riding camp instructor in her mother's handwriting, saying Gigi had carpal tunnel syndrome— she was proud of that excuse—and wouldn't be attending riding camp this summer because her wrists needed to be strong for field hockey season in the fall.

Ha. Field hockey. As if.

The only problem was that now her days loomed long and empty. Gigi couldn't hang at the club pool; most kids her age were away at camp, so it would just be her and the little kids. Besides, she couldn't risk any of the other moms calling hers.

And she couldn't stay anywhere in the neighborhood, on the very off chance that her mother left the house or that Uncle Simon, the only one in her mom's family who seemed to think Gigi was worth talking to, stopped by to visit.

So Gigi mostly pedaled her bike aimlessly around. Some days she'd cross the bridge and head into Amesbury, where she sat by the waterfalls and ate frozen yogurt, then maybe went to a matinee at the cinemas on Route 110. Or she would bike south from Newburyport to sit on the banks of the Parker River and draw the great blue herons and egrets in her sketch pad. Once, she had even seen a sandhill crane. She could draw, like, for fifty hours straight, if only her teachers would quit harassing her about things she wasn't remotely interested in, like physics and algebra.

School was for morons. She couldn't understand those girls who tested themselves on Quizlet or made color-coded note cards and never missed a help session, posting things on Facebook like *Two tests tomorrow, might as well kill myself now, so stressed!*

Today she had ridden her bike out to Beach Plum Island to see where Ava lived. Not that she could even *think* of her as a sister. God, she was older than her own mom! Still, Gigi was curious about her and about Elaine, too, after that freak show at the service.

She had met them before, of course. Mom used to always invite them for holidays or whatever. "They're family," she'd insist when Gigi rolled her eyes and pointed out the obvious, that Ava and Elaine wanted nothing to do with them. "They should know they're always welcome in their father's home."

Today, after Ava caught her snooping around the studio—she would have liked to have seen more, but she didn't need any *lectures*—Gigi biked over to the beach by the Beach Plum Island lighthouse. This beach was across the Merrimack River from Salisbury Beach on the mainland, a place her mom refused to go, saying it was filled with "transients," and probably even "real Gypsies." But Gigi and her dad went to Salisbury anyway.

"Let's go to the honky-tonk side of town," Dad would announce on certain steamy summer weekends, and off they'd go to Salisbury Beach, where they'd bodysurf the waves or wander through the chaotic campground with its flocks of sticky kids.

Then they'd hit the boardwalk and hang out at the arcades. Her dad was amazing at the old pinball machines. For dinner they'd eat slices of limp pizza sold out of a window. They'd finish the night with go-karts and fried dough powdered with sugar and so sweet it made Gigi's teeth ache. Her dad always made her arm-wrestle him for the last bite.

Gigi's eyes filled. She swatted away the tears, wishing she could smash them like flies. She hated God for letting Dad die. More proof that God sucked. As if the hurricanes and earthquakes, terrorist bombings, and school shootings weren't enough proof that God was totally insane.

She locked her bike to the chain-link fence by the playground, slipped off her sandals, and carried her sketch pad down to the water, where she sank cross-legged onto the sand and fiddled with her lip ring. She'd gotten her ears pierced when she was twelve. Her mom took her to a doctor and winced when the doctor put gold studs in Gigi's ears, despite the fact that he'd numbed her ears so completely, Gigi felt like her head was wrapped in duct tape.

After Dad got sick, she'd bribed Miguel, one of the janitors at her school, to take her to New Hampshire in his rusty truck for more piercings. Miguel knew lots of places where people didn't care how old you were. You could buy tattoos, fireworks, lip rings, and even guns in New Hampshire if you had the money and knew where to go.

She'd pierced her eyebrow and then her lip out of solidarity with her father. By the end, Dad had looked half machine, connected to tubes that dripped medicine into his body like a leaking faucet. Only it seemed like maybe the faucet was dripping the wrong way, because her dad's life was leaking out of him.

After getting her lip pierced, Gigi had ridden her bike to the hospital. Her lip was swollen and red. At the sight of it, Mom said, "Oh, Gigi, that's the last straw, honestly, your poor beautiful mouth," and started to cry. She left the room "to get a little air."

But Dad, who was having one of his good days, sitting up and drinking something orange with a straw, asked her to sit on the bed beside him. His face was so thin by then that he'd been joking with Gigi about it lately, saying, "Finally, I look like Mick Jagger instead of a fat banker."

"Does it hurt?" he'd asked, reaching out to almost, but not quite, touch her lip.

"More than my ears or my nose," she admitted. "That's okay. I wanted it to hurt."

"Why, honey?" Dad dropped his hand, his fingers landing on her wrist like a bird's scaly cold foot.

"I wanted to know what you're feeling." She pointed to the needle in his arm that connected to his tubes.

He smiled. "Thank you. I wish I could dye my hair blue and know what you're feeling."

"I could dye it for you," Gigi said, pretending that her dad still had his hair, when in fact his head looked like a baby's now, pink and smooth, with a few random cottony bits.

"Maybe next time. Listen, there's something you need to know before I leave you, G-girl. Something very important."

"Okay," she said, even though her stomach had knotted. Having her dad die was important enough, it seemed, without having to know anything else. "What?"

"I love you, and I know you love me. But I have a feeling you're going to forget me after a little while."

"I won't!"

Dad blinked hard. "Okay. Even if you don't, though, I want you to know that you won't be alone in the world after I'm gone."

"You're not trying to tell me to believe in God and angels or anything like that, are you?" she'd said. "Because this would be a really bad time to try and convince me that God has a plan."

"I hear you, G-girl. No, no. I want you to know you have other people in your family."

She nodded. "Right. Mom and Gramma are around every day, and now Uncle Simon is back from China or wherever."

"Yes, but you have other family, too." Dad took a deep, shivery breath, his whole chest caving in. "On my side."

"You mean Ava and Elaine?"

"No. I mean your brother. You have a brother, Gigi."

"I do?" Gigi was so stunned that she'd stopped fiddling with her new lip ring. "You had another wife, not just Mom and Suzanne?" She'd heard all about Suzanne from her mom, who said Dad's first wife had "gone off the deep end." This sounded exciting, though not the way her mom said it.

Dad shook his head. One eyelid was twitching like it always did when he got tired. "No more wives. Two were plenty for me. And I could never, ever love another woman the way I love your mom, honey. Never forget that. But Suzanne and I had another child when we were very young, not much older than you." His voice had faded to a whisper. "Named Peter. He would be so proud of you, honey, just like I am."

Gigi's heart had started pounding. Could this be true? She knew all about her dad's medicines and how her mom said sometimes he didn't make sense. On the other hand, he'd never seemed confused about anything when she was around. "Does Mom know?"

"She knows a little bit." He coughed for a long time, then added, "You know how upset she gets these days. I didn't want to bother her with any of this stuff. But I wanted you to know about Peter so you can look for him."

"Where is he?"

At that, her father had closed his eyes and said, "I don't know. There was something wrong with him. Suzanne couldn't take care of him. It was a terrible thing."

He'd just managed to get these words out when the machine that tracked her dad's heart and blood and breathing, the one with all the colored lines on the computer, started beeping like a pinball machine when you've won an extra game. A nurse had come running in, saying to Gigi, "Sweetie, I'm sorry, but we need to give your dad some special medicine now. You'd better go find your mom."

Gigi had stood up, frightened. "Dad?"

"It's all right," he'd said without opening his eyes. "Find your brother. It wasn't my choice to give him up. I would have loved your brother no matter what. If he's still alive, tell him that for me. It's important. Promise?"

"I promise," Gigi whispered.

Her dad didn't die that day, so at least Gigi didn't have to feel guilty about killing him. He'd fallen asleep, though, and wasn't awake much after that. Only his fluttering eyelids told Gigi he could hear her.

Gigi's breathing was ragged now, as she sat on the beach and tried not to cry. She didn't want to think about Dad anymore. She started drawing, focusing intently on the whorled designs in the sand. The tide had gone out, leaving the sand as rough as fish scales arranged in circles around silver tidal pools.

The circles were calming to look at. Hypnotizing, even. She copied the designs in the sand, then amplified them, shading the curves. Her breathing, so shallow and harsh a minute ago, began slowing down as she breathed in and out with the steady rhythm of the waves lapping against the shore.

Eventually Gigi wasn't just drawing designs, but turning them into bowls and jars, exploring the relationships between circles and squares. The jars she liked best were the ones she'd drawn as squat and round as birds' nests. To these, she'd added square, flat lids instead of matching circular ones. The jars looked like she felt right now, pushing upward, struggling to free themselves from the lids, maybe pop them off with a scream.

"Hey, those are pretty cool drawings."

It was like the voice inside her head was talking to her. Startled, Gigi slapped the sketchbook shut and scrambled to her feet.

Ava stood on the beach behind her, looking as wild as Gigi felt:

windblown tangled hair, feet tucked into scuffed sandals, torn blue jeans, a T-shirt stained with colored glazes. Even her bare arms were spotted with colors, as if Ava were some kind of exotic beach animal. Her green eyes were freaky, glowing like sea glass.

"What are *you* doing here?" Gigi demanded.

"I live here," Ava said.

"Not *here*."

"Close enough. Which you apparently already know, since you were snooping around my studio. What are *you* doing here?"

Ava didn't sound angry, only curious. Gigi sighed. "I didn't touch anything."

"You weren't looking for a smoke?"

Gigi felt her neck and face get hot. "I don't really smoke. Only sometimes."

In truth, she'd started buying cigarettes in seventh grade, but her father had made her promise to quit after he got sick. He'd made her promise a lot of things, but this was something she could actually do for him. So she'd been smoking less and less, despite the fact that she loved how the nicotine got her blood racing and cleared her head.

"I'm glad to hear it," Ava said.

"Why did you follow me?"

"To ask what you were doing at my studio. I thought you might be looking for me."

"No way!" Gigi stared down at her bare feet in the sand. She'd painted her nails blue to match her hair, but most of the color had chipped off by now. Her toes looked diseased. "Why would I look for you? I don't even know you."

"You could, though. I'd like that."

Ava's tone was so warm that Gigi actually looked up and met her sister's eyes, something she tried not to do with most adults. Grown-ups had all the power. She hated that.

But Ava's green eyes were soft and kind. She wasn't very tall, but she gave the impression of being tall because of her posture. She carried her head high and her shoulders back. Gigi had shitty posture and hated that about herself. It was probably from her school backpack, which weighed as much as a *car*. She hated that, too. She hated pretty much everything and everybody right now. Everybody hated her, so why wouldn't she hate them back?

This thought made Gigi's throat clog as if a whole sandstorm had blown into it. Her eyes were watering with the effort of trying to breathe. She couldn't speak.

Ava reached out and touched her arm, her fingers cool on Gigi's sun-warmed skin. "Come on," she said. "I have my bike, too. Let's ride to my house and get some lunch. I'll show you my pottery and you can show me your drawings."

Miserably, gratefully, Gigi followed her sister home.

# CHAPTER THREE

It was a typical manic Monday for Elaine: problems with one of the printers, reviewing an admissions video, scheduling school visits for Tony next week. It was Tony's college marketing company; he had started it ten years ago and managed it now with the joy, fury, and stalwart determination of the rugby player he'd been during college, where they'd met in a statistics class.

Tony was gay, so Elaine had never been tempted to sleep with him, thank God. One less buried land mine of a mistake to side-step. Five years after earning her MBA, she was working as the public relations director for a big software company west of Boston. She'd run into Tony at a class reunion and he had lured her into his company.

"Look, honey," he'd said, "the high-tech bubble has popped in Boston, but you can't throw a rock in this town without hitting a college. And every college is scrabbling to create an online presence, since that's the way kids shop for everything these days. Time to get digital, baby."

She'd been worried, at first, that she wouldn't fit in, since she'd been in high tech for so long, but Elaine soon discovered that her skills transferred easily enough. And Tony was right: the colleges needed them desperately. Schools were all rushing the Internet gate and crying, "Save me!"

Tony still went on the road every week to put in face time with clients, but really, their services sold themselves. Elaine loved being in a company where it was just her, Tony, and five account managers, plus two copywriters and the designers who worked in the adjoining office suite. The rest of what they did was easily jobbed out; you couldn't throw a rock in Boston without hitting cafés jammed with hungry freelance writers and videographers, either.

Of course, there were times like today when Elaine wished she'd never again have to hear precious education-marketing-speak like "individualized attention" and "experiential learning." Like right now: the writer of the video script she had received this morning should be shot.

She slashed her virtual red pen through the script and wrote, "This reads like you cut and pasted every other college's catchphrase. We need something original. Don't make me yawn."

She e-mailed the document back to the writer, then made herself another coffee. Elaine was taking the first fragrant sip of Hazelnut when the phone rang. It was Ava, who had left her three messages since the memorial service. She'd have to talk to her eventually; it might as well be now. She had eleven minutes until the afternoon staff meeting.

"What?" she said.

"You *know* what." Ava's voice was mild but firm. It was the same voice she'd been using with her boys since they were born, the voice of reason, that teacher's tone that expected everyone to nicely use their words and take turns on the slide, even the bully and the crippled kid.

"I am *not* apologizing," Elaine said, and took another sip of coffee.

"Oh, really?" Ava asked. "You don't think your behavior on Saturday might warrant even a teeny little note to Katy, saying you're sorry for behaving like a complete jerk? To mend fences, so we can hold our heads up here around the North Shore?"

"I never go north except to see you on Beach Plum Island," Elaine pointed out. "Which, may I remind you, is an *island* and has a river running between it and Newburyport. I never need to see those people again."

"I do my grocery shopping in Newburyport," Ava pointed out. "My dentist and mechanic are both in Newburyport. I sell my pottery through galleries in Newburyport! Look, this is the big-girl thing to do, Elaine, and you know it. Apologize! Get it over with and give your conscience a break. I know you must feel bad about it."

Elaine was silent, lining up the pens on her desk. She liked to keep the black ones to the left of her desk blotter and the red ones to the right; she couldn't hear herself think if they were out of order. She hated having Ava remind her of the memorial service, because it brought back the sight of Katy's pale, ravaged face. Elaine hated it even more that Ava was right: she did regret what she'd done.

"Oh, for Christ's sake," Elaine said. "Fine. I'll write to her. I am sorry about the way I acted, actually. Katy did seem pretty flattened."

"She was. Gigi, too."

Elaine frowned, trying to recall Gigi at the funeral. "Was she the kid with that awful blue hair?"

"Yes."

"God, I didn't even recognize her."

"I think she's really hurting," Ava said. "I'm worried about her."

"Why?"

There was a brief silence. Elaine tried to imagine what Ava was doing. Folding laundry, probably. Ava always folded laundry while she talked on the phone, and often kept her cell phone on top of a full basket of clothes, where it sank into the cotton vortex as Ava piled more clean laundry into the basket without emptying it first. Elaine didn't understand why Ava didn't make those great big hulking kids of hers do their own laundry. But that was her sister for you, always the enabler.

"Gigi came to see me today," Ava said.

"You're kidding!" Elaine set down her coffee mug.

"Well, not to see *me*, exactly, but to see where I lived. I caught her snooping around the studio."

"Be careful. That kid has 'pyro' written all over her."

"No, I don't think so. Gigi left as soon as I tried to talk to her. I had to follow her to the other end of the island and invite her back."

"Why the hell would you do that?" Elaine felt outraged. She'd like to think she was angry on Ava's behalf, because Ava always did too much for other people. But, if she was truthful, she'd have to admit she was irritated by the very idea of her father's other family circling anywhere near her own.

"I feel sorry for her," Ava said. "Gigi really seems distressed. Not just about Dad, but about life. She's only fifteen but she looks like she's carrying the whole world on her shoulders. It also seems like Katy doesn't know where Gigi is half the time."

"Did our mother know where *we* were when *we* were fifteen?"

"That's my point," Ava said. "When I asked Gigi about her mother, she said Katy isn't leaving the house or taking showers, and she's hardly eating. Remember how depressed Mom was after her own parents and brother died? And look how she spiraled out of control after Dad left."

"Don't remind me." Elaine glanced at the clock. "Okay, I'll write Katy a note. You feed the kid and talk her off the ledge. Listen, I have to go."

"Wait! I need to tell you something else."

"Make it fast. Some of us are actually working today."

"Remember how Dad said that weird thing to me before he died? About us having a brother?"

"Yes. I also remember reminding you that Dad was hopped up on drugs."

"I know, but what if he really was trying to tell me something? I had that same dream again last night. You know, the one about the kid in the locked room. What if those two things are connected and that was our brother? Maybe it's not a dream at all, but an actual memory."

"You've been sniffing too many glazes." Elaine ran a hand through her hair. "Ava, we didn't have a brother. Dad might have been able to play that card close to his chest, but Mom for sure would have let it all come howling out."

"I guess. It's just that Dad sounded so clear and determined. Really focused. I've been worrying about it."

"Don't waste your energy. Dad was delusional, out of his mind on morphine. Or maybe he did have another child with somebody else, long ago. How would we know? And what does it matter at this point? Look, I really have to go. I'll come up this weekend."

"That would be great. Thanks for writing to Katy."

Elaine hung up and shot another look at the clock. Three minutes to get her act together and be ready with that presentation on the ad campaign for Pineville College.

She was never, ever late to meetings. She liked to set a good example. Today, though, Elaine wished someone else would run the meeting while she sat back with her eyes half-closed, zoning out.

Just enough time to zip into the restroom, pee, and check her makeup. Elaine grabbed her purse and headed for the bathroom, not the one closest to the elevators and most often used, but the farthest, quieter bathroom down by the supply closet.

Someone else entered the bathroom after she'd closed the stall door. Thankfully whoever it was turned the faucet on full blast. Elaine finished her business and headed for the double sink, keeping her head down to avoid conversation. Nothing worse than having your employees hear you peeing. At least she hadn't done anything more embarrassing than that in here.

Then she realized something odd: the faucet was on, but nobody stood at the other sink. Elaine rinsed her own hands, then turned off both faucets and looked in the mirror. In the far corner of the bathroom, next to the bucket and mop, a woman was huddled on the floor, her face pressed against the knees of her black slacks.

By the short gray curls and thick-soled black shoes, Elaine recognized their newest copywriter. She was a former journalist Tony had hired when another one of the small daily suburban newspapers shuttered its doors. Of course Tony called her a "content provider," not a copywriter, given the online nature of their work. What was her name? Joy? Jane? Some plain doughnut name that went with the woman's plain, round face.

The woman hadn't made any sort of impression on Elaine in the month since she'd been hired, other than the few times Elaine had passed her in the hall and overheard her talking on her cell to one of her kids at home. Elaine hadn't said anything; she knew working mothers had it tough. She'd seen Ava go crazy whenever one of her kids was sick and she had to miss work, and summers weren't easy when the boys were small. Elaine sympathized. But she also didn't want kids compromising the workplace by taking their parents' attention off the jobs at hand. If she saw this woman doing it again, she'd have to speak to her.

Elaine rubbed her hands beneath the dryer, trying to decide

what to do. She didn't have time to play nursemaid, but she could feel Tony's conscience guiding her. He always made it his business to find out why an employee was unhappy. "Are you all right?" she finally asked, turning around and leaning her back against the sink.

The woman shrugged but didn't lift her head. "I will be. I just need a minute."

Elaine hesitated. She'd done her duty; perhaps the woman would recover better if left alone. That was certainly Elaine's preference. She hated anyone seeing her out of control. On the other hand, this was her employee and something was nagging at her about this woman's name. What was it?

Then she remembered: Joan Toledo. And that led her to realize this was the same writer—sorry, Tony, "content provider"—whom she'd e-mailed that harsh critique to an hour ago. Her stomach dropped. It was because of her, probably, that the woman was sobbing in the bathroom.

"You're Joan, aren't you?" she said.

The woman raised her head and, with a sigh, pushed herself up to a standing position, brushing off the back of her slacks. She was fifty if she was a day. The kids at home couldn't be young. "Yes. Joan Toledo. Go ahead."

Elaine frowned. "Go ahead with what?"

"With firing me." Joan scrubbed at her face with both hands. This had the unhappy effect of turning her cheeks brick red and leaving a trail of mascara. "It won't be the first time. I know the drill."

"Well, you're obviously asking for it, acting like this," Elaine said.

Good. That made Joan lift her chin and narrow her brown eyes.

"Yeah? Am I? And what would you do, if you had two kids in college and a husband out of work?"

"I'd probably drink myself to death," Elaine said truthfully.

Joan gave her a startled look, then laughed. "Well, that's one thing I haven't tried, anyway."

Elaine grinned. "Then you're a better woman than I am. Seriously, why were you crying? Was it because I critiqued your copy?"

Joan pulled a tissue out of her pocketbook and blew her nose. The sound trumpeted off the bathroom walls. "You didn't just critique it. You *shredded* it. Then you ran it over with your car!" Joan blew her nose again. "I'm crying because you were right. It was awful copy. I suck at this job."

"Right now you do. But you've only been here a month," Elaine pointed out. "We usually let people suck at least six months before we fire them. Tony's a marshmallow that way. And I'm betting you can rewrite that copy. You were a journalist. You've got skills."

Joan snorted. "Skills nobody wants."

"What do you mean?" Elaine demanded. "Marketing writers are essential in the business world. We depend on people who can string together literate sentences and make old ideas sound fresh. It's like being a plumber or an electrician. You've got a trade, girlfriend, and it's a useful one. Now get out of that corner, wash your face, and go to work. Give me a new draft by four o'clock. I'll help you whip it into shape."

Joan looked shy now, and suddenly seemed younger. She stepped out of the corner and joined Elaine at the sink. "I like your lipstick," she said suddenly.

"War paint," Elaine said. She opened her purse, fished out a tube. "Here. I always carry a few spares. Take one."

"I couldn't."

"Why not?" Elaine gave her a frank look. If anyone needed

color, it was this woman. "Lipstick is the best way to let the world know you're on top of your game."

"Ha. As if."

"Pretending to be in charge is half the battle."

Joan gave her a thoughtful look, then held out her hand. "All right. Thank you."

"Sure," Elaine said. "I'll see you in the conference room." She left Joan examining herself in the mirror, the lipstick in her hand, hearing the sharp staccato sounds of her own heels on the tiled floor.

Ava parked behind Port Pleasures, her friend Caroline's gallery in Newburyport, and lugged her boxes into the store. Caroline was barking shipping orders into her phone, but greeted Ava with a hug and gestured for her to set the boxes on a worktable in the back room.

Caroline's gallery specialized in crafts by local artists. Ava paused to admire a hand-carved cherry sleigh bed. A woven carpet in rich reds was laid out beside it and the bed was covered in a patchwork quilt in cool greens and blues.

Ava had a sudden urge to fling herself onto the bed and burrow under the quilt. She'd been tired down to her bones since the memorial service. She thought fleetingly of Katy, wondering how she was coping, and hoped her call to Elaine yesterday had done some good. She wondered, too, where Gigi was. She had invited her to the studio today, but the girl had been noncommittal, evasive.

"All set," Caroline said briskly, poking her head out of her office. "What can I get you? Soda? Iced tea?"

"Water's fine."

"Come sit down for a minute. Watching you carry all of those heavy boxes wore me out."

Caroline's office was tucked beneath a staircase leading to the shop's second floor. Unlike the painstakingly arranged tableaux in her store, the office looked inhabited by a college fraternity. Stacks of papers and photographs rose from every horizontal surface; the hat rack was barely visible beneath layers of clothing; and a gym bag gaped open on the floor, spilling workout clothes.

"I didn't know you were going to the gym again," Ava said.

Caroline made a face. "I wish I were, but I can't seem to find the time. I'm reduced to paying gym membership fees like I tithe at church, hoping for salvation. Good intentions must count for something, right?" She lifted a tower of file folders off her desk chair and sat down, gesturing to a stool in the far corner for Ava to use. "Hungry?" She pulled open a desk drawer and started rummaging.

Ava shook her head. "I had breakfast. Besides, I'm too stressed to eat."

"That's the difference between you and me. Stress makes you thin but puffs me up like a pigeon."

Ava laughed. Caroline continued fishing through her desk drawers and talked about her kids and the latest on the city's new waterfront development plan. It was true that her friend had thickened around the waist and hips, but that was hardly surprising. Caroline was content and settled. She'd married her high school boyfriend, just as Ava had married hers.

The difference was that Ava and Mark slowly drifted apart as the kids grew older, until eventually Mark had a brief affair with the secretary in his civil engineering firm. Elaine and her friends couldn't understand how she and Mark had settled into such an amicable relationship after the divorce, given Mark's affair, but Ava knew the divorce was at least as much her fault as his. He had failed to honor their marriage vows by straying physically, but she had abandoned him emotionally long before that.

They had mediated the divorce without arguing about furnishings, custody, or money and remained friends, a fact that had made Caroline say, "Good Lord, you two get along better than most married couples I know."

Ava knew Caroline didn't get it. Neither did most of her other friends, especially when they happened to drop by while Mark was helping her with things around the house or called to ask for advice about his father, now eighty. "We raised each other," Ava told them. "We'll always have a connection because of the boys."

This was true. Yet sometimes she wondered if she'd done the right thing, if perhaps leaving Mark had been harder on the boys than it seemed, despite being selfishly thrilled to be on her own, at last, without having to feel like she was failing as a wife.

The only serious relationship she'd had since the divorce was with an architect she'd met two years ago. Jack had a pale Irish complexion and blue eyes, and a way of looking at Ava that made her knees buckle. He'd been determined to crowbar Ava out of her "comfort zone," as he'd put it after hearing she'd never been with a man other than her husband.

Once, after drinking too much frothy stout at a fishermen's bar in Gloucester, Jack had made silent, urgent love to Ava on a damp tangle of fishing nets on one of the docks. He'd taken her to his weekend house in Vermont, too, where they'd swum in waterfalls so icy that her skin burned when she clung to him in the water.

She had started to feel like a different person with him. Sensuous. Desirable. *Desiring.* She had never felt this electrical physical excitement with Mark. There was a change in her work, too, as Jack showed her how to look at buildings as art and encouraged her to think about creating pottery in ways that went beyond the functional.

Then they'd reached a crossroads. Jack was offered a job in California and asked Ava to come with him. Not to marry him—he wasn't ready for that, he said—but to join him for a year to test the waters. "You'd love Berkeley," he said. "We could find a place with enough room for you to have a studio. You wouldn't even have to teach."

"What about the boys?" she had asked.

He'd looked confused for a minute. This was partly Ava's fault. For the six months they'd been dating, she had scheduled their time together to coincide with weekends the boys spent with their father, not wanting Evan and Sam to become attached to Jack in case things didn't work out. Jack clearly hadn't given the boys any thought, and why should he? He hardly knew them.

Jack had valiantly tried to rally. "Of course Sam and Evan could come to California," he said too heartily, while pointing out that the boys would probably want to stay in the same school with their friends. "What if they live with their dad and visit us on holidays?" he'd said. "Would that be possible?"

It would have been. But Ava knew she couldn't do it. She hated sending her sons to their father for even two weekends a month. The house echoed around her without Evan and Sam to fill the rooms. Whenever the boys were gone, every baby she passed reminded her of how her own children had looked as infants with eyes squeezed shut against the light, wrapped like croissants in their blankets.

It was as if she were only partly real without her children. The boys gave shape to her days. Caring for them was exhausting, yet it created a rhythm she desperately missed when it was no longer there.

The only thing that got her through those awful weekends alone in the house was knowing that, on Sunday night, Evan and Sam would come bouncing back in like a pair of golden retrievers, damp and smelly and happy to see her. And how could she tear the boys away from their father, even if Mark agreed to the move? Mark was the only person in the world who loved the boys as much as she did.

"I'm sorry," she'd told Jack. "I can't. I need to live with my children, and they need to be close to their dad."

Jack had gone west without her. She hadn't missed him as much as she'd worried she might; she supposed now that she hadn't ever really fallen in love with him.

Caroline emerged from the desk, triumphantly waving a bag of corn chips. She tore the bag open with her teeth and munched a handful of chips. "So, ready to wow me with your new masterpieces?"

Ava felt suddenly tentative. "I don't know. I'm feeling anxious now that I'm here."

"Don't be an idiot. You know I'm your biggest fan."

"You might not be, after seeing these bizarre things." Ava followed her into the back room.

"Why? What's so bizarre about them?"

"They're just not me," Ava said, standing with Caroline in front of the worktable where she'd put the boxes. "I start to throw my usual mugs and pitchers and bowls, but lately something weird happens. It's like my hands are possessed or something. I'm turning out things that look like they're made by someone else."

"Maybe you got bored with playing it safe."

"Maybe," Ava agreed, but the remark stung.

She hovered anxiously while Caroline used an X-Acto knife to slice through the tape on the boxes, removed the half-dozen pots, and set them on the table. Then Ava narrowed her eyes and tried to see her work as if another artist really had created it.

She had thrown the bases of these pots as giant bowls, using two cylinders she attached together before widening them. Then she'd hand-built the top half of each pot using a combination of coils and tiny sculptures. Three of them had sculptures of women only, their hair crafted out of spaghetti-sized coils, their breasts and buttocks carved to protrude from the walls. The other pots had sculptures of entire families, the babies held aloft by their mothers to form the curvy rims along the edges of the pots. Ava had used iron oxide alone on the bottom halves, then glazed the top halves in brilliant blues and greens.

Caroline spun around to give Ava a hug. "They're brilliant!"

"You think so?" Ava allowed herself to smile.

"I do. These are pots with personality! Let me try to sell them before you take them anywhere else."

"All of them?" Ava asked in disbelief. Caroline typically took only a few of her larger decorative pieces at a time. "Not everyone wants pots with personality. Most people just want a reasonable casserole dish."

"True. But people also buy art that's emotionally expressive. And you know what I love best about these?" Caroline put her hands on Ava's shoulders, her hazel eyes solemn. "For once, you've made pots that express something about *you*." She took a small notebook out of her pocket and began jotting down descriptions of the pots to give Ava as a receipt.

Ava, meanwhile, wondered what these strange new clay creations—so crowded with men and women and children—could possibly say about her.

Afterward, she drove back to her studio to meet Sandra Judd, a photographer Caroline had recommended. Elaine had convinced Ava to invest in a Web site; she'd even offered to design it. Sandra, who arrived at Ava's studio a few minutes later in a white van full of camera equipment, was going to shoot photographs for it. She was a squat brunette in blue jeans and a red T-shirt, a bulldog of a woman who said little but worked efficiently.

Caroline stopped by at lunchtime to check on their progress. They'd nearly finished shooting when Olivia, a painter who lived on the basin side of Beach Plum Island and was one of Ava's dearest friends, came loping toward them wearing a sweat suit that must have been one of her son's castoffs. Ava and Caroline stared in amazement as Olivia dropped to the beach in front of them and did twenty push-ups, then stood up and succumbed to a coughing fit.

"I think she's losing a lung," Caroline said.

Ava patted Olivia's back. "Are you okay? Why in the world are you jogging?"

"I could hardly button my jeans this morning," Olivia wheezed. "Damn that menopause middle."

Caroline laughed. "Welcome to my world. And I've got ten years to go before the Big M."

"Right, rub it in now while you can. Don't worry. Your invitation to Cronesville will come." Olivia reached into the pocket of her gray hoodie, pulled out a pack of cigarettes, and lit one, ignoring their cries of disbelief. "So what's all this?" She gestured toward Sandra, who had placed one of Ava's pitchers on a small hillock of sand and was kneeling in front of it with a light meter.

"Portfolio shots for my Web site," Ava said. "We're doing the mugs next. Any ideas?"

Olivia cocked her head at the row of mugs Ava had lined up on the bench outside her studio. "They look like birds, because of those bright glazes and the feathery swirls on the handles. What if we play with that?"

"I'm not sure what you mean," Ava said.

"Here." Cigarette dangling between her lips, Olivia carried the mugs from the bench to a hunk of driftwood, where she arranged them on the log with the handles facing outward like birds on a fence, tails in a row.

"Perfect!" Ava said, grinning at Olivia.

"Not completely terrible," Caroline said.

Olivia snorted. "High praise from the High Priestess of the local art scene."

Ava called the photographer over. "What do you think, Sandra? If you shoot these mugs from down low, in front of the driftwood, maybe we can get the grass in the background, too."

Sandra nodded. "That should work." She shot the mugs from various angles, then packed up her equipment and said she'd have the pictures ready in two days. Caroline said good-bye as well and followed her out of the driveway.

Olivia had regained her composure after a second cigarette and somehow managed to look put together even in the oversized sweatshirt. Her hair was the same shade of gray as the fabric and had escaped from the hood to fall in long tendrils around her narrow face. "Who's your little stalker?" she asked, gesturing behind Ava.

"What?" Ava started to turn around, but Olivia put a hand on her arm.

"No need to be so obvious," Olivia whispered. "You don't want to spook the wild critter. It's a girl, and she's up by your studio on a bike."

"Oh! That must be Gigi, my half sister."

Olivia pursed her lips. "That's some hair color."

"Yes, well. Wait until you see the rest of her. Come on. I'll introduce you. She needs friends. Just put out that cigarette, will you, please? Gigi's trying to quit."

"Oh, great. Another self-righteous reformed smoker. Just what I need in my life," Olivia grumbled, tossing the butt onto the sand.

"Hey! You shouldn't litter," Gigi called from the studio doorway.

Ava was startled into laughing, but Olivia scowled. "It's biodegradable," she yelled back.

"Those are toxic chemicals!" the girl argued. "And if everybody littered, the beach would be like one big ashtray!"

Olivia rolled her eyes at Ava. "Is she always like this?"

"I don't know," Ava said. "I certainly hope so."

They walked up the beach to the studio, where Gigi straddled her bike with a defiant look. She wore a torn black T-shirt, baggy green shorts, and neon orange sneakers. Her short hair was no longer blue, but glowed a bright orange with magenta highlights. She looked like her head was on fire.

Ava wondered where Katy thought her daughter was right now. "Want to come in?"

"What for?" Gigi glanced over her shoulder, as if she were afraid of being surrounded.

"Well, have you had anything to eat this morning?"

Gigi shook her head.

"All right, then," Ava said. "How about coming in for some French toast?"

"You don't have to ask *me* twice," Olivia said.

Ava rolled her eyes. "I didn't even ask you once."

"Guess I'll have to ask myself, then," Olivia said, which made Gigi laugh, a giggle that made both women smile and then duck their heads to hide it.

The girl ate as if she had skipped not only breakfast, but dinner and lunch the day before as well. Ava made an entire package of bacon and turned half a loaf of bread into French toast, serving it in the dining room with Vermont maple syrup, bananas, and whipped cream. They talked about Ava's pottery, which was on the table and scattered around the house.

Then Gigi turned to Olivia. "Are you an artist, too?"

"Some might call me that. Right now I'm doing some river landscapes like that one," Olivia said, gesturing to the painting hanging above Ava's head. It was an oil painting of the salt marsh rendered in deep reds and plums and oranges. Ava had hung it on the back wall to give the room more depth, as if there were another window opposite the sliding doors opening onto the patio and the beach beyond it.

"She's much more famous than I am," Ava said.

"That painting has cool colors," Gigi offered.

"Gee. Thanks," Olivia said. "Sadly, the landscapes I'm painting now are tedious to look at."

"Your new work is *not* tedious," Ava protested.

"Yes it is. My palette is too muddy these days," Olivia said. "I still can't believe anyone would want to suffer through those brooding colors. Looking at them makes me feel positively Dutch."

"Well, even if they're horrible, people always want to buy landscapes," Ava said.

"Right, and there's nothing better than pandering to the tastes of weekend tourists." Olivia stood up and gestured to Gigi. "Come on, kid. Ava cooked. That means you and I are stuck with kitchen duty."

To Ava's surprise, Gigi went along cheerfully, talking to Olivia nonstop about drawing and painting: *Are landscapes harder than people? Are oils more fun than acrylics and watercolors? What happens if nobody ever buys your paintings?*

At that last question, Olivia cackled and said, "Then you get yourself a day job and paint at night. I once spent an entire summer proofreading telephone books for money. Of course, that was before you were born," she added. "Back in the days when people actually *used* telephone books."

"Back when we all had telephones attached to our kitchen walls and we couldn't walk more than six feet away from the wall if we were having a conversation," Ava added, then laughed at Gigi's horror-stricken expression.

Olivia went home once the kitchen was clean, saying that Gigi had inspired her to get out her watercolors and leave the oils alone for a while.

"She's pretty cool," Gigi offered. "Is Olivia your best friend?"

The girl sounded so wistful that Ava wanted to hug her, but didn't dare. "One of them. I've known her a long time. Friendships take a while to grow." Ava wanted to ask Gigi if she had any friends, but she didn't dare do that yet, either. "Would you like to try making a pot? Maybe like one of those jars you were drawing on the beach?"

"For real?"

"Of course. And let me tell you this right now: I don't let just anyone work in my studio and touch my tools. Only people I trust."

"Wow. That would be so sick!"

Whenever Gigi smiled, as she was doing now, Ava could see how much she resembled their father. She felt a pang, seeing her dad's same dark brown eyes and the dimple in Gigi's left cheek.

Gigi mastered hand building quickly. Her deft fingers quickly formed the coils for her first jar. She painstakingly followed Ava's instructions about smoothing the walls with a flat wooden tool as she rounded its belly and did a decent job on the lid, too, making a square lid for a round pot. An interesting choice, Ava thought, though who knew what would happen in the kiln.

Ava showed Gigi where to put the pot on the metal shelves with the other greenware, then explained how it would need to dry for two days before she could fire it. "Once I fire it in the kiln, you can come back to glaze it. Then it'll go in the kiln one more time, at a higher temperature, so the glaze turns into glass. After that, you can take your pot home."

"This is so awesome," Gigi said. "Thank you."

"You're very welcome." As Ava watched the girl diligently rinse the tools in the sink, she asked, "So where are you supposed to be right now?"

Gigi didn't turn around, but by the defiant toss of her head, Ava knew she was about to lie. "Nowhere. It's summer, remember?"

"Don't even try to lie to me. I'm a high school teacher and I have two sons older than you are," Ava reminded her. "I won't be mad. Just tell me the truth."

The girl spun around, her cheeks almost as pink as the tips of her hair. "All parents say they won't be mad when you tell them the truth. Then they are anyway."

"First of all, I'm not your parent. I'm your sister. Second, I really care about you. I'm sure your mom does, too. She just wants you to be happy."

"That's what all mothers say."

"No. Some mothers actually drown their children, or shoot them or shake them or give them away."

Gigi looked startled, then giggled. "*God.* You're even more morbid than I am."

Ava doubted that. "I'm telling you the truth. I care about you, and about your mom, too."

"Uh-huh. That's why you were at the house every day Dad was dying."

"I *wanted* to come. Your mom made it clear she didn't want me around."

"I believe you," Gigi said with a sigh, her narrow shoulders slumping. "Mom didn't want anybody around, especially not you or Elaine. I didn't blame Elaine for doing what she did at the funeral, you know. If I were you guys, I'd be pissed off at my mom, too, for stealing your dad."

"Oh, honey. Your mom didn't steal him. Our dad hadn't been happy for a long, long time." Ava bit her lip, wondering what she could say that would be true without being too honest. "Everything that happened with our parents was long ago. It had nothing to do with you, me, or Elaine. Nobody outside a marriage can really know what's happening on the inside of it."

She stopped talking, reminding herself that the girl was only fifteen. If Gigi had been older, Ava might have said that falling in love was like visiting a foreign country: Occasionally, you felt so at home in a new place, you wanted to stay there forever, adopting new customs as your own. More often, things went stale. If you were lucky enough to get out, you could search for a new country to visit. Or maybe you'd quit traveling to new places altogether, as Ava had done.

"There are more mysteries about love than you and I could solve in a lifetime," she told Gigi. "What I want to know is what you've told your mom about where you are."

"She still thinks I'm at riding camp."

"*Riding* camp?"

Gigi glanced up at Ava's incredulous tone. "Yeah. You know. Horses? My mom has this thing about them. Like, horses are her obsession."

Ava chewed her lip, trying not to laugh at the look of disgust on Gigi's face. "So I'm guessing you don't love horses like your mom does."

"That's not true! I probably love horses more than I love people, actually. But I hate competitive riding. And the people who do it," she added.

"So how did you get out of going? Doesn't your mom drive you there every morning?"

"No. I ride my bike. Mom doesn't leave the house, not ever. Not since Dad died, except for the funeral."

"Not at all?" Ava touched her own forehead, imagining Katy's pounding head, cottony with grief. "That poor girl. I should stop in on her."

"She wouldn't see you."

"Maybe not, but we need to go to your house and at least tell her where you are."

"No!" Gigi looked stricken. "She'd kill me if she knew!"

"Why? Does she really hate us that much?"

"I don't know. But she doesn't *like* you. She thinks you and Elaine have been bitches to her. Not that Mom would ever say the b-word," Gigi added quickly.

"I don't blame her," Ava said. "We haven't been very nice to her in the past. But I think she might really need some help, don't you? The kind of help you probably can't give her by yourself."

A long silence followed, while Gigi chewed on a fingernail. Finally she nodded and said, "Okay, I guess."

Ava's car was ancient, so old and sketchy it was easy for Gigi to imagine they were leaving a trail of rusted-out car parts behind them as they rattled over the bridge from Beach Plum Island toward Newburyport. She wondered if Ava was poor and then felt bad about wondering. If Ava was poor, wouldn't that mean Dad hadn't taken care of her, when he'd always given Gigi everything?

But Ava was a grown-up. A mom. Gigi had seen Ava's sons— her nephews!—at the service, two blond kids older and taller than she was. She was curious about them, not just because they were guys and went to public school—always an attraction, since the kids in her prep school were mostly posers—but because Ava's sons clearly loved music as much as she did. There were guitars and amps and sheet music all over Ava's living room, and even a drum set. She had kind of been hoping the boys would come home while she was there.

Now Gigi was glad they hadn't shown up. They would probably hate her anyway because her mom had stolen their grandfather. And she would have been totally humiliated to have them see Ava driving her home. She couldn't quit chewing her nails, wondering what would happen. Mom could be in one of those painkiller comas and not even wake up when they arrived. Or maybe she'd go totally ballistic when she discovered Gigi had been hanging out with Dad's other family instead of riding. She was relieved when Ava put on some chill tunes, a burner CD, so they didn't have to talk.

Mom was upstairs in her bedroom, where she always was these days, lying under a blanket like it wasn't the last day of June and eighty degrees. She looked like a little kid, her pale hair knotted and her face puffy and pink. Beside her was a whole blizzard of crumpled Kleenexes.

The maids cleaned twice a week, a trio of Brazilians that sounded like parakeets when they flitted around the house, talking in their singsong way and cleaning things Gigi would never think to clean, like the tops of picture frames, and folding the toilet paper ends into triangles. The cleaners had been here today, judging by the slick sheen on the counters and wood floors downstairs, but her mom hadn't let them into her bedroom since Dad died. Her bed was a mountain of blankets and pink sheets; there were so many clothes on the floor that it looked like her dresser had exploded, and there was a tray on her night table that smelled like cat food. Gramma Dawn must have left the food but not been back yet to retrieve the tray.

Gigi's scalp prickled with shame, having Ava see her mom this way, as helpless as an abandoned kitten. Before Dad got sick, Mom was prettier and more fun than any of her friends' mothers, and Gigi was proud to belong to her. Dad was, too.

"Your mother's the sun and I'm her moon," Dad always said. Then, to crack Gigi up, he'd add, "Not that I plan to moon her with you in the room, though. I'll save that for later."

"Bob! Do you always have to be so inappropriate?" her mother would say, but she'd be giggling, too, like she was hardly older than Gigi.

Gigi left Ava in the bedroom and carried the tray of food downstairs. She set it on the counter and stood at the sink, her nose and eyes running as she stared out the window. Rain spattered like handfuls of gravel against the glass, as if the sky were crying, too.

She scraped the plates into the trash, rinsed them, and loaded them into the dishwasher. This kitchen, with its gleaming giant stove and a refrigerator big enough to fit a cow inside, was the opposite of Ava's tiny kitchen, with its painted yellow cupboards and small white wooden table. Ava's felt like home. This one embarrassed her, suddenly. It looked like it should be inside a hotel, not a house. No wonder her mother stayed in bed. The two of them were rattling around in this house like dice in a bus.

She went back upstairs. Outside her mother's bedroom door, Gigi was amazed to hear Mom actually talking to Ava. *Talking.* These days Mom never talked, not even to Gramma Dawn, unless it was to ask for another glass of water and one of her "nerve pills." Mom's friends had pretty much stopped coming around or calling. This was a relief, sort of, since Gigi was the one who mostly had to answer the phone and say, at her mother's insistence, "Mom can't come to the phone right now. She's resting."

It sounded like Ava had pissed her off: Gigi could hear a thrumming tension in her mother's voice. Well, fine. Mad was definitely better than sad. Gigi slumped to the floor, her back against the cool wall, and listened.

"You don't understand. She *has* to go back to that camp," Mom was saying. "I can't have her running all over town unsupervised. She's only fifteen, for God's sake."

"But she hates the camp," Ava said. "Why make her go back? Can't you get the money refunded?"

"This isn't about the money! This is about what's best for Gigi! She needs structure over the summer and she needs to conquer her fear of riding. I know she loves horses. It's just a matter of getting enough experience and building confidence."

Gigi heard a rustling sound. Was her mother actually sitting up? She was afraid to look.

"She does love horses," Ava said. Her voice was soothing and warm, the way it had been with Gigi that first day. Ava's kids were lucky, knowing their mom wasn't going to fly off the handle and slap them, or crumple and cry in front of them, the way Mom started doing after Dad got sick last year. "But I think the camp environment might be too stressful for her right now."

Gigi sighed with relief. Thank God Ava didn't say anything about her not wanting to ride competitively. Mom was so sure Gigi had what it took to be an Olympian, or to at least compete in the Grand Nationals. Gigi would rather set herself on fire than do that.

"*Everything* is stressful right now," Mom said. "Gigi misses her father. She has to get back in the saddle and keep going."

There was a small hesitation, as if Ava was struggling not to say the most obvious thing: *Oh, like you're doing, lying here day after day? Is that what you mean by getting back in the saddle?*

But Ava wasn't mean enough to say anything like that. Instead, she said, "Maybe she could go back to camp next summer, when she's had time to grieve. I think Gigi needs a complete change of scene for a little while, something that doesn't remind her so much of her dad."

Gigi was startled by this idea. What did it matter what she did? She thought about Dad all the time anyway, no matter where she was or what she was doing.

"Like what?" her mom said, sniffing.

"How about art? Gigi seems very creative."

Her mom actually laughed. "That's an understatement." There was another rustle of blankets. "I remember one teacher who taught Gigi's class how to make gingerbread houses at Christmas. You know, the kits you can make with graham crackers and canned frosting and candy? Well, every one of the kids in that class made a tidy little A-frame cottage, just like the picture on the box. But not Gigi! Oh, no. Her house was all different levels and flat roofs. When the teacher tried to apologize for not being able to make Gigi follow directions, Bob stopped her. He said it was the only gingerbread house Frank Lloyd Wright might have made, and he was damn proud of Gigi for making it." Her mother was crying now, a little huffing sound. "Bob understood Gigi, but I never have."

That was true, Gigi thought. How would the two of them ever get along without Dad around, acting like one of those rubber bumpers that keeps ships from crashing into docks?

When Gigi peeked around the corner of the doorframe, Ava was picking up the tissues on the floor and throwing them away. Then Ava sat down next to Mom and smoothed her hair. "Raising a child is never easy. It's like making art."

Her mom sniffed. "If you mean it's like molding them into pleasing, useful shapes, then I'm a dunce at it."

"No." Ava shook her head, her long streaky hair moving softly around her shoulders. "Being a great artist takes good technique. But you have to be open to your instincts and emotions, too. You have to stop trying to force a piece and let it evolve organically."

"And what does Gigi need to be? Organically, I mean?" Her mom was looking at Ava, really looking at her, with her beautiful gray eyes glimmering like tide pools.

"Herself," Ava said.

Gigi pressed a hand to her mouth and scrambled downstairs, not wanting to hear any more. How could she be herself, when she didn't even know what that was?

When she sat down to write to Katy, Elaine let herself say everything she felt, crumpling pages of stationery one by one and burning them in her sink. It was the Fourth of July; rather than drive north to Ava's and fight traffic, she had gone to a rooftop party in Boston with Tony and his new boyfriend, a swanky lawyer who probably owned more shoes than she did, to watch the fireworks. Now she was alone and melancholy, missing Dad because the Fourth was his favorite holiday.

Every year he'd drag them to Rockport, that ridiculous toy of a town at the tip of Cape Ann with its too-often-painted red fishing shack, its bright buoys dangling like earrings from its clapboards. Dad always insisted on a lobster picnic, despite the fact that she and Ava hated lobsters. They'd eat the lobsters cold on Back Beach with whatever rank potato salad they could buy in town, and stay for the parade of fire trucks and out-of-tune high school bands and bagpipers. Rockport always had a bonfire, too, with something like a pirate ship at the top of it that threatened to topple onto the eager crowd.

Now Elaine poured herself another glass of wine—it was the Fourth, after all—and pressed her pen to a fresh sheet of paper. "Dear Katy," she wrote, then:

*I'm sorry that my dad died and left you a widow and I acted
like a punk about it.*

*I'm sorry that my dad left my mom and I lost a year of my life
and wanted to kill you.*

*I'm sorry that you were ever born. You're the reason my mom
died of a broken heart.*

*I'm sorry that I'm so petty and mean and jealous.*

*I'm sorry that I never knew my dad the way you and Gigi did.*

This last line made her hand tremble as she lit a match to the
page.

Why hadn't she known her dad? They were too different. Everyone said so: Elaine was dark and high-strung and delicate, like Suzanne, and Ava was Bob's scrappy outdoorsy girl, the son he never
had. Dad and Ava loved to hike and make up stupid limericks and
songs. They loved things like Salisbury Beach and the Topsfield
Fair, that horror show of racing pigs, puke-inducing thrill rides,
and fried dough.

Dad was proud of his working-class roots and flaunted them,
making people—especially Elaine, as she got older—uncomfortable
with his childhood stories about stuffing rags in the walls of his
family's home for extra insulation and eating roadkill. Meanwhile,
Mom, whose family had no more education than Dad's but more
money, thanks to Grandpa's car dealership, was still just a small-
town girl from Bumfuck, Maine, and practically killed herself trying to fit in with people at the country club. She joined the PTO
and the garden club, volunteered at the hospital, learned golf and
bridge, and ordered her clothes out of the right catalogs. She loved
her children, Elaine knew, and tried her best to play the part of a
good mother. Mom was always home when they returned from

school, even if she was just parked on the sofa in front of her soaps. She read stories to them at night, took them shopping for sports equipment or just the right outfit for a party, and displayed their school papers and drawings on the fridge.

Yet, even as a child, Elaine was acutely aware that Suzanne was doing some sort of memorized dance, counting steps as she parented with the tense, distracted air of someone looking over her shoulder to see if she, herself, was earning a positive report card. By the time Elaine was leaving elementary school as a skinny, determined fifth grader, Suzanne seemed unable to cope with even these clearly earmarked mothering tasks and increasingly handed them over to Ava.

After Dad left, Mom fell apart, transformed into the kind of woman Elaine would have crossed the street to avoid: an unwashed hoarder, a timid agoraphobic, a woman who might burst into tears or crumple to the ground if you even looked at her cross-eyed.

Elaine hadn't been able to avoid her, of course. It had fallen to her to care for Mom after the divorce. She'd worried the whole time that Mom would never get better.

And guess what? She was right to worry. Mom never did get better. That knowledge was like a flickering match leading Elaine down a dark tunnel to an even damper, more shameful fear: that she might look as much like her mother on the inside as she did on the outside.

Elaine didn't have to deal with their mother while Ava lived at home, because Ava, five years older, had always cooked and helped Elaine with homework. Elaine got to be a kid, with her own agenda: school, field hockey, boyfriends. Then, when Elaine was fifteen, Ava married Mark and moved out of the house. She remembered feeling angry and hurt and abandoned, just as Gigi must be feeling right now. Entitled brat or not, Gigi couldn't find it easy, losing her father at fifteen.

Their father.

Elaine sighed and started over on a fresh sheet of paper.

*Dear Katy and Gigi,*

*I am sorry for your loss. Dad was a powerful presence in all our lives. I know he was a good husband and father to you, and that you were close to him in ways I never was. I guess maybe that's why it hit me so hard when he died: I never really got to know him, and I will regret that forever.*

*I want to apologize for acting the way I did at the service. I would like to blame my atrocious behavior on the wine.* [Here, Elaine barely refrained from adding, "Which could have been better, by the way."] *But I hold myself fully accountable for my outburst. You were trying to honor my father with the memorial service and I greatly appreciate the effort you made. You were generous to include us, and I thank you.*

*I hope things will get easier for you over time. I promise to behave more like an adult if our paths ever chance to cross in the future.*

*Sincerely yours,*

*Elaine Barrett*

Then, before she could change her mind or spend any more time fretting, Elaine neatly folded the paper in thirds, slid it into a matching envelope, and put a stamp on it.

The deal Ava made with Katy after the Fourth of July was simple: she would offer Gigi a job in her pottery studio and keep an eye on her.

Katy didn't seem to have gotten out of bed since the last time

Ava was here a week ago. She looked up at her with gray eyes wreathed in plum shadows. "What if Gigi hates pottery, too?"

"She won't," Ava said with confidence. "But if she does, we'll think of something else. Is Gigi close to anybody else in your family?"

"Not really. Only my brother, Simon, maybe. I hear her talking to him sometimes when he visits."

Ava felt her cheeks grow warm, remembering how Simon had held her as she cried after the service. He would want to be aware of how his sister was struggling; on the other hand, Katy probably didn't want him to know. How could she get Simon here without making Katy feel embarrassed or defensive?

Then Ava had a thought. "Maybe Gigi would like to see Simon. If you give me his number, I'll call him and let him know what's going on. He could check in with Gigi from time to time."

"Okay." Katy's voice was listless, but at least she wasn't objecting.

Ava found an old envelope on Katy's dresser amid the rubble of clothes and jewelry and wrote down Simon's cell phone number. "All right, then," she said. "I should get back. The boys will be home soon and they've started a band. I like to be around when they're practicing just in case groupies show up."

"Your dad would have loved that," Katy said. "He always wanted to be in a band."

Ava was so surprised that she stopped and turned around. "He did? I never knew that."

"Oh yes. He was a frustrated musician. Maybe next time you come, I could show you a video of him singing with Gigi." A pair of frown lines appeared, marring her pretty forehead. "You will come back, won't you?"

"Of course," Ava said.

She went downstairs and said good-bye to Gigi, who looked panicked by the news that Ava was leaving. "It's all right," Ava said.

"Your mom and I talked. You can come to the studio tomorrow. I'm offering you a job if you want it. Do you?"

The girl nodded so hard that her pink and orange hair flopped over one eye. "Do you really have work for me to do? Seriously?"

"Don't worry," Ava said, waving a hand. "I'm a slave driver. I promise you won't be bored. And you'll learn more about pottery than you ever wanted to know."

When Gigi smiled, as she did now, she was so startlingly pretty that Ava could almost overlook the lip, nose, and eyebrow piercings. "Also, I'm calling your uncle Simon so he can look in on your mom," Ava added. She gave the girl a quick hug.

Outside, Ava dialed Simon's number from the car. When his voice mail picked up, she stammered through her message. "I was really grateful to you for comforting me during my dad's service," she said, hating the stiff way her voice sounded. "I hope you don't think it's too weird that I'm calling you, but Katy and Gigi need you to come around more if you can. Like you said, we're family and we need to help each other through hard times."

She hung up then, before she could make an even bigger fool of herself than she already had.

## CHAPTER FOUR

Ava had e-mailed the portfolio shots two days ago, but Elaine had been too overwhelmed at work to sort through them or do anything about starting to design Ava's Web site. This made her feel guilty, but there wasn't much she could do about it. *Know your priorities*: that was one of her key mantras.

When Ava called midweek to invite her to dinner on Friday night, therefore, Elaine said yes despite her plan to go clubbing and maybe hook up with someone for the night. Maybe she could do both: she'd review the photos and design the Web site at Ava's house, with her sister's input. It couldn't possibly take more than an hour or two. Choosing pictures of pots had to be easier than selecting photos for school Web sites, where you had to tediously toss out shots of homely kids, professors with their eyes closed or scratching their butts, and any photos that revealed graffiti or crumbling buildings.

"Why don't you spend the night?" Ava suggested. "I mean, if you can stand the music. Evan and Sam have turned my living room into a practice studio."

Elaine hesitated. Hanging out at her sister's overnight would definitely be a healthier choice than her original plan to cruise the Matchbox Bar, but a lot less fun. "Let's see how late it gets," she hedged. "I'll bring the wine. What are you cooking?"

"Probably spaghetti, since the boys are with me this weekend, along with who knows how many of their friends."

"Wait. Wasn't last weekend your weekend with them, too?"

There was a slight hesitation; then Ava said, "Yes, but Mark is seeing somebody. He doesn't want the boys to meet her yet."

"They don't know, but you do? That's a little twisted, don't you think?" Elaine regretted the words as soon as they left her mouth, but she'd never understood how Ava could have forgiven Mark for cheating on her and making her look like an idiot. If any guy did that to her, she'd for sure find a way to ruin his life, if only by posting egregious photos on Facebook.

"I fixed him up with this woman, actually. She and I play tennis once in a while."

"Oh. My. God. You did *not* fix him up. What planet are you from? Your own husband!"

"Ex," Ava reminded her. "And why not? Mark's a good guy. Besides, if Evan and Sam are going to have a stepmother, I'd rather help pick her out."

They hung up shortly after that. Elaine sat at her desk and stared sightlessly at her monitor for a few minutes, thinking about how Ava had once told her that most divorces happened long before the marriages were over.

Life was too short to let things slide by, yet that's what people did. The human condition was just plain tragic when it came to relationships. Maybe you loved a few people and did some good work, added some new souls to the planet. You felt useful for a while.

Then, when you were done with accomplishing the requisite goals society considered signs of success and responsibility, you breathed a sigh of relief and thought, *Okay, now I can do what I want.* Only by then you'd run out of time. Your marriage was on the rocks, you got laid off, or your kids had turned out all wrong. You spent your last years wading through a swamp of regret, crippled by anger or struggling for salvation.

Even if you avoided most of life's dismal pitfalls, even if things did go well for you, then what? What did it matter if you loved certain people with your whole heart and soul, your fingers and lips and words and tears, and had been loved in return? You still died alone and left them behind. Or they left you first, paralyzed by grief until the day your heart stopped beating.

Ultimately, no matter how you lived, you were faced with the same profound, pitiful, and unanswerable questions: Why are we here? Why do one thing and not another? Why love one person and not someone else, or anyone at all, if everyone's story ends the same way?

Elaine gave herself a vigorous mental shake and opened a new document. She didn't have time for pointless navel-gazing.

She stayed late at the office and then went to do her shift at the suicide hotline. She'd been volunteering for over a year now, at Tony's suggestion, when Elaine finally decided the third therapist she'd seen after her mother died had nothing more to offer. Through the years, she'd literally heard it all, every stage of grief mapped out in painstaking detail, as if Lewis and Clark themselves were cataloging her thorny, swampy trail of dissolution with their explorers' zeal. At Tony's insistent urging, she had volunteered to talk people off the proverbial ledge—well, the literal ledge, in the case of one guy who wanted to jump out of his apartment window after losing his job—mainly to prove she wasn't as pitiful as most of the nutters out there.

Instead, Elaine had been fascinated, horrified, intrigued, saddened, and terrified by the level of misery swirling about in the world. Everyone, it seemed, had something going on. Only the rigors of daily life kept you above the black muck rising around your ankles and threatening to swallow you whole.

"We don't expect you to be an expert," said Katrina, the woman who trained her. "But you being here to answer someone's call might make the difference between life and death. Fewer than a third of the thirty-two thousand people who commit suicide in the U.S. each year are seen by mental health professionals. We really can guide people to make different choices."

Despite her honeyed voice and name, Katrina was the opposite of a blond bombshell, built more like a linebacker and with so many tattoos on her beefy arms that Elaine had thought at first the woman was wearing long sleeves. "Your job is to just listen, and maybe help the caller feel less alone." She had instructed Elaine to collect as much information about the person on the phone at the beginning—such as where the caller was and whether he or she had abused any substances—to prioritize the calls they might share with emergency services.

"Then you want to build rapport," Katrina had continued. "You may have a chance to direct them to mental health resources later. In the meantime, let them explain, vent, rage, whatever. Your job isn't to cure people. All you can do is offer support, so the callers can maybe get through this one bad day to live another, better one. Sometimes we get enough information to warrant calling 911, but usually not. If no medical intervention is necessary, or if you can't get the caller to tell you where she is, the main thing is to thank her for being brave enough to make that call. That alone might give her a reason to keep going."

"That's it?" Elaine had asked, stunned. "That's all we can give people? A temporary reprieve?"

Katrina had raised one penciled eyebrow. "Isn't that enough?"

The fact was, except for the few callers Elaine heard from over and over, she never knew if she had an effect on the people who phoned asking for permission to end things or a reason not to. She took calls from women whose boyfriends beat them, from drug addicts and cutters and alcoholics and some whose words she couldn't understand between the sobs.

The calls picked up over the holidays, whenever there was a full moon, during heat waves and blizzards that kept people indoors. Elaine found that sometimes the most helpful thing wasn't just to listen, with some of these callers, but to tell them about her mother, or about her own struggles with depression, and how she managed to keep going. She prescribed exercise, the pleasure of trashy television reality shows, and going to bed early.

"Forgive yourself," she told people over and over, hoping that someday the words would sink in and she could do the same.

On Friday morning, Elaine went into work again early, after a hard workout in her favorite spin class, so she could leave for Ava's before four o'clock. Traffic was light; it was the third week of July and most people were either already on vacation or leaving for their precious weekly rentals in New Hampshire and Maine.

You couldn't pay her enough to be part of that scene, loading up kids and bikes and sitting in traffic with the destination being nothing more than an overcrowded beach where you had to withstand other people's radios or a weedy green lake where the moms wore bathing suits with skirts, the dads wheeled coolers of beer, and the kids never stopped eating.

No, Elaine's idea of a good vacation was the one she'd taken last year to a high-end resort in Mexico that catered to singles, a place where she could soak up some sun, sleep, and hook up to her heart's content.

On that vacation, she'd seduced a noisy Texan. It hadn't been difficult. She had deliberately waited until the man took a chair on her side of the pool. Then she untied the top of her bathing suit and turned onto her stomach, arching her back as she adjusted her butt on the lounge.

The Texan bought her margaritas made with a cheap mix that left a chalky aftertaste. The waiter brought the third drink with a disapproving shake of his head. When the Texan dove into the pool with an expert racer's dive that barely rippled the water's surface, the waiter bent low over Elaine's chair to say, *"Cuidado, el Tejano es un hombre sin vergüenza."*

*Be careful, the Texan is a man without shame,* was how that sentence literally translated. Though Elaine—always precise in her Spanish classes—knew it could also mean, *The Texan is a bold man.*

Either way, that's exactly what she was looking for in a vacation fling. She wanted a man with no shame because she wanted to do shameful, naughty things. And she wanted a bold man who wouldn't be intimidated by a woman with an appetite in bed.

When the Texan, a man with a satisfyingly flat stomach, broad shoulders, an expensive wristwatch, just the right amount of chest hair, and a thriving import-export business, returned to his chair, Elaine had turned over again lazily, pulling her swimsuit top up over her breasts almost too late.

"It's so hot out here," she murmured. "I think it's time for me to get out of this sun."

They went to his room. She didn't ask his name and she was grateful that he didn't ask hers. They'd showered first, and he had soaped Elaine up and down, admiring her body with words she'd never actually heard anyone use other than in porn movies. At one point, he'd slapped her ass and let out a whoop of joy.

Elaine was still smiling over this happy memory when she

pulled up in front of Ava's cottage, a gray shingled bungalow that squatted like a gull on the beach. She could never live here, an hour from Boston on an island with more piping plovers than people, but it was a breathtaking spot. The gray shingles of the cottage were tinged lavender from the sunset, the sand around it sparkling diamonds.

She sat in her car for a minute and admired the rushing sound of waves breaking on the beach. For a minute, she felt envious of her sister's life on this beautiful island. Ava had no idea what it was like in the real world, where information came at you so fast it was like being tarred and feathered with factoids every day.

Elaine closed her eyes, took some slow deep breaths, and reminded herself of everything she'd accomplished. Tonight, she and Ava could relax together. They would share a bottle of wine and she could help Ava with her Web site. They'd talk about the boys and Ava's pottery. Whatever differences she and Ava might have, they were sisters. They had to stick together, especially now that their parents were gone.

Suddenly, Elaine's peaceful mood was shattered by raucous music: an electric guitar, a bass, drums, and the wailing of a girl who sounded as if her heart were breaking. Shit. This must be Evan and Sam and their new band. She hoped Ava planned to kick them out of the house before dinner.

Then she remembered what Ava had said about making spaghetti for the boys and their friends, and groaned. Even the Matchbox Bar in Cambridge had to be quieter than this.

Elaine grabbed the wine, climbed out of the car, and diligently locked it, leaving her laptop in the trunk. Inside, she took off her shoes in the kitchen and wiped her feet carefully on the mat.

Though, from the looks of things, whatever she did or didn't do with her feet would hardly matter. The linoleum floor was gritty with sand and the counters were stacked with cooking pots and dishes. There was a bucket of compost on the counter, too, filled to overflowing. Ava insisted on loading leftover food into that bucket and kept some kind of bin contraption out back, where worms broke down the compost so she could spread it on her vegetable and flower gardens. In Elaine's opinion, there was such a thing as being too organic.

The floor was an obstacle course of shoes, at least fifteen pairs, most of them clown-sized and reeking. How many people were in this band? Elaine said a little prayer of thanks for her own peaceful condo with its garbage disposal, beige walls, and white shag carpet, uncluttered except for some tasteful linen pillows and a few bits of Ava's pottery.

Ava, thankfully, was setting the dining room table with only two places and had shut the door between the dining room and living room. She wore her usual glaze-splattered overalls over a yellow T-shirt, her hair twisted in a blue bandanna.

"Oh good, you're here," Ava said. "I just fed the kids. If it gets too loud in here, we can take our plates out to the patio. It's warm enough, don't you think?"

What Elaine thought was that she'd rather sit outside, away from the mess and noise, even if she had to wear a ski parka. But something in her sister's expression—an anxious look in her eyes—stopped her from saying so.

"Wherever you want to eat is fine with me," Elaine said, just as the girl stopped singing and the drummer went into a crashing, frenzied solo.

This was enough to make Ava load everything onto a tray and carry it out to the patio. Elaine followed with the wine, a pair of glasses, and a corkscrew. She opened the wine while Ava served their plates. They balanced their food on their laps and ate as the sun went down, turning the sea from green to blue to cobalt. By the second glass of wine, the music was tolerable.

They talked about Elaine's work and Ava's Web site. Then Ava told her about the visit to Katy, avoiding Elaine's eyes.

Elaine stabbed at a meatball. "It's not like they're family anymore. That ship has sailed. You've got enough on your plate with the boys and your studio. Why get involved in their problems? Let Katy's family take care of her. That's who she needs!"

"I know. I did call her brother after I left."

By the way Ava was concentrating on her plate, Elaine suspected there was something else her sister wasn't telling her. She didn't want to know what it was, so she didn't ask. She hated having Ava angry at her, and she knew whatever she said about Katy was bound to be the wrong thing.

After dinner, they carted the dishes into the kitchen and stacked them on the counter with the others. Then Elaine went out to the car to grab her laptop rather than use Ava's computer in the living room, where the band was now playing a surprisingly melodic version of "Californication."

"What do you think? The band sounds pretty good, right?" Ava said as Elaine booted up her laptop on the dining room table. "That's Sam on lead guitar and Evan on bass."

"Not bad," Elaine agreed. "It's just a shame they don't have a volume control. You do have a curfew, right, so you can get some sleep?"

"Oh sure. None of them have cars and the parents have all promised to pick them up by eleven o'clock on weeknights."

"Friday's a weeknight now?" Elaine looked up, teasing, thinking of her own high expectations for the Matchbox Bar later.

"It is for me," Ava said. "I have a big order to finish tomorrow."

They spent an hour setting up the Web site. Elaine showed Ava how to navigate the template and upload content onto different pages. She also talked her into writing a short newsletter and adding an e-mail subscription feature. "You can send out news about your gallery events and sales that way," she said.

Ava learned quickly and readily agreed to everything, making Elaine wish all her clients were this smart and amenable. They had the site up and live in less than two hours. It wasn't even nine o'clock. She shut the laptop and packed it away.

"Thanks for the sleepover invite, but I think I'll head out," she said. "There's this band I want to hear in Cambridge."

Unfortunately, Ava knew her too well. "I really wish you'd stop trolling for hookups," she said. "I worry about you bringing home the wrong guy. Or the wrong STD. I don't understand why you take such risks."

Elaine held up a hand. "Stop! You know I play it safe. I never bring anyone home, I always have my own wheels, and I carry condoms and pepper spray. You can't possibly understand what I'm doing because you've only ever been with two men in your whole life. You say you don't understand me, but I don't get you, either! I can't believe you don't have needs. Why don't you come with me?"

"The boys are here," Ava said.

"They're old enough to take care of themselves."

"Yes, but now they're old enough to take risks themselves, and I'm not about to leave a houseful of teenagers unattended. Anyway, I do have 'needs,' as you so tactfully put it, but I don't think those could possibly be met with one-night stands."

"How do you know unless you try it?" Elaine was warming to the idea. This was just what her sister needed: to change out of those crappy overalls and get off mother patrol. "Or I could help you use one of the dating sites. That way, you'd know a lot about somebody before even meeting him."

"No, I wouldn't," Ava said. "I'd only know what the guy chose to share online. I wouldn't really know *him*. Knowing somebody has as much to do with physical chemistry as it does with knowing whether he loves bicycling or sci-fi movies."

"Exactly! That's why I'd rather meet a man in person before I sleep with him. If I see him with my own eyes, I can make a decision based on how he holds his wineglass or what kind of clothes he wears."

"But that's just the point, Elaine. You're meeting men not because you want to *know* them, but because you want to *sleep* with them."

Elaine laughed. Sometimes the five-year gap between their ages seemed more like five decades. Ava was so off the social grid, it was like dealing with Jane Austen. "Crawl out of your cave. Men have been choosing women based on our appearance since time began. So have women. The difference is now it's okay for us to say we want the same thing they do."

"Which is what?"

"A little pleasure with no strings."

"God. You make it sound so *soulless*." Ava must have seen something in Elaine's expression, because she quickly apologized. "I'm sorry," she said. "I didn't mean that the way it sounded. I'd just like to see you in a real relationship for once. You're worth more than this."

"It's not about what I'm worth. It's about what I want," Elaine said. "And I'd like to see you in a real relationship, too, so we're even." She couldn't decide if she was angry or not. She knew Ava only wanted her to be happy, so Elaine chose not to give in to her temper. Instead, she kissed her sister as she stood up and said, "I'll just say good-bye to the boys, and then I'm off."

"Don't bother," Ava said, standing up. "Evan and Sam are so

busy with their friends, they won't even know you've been here. Besides, the living room looks like a bomb went off. See them next time."

Elaine stared at her, confused. If she didn't know better, she'd think Ava was deliberately standing between her and the door to the living room, blocking her way so she'd have to leave through the kitchen. Her sister's mouth looked practically stitched shut. "What's going on? You're always so big on manners. Of *course* I should see the boys. They'll think it's weird if I just sneak in and out."

"No they won't," Ava said too quickly.

That did it. "Move!"

"Wait. I need to tell you something. But first promise you won't be mad."

Elaine snorted. "Why wouldn't I be mad, with you shooing me out of your house like a Jehovah's Witness?"

"I am not!"

"You are so!" Elaine was incredulous. Her sister still wasn't getting out of the way. "What the hell is in the living room that you don't want me to see? And no more lame excuses about the house being a mess! This is *me* you're talking to. I've seen your house look so bad, I'm surprised the board of health wasn't here posting notices."

Ava folded her arms, her green eyes hard. "Thanks a lot. I'm used to you acting childish, but I don't expect you to be *mean*. At least not to me. What did I do to deserve that?"

"I'll tell you in a minute." Elaine darted to the living room door and yanked it open before Ava could stop her.

There were teenagers on every surface, their blue-jeaned or bare legs draped over the sofas and chairs and floor. Evan and Sam were on their guitars, a shaggy drummer doing his thing behind them.

In front of the band, the singer held a microphone attached by a long cord to a speaker. She had her back to Elaine, a small girl in a shredded pink T-shirt that matched the pink tips of her orange hair. The T-shirt didn't quite reach her hip bones, where her baggy white shorts were cinched with a rainbow belt. She was barefoot.

Evan and Sam started playing. It took Elaine a minute to recognize the opening chords as Nirvana's "Smells Like Teen Spirit." Then the singer turned around, her lovely slim pale arms pinwheeling as she danced and started singing, her voice rough and sweet and teasing, a slight vibrato in it.

The scene came together then, rooting Elaine to the spot. It was Gigi, singing. Gigi with her eyes closed, Gigi with their father's smile and dimple, Gigi in Ava's living room, singing and happy and so mesmerizing nobody could take their eyes off her. Especially not Ava's boys, who didn't even notice Elaine standing there.

Elaine spun on her heel and fled through the kitchen, her laptop case banging against her hip. Ava followed, shouting, but Elaine kept going and pressed the button on her car key, frantically trying to unlock the BMW and slip into its safe white leathery sanctuary before Ava could reach her.

She failed. She'd pushed the wrong button and now the trunk gaped open. Elaine ran to slam it shut before getting into the car. But Ava, always faster and stronger, was practically on top of her, pinning Elaine against the car.

"Stop being such a damn baby!" Ava said. "Even if you don't want to talk to me, at least come inside and calm down before you drive off and kill somebody."

Elaine felt so much pressure on her chest, it was as if it weren't Ava holding her in place but a tree. A giant redwood falling out of nowhere, slamming against her torso, making it impossible to breathe. She couldn't get the image of Gigi dancing in her sister's living room out of her mind, swiveling her hips and shaking her head so that the hair looked like flames, pink and orange catching the overhead light.

Gigi's powerful voice carried out the window, surrounding Elaine until she wanted to cover her ears while at the same time admiring its throbbing emotional intensity. How did such a skinny little girl manage to combine tone, power, and longing to make singing seem so effortless? So *fun?*

By practicing with their father. By singing with him for hours and hours. Elaine could almost hear Dad's voice right now, accompanying Gigi, the way the noise of the surf, angry and unpredictable, always lay beneath the shushing sound of a summer wind swirling sand around your feet.

"Let me explain," Ava was saying.

"You don't owe me an explanation," Elaine said, her words falling out of her mouth like wooden blocks, clunking onto the driveway. "Who you invite into your home is your business."

Ava blew out her breath so hard that a lock of her hair lifted from her face and touched Elaine's cheek. She didn't let go of Elaine. "Of course it's my business, you idiot," she said. "But that doesn't mean I want to see you upset. I wanted to talk to you about Gigi tonight. That's why I invited you to dinner."

"I thought you wanted my help on your Web site." Elaine was proud of herself, speaking without shouting despite the emotional fog starting to cloud her vision.

"Sure, of course," Ava said, backpedaling. "But I could have waited. I wanted you to come over because I was hoping we could discuss Katy and Gigi. Katy's still in a bad way, so I've been looking after Gigi by having her work with me in the studio."

"*That*," Elaine said, lifting an arm to point to Ava's house, "is not your *studio*."

Finally, Ava looked flustered. "I know. It's just that Gigi and the boys hit it off, and Evan and Sam needed a singer. You heard her. Gigi's good! They just booked their first real gig, a free concert at the farmers' market next month! I was hoping you'd come."

Elaine locked eyes with Ava, allowing herself, just for one moment, to hate the pride shining in her sister's green gaze, to abhor that generous love for her children and every single amazing thing they did. When she could speak, she said, "Thanks for the invite, but I'm busy next month." She lifted her arm again, this time to remove Ava's hand from her chest. "In fact, I'm pretty tied up for the whole summer, actually. Work and stuff. You know."

"Don't be like this!" Ava's eyes filled with tears. "I'm really sorry. Gigi was hurting. I had to do something to help her. She's our *sister.*"

Elaine stepped away from the car. To her relief, Ava backed up. "You did what you thought was right and I'm sure Katy is grateful. Having Gigi hang out here is probably a million times cheaper than camp. Anyway, I've got to go. The band I really want to hear is at a bar in Cambridge. I'm already late for the first set."

"I didn't mean to upset you. I'm really sorry," Ava said again.

"Yeah, well. Me, too."

This time, Elaine pushed the right button on the car key. She got into the car and backed out of the driveway slowly, her hands steady on the wheel, her sister's waving figure growing smaller and smaller.

With the sea cresting white behind her, it was as if Ava were on a ferry, headed out to sea, and Elaine was the one standing still. She didn't wave back.


Ava got up at first light on Saturday and went out to the studio. She'd had a bad night's sleep, thinking about Elaine. Her sister's fury and hurt had been more controlled than usual, but honest to God, sometimes Elaine acted like a three-year-old on a bender.

It didn't help that she was partly to blame. She should have talked to Elaine about Gigi right away. Elaine might have been more reasonable if Ava hadn't sprung things on her. For all of her pragmatic, sometimes icy businesslike demeanor, Elaine had a kind heart and was often surprisingly generous.

Instead, Elaine had been shocked, seeing Gigi with the boys, and the look on her face had been one of absolute devastation. As children, Ava had mothered Elaine because their own mother couldn't. Now she'd let her down at a time when Elaine was clearly in so much pain. She wondered if Elaine had still gone to a bar last night and picked up a man. If so, Ava hoped it had at least brought her some comfort.

Ava couldn't imagine ever doing such a thing. But she didn't harbor that same poisonous, leaden black core of loneliness that Elaine carried. Having children had cleansed her of it. Being a mother was like being a ship's figurehead: you had to keep moving forward through the waves and weather, your head high, even when an iceberg was clearly on the horizon, too big to go around.

She began wedging a block of clay, furiously pressing the heels of her hands into the cold gritty stoneware to pop the bubbles of air that could cause the pieces to explode in the kiln. No, she didn't need a man. Her life was full enough between teaching, her studio work, and the boys. Besides, now there was Gigi, too.

Despite Elaine, thinking about Gigi made Ava smile. True to her word, the girl had arrived promptly every morning since the day Ava hired her. Whether she asked Gigi to sweep the studio, load the kiln, prepare clay, or mix glazes, the girl was remarkably quick and curious, eager to learn, and good company besides.

Then, two weeks ago, Ava had returned from the grocery store one afternoon expecting Gigi to already be gone and found her in the living room with Evan. Evan, usually so shy, was sitting next to Gigi on the couch, his blond head bowed and almost touching Gigi's pink and orange one. The two of them were humming a song they were listening to on Evan's iPod, each wearing one earbud of Evan's headphones. It had been only natural to invite Gigi to dinner.

During dinner, Gigi and Evan had surprised her again by asking Sam if Gigi could try singing with the band.

"I don't know about that," Sam said. He had appointed himself the band's unofficial manager, creating a Facebook page and posting YouTube videos.

"But we need a singer, dude," Evan said. "You're the one who said so."

"Yeah, but I meant a *good* singer." Sam didn't say this unkindly; he took his role as older brother seriously and was always kind to Evan. But he was honest. If Gigi didn't cut it, Ava knew Sam wouldn't let her sing with them.

"She's got a great voice," Evan had argued. "She really does."

Ava had to pinch herself, hearing Evan, typically so unsure of himself, stand up to Sam. Sam wasn't only a year older; he was also more popular at school than Evan, a better student, and a double varsity athlete who played soccer and lacrosse.

Sam must have been as surprised as she was, because after a stunned silence, he'd agreed. "Okay, dude. Let her try out for the band. But she has to wait until Les is here. He gets a vote, too."

Les, an acne-scarred kid with braces, had been a drummer since elementary school and was already attending summer classes at Berklee College of Music. He was definitely the highest authority on music in Ava's household. When he arrived, the band assembled and Gigi sang.

To Ava's astonishment, Gigi didn't just sing. She became another person altogether. She wailed and growled and soared, whether they tried her with Aerosmith or the Rolling Stones or Pink Floyd. Where in the world had a girl that age learned to sing those songs with such authority, such emotional resonance?

Then it dawned on her: their father had taught her, of course. Knowing this had made Ava's knees feel as if they had come unbolted.

Since that impromptu audition, Gigi had been staying at Ava's almost every day after finishing in the pottery studio, waiting for the boys to come home from their summer jobs so they could practice. Katy had agreed to this; amazingly, Gigi had even managed to talk her grandmother into picking her up in the evenings because Katy was still taking antidepressants and reluctant to drive.

Gradually, some of the other kids in the neighborhood had started coming around. Word spread fast that it wasn't just three boys fooling around on instruments and doing whatever, but a live band with a singer worth listening to, a girl with pink and orange hair who could rattle the windows with her voice.

It was a productive morning. Ava threw forty-five mugs in three hours. The boys had come and gone, telling her they'd had cereal and were riding their bikes to work. It was heavenly to be alone.

The studio was so warm from the kiln that Ava pulled off her sweatshirt and worked in her tank top and jeans as she finished trimming the last mugs. She was straightening up to stretch her back when the screen door slapped open. Simon Talbot stood in the doorway. Silhouetted in the rectangle of bright sunlight streaming behind him through the screen door, his hair was a pale halo and she couldn't make out his expression. Then he approached the wheel and she saw him in more detail.

Simon's blue eyes were heavily creased at the corners; his nose was more prominent than graceful; and he had a small, moon-shaped scar on one cheek. He was dressed in khaki shorts, a navy polo shirt, and worn moccasins. He was very tan, his skin nearly the same golden brown as his khakis, his hair a shade lighter, wheat-colored and too long over his eyes.

"Hey," he said. "Can you talk?"

"Sure. What's up?"

Simon flashed a quick smile. "I came to thank you for looking after Katy and letting me know the situation."

"And what is the situation now?" she couldn't help asking. Simon had such a funny, clipped, almost British way of speaking, as if he were acting out his lines. She supposed that came from living in Hong Kong. Or maybe he was shy, she thought, as he ducked his head to hide his eyes.

"Things aren't as dire as last month, thanks to you," he said. "My mother and I are taking turns dropping in on Katy. And we all really appreciate what you're doing for Gigi. I hope she's not too much trouble."

"Not at all. Gigi's fun to have around."

Simon looked up, smiling again. "She is, right? That girl floors me."

"Me, too. Have you heard her sing?"

He nodded. "She's been singing since she could talk. And now she tells me she's in a band with your sons?"

"That's right. They're calling themselves 'the Misfit Toys.'"

To her surprise, Simon didn't laugh at the name, but said, "Good for her. Gigi must get her talent from your side of the family. None of us can carry a tune."

"We can't, either. I mean, other than my dad. He loved to sing." Ava had to swallow around the hard lump in her throat. "Dad used to play his music—rock and roll, mostly—whenever our mother wasn't around. He taught us his favorite songs. Gigi must have learned them the same way."

"That's a nice legacy."

"Yes." Ava nervously lifted the bat off the wheel and carried it over to the other bats of mugs she'd made that morning and stored on open metal shelves. She switched on a portable fan to dry them faster.

"Did you make all these?" Simon came over to stand beside her.

"Everything but those." She pointed to Gigi's shelf, filled with about two dozen hand-built jars of all shapes and sizes. "Those are Gigi's. She wants to try the potter's wheel. I'll probably teach her how to use it this week."

"No wonder she loves hanging out here." Simon walked around the shelves, examining the pieces in more detail. "How long did it take to make all these mugs?"

"About three hours."

"My God. You're like a little factory."

"It's not hard. Throwing pots is like dancing or playing the piano. Once you learn a shape, it's locked in your muscle memory. Your body just goes through the steps. No matter how perfectly you make something on the wheel, though, the kiln can be unpredictable. Which reminds me: I'd better check mine."

She crossed the studio to the separate room housing the gas kiln. She had finished the kiln room in a double layer of fire-resistant Sheetrock. For most of her bisque firings, she actually used a pair of electric kilns that she could set and forget, she explained to Simon, "but I get better results with glazes using this gas-fired kiln."

"Fascinating," he said, but he wasn't looking at the kiln. He was looking at her.

Ava was suddenly, uncomfortably aware of her clay-damp jeans and skimpy tank top as she checked the temperature cones through the kiln window. "Why aren't you at work?"

"It's Saturday," Simon reminded her. "I was in Newburyport visiting Katy. Anyway, I have my own company and make my own hours."

"What kind of company?"

"We develop and support software for different manufacturing companies."

She was surprised. Simon looked nothing like any engineer or computer scientist she'd ever known; she would have guessed he was in finance or marketing. Or maybe one of those adventurers with his own TV show. "Do you live near here?"

"I have a condo on one of the wharves near Faneuil Hall, overlooking Boston Harbor. I paid through the nose for a waterfront view. But I wanted a place convenient to work. My office is near South Station."

Ava nodded, wondering whether he was married. She glanced at his left hand. No ring. "Sounds like a nice place."

He shrugged. "I'm still not sure I did the right thing. I wanted a place on the water so I could own a sailboat. But having a boat is like a second job. I hardly have time to care for it, much less sail it. The other problem is that the condo has one wall that's all windows, and there's this spiral staircase leading up to my bedroom. Sometimes I get vertigo coming downstairs, like I could plunge through the windows and plummet right into the water. I've only been there a year, but I'm already thinking I'll have to sell."

Ava was having trouble keeping up with this outpouring of information. The men in her life—Mark and Jack, admittedly a small sample size—tended to talk in single syllables. Why was Simon telling her all this? "I'm sure you'll do the right thing. Maybe you could find someone to share your boat and half of the expenses."

"Not a bad idea," he said, and pointed to the shelves of finished pottery. "These are beautiful."

"Thanks. Those are some of the pieces I'm taking up to a gallery in Portsmouth next week."

Simon picked up a lamp glazed in a midnight blue and a pitcher finished in her signature Shino glaze, a warm reddish brown. The texture on the pitcher was rough; she'd scratched the finished pot with a comb and dripped white glaze over the brown rim.

"I like both of these a lot," Simon said. "Could I buy them from you?"

She raised an eyebrow. "They hardly go together."

He laughed. "Well, I don't have much in my place other than a few sticks of furniture, so it doesn't really matter. They don't even have to live in the same room." He glanced down at the objects in his hands. "How do you decide what to make?"

"I think I go more by instinct than any rational decision-making."

"Yet you must make choices with every piece about size, texture, and glaze. Do you do that ahead of time, or as you go?"

Ava considered this. "I don't know. When I first created that pitcher, I was thinking about the fields in Prince Edward Island, Canada, where my mom's family is from, and how the wind used to mix the snow and dirt in swirls, like little red and white tornadoes. I think most of the pottery I make is a way of trying to re-create landscapes. We all carry our inner landscapes, don't you think? Our memories can't help but inform the objects we create."

"For some of us, that information might fit on postcards."

She smiled. "Postcards can be great art. Anyway, you can have that lamp and the pitcher. You don't need to pay me."

"Thank you. That's very generous."

To her surprise, Simon was blushing. The pink flush started below the open buttons of his shirt collar, where his skin was dusted with freckles. She had a sudden impulse to touch him at the base of his throat, to feel his pulse beating beneath her fingertips.

"Want to take a walk?" he asked. "I thought maybe I'd explore the beach a bit. I've never actually been on Beach Plum Island. It would be nice to have company."

Ava hesitated. What if Simon could guess by her expression that she'd been thinking of touching him? Him, *Katy's brother*? My God. That would drive Elaine completely around the bend. Katy and her mother probably wouldn't like it one bit, either.

Well, Simon was asking her on a walk, not a date. No big deal. And a walk would certainly help loosen her back.

"Sure," she said. "Let me just run inside and change."

He waited in the kitchen while she dashed upstairs, stripped off her damp clothes, washed her face and hands, and rummaged through a basket of clean laundry. She dressed in a green T-shirt and a pair of Sam's board shorts, then ran a comb through her hair. Her hair was as disobedient as ever. Well, never mind. Whatever she did with her hair, the wind would undo in seconds.

Downstairs, she found Simon seated on one of the rickety wooden kitchen chairs, his legs sprawled in a way that reminded her of Sam and Evan, of how her boys always stretched to occupy every inch of space in a room. "Great kitchen," he said.

Ava followed his gaze around the room, taking in the yellow cupboards and cream walls, the broken bits of pottery she'd transformed into a colorful mosaic behind the stove, the African violets and geraniums growing in pots she'd made, and the pile of shoes by the door. The pile expanded day by day, making her suspect that some of the teenagers who were friends with Evan and Sam routinely forgot their shoes and walked home barefoot. Their mothers must be wondering where all those shoes were.

"I love this room, too," she said. "I spend most of my time here when I'm not at the studio. A habit left over from when I worked for a caterer, I guess. That's the first job I took when Mark and I split up, before I started teaching. I moved here with the boys and he kept our house in Newburyport. The oven was always on when I was catering, so the kitchen was the warmest room in the house. Money was tight back then."

"Not now?"

Ava studied Simon's long, serious face and remembered the granite counters and tony restaurant appliances in Katy's kitchen, and what he'd told her about his condo on the wharf. She must look completely impoverished to the Talbot family. "No," she said. "We're doing fine now."

"Good."

Simon's blue eyes were ringed in a darker blue, almost slate. He was studying her face so intently that Ava wondered whether there was glaze on her cheek. Probably. There usually was.

"It must be difficult," he said, "being on your own with two boys."

"I'm lucky. My boys are easy and I love my work." Ava felt the heat rising in her neck and face. She didn't need anyone's pity. "What about you? Married? Kids?"

"Divorced. Almost ten years now." He shifted, making the chair creak. "One son. Brook is seventeen and will start his last year of boarding school this fall in Connecticut. He's spending the summer coaching hockey at a camp in Vermont."

"Did you see him much before he went away to school?"

Simon looked confused. "I don't understand. What do you mean?"

"Custody arrangements. I assume he lived with his mother."

"Oh. No. He lived with me after his mother and I split up."

Simon was frowning, probably offended by her assumption. She couldn't blame him. Still, it was unusual for a judge to grant full custody to a father, especially if the father traveled like Simon did. His ex must have been unhinged. Either that or Simon had a great lawyer.

"You must miss him," Ava said.

He nodded. "I wanted Brook to live with me through high school, but he really wanted to go away. Boarding school allowed him to stay in this country while I was working abroad. It was the right choice. It kills me that he's applying to colleges in California, though."

"I bet." Ava couldn't unleash her mind in that direction. She hated the thought of Evan and Sam leaving home, moving on in their lives without her.

They left their shoes on the patio. As they walked toward the refuge beach, Ava told him about the island's history, explaining that the first settlers in the area were English, arriving by ship in 1635. The settlers had learned from Native Americans how to make preserves out of the small, sour beach plums that grew on the short gnarled trees populating the dunes. The sand was purple because of the crushed garnet stones, Ava added, and no bridge had connected Beach Plum Island to mainland Massachusetts until the 1880s.

"Before that, Beach Plum Island was a refuge for the ill, the brave, and the unlucky," she said. "Smallpox and polio victims were sent here. Revolutionary War soldiers and shipwreck survivors landed here, too."

"And you? Why are you here?"

She shrugged. "It was a cheap place to buy a house back when I got divorced."

"And now you're a saltwater woman, living on the beach."

Ava smiled, embarrassed but pleased by the phrase "saltwater woman" and what it conjured for her: a woman who lived her life in rhythm with the sea, the shifting dunes, the whispering sea grasses.

Simon stopped to pick up a sand dollar. To her surprise, he tucked it into his pocket. "Can I ask you something?"

"Of course." Ava looked up into Simon's blue eyes, then had to lower her gaze. She was so attracted to him that it was easy to imagine that he could hear her heart pound above the surf. *This is Katy's brother*, she reminded herself. *Off-limits.* "What is it?"

"I need to know why you're being so nice to my family."

"What?" She was startled enough to look up at him again.

Simon's expression was guarded now, his eyes narrowed and wary. "Why are you being so nice?" he repeated. "Katy obviously broke up your parents' marriage. That must have been hell on you. We weren't happy about it in our family, either. My mother was certain your father was after Katy's money, and we all hated to see her marry a man she'd probably end up nursing on his deathbed, which is exactly what happened. But we love Katy, so we accepted her choice, unlike you and Elaine."

His words felt like sand thrown at her skin, unexpected and stinging. Ava dug her fists into the pockets of her shorts. "Don't you dare lump me in with Elaine! Sure, I was upset by the divorce and its effect on our family, but I got over it. I've always treated Katy with respect, and if she says anything different, she's lying."

"She hasn't said an unkind word to me about you. Or about Elaine. Ever." Simon lifted his hands, palms up, shrugging his powerful shoulders. "But how could you be over it? If I were you, I'd be livid!" His voice was getting louder. "Your parents were struggling through your mother's depression, as I understand things, and then Katy, this blond riding instructor—still a girl, really, barely out of college—busts your family apart like a grenade! How can you *not* hate Katy? Or at least resent her? And Gigi, too?"

Ava was so taken aback by his outburst that tears pricked her eyes. "Because I'm not like that! And this all happened years ago! Why do you sound like you're accusing me of something? What have I done?"

"I'm sorry." Simon ran a hand through his hair. "I didn't mean to get excited. It isn't what you've done, Ava. It's what you *might* do. I can't stand to see my sister in any more pain than she's already in. Frankly, I doubt she'd survive it. If you turned on her, or hurt Gigi in any way, that would be the end of Katy, and I love Katy and Gigi more than I love myself. I need to protect my family from whatever it is that you and Elaine might want from us."

"I don't want anything!" Ava shouted. "Everything I could have wanted is already gone! Can't you see that? My parents got divorced and we lost our house. Now my mom and dad are both *dead*!" Tears were streaming down Ava's face. She turned around and started running home, not caring if Simon followed or not.

He did, of course, and grabbed her arm. She struggled to break free, but his grip was too strong. "Look at me!" he commanded.

She wanted to slap him, to wrestle Simon into the sand and kick him in the head. But Ava didn't have any choice. Simon wouldn't let go.

She glared up at him, not caring that her face was stinging with tears. "Are you happy now? Was this your goal, to make me miserable, too? Just like Elaine, Katy, and Gigi? Is that what you wanted?"

"Oh, shit," Simon said. "I didn't mean to make you cry."

She snorted. "Well, thank God. I'd hate to see what you'd do if you *meant* to make me cry."

Simon made a noise low in his throat and pulled her close. Ava rested her head against his chest, smelling his scent mixed with the sea and realizing that, once again, she was going to dampen Simon's shirt. "Oh, shit, is right," she said. "What a mess."

He stroked her hair. "I just had to find out if you're for real," he murmured. Then he tipped her chin up and looked into her eyes, frowning a little, as if he was desperately memorizing her face.

Ava tried to pull away again, but Simon still wouldn't let go. Instead, he leaned down and brushed his lips across hers. She tasted mint and the sea and something else, too, something so foreign on his lips that it took her breath away: desire.

Or maybe that was the taste on her own lips as she kissed him back, hard, holding on to Simon as if, at any moment, a rogue wave might carry them both out to sea.

# CHAPTER FIVE

Elaine groaned and rolled over. Or tried to, anyway, but something heavy was holding her in place.

For a minute she panicked, remembering how Ava had pinned her against the car last night and the terror of not being able to breathe. She started choking and opened her eyes.

She wasn't with Ava. She was in her own bed, her favorite pink sheets and beige comforter tucked high up under her chin. How had she gotten here? She didn't even remember driving home.

Elaine blinked and tried to sit up, discovered she could not. Somebody was pounding spikes into her temples. Gingerly, she lifted the covers and let out a gasp, blinking hard to clear her clouded vision. She had on the same clothes she'd been wearing last night, and the thing strapping her down was a man's hairy arm.

Jesus Christ! What was a man doing in *her* bed? She never, ever brought men home! That was her cardinal rule!

Well, she'd just have to get rid of him fast. Then she'd start her Saturday the way she always did, with her favorite seven a.m. Zumba class and a smoothie from the yogurt place on the corner. She needed to sweat.

There was just one problem: by craning her neck and squinting at her bedside clock, she could see that it was already well past ten o'clock.

Elaine shook her head hard, as if she could somehow shake off her headache like a hat, but no. That just made her vision go blurry again.

She dropped her head back onto the pillow and closed her eyes, too afraid to turn around and see who belonged to that hairy arm.

Gigi wasn't supposed to go to Ava's on Saturday. Ava only expected her to work five days a week, four hours a day, for which she paid her the minimum hourly wage. Gigi would have gladly worked a million hours a week for free. That's how much she loved pottery.

Today, though, she was going to Ava's not to work or practice with the band—something else she couldn't believe was happening, it was so freaking cool—but because Evan had finally invited her to see his drawings.

"Sam won't be here and Mom always makes French toast for lunch on Saturdays," Evan had added, as if Gigi needed any other reason to ride her bike to Beach Plum Island on a day as supremely fabulous as this one, with streamers of white cloud waving across a sky the color of pansies.

Evan liked to draw as much as she did. One day he wanted to create graphics for computer games. Gigi had shown Evan her sketchbook, but so far he'd refused to share anything of his.

"You'll think they're stupid," he said. "Sam does."

"Sam isn't me," Gigi had pointed out. "And Sam doesn't do art."

This was true. Sam did a lot of things well. He could run fast and hit balls with sticks, make cool videos, and figure out how to play songs on his guitar after listening to them on the radio. But Sam didn't do art. And, in Gigi's opinion, that made Sam nice, but less interesting than Evan.

"You think Sam is less interesting than me?" Evan clearly didn't believe her.

"Would your own auntie lie to you?" she'd teased, elbowing him in the side.

They planned to look at Evan's drawings together, before his dad picked him up for the rest of the weekend. Sam would still be at Les's house, where he'd spent Friday night after practice because he and Les were coming up with a set list for their first show. Gigi had already picked out the perfect performing outfit—a striped blue and white tunic over black leggings, with her rainbow belt—and planned to dye her hair black.

Sam and Evan had talked her into taking out her lip ring, saying they could understand her better when she sang without it. That meant she might be able to wear lipstick for the gig, too, if she could borrow some of Mom's. Mom had like three hundred tubes of the stuff, so she probably wouldn't mind.

It was already hot by the time Gigi left her house to ride to Ava's, but at least there wasn't much beach traffic in the middle of the day; it was so hot everyone was probably already there. She didn't mind biking the five miles from Newburyport to Beach Plum Island. She especially loved passing the little airport, where the small planes taking off and landing there looked like toys. She liked cruising through the marshes, too, where the tips of the whispering tall grasses were as puffy as lions' tails and great blue herons stood at the edge of the marsh, feathers glinting silver in the bright light.

The only part Gigi hated was riding over the bridge. If there were cars, it was hard to stay far enough over and not get mowed down. But she was good about wearing her helmet, not a goofball like some idiot kids. She'd like to keep her brains intact, thank you, especially now that life was way less boring.

Ava was in the kitchen when she arrived, loading the dishwasher. She glanced over her shoulder and smiled. "Go out to the patio where it's cool," she said. "I've already eaten, but Evan's out there. Want some French toast?"

"Sure."

It was weird that Ava's house didn't have air-conditioning. Gigi had never been in a building without it. Ava had these giant ceiling fans and every one of them made a different noise. The living room fan looked like palm leaves and creaked. The white kitchen fan fluttered like bird wings. You could tell where you were in Ava's house even with your eyes closed. Gigi liked the fans and breezes in Ava's house better than the air-conditioning in her own. She ended up wearing a hoodie inside her own house, it was so cold, but she couldn't open a window or her mom yelled at her for wasting electricity.

Evan was sitting cross-legged in one of the Adirondack chairs and drawing. Ava's chairs were wooden and painted a soft green, with stars and moons cut out of the backs of them. Gigi loved them; sometimes she sat out here drawing whenever she was finished with her work in the studio and waiting for Sam and Evan.

Sam wore his hair buzzed short like a jock's, but Evan's was longer and straighter than Gigi's. His bangs slipped over one eye as he looked up and smiled. "I brought it downstairs," he said, tapping the cover of a black sketchbook.

Gigi held out her hand. "I'm ready."

They spent an hour examining his drawings. At some point Ava brought her a plate of food and a glass of orange juice; Gigi handled the book carefully, wiping her hands every time she took a bite of Ava's amazing French toast before touching a new page.

Evan's book was good enough to be in a museum. He drew cartoons, but not like the ones you saw in comic books. These were detailed pen-and-ink sketches of fantastic creatures and scenery from whole worlds Evan imagined in his head, done in different inks and with such careful details that the signs on the storefronts had letters on them. You could even see things reflected in the eyes of the giant sandworms and ogres.

Evan's dad showed up after a while. This was the first time Gigi had met him. Mark was pretty cool, a skinny guy with a long face and bony fingers like Evan, but thick eyebrows and a bouncy walk like Sam. He was bald and smiled a lot.

Gigi couldn't imagine Ava being married. She was so self-sufficient. Not at all like her mom, curled in a ball of grief after Dad died and only now starting to get out of bed on any regular basis. Still, she had been prepared to hate Mark for divorcing Ava, but she didn't. She found herself smiling back when Mark grinned at her and said, "So you're Ava's sister. It's nice to finally meet you."

She was relieved when Mark shook her hand and went right on talking to Ava in the kitchen, leaving her alone to nerd out with Evan and finish looking at the drawings. But her relief turned to something dark and shiny and sharp when Mark told Evan it was time to leave.

Evan shut his book of drawings, shrugged, and said, "My dad's taking us to the Cape to meet his new girlfriend or something. Ugh. Guess that means I won't see you until Monday."

Gigi lifted a hand and gave a lame little wave. "Yeah, see you."

Ava startled her a minute later, coming out to the patio and wiping her hands on a dish towel. "Want to take a swim? It's already broiling out," she said. "I'm going to dunk my head before it's too hot to walk on the sand."

"I don't have a suit," Gigi said.

"I can give you a T-shirt and shorts. Come on. Just a quick dip.

Then I'll drive you home so you don't die of heatstroke on your bike."

"Okay."

They walked past the last house before the refuge, then waded into the water. Gigi had never been swimming on Beach Plum Island despite living nearby all her life. There was a steep drop-off, so they weren't more than a few feet out before Gigi was in over her head. The waves were big and green and humped like a serpent's back roiling along the shore; the water was so cold, Gigi had to work hard to breathe and her legs and arms went immediately numb.

There was a powerful undertow, too, which was why Mom never let her swim here, only at Crane Beach in Ipswich, where you had to wade out like a mile before you were in water over your head. At Crane's, the waves were more like ripples in cloth than real surf like here.

Gigi got sucked under at one point and came up coughing and choking, panicked because she couldn't stand up and certain she was being swept out to sea. Then Ava was touching her shoulder and paddling next to her.

"Just float," Ava said. "Don't fight the undertow. Stay on top of the waves."

Ava held Gigi with her eyes, her eyes as green as the water around them, as if Ava had become part of the ocean, like those selkies who were half-woman, half-seal. She held Gigi up with her eyes and voice until they were both floating on top of the water, rocking like they were lying in a giant cradle, and Gigi wasn't scared anymore.

"Did Dad ever come swimming here with you and Evan and Sam?" Gigi asked as they floated together just beyond where the waves broke, the sea swelling beneath them like one of Evan's dragons rippling its back.

"A few times."

"He must have loved it. Dad hated the pool at the club. He always talked about some lake in Maine where he used to swim as a kid."

"Moosehead Lake," Ava said.

"Right. Did he ever take you there?" It wasn't the real question Gigi longed to ask, but she was determined to lead up to it; out here, with the two of them alone in the ocean, it finally seemed safe to ask.

"No," Ava was saying. "Dad always talked about taking a vacation on Moosehead, but Mom never wanted to go there. Too close to the town where they grew up, I guess. Though that's where she ended up living at the end."

Gigi noticed Ava's mouth tightening and felt terrible. She'd forgotten Ava's mom had died in Maine. "I'm sorry," she said.

"It's fine. It was a long time ago," Ava said

Gigi knew she didn't mean it. She could tell by Ava's expression, by the way her green eyes looked like someone had drained the light out of them, that her grief for her mother was with her every day. Gigi understood; she felt that way about Dad. She supposed you never stopped missing the only people who'd known you all your life.

Her face was so numb with cold that her skin burned hot and she imagined her lips had turned purple. It was hard to speak because her teeth had started to chatter, but she made herself keep talking. It might be a long time before she and Ava were alone again. "So did Dad ever tell you about our brother?"

Ava lifted her head out of the water to stare at her. "What did you say?"

Gigi bit her lip. "It's kind of crazy."

"Try me."

Now Gigi felt nervous. Maybe telling Ava this would ruin everything. What if Peter was dead or something shitty like that? The last thing she wanted to do was hurt Ava.

On the other hand, Dad had wanted Gigi to find Peter, and Ava was the only one who might help.

Gigi rolled onto her back, took a deep breath, and said, "Just before he died, Dad told me I had a brother. A brother older than you. His name was Peter." She pressed two fingers to her salt-burned lips, then added, "Dad wanted me to find him and give Peter a message."

"Peter," Ava said softly, as if the name were a prayer. "What kind of message?" Her green eyes were so wide that Gigi could see herself reflected in them, like the eyes of the mythical creatures in Evan's drawings.

Gigi frowned, trying to remember the exact words. "Dad wanted Peter to know he loved him and it wasn't his choice to do whatever he and your mom did, even though something was wrong with him."

"Something was wrong with who? Dad or Peter?"

"Peter. From the beginning, Dad said."

By this time they had floated close to shore. "Come on," Ava said. "I can't concentrate out here. I'm too cold. And I need to hear this again."

Back at Ava's, they used the outdoor shower to rinse off before changing into their clothes, Ava upstairs and Gigi in the downstairs bathroom. The bathroom was so small that Gigi had to practically keep her arms pinned to her sides when she turned around, but she loved the tiny hand-painted sink Ava had made for the corner. She ran her fingers through her hair, her skin still stinging with salt.

After Ava had joined her outside, carrying her wet towel to hang on the line, Gigi said, "You know, even if I don't really have a brother, I'm glad you're my sister."

Ava's smile was quick and very white against her sunbrowned skin. "I'm so glad you're my sister, too." She sank into the other Adirondack chair, her long wet hair spread like seaweed across her tanned shoulders. "Now tell me again," she said. "Everything Dad said."

Gigi did. "You don't think he was imagining things?" she asked afterward. "Did Dad tell you about Peter, too?"

Her sister's face was a mask of concentration, her mouth a thin line, her eyes narrowed and serious. "Yes, but he never gave me any details. I thought he must have been out of his mind on drugs to say something that weird. Now I don't know."

"Me, either," Gigi said, mainly because she wanted to agree with Ava, even though she didn't really think her dad was lying or confused.

Ava shook her head so hard that droplets of water from her hair stung Gigi's face. "I can't believe my mother wouldn't have said something to me about having another baby. Maybe Dad had a baby with another woman. Or maybe he was confused and talking about *his* brother, who died ages ago. People's memories aren't too reliable when they're on certain drugs."

"No. Dad said he had the baby with your mom. He never seemed out of it, either. So why would he be confused about having a son?" Gigi had a headache; she was concentrating so hard. "What was Dad's brother's name? Was it Peter?"

"No. John."

Gigi noticed that Ava was pressing her fingers to her lips just like Gigi had been doing a minute ago. She wondered whether this was their dad's nervous habit and she and Ava had both inherited the behavior. Or had they seen him do it and learned to imitate him, the way chicks imprinted on whatever they saw first when they hatched?

Gigi couldn't remember her father touching his mouth when he was thinking. Then again, she had forgotten a lot of things about Dad already. Terrifying, to feel him slipping away.

To Ava, she said, "So maybe we really *do* have a brother named Peter and he's still out there somewhere! Maybe Dad wanted us to find Peter together. Did he talk to Elaine about it, too?"

"I don't think so. Did he say anything else to you? Like where Peter's living now?"

"No." Gigi's stomach did an unhappy lurch. "What if it's too late and Peter's already dead or locked up in prison or something?"

Ava sighed. "Then that would be horrible. I wonder if Dad told your mom anything about this."

"I think so, but when I asked, Mom said it all happened too long ago to matter."

"Maybe to her, but not to us." Ava stood up. "Come on. Let's go talk to her."

The hairy arm belonged to a man Elaine could have sworn she'd never seen before in her life. Yet here he was, wandering around in striped boxer shorts like it was his condo instead of hers. She must have fallen asleep again, because she hadn't heard him get up and now it was past eleven o'clock. She hadn't ever slept this late before in her *life*, not since having mono when she was a teenager.

The man approached the bed and handed her a mug. "Coffee?"

When she didn't take it, he set it down gently on the table beside her. It was her special hazelnut; the man had obviously been up long enough to find his way around her kitchen and tame the cranky Barista.

Elaine sat up, pulling the covers up to her chin despite being fully dressed, and stared at the stranger while he plucked a pair of jeans and a black T-shirt off the floor and put them on. Her worst fears were realized when she saw a Habitat for Humanity logo on the shirt. She never invited men to her place until they'd gotten to know each other and established ground rules. And, whenever she *did* invite a man to stay over, it certainly wasn't some knee-jerk liberal wearing a shirt advertising a hopeless cause.

"Who the hell are you and what are you doing in my bedroom?" she demanded.

He raised his black eyebrows and laughed. "Morning, sunshine. I'm Gabe, and I brought you home so you wouldn't do something you regretted."

She had already done something she regretted, waking up to find this guy in her bed. Elaine sipped the restorative coffee while studying Gabe under her lashes. He had a kind face and a great laugh, actually, a gravelly, sexy chortle that might have caused Elaine to turn and look at him in a restaurant if she'd heard it.

Of course, they weren't in a restaurant, they were in her bedroom! And if she *had* turned to glance at him in a restaurant, she would have looked away immediately to avoid sending false signals.

Gabe was *so* not her type. Her type was young and sleek, clean-shaven and prosperous. Her lovers went to the gym with the same religious fervor she did. Or, if not, they trained regularly to compete in some rigorous but acceptable sport. No mountain bikers or skateboarders, for example, but skiers and marathoners were acceptable, provided they had day jobs.

Gabe had no facial hair, thank God, but otherwise there was nothing sleek about him. He wore black-framed glasses, the sort that bass players in funky indie bands seemed to buy in bulk, and his dark hair sprang from his head in corkscrew curls. He was average height, and from his build, Elaine would guess his exercise regime probably consisted of walking to the corner bakery. No potbelly, but definitely going soft around the middle.

He was by far the oldest man she'd ever been with, too. At least forty. She avoided men that age. After a certain age, men came with relationship baggage they were bound to dump out on your living room floor, hoping you'd pick it up and organize it for them.

Yet Gabe's eyes stopped her. She couldn't help but linger on his face, on those eyes, lighter brown than her own and warmly affectionate even when he wasn't smiling. His mouth, too, was appealing, generous and curved in a way that suggested he might laugh at any lame joke. Not because he wanted to make you feel good or anything, necessarily, but because this man genuinely found life more amusing than sad. Unlike her.

"Finish your coffee," Gabe said gently. "It'll help your head."

Elaine surprised herself by obeying, keeping an eye on him as Gabe disappeared from the bedroom again. How did she even know that was his real name? She hoped he wasn't rifling through her purse. Well, identity theft was the least she deserved for being such a moron and drinking enough to black out.

The coffee was just the way she liked it, black and strong. How had he known?

More important, where did they meet? Where was her car? And how the hell had this man talked her into letting him bring her home and breaking her own rules?

Gabe reappeared, carrying a plate of toast thick with butter and strawberry jam. Elaine's stomach rebelled at the idea of food, especially carbs. Never mind the gym. She hadn't even gotten up to walk to the bathroom this morning! Yet somehow Gabe calmly chided her into eating a piece of toast.

He sank cross-legged onto the floor—all right, he was flexible, so maybe he did yoga, that was a small plus—and chewed his own toast in a companionable way, catching the crumbs in the palm of his hand. His feet were bare.

This guy would be perfect for Ava, Elaine thought, then felt her face flush as she remembered the unpleasant scene from last night: Gigi dancing in her sister's living room and singing Nirvana's "Smells Like Teen Spirit." The worst part was that Elaine knew the lyrics by heart because it was one of Dad's favorite songs.

Gigi's father's, too, obviously. *Crap.*

Elaine's hand started shaking so badly, she had to set the empty coffee mug down on the table. She moved too clumsily and missed the table altogether.

Gabe magically appeared beside the bed and caught the mug before it hit the floor. "Whoa. You okay?"

His voice was deep, as appealing as his laugh, but she was determined not to like it. Or him, with his Jedi mind tricks. Gabe needed to leave her condo so she could think. He needed to leave *now.*

She must have said these words aloud, because Gabe bent over and started strapping on shoes. Sandals, naturally, the sort of thick-soled, wide-strapped leather sandals a camel trader would wear. "Okay. If you're sure you're feeling all right, I'll get out of your hair," he said. He was almost, but not quite, smiling.

She glared. "I am totally *fine.*"

"You're vertical, anyway." Gabe hovered at the foot of her bed. "But if you don't mind me saying so, you don't seem *fine* at all."

"I do mind," Elaine countered, "since you don't know one thing about my life upon which to base your opinion."

"'Upon which'?" he repeated, grinning.

"Yes," she said. "What's wrong with that?"

Gabe laughed. "Nothing! I'm delighted to meet a woman who knows her way around a prepositional phrase. That's why I stopped going online to meet women, you know. I couldn't stand wading through that sulfurous grammar bog."

"I know what you mean," she said, then clammed up, afraid of appearing too agreeable.

Little chance of that. She was too hungover. Bits and pieces from the night before were starting to soak through her consciousness now, as if a layer of paper towels had been pressed onto her damp brain and the contours of last night's events were only now seeping through it.

Fact: she had been to not just one bar, but two.

Fact: she had driven crazily from Ava's to the Matchbox Bar, testing how long the yellow lights stayed yellow, only to be escorted out the door by a bouncer because she'd started yelling at some guy about something she couldn't even bear to remember right now.

Fact: she had driven home, ditched her car, and walked to the Foggy Tavern around the corner from her apartment.

She'd never set foot in the Foggy Tavern before. In fact, she typically crossed the street to avoid it. It was the kind of neighborhood bar with Christmas lights strung up year-round, neon 3-D beer signs, motorcycles parked outside, and a karaoke machine in the corner. How had she ended up there, for God's sake? What primitive part of her cerebral cortex had fired up to make her think *that* was such a brilliant idea?

Gabe was watching her closely with those unnervingly sympathetic eyes, apparently tracking her thoughts. "How much do you remember?"

Elaine waved a hand, hoping it wouldn't tremble. "Enough to know we didn't sleep together."

"You don't really know that." His voice was pleasant. "I could have had my way with you and dressed you afterward. You were really out of it."

The same horrible thought had crossed her mind, too, of course, but she had dismissed it. Somehow, Elaine couldn't picture a date rapist in sandals and a Habitat for Humanity T-shirt.

"You're not the type," she said.

"Lucky for you. But the next guy who picks you up in a bar might be."

Gabe now sounded as stern as Ava. One thing was clear: this guy was a caretaker. Probably the adult child of an alcoholic or the oldest brother of a dozen kids.

"Are you lecturing me?" She squinted at him, bringing him into focus, her head swimming.

"Nope. I wouldn't dare. But honestly? Do you remember anything about last night? I practically had to carry you home."

Elaine felt a slight tremble in her lower lip and put her fingers up to stop it. "Not really." She wouldn't let herself whisper, hang her head, or close her eyes. In her experience, refusing to act ashamed was the first step toward moving on from a bad decision instead of wallowing in guilt. "Where did we meet?"

"In the karaoke bar around the corner. You were singing an Aerosmith song."

"That's impossible. I can't sing."

"I didn't say you were any good."

Elaine winced at the idea that she might have been bellowing into a microphone as some reflexive, ridiculous, ineffective revenge for Ava letting Gigi sing in her house. Jesus. Was she really that jealous? That pathetic?

She was, obviously.

"Then what? How did you end up in my condo?" She couldn't bring herself to say "in my bed."

"It wasn't easy. I thought you were going home with that motorcyclist in the red bandanna. The guy with all the tattoos. Remember him?"

Elaine groaned. It was all starting to come back like a down-loaded YouTube video playing in halting segments: some bald Ne-anderthal in a red bandanna had actually picked her up and slung her over one shoulder. He'd tried to carry her out of the bar. This much Elaine remembered because she could recall the dizzying, sickening sensation of the world being upside down, a world of blue jeans and sneakers and peanut shells on the floor.

Then what?

It was all a blank. "We didn't sleep together." She wanted to be absolutely clear on this point.

"No." His light brown eyes crinkled again. "I only ravish women who are awake."

"I've never done anything like this before. This isn't me."

Gabe had stopped smiling. "Glad to hear it." He put on his denim jacket—seriously? A denim jacket? Who wore those, other than models posed against mountain backdrops in catalogs?—pulled a card out of his wallet, and placed it on the table beside her. "Call me if you ever need a bodyguard for one of your nights on the town. Or a lunch date."

She picked up the card and squinted at it. *Gabriel Blaustein*. Oh, God. The knight who'd come to her rescue was a chubby Jew in a jeans jacket who, for some reason, had been in a karaoke bar with Christmas lights and defended her honor in some mysterious, mis-guided attempt at chivalry. And she had no ethical choice but to be grateful. Or to act grateful, anyway, even if she'd rather have him just beam up to wherever he'd come from.

"Wait," she said.

Gabe turned around, his eyebrows raised above the frames of his black glasses.

"It's nice to meet you, Gabe," she said. "My name is Elaine." Out of habit, she didn't offer her last name.

"I know."

"How?"

"I had to go through your purse to find your driver's license, so I'd know where to carry you home after you passed out."

"Oh my God." She put her head in her hands and closed her eyes, humiliation rising like a cloud of unpleasant scent to choke her.

She felt the side of the bed sink as Gabe sat down. He reached over and stroked her hair. "Everybody's entitled to one bad night," he said. "You got lucky on yours. But don't do that again, okay? Or if you do, keep that card in your wallet so you can call me. Promise?"

"Don't touch me," she hissed, clenching her eyes shut.

"Why not?" Gabe continued to stroke her hair, his fingers gentle.

Elaine didn't have an answer to that, so she said nothing. It was taking all the energy in the world not to cry.

They found Katy in the garden. She looked remarkable, Ava thought, nearly healed. Her pale hair was brushed straight back from her forehead and held in place with a tortoiseshell hair band. Her gray eyes were serene. She was wearing black capris and a pink tank top, and she was weeding one of her perennial gardens, tossing plants into a green plastic tub.

Katy stood up and shaded her eyes as they approached. "Oh, hello! I didn't even know you'd gone out," she said to Gigi. "No wonder you didn't answer when I called to see if you wanted breakfast."

As Gigi explained about riding her bike to Ava's house to see Evan's drawings, Ava wondered how it was that a mother wouldn't know if her fifteen-year-old daughter had left the house. Of course, as Elaine had pointed out, their own mother never knew where they were, either. Maybe that was the result of having a house big enough that your bedroom was on a separate floor from your child's. Ava could still remember the heady thrill of sneaking out of this very house in high school to meet Mark in the middle of the night.

"Mom, Ava and I need to talk to you about something," Gigi said.

"Okay." Katy's expression was suddenly wary.

Ava felt sorry for Katy, who clearly was imagining all sorts of new problems, now that she'd entrusted Gigi to Ava. Katy probably thought she was a nice but slack hippie who played with clay in a beach house; she wouldn't be far off the mark, either.

Ava remembered Simon's words then—"a saltwater woman"— and felt herself flush with pleasure. She hoped he'd thought of her even half as often as she'd been thinking about him, despite how impossible it was to pursue a relationship. They had both agreed on that point before parting. Still, that didn't stop Ava from replaying the feel of his mouth on hers.

To Katy, Ava said, "It might be better if we all sat down."

Katy nodded and led them into the kitchen. Ava and Gigi sat on metal stools at the granite counter. The house was so cold, it was like walking into a meat freezer; now Ava wished they'd stayed in the garden.

"Water?" Katy asked.

"Sure," Ava answered.

Katy brought bottles of citrus-flavored water out of the refrigerator. Gigi uncapped all three bottles with a bottle opener shaped like a mermaid while her mother stood on the other side of the counter, hands braced against it. Ava tried to imagine her father using that mermaid to uncap his nightly beer but failed.

Katy still wore her gardening gloves, which were blue and elbow-length. "Poison ivy," she said, as she followed Ava's gaze and removed the gloves. "I'm so allergic I swell up like the Elephant Man if I come within ten feet of it. So what's up?"

Ava eyed Gigi, but the girl stared at her bottle of water. Ava cleared her throat. "This morning I found out that Dad told Gigi something about having another child. A boy. He told me the same thing. I need to know if he said anything to you about this as well."

Katy's face relaxed a little. "Oh, that."

Her nonchalance was irritating. "Yes, *that*," Ava said. "It's a shock to me, as you can probably imagine."

"Really?" Katy seemed genuinely surprised. "I'm sorry. I thought you must have known." She bit her lip, studying Ava and Gigi across from her. "Wow. I never realized how much the two of you looked alike until just now." Her voice sounded strained. "I can really see the resemblance, with both of you staring at me like that."

Gigi and Ava glanced at each other. Gigi flashed a quick smile, then turned to Katy again. "Mom," she said gently, "we're not trying to upset you or anything. We just need to know if you can help us find our brother."

"I don't know where he is." Katy sighed. "Truthfully, I never knew a thing about him until your dad's last weeks. Then he started telling me all these things he thought I should know. A lot of it was hard to hear. Especially that."

Ava's heart went out to her. She knew how debilitated she'd been by the divorce; after Mark moved out, there were entire weekends when all she could manage was a trip to the grocery store, and sometimes not even that. She couldn't imagine the pain of losing a spouse. And what if your husband had lived a completely different life before he met you? A life with children, a wife, a career. Fifteen years was nothing in the lifetime of a marriage, when one spouse was as old as Dad.

"Is there anything he told you about my brother that might be helpful?" she asked.

"You need to tell us if he did, Mom," Gigi said. "He's my brother, too."

Katy pulled one of the stools around to her side of the counter and sat down. "I don't know much that could help you," she said, looking at Gigi. "Dad was scared to tell you himself, honey. He didn't want you to hate him because he'd given up a child."

"I wouldn't!" Gigi said quickly.

"I know," Katy said. "That's why I encouraged him to talk to you before he died, about anything he wanted you to know. Even things he wanted to share with you, but not with me. I knew there probably wouldn't be another chance." Her voice caught; she had to stop and sip her water. "Your dad told me your mother got pregnant sophomore year of high school. Of course their parents were horrified, especially when the baby was born with problems." Katy gave Ava a curious look. "Suzanne never told you any of this?"

"No. Nothing." Ava felt the tiny spots and sparkles on the granite counter swimming up to meet her. She clung to the edges of the stool with both hands. "Why didn't they get married then?"

Katy looked surprised again. "Suzanne's parents—your grandparents—didn't want them to get married. They thought Bob was beneath your mother. He came from a farming family outside of town, as I'm sure you know. Your grandfather on your mom's side owned a car dealership and made a good living. They sent your mom away to have the baby, but something went wrong. The baby was born blind, barely breathing. Suzanne's parents told her he was born defective because she'd had sex out of wedlock and this was God's punishment for her sin."

Ava put a hand to her mouth, imagining her poor mother as a girl Gigi's age, going through this. "That's awful."

"I know." Katy's gray eyes were soft. "Bob told me Suzanne gave the child up before he even knew it was born. I can't blame her." She glanced at Gigi. "She wanted to please her parents, I'm sure."

"So she put the baby up for adoption?" Gigi was leaning forward now, resting her elbows on the counter, hanging on every word. Even her hair seemed to be listening, the pink and orange tufts quivering like antennae.

"They gave the baby to somebody in Suzanne's family." Katy frowned. "Your dad wasn't involved in that, either, so he wasn't sure who. An aunt, he thinks. But then she gave the baby up, too."

"Where did he go after that?" Gigi gnawed at a ragged bit of chipped blue fingernail.

Katy sighed. "I don't know, honey. I don't think they had orphanages anymore in the nineteen seventies, but I could be wrong. He was probably placed in foster care or an institution."

"That's harsh," Gigi said.

"It's what people did back then." Katy patted her daughter's hand.

Ava was clenching her teeth so hard her jaw had started to ache, but her thoughts wouldn't stop pinging in all directions. "You don't know any more?"

Katy frowned. "I don't think there's anything else to the story, really. As soon as Suzanne turned eighteen and she could leave home without being worried her dad would stop her, Bob convinced her to leave Maine, the Catholic Church, their families. Everything. They eloped and moved to Boston."

"Dad put himself through college and worked, while Mom stayed home with Elaine and me," Ava said. "She was always fighting depression in some way or another. I guess this might explain why."

Katy collected their water bottles. "I don't know much about your mother's state of mind."

Ava let this statement hover in the air between them for a minute, feeling the cold unspoken words about what part Katy had played in breaking up her parents' marriage. She could see the weight of those words on Katy's narrow shoulders, in the way Katy curved her body forward and leaned more heavily on the counter. Ava felt sorry for her, but that emotion was mixed with anger.

"Who did you say they gave the baby to?" she asked.

Katy frowned and adjusted her hair band. "I don't know. Bob never told me her name. An aunt of your mother's, I think."

"It must have been Great-aunt Finley," Ava said. "She and Mom were pretty close. Finley had an apartment in her house near Moosehead Lake and that's where my mother went to live after Elaine moved back to Boston. I haven't seen Finley since Mom died, and I hardly saw her before that. She's a little strange."

"No wonder she and Suzanne got along," Katy said, then clapped her hand over her mouth. "God. I didn't mean to say that aloud. Sorry."

Ava was startled enough to laugh. "It's fine. I'm used to Elaine, remember? She has fewer filters than most."

Katy picked up the sponge next to the sink and began rubbing furiously at invisible spots on the counter. "That sister of yours should learn some manners."

"Yeah? And who's going to teach her? You?" Ava said.

For a minute, she thought Katy might throw the sponge at her. But then she sighed and said, "I'm sorry, Ava. For everything. I hope you know that."

"I do," Ava said. She had never blamed Katy, but it was only recently that she'd begun to see why her father had been so drawn to her that he would risk leaving his old life behind to start over.

Gigi jumped down off the stool. "Come on!"

"Where?" Ava asked.

"We need to call this aunt and ask about the baby!"

Ava shook her head. "We can't. Finley doesn't have a phone."

"That's stupid. Everybody has a phone."

"No," Ava said. "Finley didn't believe in phones. She was always afraid the government would listen in on her conversations or something." She didn't say the rest of what she was thinking, which was that if Finley had put in a phone all those years ago, her own mother might have gotten help in time and not died of her heart attack.

"Then we should drive to Maine," Gigi said. "Right now!"

"I can't," Ava said. "The boys."

Gigi rolled her eyes. "They're with their dad this weekend. And Maine isn't that far, right?" She looked from Katy to her mother.

"No," Ava said, thinking, *Only on the other side of the world.*

## CHAPTER SIX

Elaine was still arguing with Ava, ranting about how the two of them should drive to Maine without Gigi. "You know how much Finley hates visitors!" Elaine was saying. "We don't want to overwhelm her."

How could Elaine keep acting like Gigi wasn't even here, or fail to see that Ava wasn't going to cave? Gigi could spot Ava jutting her chin out a mile away. Elaine should just shut up now and get in the car.

Ava had somehow convinced Elaine to drive to Beach Plum Island, but by the time she roared into Ava's driveway it was nearly three o'clock. Gigi knew they had to hit the road fast if they were going to make the four-hour drive before Great-aunt What's-Her-Name went to bed. If she was old enough to be Suzanne's aunt, she could be, like, ninety.

"Look, I will say this exactly one more time." Elaine put her hands on her hips and leaned forward, nearly nose to nose with Ava. "That. Kid. Is. Not. Coming. With. Us. What do you suppose Finley would do if some child of Dad's shows up? Have you considered *that*? Finley hasn't let anyone say Dad's name in her house since the divorce!"

"There's no reason Finley has to know," Ava said. "Gigi and I agreed to say she's a friend of the family, that's all."

Elaine snorted. "Like that will fly. Gigi looks just like Dad." She cut her eyes over to Gigi, then glared at Ava again. "And you. She's like a little clone."

"Finley won't see that. She was already having problems with her eyes the last time I saw her, and that was years ago," Ava said.

Ava must be such a cool high school teacher, Gigi thought. She hadn't freaked out at all, even when Elaine started getting all super tantrumy and ridiculous.

Watching her sisters butt heads, Gigi also knew that Suzanne must have been smoking hot if Elaine looked like her, which was what Mom said. Elaine was tall and gorgeous and almost too thin, except she still had boobs and curvy hips, like one of those magazine models who look like another species. Her brown hair was straight and long, as shiny as a Thoroughbred's. Today Elaine wore jeans that Gigi knew must have cost over a hundred bucks, since some of the girls at school had them and were always bitching about the price, like their parents didn't buy them.

Despite the broiling July heat, Elaine also wore high-heeled boots and a long-sleeved white blouse. She should have looked wrinkled and sweaty, but she looked like she'd just stepped out of an air-conditioned hotel. Ava was the one whose hair was flying around all crazy and gold, as if she had a lion's mane instead of hair.

Ava was acting calm but she was upset inside. Gigi knew this by the way Ava's hands were bunched into fists. Seeing this made Gigi want to punch Elaine in her flat belly.

"Hey!" Gigi yelled suddenly. "Leave Ava alone! I'm right here, you know. If you've got something to say about me, say it to my *face*."

Both women turned to stare at her, openmouthed as guppies.

Gigi took advantage of their momentary paralysis to march up and insert herself between them. "You are not the boss here, Elaine. We could already be on our way to Maine right now. We didn't even have to *call* you! But Ava thought you should come with us because Peter is your brother, too. Just like he's *mine*." She folded her arms. "So make up your mind. Are you coming or not?"

"The question isn't whether *I'm* coming," Elaine spit back. "It's whether *you're* coming, you entitled little brat. He's only your *half* brother, like we're your half sisters."

Behind her, Gigi could feel Ava nearly fly up off the ground, she was so ticked off. "Elaine Barrett, you should be ashamed. Do *not* talk to your sister like that," she said. "Not in front of me, and not ever!"

Elaine actually fell back a step. "Why are you always taking *her* side?"

"I'm not," Ava said. "I'm just trying to get the three of us to work as a team, and frankly, I'm running out of energy."

Elaine was scared, Gigi decided, risking a glance at her pale, pinched face, but of what? Of her? Or of actually finding a brother?

"Look, I'm sorry you hate me so much," Gigi told Elaine, struggling to make her voice sound as calm as Ava's. "You can just ignore me. I'll ride in the backseat and listen to my iPod or whatever. Pretend I'm not even here. I mean, don't you want to come with us? Aren't you even a *little* bit curious?"

Elaine opened her pretty pink lipsticked mouth wide, like she might start yelling again, then closed it and sighed. "I don't know. I still think this whole thing is a hoax, frankly."

"How can it be a *hoax*?" Ava demanded. "Why would Dad try to trick us?"

"Not *Dad*," Elaine said, gesturing with her chin at Gigi.

"Yeah, well, Dad told me about our brother, too," Ava said.

"There's no way to know whether this is a hoax unless we visit Finley. Even if she didn't take the baby, she'll know what happened." She glanced at her watch. "All right. I'm done here. I'm driving to Maine. Whoever wants to come better get in the car *right now* or I'm leaving without you."

Gigi started for Ava's Honda, but Elaine laid a manicured hand on her arm, the nails like brittle pink petals. "Do not get in that car," she said.

Gigi shook her off furiously. "You can't make me stay here," she said. "Ava wants me to come!" She was so mad that she was afraid the tears pricking her eyelids might start running down her face. If only she were older and had her own car, she wouldn't even need her sisters.

Elaine rolled her eyes. "No, you idiot," she said. "What I meant was, we're not taking Ava's rattletrap Honda all the way up to Back of Beyond, Maine. If we're going on a treasure hunt, we're riding in style."

Gigi grinned. She had always wanted to ride in that sweet red BMW.

Three hours into the trip, Elaine stopped to fill the car with gas while Ava and Gigi used the restroom. When they came back, she went into the station to pay and took her turn in the bathroom.

Alone beneath the too-bright, buzzing fluorescent light, Elaine peed and washed her hands and tried not to scream. Though, judging from her appearance in the wavy piece of steel some joker had put up for a mirror, she wouldn't even need to scream for people to know she was falling apart.

Her brown eyes were bloodshot, she'd chewed off most of her lipstick, and the clean white blouse she'd ironed this morning was so stained and wrinkled, it looked like she'd been storing it in the bottom of a boat. Maine always had this effect on her. She already felt defeated and things could only get worse from here.

She splashed her face with cold water, then tried to sponge off the worst of the stains. This had the unhappy effect of turning the stain darker and making it spread across the front of her blouse. Now it looked like a map of Italy.

It was probably that brown mustard. Ava, always the den mother, had insisted on packing sandwiches for the ride. Ham sandwiches with butter and mustard! And chips! A bag of chips for each of them! And she'd eaten all of hers! Jesus. She'd have to work out an extra hour at the gym tomorrow just to lose half those calories.

As she scrubbed pointlessly at the blouse, Elaine gave herself a stern lecture. No more meltdowns. So what if she was the only one Dad hadn't told about some phantom handicapped brother? That didn't prove anything, except maybe that their brother didn't exist.

She slammed the flat of her hand down on the sink, then for good measure pounded her own thigh to punish herself for letting her emotions loose in front of her sisters, who were absurdly tight, acting like they were the ones who grew up together and not her and Ava. Fine. Gigi could be the sister Ava had always wanted, barefoot and messy and artsy. The two of them probably even loved using that crap outdoor shower at Ava's cottage. Not a civilized bone in their bodies.

From now on, no matter what happened, Elaine would keep a grip on herself. She would do the right thing for Ava's sake and drive the car to Finley's, where they would find out either their brother had never existed or he was defective. Probably autistic, a Down's baby, or a schizoid mutant. Maybe he had died young. These things happened. Especially in Maine.

Elaine stroked on bright pink lipstick. Instead of perking her up, though, the bold color made her look like a weather girl on cable. She rubbed it off with a tissue and applied nude lip gloss instead.

It was after six o'clock. Maybe Finley wouldn't even answer the door. She would be what, eighty-five? She could be asleep by now. Or lying dead in her apartment, just like Mom.

Not that Finley deserved that fate, but let's be honest, Elaine thought. Finley had chosen to be a recluse, and that's what happened to women who lived alone: nobody knew when they died.

That's what happened to women who lived alone and *didn't work*, Elaine hastily amended, thinking of her own condo, high above street level and so thickly carpeted and well insulated that nobody would likely find her, either, if she keeled over in her kitchen.

Women who died alone either got eaten by their pets or were eventually found by a neighbor who jimmied open the door, recoiling in horror at the sight of a body on the floor. It was a neighbor who'd found Mom. Finley couldn't climb the stairs with her lung problems; she'd gone across the street for help when she realized she hadn't heard a noise upstairs in over twenty-four hours.

"Oh, goddamn it to hell," Elaine swore under her breath. Here she was crying again, and she'd just reapplied her mascara. What a fucking mess she was, and for what? Tears couldn't bring her mother back.

The only thing crying did was make her look weak. Elaine shuddered, remembering that melodramatic scene with Gabe in her bedroom this morning. She'd sobbed on his shoulder until she finally pushed him out the door, telling him she was going to puke and he'd better just hoof it in his Habitat for Humanity T-shirt.

Then, just as she was collecting her wits and trying to make herself go to the gym, Ava had called to tell her about Dad's deathbed confession to Gigi—to Gigi, of all people!—and to ask if she'd drive with her to Maine. Elaine had said yes at once, wanting to make up for leaving Ava's house last night in such a huff. Of course Ava had neglected to mention Gigi would be tagging along with them.

Elaine rinsed her face again, carefully wiping away her mascara and smoothing concealer under her eyes. Ava and Gigi weren't wearing makeup. In fact, no women in this part of Maine seemed to bother with makeup. So she'd join them and go about her business, bald-faced and brave, until she could finally get back to civilization. This day couldn't last forever. All days were the same length, she reminded herself. At the end of it, she could have a drink.

The final hour of the trip was an excruciating series of winding roads skinny as ribbons, through towns too small and broken to name. Coastal Maine was cluttered with well-heeled escapees from Boston or New York. They clogged the winding roads by driving too slowly in their giant comfy sedans, but breathed life and color into the historic homes and actually needed restaurants and shops to survive. Here, though, in western Maine, the old farmhouses were beyond weathered and on to desperate, the shingles flaking off them like dead skin. Between them squatted trailers surrounded by skinny dogs and fat kids and flapping laundry.

In front of one trailer, Elaine glimpsed a motorcycle parked next to an empty space in the driveway with a sign that read, BITCH PARKING ONLY HERE. The only restaurants were diners sure to serve greasy food with gravy on the side. Probably even the fries came with gravy, this close to Canada.

"It's so beautiful here," said Gigi, who had been plugged into her iPhone the whole time and had, impressively, kept her mouth shut until now, except for the one time she started singing and Elaine told her to shut it.

"It really is," Ava agreed. "I love the rolling hills and pine trees. And the wildflowers, wow. Look at that field."

"Don't forget the rusted trucks, caved-in barns, and plastic on the windows," Elaine couldn't help adding. "Those definitely add to the picturesque effect."

"I love the cows," Gigi said. "But why are they lying down?"

"Means it's going to rain," Ava said.

"No it doesn't. That's just an old wives' tale," Elaine said, but wouldn't you know it, a handful of raindrops splattered against the windshield of the car just then, even Mother Nature pranking her now.

She put on the wipers, silently daring Ava and Gigi to say a word. They didn't.

Great-aunt Finley's house looked just as dismal as she remembered. It was a two-story, flat-roofed house painted barn red. Even the trim and porch floor were that same shade of tired rusty red, giving the house the look of a brick standing on end.

The front porch was flanked by ancient hydrangea bushes laden with supernaturally huge blue blossoms. Elaine shut off the car and stared at the bushes, remembering the photograph of her mother by the hydrangeas at the cabin they'd rented closer to the lake. Afterward, Mom had picked some of the blooms and brought them inside, discovering too late that the flowers were covered with ants. She'd spotted a line of ants crossing the kitchen floor and become hysterical, convinced the ants were after her. Was that because of the alcohol, the pills, or her own poor fizzling brain?

Why didn't Dad or Finley know enough to have her hospitalized? Why hadn't Elaine tried to get her more help? Why didn't Ava ever come?

Pinned in place by fury and remorse, Elaine wanted to sit in the car and howl, but Ava and Gigi were already headed up the brick path to the house. They paused on the porch, both of them turning to look at her at the same time. Elaine was struck again by how similar they were in build and profile, both like their father, slender and not too tall, yet strong and imperious-looking just the same.

She slid out of the car, looping her purse over one shoulder and locking the BMW behind her with a comforting beep of the key. She'd soon be getting back in her car and returning to Boston, with this house fading in her rearview mirror.

Elaine wouldn't let herself glance up at the blank upstairs windows of the apartment where her mother had died. She could smell the cigarette smoke from here. They were five miles from Moosehead Lake, but the scent of lake water was a pungent grace note to the cigarettes.

"Okay, troops. Who's got the cue cards?" she asked, forcing herself to smile and trot briskly up the sagging porch steps.

Ava smacked a hand to her forehead. "God, you're right. We should have thought about what to say. We don't want to give poor Finley a heart attack." She glanced at Elaine. "Oops. Sorry. Poor choice of words."

Elaine shrugged. "Fine by me. She was your mother, too."

"We should just tell her what Dad said and ask what happened to Peter," Gigi said impatiently. "How hard is that?"

"Ha. You don't know Finley," Elaine said. "She's not exactly Miss Hospitality. And, no offense, but your dad is pretty much at the top of her blacklist since he walked out on Mom."

"He was your dad, too." Gigi pressed two fingers to her bottom lip. It was only then that Elaine noticed she'd removed the lip ring. You couldn't even see the hole. She was at least slightly less psychotic looking without the lip ring, maybe even cute, but that spiked hair still gave Gigi the appearance of a belligerent hedgehog.

"Could you please call a truce, you two?" Ava was saying. "We're in this together." She knocked on the door.

Elaine hadn't been aware of the tinny sound of the television until the noise was suddenly muted. They heard shuffling footsteps; then the door opened a crack. The smell of smoke was so strong with the door open that Elaine imagined blue strands of it curling out of the house in the shape of a huge hand, like in a cartoon.

"Hey, Aunt Finley," she said. "It's me. Elaine."

"And me, Ava." Ava looped an arm around Gigi's skinny shoulders. "This is our friend Gigi. We were passing through town and thought we'd stop by."

*Lame*, Elaine thought.

A hay loader rattled past on the narrow road behind them as Finley grunted and fiddled to unlatch the door. Finally she managed it. The door swung open onto a foyer crammed with boots, a bag of cat litter, a bucket of salt, an ice scraper, and a snow shovel. It might be July in Maine, but Finley was clearly still prepared for the sky to fall.

"Well, don't just stand there and let the flies in," Finley said. "Come in and shut the door." She turned and made her hunched way back into the house. She wore a blue cotton bathrobe and tan mules, her cracked dry heels hanging over the backs of her slippers like a pair of corks.

The apartment was as dark, smoky, and pine-paneled as a VFW bar. Finley had the woodstove going in the living room despite the sultry midsummer heat that had slithered its way even this far north. Elaine immediately broke into a sweat and again regretted her blouse, jeans, and boots. She shot an envious look at Ava and Gigi, who both wore shorts and T-shirts and sandals. There was something to be said for letting your standards slip at the height of summer.

"Have a seat, girls," Finley wheezed. She settled herself on a plaid recliner with cat-scratched fabric; the chair looked like it had been dragged in off the street. "I'd offer you a pop, except I haven't been to the store." She picked up the cigarette smoldering in the ashtray and took a long drag of it, smoke swirling out of her nostrils. Judging from the number of butts in that ashtray, it was no wonder the woman's skin had the texture of a walnut shell.

The rest of the living room furniture consisted of a sagging brown tweed couch and a coffee table with so many water rings on its surface, it looked like a deliberate helix design. There was a wooden lamp, its base carved like an owl, and magazines were stacked all over the floor and on top of every horizontal surface, even the TV. Navigating the living room was like walking through a miniature city of paper skyscrapers. Glancing down, Elaine made out the date on one *National Geographic*: 1969. Finley probably had every issue dating back decades; she could put this collection on eBay and pay her rent for a year.

In this dim light, and despite her rough brown complexion, her great-aunt didn't appear to have aged much since the last time Elaine had seen her eight or ten years ago. She was still stout and her pewter hair looked like she'd cut it herself around a cereal bowl. Despite this, she had surprisingly feminine features: a pretty upturned nose, a doll's pert mouth, and small ears that gleamed like pink seashells through the strands of her sparse gray hair.

Finley had been eating her supper, the remains of which were on a folding table next to the recliner: a half-empty bowl of soup and a sleeve of saltines. "I could get you some water," she offered. "There's always water."

"Oh, don't bother. We're fine," Ava said. "We just popped in to say hi because it's been so long since we've heard from you."

"Last I checked, I'm still here." Finley's face wrinkled into a smile. "I read the obits every morning just to make sure I'm not listed." When Gigi giggled, Finley gave her a rheumy look. "Who are you again?"

"Gigi works for me and plays with my sons in a band," Ava answered smoothly. "Do you remember Evan and Sam?"

"Not likely," Finley said with a dismissive snort. "Haven't seen them or you since that memorial service for your mother. The little one was in that sling contraption you carried on your back. Bigger 'n' you by now, I expect."

"Oh yes. They're both tall like my husband," Ava said.

"Don't remember him, either, except he was losing his hair," Finley said. "I don't know how you stood it. Some women think a bald man is sexy, but I never did."

"We're divorced now," Ava said.

Finley nodded. "Well, that's too bad, but at least you don't have to look at him anymore. I'm sure he didn't grow more hair as he got older." She swiveled her gray head owlishly in Elaine's direction. "And you? How you been keeping? Still working in Boston?"

"Yes."

"A miracle you haven't been shot, from what I see on the news. Gangs and drugs everywhere you go. Bombs, too. What kind of job do you have?"

"I'm in marketing." Elaine had forgotten Finley's shotgun approach to conversation; it was as if the woman had studied how conversations were supposed to go, but never quite practiced the techniques enough to master them.

"My. Marketing what?"

"Colleges."

"College, ha!" Finley laughed, showing the pink gums where several teeth were missing. "Only billionaires can afford them now. Even the state university! And why send your kid to college anyway? To listen to a bunch of liberal professors talk like Commies about global warming? No, thank you."

"College costs are definitely on the rise," Elaine said, scrambling to stay on neutral ground.

Finley stabbed her cigarette butt into the pile of ash on a chipped flowered saucer. "Married yet? Kids?"

"No." Elaine shifted her weight. She was suffocating in here, breathing smoke, sweating, the ceiling pressed too close to her head. Did her mother die in the room right above this one? She'd never thought to ask where in the upstairs apartment they'd found her.

"Good on you. You're a smart one. Men marry you just so's they can control you." Finley narrowed her cloudy eyes at Gigi. "Make a note of that, girl. When it comes to men, you can never be too quick or too careful."

"Yes, ma'am." Gigi sat up a little straighter on the couch.

Finley smacked her lips. "Well. Somebody's brought you up right, I see."

That was enough banter, Elaine decided. Time to get what they needed and get out. Finley was smart; she'd have to know they hadn't driven four hours to see her on a whim. "We actually came here to ask you something," she said.

"Ah. Not purely a social call, then. Figured as much." Finley lit another cigarette and continued squinting in their direction, her eyes so hazy and blue with cataracts that Elaine wondered how clearly she could see. "You never did think much of Maine. Just like your dad, the pair of you, thinking you're too good for us all. He left this state behind him as soon as he could and never looked back. Took your mother with him and ruined her life."

Elaine swallowed hard and felt Ava's thigh muscle tense up against hers. "We're sorry we haven't had time to visit lately," Ava said, "but we've both been busy with work. It's hard to get away."

Finley waved a hand. "No excuses necessary," she said. "You know I'm not much for visiting anyhow. Ask what you came to ask and be quick about it. It's nearly bedtime." She stared fixedly at the muted television, where a woman was openmouthed in horror at the sight of her son's stained jeans, reminding Elaine of her blouse.

Ava glanced at her, waiting for a cue. On the other side of her, Elaine could feel Gigi jittering; she wanted to put a hand on the girl's knobby knee to stop her foot from bouncing, but couldn't bring herself to actually touch her.

Elaine couldn't speak. Her brain was overloaded with memories, the circuits fried. She looked back helplessly at Ava.

"Well," Ava said, "first I want to ask whether you got that card I sent, saying Dad died."

"Sure I did," Finley said, with a quick sideways shift of her eyes.

Elaine followed her great-aunt's glance to an old pine table in the corner. There was a basket on top of it, overflowing with mail. Ava's card was probably buried in there someplace and maybe even unopened, if Finley couldn't see well enough to read anymore. Not that Finley would have cared about Dad being gone anyway; she probably would have danced a jig, hearing the news. Or at least bought a fresh pack of smokes to celebrate.

"The thing is," Ava went on, "just before Dad died, he told us we have a brother. He said Mom had the baby before I was born."

"He did not say that." Finley jabbed her cigarette into the ashtray, though it was still long and white.

"He did," Ava said gently. "Dad said they had to give the baby up. A little boy. I heard they gave him to you."

It was a bold stab in the dark, Elaine knew. She was prepared for their great-aunt to be as mystified as they were, or to deny it all and shoo them out the door.

But Finley's face crumpled like a damp paper bag, her eyes

nearly disappearing in the folds of her skin. "I told Marie it was too much," she whispered.

Jesus, Elaine thought with a horrified shiver. So the rumor was true. Her mother had another child, gave him up, and kept it from them all this time! From *her*, even though she'd been living here, alone with her mother, for an entire wretched year! She felt her own face crumple like Finley's, feeling hurt and betrayed.

Ava heaved herself up off the sagging couch to kneel on the floor between stacks of *Ladies' Home Journals*. She awkwardly embraced Finley around the old woman's thick waist. "I know it must have been difficult," she said softly. "Tell us about it. It's okay to talk now. Everything happened so long ago. It wasn't your fault. We know that."

Did they really know that? Elaine was nearly holding her breath now; beside her, Gigi had gone completely still.

"Your mother, she was such a beautiful girl. Pretty as this one." Finley lifted a finger and pointed right at Elaine. "Dark and thin, quick as a fairy. Her parents treated her like a princess. They brought her up in the Catholic Church, bought her nice clothes, made sure she knew her manners. Then she started over at the high school and all that went out the window. Just about killed my sister with what she did." Finley looked longingly at her pack of cigarettes but didn't light another one.

"Our parents fell in love," Elaine said. She felt like somebody had to speak up on her mother's behalf. "Mom wasn't trying to hurt anybody. Dad was her whole life, she said, from the first minute she saw him."

Finley was nodding, staring into her lap, her gnarled fingers twisted together. "That was true. Once Suzanne met Bob, you couldn't talk a grain of sense into that girl. Your grandparents didn't see the trouble coming, but I did. Then, when it was too late, your mother didn't want to tell them she was in a family way. She was a good girl and knew it would break their hearts."

Ava asked what year the baby was born, but Finley shook her head. "I don't rightly remember. It was just a couple of years before they eloped and then you came along."

Elaine tried to calculate the year: 1970 or 1971, probably. "I don't understand why getting pregnant was such a big deal. The women's movement was well under way by then."

"Not here," Finley said. "Nowhere close to here, anyway. Feminists would've been run out of Maine. Back then everybody was sure feminists must be lesbians. Lesbians weren't welcome anywhere, except maybe California and New York City."

Elaine understood, suddenly: Finley was gay. All these years, and she'd never guessed. Had she been with other women? She must have tried, judging from the bitterness in her voice.

"What about abortions?" Ava was asking. "They weren't legal then, but women had them."

"Not in Maine," Finley repeated. "Besides which, our family was proper lace-curtain Catholic, so that wouldn't have been a solution even if it hadn't been too late for that by the time your mother faced the music and told them. She should have told someone sooner, of course, but Suzanne knew she was going to bring shame on her family. Especially after your grandfather worked his fingers to the bone making a success of that Pontiac dealership and getting himself into the chamber of commerce. Suzanne hid the pregnancy for as long as she could, pinning her skirts and eating a lot, pretending she was just gaining weight. I knew, though. The poor thing looked like a marshmallow on toothpicks by the time she told my sister."

Elaine didn't ask why Finley had kept quiet. She knew the answer would be complicated: Finley didn't get along with Marie, their grandmother, for reasons that probably went as far back as them sharing a bedroom growing up in Prince Edward Island.

"Where did she have the baby?" Gigi asked.

The girl was like a bloodhound, going straight for the facts, Elaine thought with grudging respect. If there was a brother to be found, this girl would find him. Elaine still wasn't sure how she felt about that.

"Not anywhere close to here. My sister Marie, she was broken in half by the whole scandal," Finley said. "She was convinced that having a bastard child was the biggest sin there was, short of murder, and sometimes she acted like even that might not be as bad. She kept up the lie about there being no baby and sent Suzanne away."

"Where?" Ava asked.

"To a Catholic home for unwed mothers over in Bangor." Finley sighed. "Not a nice part of Bangor, either. Marie and I drove your poor mother over there at night, making her lie down on the floor so nobody could see she was pregnant. Suzanne had dropped out of school by then to keep people from talking, saying she was ill, but of course there was some talk."

They left her in Bangor, Finley went on, her voice a determined rasp, expecting Suzanne to deliver the baby and give it up for adoption, then come home and return to school like nothing had happened. She'd get on with her life and go to college, knowing she'd done the right thing for her family and for the baby, too.

"Your mother wasn't supposed to see the baby after she delivered," Finley said. "That's the thing that went all wrong: one of the nurses brought the child to her. Suzanne told me later that it was like he knew her already. The baby stopped crying right away when she held him. He turned his head to nuzzle her breast, and that did it."

"What do you mean?" Elaine asked. "Did what?"

"Sealed the deal. Suzanne told me later that she couldn't even imagine giving her little boy away once she'd held him in her arms, so she came home with him instead of going back to the nuns and signing him over." Finley shook her head. "I couldn't believe it when your grandmother called to tell me she was back in her father's house with that baby. Then again, what else could the poor girl do? She had no money, no place to go. The rest of the family was all in Canada. Your father had no idea where she was, or even that she was pregnant. Her parents had made her break up with him and wouldn't let her talk to him, even though he camped out in his car in front of their house until the police chief had to chase him off."

Marie wanted Suzanne back in school and convinced her the best thing would be to have Finley care for the child. Finley lived half an hour away, in another small town entirely; bringing up the baby there would keep him in the family while preserving Suzanne's reputation. She had given Finley money every month so she could quit her job at the paper mill and stay home. Marie, Finley, and Suzanne didn't tell anyone where the baby was, not even Suzanne's father, and certainly not Bob, who might have made trouble.

"The baby was tiny, born a month early, and he had problems right from the start. Cried like somebody was sticking him with pins. Colic, I suppose. Later of course we realized he was blind as a mole," Finley said. "Even so, he walked early and was always trying to climb things, feeling his way around this house. I was sure he'd kill himself. I was all alone, and he was too much! I tried my best. I did! But I ended up giving him away, too." She doubled over in the recliner, her head nearly pressed to her knees.

"I'll make some tea," Ava said, and sprang to her feet.

Stunned, Elaine could only stare at Finley as she rocked and rocked with her chubby arms wrapped tight around her knees, looking like an abandoned child herself.

Her aunt's kitchen was even filthier than the living room. Those crusted dishes in the sink had probably been there for weeks, and the floor was so sticky that Ava's sandals adhered to the linoleum. For one awful, absurd moment, she remembered Mark putting sticky paper down for mice in their house, and how she'd found a frantic mouse trapped on it, its poor little foot nearly torn off after a night of trying to chew itself free.

Ava rummaged through the dusty cupboards for tea bags. She found an old stash in a plastic bag, probably filched from a restaurant, and set a saucepan of water on the stove. While she waited for it to boil, she went deeper into the house to find the bathroom, desperate to pee.

It was here, at the end of the long dim hallway, that the memory came rushing back. Definitely a memory now and not a dream: She had walked down this hallway and reached up to open the door to the farthest room on the right. The child had come shooting out of the room, clawing at her and making weird high-pitched squeaks, babbling a few words.

What had he said to her? The words came back now, like gravel flung at her face: "You home now, I come out!" Then, after clutching her neck and feeling her face, the boy had sprung back as if burned and then, absurdly, he'd laughed. "Who you?" he'd cried. "Who you?"

Ava remembered now how terrified she'd been, hearing the other child's manic, panicky giggling, a sound that occasionally repeated itself in her dreams. She'd been sure the boy was laughing at *her*.

She hesitated, hand raised, then pushed open the same door. She flinched as the door creaked and then yawned open.

Ava felt around inside the room for a light switch, found it, and flicked it up. The ceiling light was an old fixture, probably original to the house, a pink glass ball etched with flowers. The bell of it was speckled black with dead insects. The room was empty but for a small white dresser and a single bed with a surprisingly elegant maple frame, the top of the headboard carved with flowers and fruit. The bed was covered with a striped Hudson's Bay wool blanket, white with orange and blue stripes. A one-eyed stuffed dog sat on the pillow. Otherwise, the room was free of clutter; not a single toy or magazine marred the bare hardwood floor. It smelled musty in here, as if the room had been closed up for a long time.

When would she have opened this door and found her brother? She was around three, so that must have been forty years ago. Peter would have been four and a half.

She shut off the light, closed the door again, and shuddered as she spotted a hook on the outside of it and an eye screwed into the frame. Finley must have kept Peter locked inside this room whenever she needed a rest or couldn't control him, figuring at least that way he'd be safe.

What was wrong with him? Why had he been born blind, and what other disabilities did he suffer?

Was he scared or delighted that night, when the bedroom door had suddenly, unexpectedly opened? Had he been kept in this room, a shameful secret stowed away, for hours at a time? That seemed likely, especially since he was too young, still, for school.

If that were the case, Peter never would have met someone his own size. What other child would he have seen? Yet he would have recognized her as a child. Children always knew other children. She'd seen that in her own boys, delighted by the sight of their own kind even as babies and toddlers. No wonder Peter had grabbed her and started babbling, trying to touch her face and hair. He must have been so shocked when she wasn't Finley, but someone who felt entirely different—someone who felt a lot like *him*. No wonder his reaction had been hysteria.

And then her mother must have heard the commotion and come running down the hall to quickly push him back into the bedroom and lock the door, dragging Ava away.

"But who is that?" Ava had asked, over and over. "Who is that boy, Mommy?"

Ava remembered this as clearly as if it had happened last week: she could see her brother running toward her in striped pajamas, his dark hair rumpled, his mouth round, issuing sharp cries like a jungle bird.

Now she opened the door to the bedroom again, stepped quickly across the room, and, with her heart pounding, picked up the little stuffed dog and tucked it into the pocket of her shorts. Then she closed the bedroom door and found the bathroom across the hall.

Ava peed standing up over the filthy toilet and returned to the kitchen as the saucepan threatened to boil over. She made the tea and added two generous spoonfuls of sugar, then carried the chipped white mug out to her great-aunt.

Gigi and Elaine were still seated on the couch, the two of them looking as frozen as if they were having their portrait painted. Nobody was talking. Finley was bent at the waist, face in her hands.

"Here you go." Ava knelt in front of Finley again. "Drink this. We've given you a shock, showing up here with our questions. You need something hot and sweet."

To her relief, Finley sat up and took the mug, cradling it between her hands. "I couldn't do it," she repeated. "You understand, don't you?" She was pleading with Ava now, ignoring the others.

"You have two sons. You know what trouble they are! I was all on my own and Peter was too much. Never gave me a moment's peace."

Ava thought of responsible, bossy Sam and sweet, timid Evan, saying a silent prayer of thanks for them both. "I'm sure it was very hard on you."

She did feel sorry for Finley. Without having married or had children of her own, this poor woman, with her anxious, reclusive nature, would have had a hard time raising any child. She'd taken the baby because that's what families did for each other.

Her great-aunt sipped the tea and made a face. Ava didn't know if this was because of the heat on her tongue or the memories. "Her mother helped her make a list, you know. When Suzanne was pregnant. They wrote the things she could give her baby on one side of the paper, and on the other side the things a real family could give him. You know what was on her side of the list? Nothing. Not a home or a wedding ring, even. On the other side were all the things two loving parents could give the baby. That's how Marie finally convinced Suzanne that she should give the baby up for adoption. I have to believe my sister did this not to spare herself any shame, but out of the goodness of her heart."

"I'm sure you're right," Ava said.

Finley shook her head. "I don't know about that now. Your mother didn't want to give him up. But she agreed to let me raise him."

"He was blind?" Elaine said. "You know that for sure?"

"Yes," Finley said. "A blind child compensates, feels his way through life if his sight is gone. Quite capably, really. But other things must have been wrong with him, too. I don't know what. All I know is that boy was so jumpy and nervous all the time, it was like he was trying to crawl out of his own skin. I did well enough until Peter started walking, but then I had to lock him up for his own good." Her aunt's eyes flicked toward the hall, and Ava knew she was thinking about that room at the end of it.

"Did Mom ever come to see him here?" Ava asked. She had to know if her memory was real.

Finley nodded. "Just the one time. You were with her, though you were just little yourself, so I'm sure you don't remember." Finley studied the floor. For the first time, Ava was aware of the cigarette ash around her chair, like a light snowfall. "I'd called Suzanne to say Peter was too much for me to manage anymore. Your mother drove up here to talk to me about taking Peter back, now that your father was making good money and they'd bought a house. She brought you along with her. She'd just found out she was pregnant again and told me she always felt wrong, giving up her first baby. I think she wanted to introduce you to Peter and reassure herself that she'd be able to finally tell your father about him, too. Instead her visit had the opposite effect. She knew at once she wouldn't be able to handle a defective child any better than I could, especially tired as she was. After that visit, your mom signed the adoption papers."

Of course she did, Ava realized: seeing her abandoned firstborn son with Ava must have shocked her mother into realizing that she couldn't let her two worlds collide ever again, or she might shatter. Which was what had happened, finally, in the end.

"She thought of him as *defective*?" Gigi was saying now.

"Well, in those days, that's what people thought handicapped babies were." Finley set the teacup down and rubbed her gnarled hands together. "We didn't have the special programs and schools they have everywhere now. A baby like that didn't usually live at home. Too difficult for everybody to cope. Doctors urged mothers to give their mistakes away."

"A mistake?" This time it was Elaine speaking, but she sounded as shocked as Gigi.

Ava glanced at Elaine and saw that her face, always pale, had gone white. Her sister's blouse looked limp and dirty, clinging to her skinny frame. Ava felt a pang of sympathy for her. It couldn't be easy for Elaine to return to Finley's house. She knew Elaine still blamed herself for Mom dying in the apartment upstairs.

"Well, he was." Finley had gathered strength from the tea; now she shook another cigarette out of the package and lit it. "I'm not talking about God's mistake. I'm not a religious woman. The hypocrisy of the Catholic Church is something I can no longer abide. No, I'm talking about how that little boy was a mistake because he should never have been born. At least not to your mother. Suzanne was a fragile little thing. The pregnancy and birth, the shame on top of that, well, that took about all the strength she had in her. Then your father leaving her finished her off."

"What happened after you gave him up, Auntie?" Ava asked, hearing Elaine suck air between her teeth in distress.

"I couldn't believe there was any family on God's green earth who'd want that child with all his problems," Finley said, drawing smoke. "My hope was that at least they'd find a foster home for him and get him into some kind of program to teach the boy how to look after himself."

"Mom must have been sick about letting him go," Elaine said.

"I'd say she was more resigned about the whole thing. Suzanne understood what had to be done. Frankly, I think it had been hard on her, knowing her child was living with me. Everything you did, Ava, every milestone—standing up, walking, talking, starting school—reminded her of the boy she gave away. In the end, she thought giving Peter up might let her focus more on the family she had and forget about whatever mistakes she'd made as a girl. But the past always catches up with you, doesn't it?" Finley was tiring, her hands trembling in her lap, her voice barely above a whisper now.

Ava stood up. "Can you show us any pictures of him before we go, Auntie?"

Finley nodded. "In that top drawer underneath the TV there's a photograph. He was mine for a little while, wasn't he? I still pray for that child." Her voice quavered. "I did the best I could by him."

"Why didn't you tell us about him after Mom died?" Elaine asked as Ava pulled open the TV drawer. Not surprisingly, it was crammed full of papers and photographs; she had to slide her hand in and press down on the papers to jimmy the drawer free.

"Not my secret to tell," Finley said, jutting her chin. "I promised my sister I'd keep their secret to my grave."

"Why are you telling us now, then?" Gigi asked. Her voice wasn't accusatory; she was just curious, Ava could tell.

Finley squinted at her. "Who are you again, young lady?"

Ava held her breath, giving Gigi the chance to tell the truth. She was relieved when Gigi said, "A friend of Ava's and her sons. That's all."

"Seeing these girls here, the two of them grown women, made me realize I don't want to be buried with this secret. Keeping my promise won't do anybody any good now."

"Did you ever hear from Peter again?" Elaine asked.

"Not a word." Finley started to cry, one slow tear snaking its way along the crevices of her cheek. "I thought I'd be able to visit the boy when my social security checks started coming regular and I could finally afford the bus to Bangor, where the social worker was who took him. But when I got all the way up there, they said he'd been removed from their system."

"*Removed?*" Ava's chest tightened, hearing this. Maybe they were too late after all. "What do you mean?" She sat down between Elaine and Gigi and dropped the pile of papers and photographs onto the coffee table. They slid across the table's water-marked surface, a mini avalanche of family history. "Did he die?"

"No, no. Nothing like that. Peter was *taken*." Finley sounded impatient now. "I wasn't allowed to know the name of his new people without your mother's permission. Even your mother didn't know who adopted him. That wasn't done back then. In those days, birth mothers weren't allowed to know the adoptive family. Everyone's privacy was protected."

"What about Dad?" Ava asked. "When did he find out about Peter?"

Finley squinted at the ceiling. "Maybe a year or so after Elaine came along, I think it was. Your mother had some kind of breakdown and told him about it then. She called me right after that, said she'd made a terrible mistake, telling him. He was that upset. I don't think their marriage ever fully recovered."

"Did Dad ever try to find Peter when we were growing up?"

"No idea. He certainly never came to me about it. Even if he had, it wouldn't have done him much good. His name wasn't even on the birth certificate and of course there wasn't any of that DNA testing back then. I suppose he could see, too, how difficult it was for your mother to cope with just you two girls, and decided to leave well enough alone."

"He was respecting Mom's wishes," Elaine pointed out.

"Maybe. Or maybe he was taking the easy way out, as men do." Finley leaned forward, sorting through the photographs on the table with her gnarled fingers until she found the one she wanted. She held the picture up in front of the three of them, her hand trembling a little.

It was a color photo of a small, serious-looking, dark-haired boy on the same sofa they were seated on now. Peter was dressed formally, in black trousers with red suspenders, a white shirt, and a little red bow tie. Was this picture taken on Christmas? Ava wondered. Or was it a photo to accompany his adoption papers?

Peter's hands were folded in his lap and he looked about five years old. He had the same square jaw and high cheekbones that Ava and Gigi had inherited from her father, but a feline tilt to his dark eyes that he—and Elaine—had inherited from their mother. Ava could almost hear Finley's voice admonishing him to "Sit still, for once in your life!" His legs were so short, they stuck straight out in front of him like a doll's as he solemnly looked at the camera.

Except he couldn't have actually been looking at anything. Peter was blind, Ava reminded herself, despite the fact that nothing about his expression suggested he couldn't see the photographer. There weren't any other obvious disabilities. He looked alert and curious. Perhaps Finley concluded he had problems because Peter was hyperactive, or suffering from anxiety. And what boy wouldn't, being closeted during most of his early childhood in a single room, with only a sedentary middle-aged woman for company?

Ava wanted to weep, seeing Peter—her brother!—posed like that, trying hard to behave, innocent of whatever fate awaited him. She felt a sense of recognition so deep, it was nearly primal: This boy was her family. Her blood. Her history.

Ava picked up the picture and, without asking permission, slid it into her pocket with the little stuffed dog.

They drove home in near silence, stopping only once at a highway rest stop when Gigi said, "I'm starving hungry! I could gnaw off my own arm! You two must be cyborgs or something, going so many hours without food."

Ava said she had no appetite. Elaine sighed and said, "I'd sooner slit my wrists than eat any crap fast food loaded with enough salt and fat and toxins to fell a herd of elephants," but she stopped anyway.

However, once they'd gone through the drive-through, the food smelled so good that both Ava and Elaine started begging Gigi for fries the minute they pulled back on the highway. They had to stop again at the next exit.

"I need gas anyway," Elaine muttered. "Might as well eat something here."

"This time, get your own dinners," Gigi said.

"Yeah? And who do you think bought yours? Santa?" Elaine snapped back.

That was the only altercation. Ava was grateful for the relative peace in the car. She was too exhausted to deal with any more drama, and still reeling from the sensation of walking through her own nightmare at Finley's house.

"Can we call places tomorrow and try to find out what happened?" Gigi asked from the backseat as they turned onto High Street to drop her off in Newburyport before continuing across the bridge to Beach Plum Island.

"Count me out," Elaine said. "I'm not ready to do this."

Ava wasn't sure she was ready, either, but she told Gigi she would. "It won't be easy, though," she warned.

Peter's last name on the birth certificate was Laurent, Suzanne's maiden name, and the father was listed as "unknown." But knowing Peter's last name might not even be useful if he'd been adopted into another family. Ava didn't know what the adoption laws were.

"What if Peter's already dead?" asked Elaine, whose thoughts must have been traveling in similar, if darker, circles. "Do we really want to know?" She sucked down the rest of her soda and rattled the ice in the cup, steering the car easily with one hand but driving too fast for Ava's comfort. "Think how horrible we'd feel."

"It didn't sound like he had anything wrong with his health, just his eyes," Ava pointed out. "And he'd only be in his early forties by now. Forty-three, if he was born two years before I was."

"We have to prepare ourselves for that possibility, though,"

Elaine said. Her profile was sharply etched against the window, as elegant as some ancient priestess's against the white collar of her shirt in the darkened car.

"Also, he might not want to see us," Gigi said, sounding glum. "Would *you* want to see the kids your dad *didn't* give up? The kids he actually stuck around to raise?"

"No," Elaine said. "I still don't, actually."

"Nice," Gigi said. "Real nice." She fell silent for the rest of the ride home.

Ava knew Gigi was hurt. By the way Elaine glanced into the rearview mirror to look at her, she knew Elaine realized it, too. She hoped Elaine was sorry, but didn't have the energy to intervene. Times like these made her wonder if having sisters was worth the effort—and why the hell she'd started this whole treasure hunt for a brother who would surely complicate their lives even more.

## CHAPTER SEVEN

Elaine and Tony had a Sunday ritual they'd started five years ago when Elaine joined his marketing company: they would meet at the gym for an eight o'clock spin class, then treat themselves to dim sum in Chinatown. This Sunday was so hot, however, that Tony called early to suggest the North End pool instead of dim sum.

"We can eat at the snack bar," he coaxed. "You'll love it. So retro."

"A public pool?" Elaine laughed. "God. I didn't know you were so *communal*."

"Are you kidding? I love that pool!" he declared. "It's the best place on the planet to ogle hot Italian guys in gold necklaces and Hugo Boss. And where else can you wear heels with your bikini? Come on. Live a little. They even have ice cream at the snack bar."

"Okay," she said. "But you're treating."

"Absolutely! The pool is three bucks for the day and the ice cream's a dollar. It'll break the bank, but you are so worth it, sweetie."

They showered and changed into their swimsuits after spin

class. Tony drove them to the pool in his green Mini Cooper, a car so ridiculously like a go-kart that Elaine couldn't even make fun of it. Besides, Tony adored it, saying it was the perfect city car: "If I can't park it, I can just put it in my pocket."

The Mirabella Pool was at the edge of Boston's North End and had a stunning view of the harbor. "See?" Tony said. "It's like Club Med in the middle of the city."

"Not quite," Elaine said, rolling her eyes at a trio of older men with brown, well-oiled barrel chests. The men were playing dominoes. "But the water looks clean enough."

The pool was deliciously cold, too. They swam laps, then floated on their backs, talking about work and Tony's new boyfriend, George, who had just moved in with him. Afterward they found an open square of concrete where they spread out their towels and slathered each other with sunscreen. Tony was olive-skinned and dark, with a strong jaw and sensual mouth; he looked like he'd grown up right here in the North End.

Finally, Elaine couldn't stand not telling him everything. Tony was her best friend and knew her better than anyone. Better than Ava, sometimes.

"So it turns out I have this big family now," she plunged. "I told you about my half sister, Gigi, right? Well, now it looks like I have this brother someplace. He was born before Ava, and my parents gave him up for adoption because they were still in high school and he was blind and disabled."

"What? Are you kidding me?" Tony sat up so fast that his sunglasses flew off his head and onto the cement. A teenage girl in a red bikini, platform sandals, and an entire chain-link fence of bracelets stooped gracefully to pick them up. She returned the glasses to Tony with a blindingly white smile.

"Jesus, I hate being this old," Elaine muttered, squinting at the girl's tight buttocks and toned legs as she pranced off to join a group of girls who looked like they could be her sisters, all ten of them.

"We all get to be young and beautiful exactly once," Tony said. "Be grateful that you and I have now moved on to become elegant and wise." He flipped over onto his stomach. "So is this really your life you're telling me about, or some Dickensian novel full of intrigue, plague, hunger, and orphans?"

Elaine laughed. "Oh yeah, I own it, baby." She told him about Ava inviting Gigi to work in her pottery studio, and about discovering Gigi at Ava's, playing music with her nephews. "I acted badly and had a little snit fit over it," she admitted. "Mainly because Ava clearly lured me up there to make nice with Gigi without having the decency to tell me anything about her being there first."

"Ava's scared of you," Tony guessed.

"Unlikely. Ava's tough. But afterward I went a little crazy, I was so mad at her."

She confessed to going out that night and drinking so much she blacked out, and about do-gooder Gabe saving her from a tattooed motorcyclist. Finally she told Tony about Dad's deathbed confessions to Ava and Gigi about a brother named Peter, and how once again Ava had tricked her into driving north, only to find out Gigi was coming along for the ride to ask Finley about their brother.

Elaine left no sordid detail unrevealed; watching Tony's expressions unfold while she talked made her feel like she was a movie he was watching. When she'd finished, she flipped onto her stomach, too.

"So much drama, and so soon after the funeral," Tony marveled. "Wow. You must be wrung out." They were lying side by side, propped on their elbows and staring out at the sailboats and oil tankers on the sparkling blue harbor.

"I am." Elaine reached around to unhook the back of her bathing suit. She wasn't about to start having tan lines now. "The other thing I'm feeling is dread. I don't want a new sister in my life. I don't want a brother, either, especially not this one."

"Why not this one?"

"Because it's all too complicated! I love Ava. That's why I went with her yesterday to Maine. I felt bad about storming out of her house just because that little freak was singing with my nephews. Plus, I knew Ava's Honda wouldn't make it that far north. I was happy she asked me. I really was. I know this is important to her, this brother. But I didn't expect her to invite Gigi along for the ride and rub that whole connection in my face. Ugh. And I don't know why we should search for some defective brother anyway."

"Because you want to know what happened to him," Tony said promptly.

"No I don't. Not necessarily." Elaine laid her head down on the towel. The hot cement made her cheek feel like she'd been slapped. "If he's alive—and that's a big if—Peter would be in his early forties and probably demented after being passed around a dozen foster families or institutionalized. He probably has hyperactivity, attachment disorder, depression, bipolar disorder, PTSD, or any number of those other horrible disorders kids suffer from when adults abuse them or lock them up."

"That *is* a long list," Tony murmured. "Like a whole year of Lifetime movies."

"Right!"

"What about Gigi, though? She's had two parents up until now. A solid start in life."

"True. And I sort of get why Ava wants to bond with her. Ava misses our dad and the two of them are like clones, all artsy and barefoot and everything, and Gigi's the same age as Ava's sons. Ava doesn't see her like I do."

"And how's that?" Tony propped his chin up on one hand to look at her.

"She's insufferable! The girl's an entitled little prep school brat who deliberately pierces herself and dyes her hair to look like some punk, when meanwhile she takes riding lessons at this fancy country club and probably sleeps in a frilly pink canopy bed. Such a poser! God!"

"She's only fifteen," Tony reminded her. "Of course she's a poser. Who knows who they are at that age?"

"I did. At fifteen, I was president of my class and thinking about colleges. Whatever. Maybe Ava needed a mini-her since I'm always at work and unavailable."

"Do I detect a snit of jealousy here?" Tony asked.

"About my brother, you mean?"

"And about the girl, Gigi. Such a sixties name. Love it."

"Probably her mother's choice. My stepmom's younger than I am. Did I ever tell you that?"

"Many times." Tony said this kindly. "And now Gigi's mom is a widow and that girl is fatherless. Could those factors have entered into Ava's thinking, when she brought the girl home and introduced her to her sons? Who would also be Gigi's nephews, if I'm following the story?"

"Oh, blow me."

"I would, gladly, but you're not my type." Tony pushed his sunglasses up so that Elaine could see his brown eyes reflecting the sunlit harbor beyond the chain-link fence. "What is it you're really worried about, sweetie? That Ava will stop loving you because she's looking after this little poser? That your brother, Peter, will somehow turn up and eat up the rest of Ava's free time, because he's in a padded helmet and has a guide dog? Is there maybe a part of you that misses Ava's mothering, now that your dad is gone and you're grieving, hmm?"

"Oh fucking hell," Elaine said miserably. As always, Tony could hold up a mirror to her life. "I suppose."

"You know, there's another way this story could go," he said.

"How?"

"Maybe your brother, Peter, survived his shitty childhood and will be glad to know he's not alone in the world," Tony said. "Maybe he was one of those kids who was resilient enough to make something of himself as an adult, despite whatever obstacles he faced."

It was only then that Elaine remembered Tony's own chaotic childhood. She closed her eyes and groaned. "Oh, God. I am so, so sorry. I completely forgot."

"Of course you did!" he said cheerfully. "But don't you see? That's how miraculously resilient the human spirit can be, that you forgot I was a foster kid." Tony rolled onto his back. "I actually loved my foster mom," he said thoughtfully. "I still do. She was the rock to my barnacled little self. Now will you please help me choose the best-looking lifeguard? Nobody has an eye for man candy like you do."

Elaine laughed. "What about George? Isn't he waiting for you at home?"

Tony checked his watch. "No. He's probably still at church, singing his little heart out," he said. "Once a choirboy, always a choirboy. Then he'll stop at the grocery store and bring us something to feast on for dinner. Did I tell you about his mango chicken?"

"Did I tell you that I'm jealous every time you tell me George is cooking for you?" Elaine said. "I always imagine him in a frilly apron and nothing else."

"George will be thrilled when I tell him that. You know, you could get yourself one of these homey, live-in boyfriends yourself someday, if you ever get tired of blacking out at clubs."

"Shut up. You sound like my sister."

"Because we both love you," Tony said. "Seriously, honey. These lifeguards are tasty to look at and so are bar boys. But you and I both know boys under thirty are only tolerable until they open their mouths. What about trying somebody maybe a tad older? A guy with something to offer you outside the bedroom?"

"You mean like a nicer car than mine?"

"I mean like somebody who can offer you a decent conversation in the clear light of day in addition to fun slutty pillow talk," Tony said. "I mean a dinner cooked at home and eaten in pajamas. When was the last time you were in bed with a guy and both of you had clothes on while you talked?"

"I don't typically go to bed in clothes," Elaine said. "My high heels destroy the silk sheets." But she was thinking of Gabe, of his warm brown eyes and deep laugh, and the way he'd held her and wouldn't stop stroking her hair.

She shook off the image. The last thing she needed was some sensitive needy guy in a nonprofit T-shirt making goo-goo eyes at her. She sat up. "Come on, hunky man. You promised me an ice cream."

"And pizza. I wonder if they have gelato here?"

Tony pulled on his T-shirt and stood up, offering his hand to her. Elaine took it and they held hands on their way to the snack bar like a pair of children at recess, so happy to be best friends they wanted the whole world to know.

They weren't going to find out anything more about their brother today. It was Sunday, Ava reminded her when Gigi called that afternoon, so offices were closed. Finley hadn't known which adoption agency had originally placed Peter with a family, but there were only a few in Maine. Ava planned to call them all, she promised Gigi.

"But not until tomorrow," she said, "so you might as well find something else to do today. Why don't you spend time with your mom?"

Ava didn't understand that her mom probably didn't even know if Gigi was here or not. Mom wasn't like Ava, who seemed tuned into everything Evan and Sam did, even though she put on a good show of pretending she wasn't. It wasn't like Ava friended them on Facebook or anything. She just asked them questions and Evan and Sam usually told her the truth, maybe because they knew Ava wouldn't blow up at them.

Gigi was in her bedroom, where she spent another hour on the computer. She'd tried Facebook first, to see if Peter Laurent was on there. He was blind, but maybe they had computers that talked to you or something. When she couldn't find him, she wondered if his new family had changed his last name. That was a horrible thought. How would they find him then? A family could even adopt him and change his first name, too.

Well, she had to start somewhere. Gigi started researching adoption resources next. There seemed to be a lot of them online. She surfed through Bastard Nation, the National Adoption Clearinghouse, and the International Soundex Reunion Registry. What all adoption registries had in common was this: You couldn't find somebody who had been adopted unless that person wanted to find you. All you could do was put your information into the registry and hope the person you were looking for did the same.

This site seemed like the best choice. It had been around since 1975 and used Soundex, a phonetic way of indexing names by sound to make it easier to find information on names that sounded alike, but might be spelled differently (Mayer, Meyer, Meier, Maier, Mire, Myer). So Soundex could help find a name in a database, even if it had various spellings. Any adoptee, foster child, or person separated from family who was over eighteen could use it.

Gigi scrolled through a few other sites, and discovered that if adoptions were finalized before 1984, which Peter's must have been, both the birth parent and the child had to file their consent for an agency to arrange contact between them. Same thing for birth siblings age twenty-one or older.

Basically, anybody looking for someone else could file information with the registry: birth parents, birth siblings, adoptive parents, foster children, legal guardians of people with disabilities. That was the line that stopped Gigi: "legal guardians of people with disabilities." Peter had disabilities, so even if he wouldn't, or couldn't, look for them, maybe his legal guardian had registered to search for Peter's family.

It was worth a try. Excited now, Gigi read on to see how it worked. The process seemed simple enough. All you had to do was register online and your form was scanned. Information would be indexed on their computer. If data matched, and the ISRR volunteers discovered a relationship existed, they'd notify both people.

Gigi called Ava to tell her all about the registry. "I can't do it because I'm not eighteen, but you could," she said.

There was such a long pause that Gigi thought for a minute her cell phone had died, or that she'd lost the connection. Then she heard a light tapping and Ava said, "I found the site. But I don't know if this will work. I don't really know anything except my mom's name. I don't even know the name of the hospital or the month and year he was born." She sounded tired.

"Well, put in your best guesses," Gigi said. "And maybe there's somebody else who can help us, right? Dad's parents are dead, but he must have cousins who are still alive or something."

"Maybe," Ava said, but she sounded doubtful. "I'll think about that."

After they hung up, Gigi wrapped her arms around her body, feeling jumpy and claustrophobic. Even if Ava put in her information tonight, they wouldn't know anything right away. The Web site said it could take ten days. They probably got lots of registrations, an organization as big as that.

And Peter, if he was blind and disabled, might not even know how to use a computer. If so, he couldn't possibly know what Gigi had managed to discover in just a few seconds on her iPad: there are ways to find your family even if they've given you away.

Which led her to other, more serious questions: What if Peter didn't *want* to find them? What if he was already dead? Or so disabled, he was one of those people you saw sometimes in wheelchairs, being fed from a tube?

Gigi didn't want to consider these questions. She flopped down on the bed and put her iPod headphones on to learn "Stairway to Heaven."

She had been singing with her eyes closed, and the music was so loud that Gigi almost screamed when she felt something shaking her arm. Her eyes flew open.

It was her mother, who almost never came into her bedroom. Mom was sitting on the edge of the bed and touching her arm, mouthing words Gigi couldn't hear over the music.

For the second it took her to pull out her earbuds, Gigi registered this fact: Mom looked good. She had washed and brushed her hair and she was wearing her favorite rose-colored sleeveless blouse, the one that set off her gray eyes and made her cheeks look pink. She smiled down at Gigi.

"What?" Gigi said, once she'd silenced the music.

"You sound good."

"Oh. Thanks." Gigi scrambled to a sitting position. "Why are you here?"

Hurt shadowed her mother's eyes, but she quickly smiled again. "I wanted to ask if you'd go riding with me."

"When? Right now?" Gigi glanced out the window. With the hours she'd put in on the computer, she would have guessed it would be dark already. But the sun was still blazing, trapped in the branches outside her window.

"Won't it be too hot in the ring?" she asked, not daring to add, *Are you friggin' insane? I'm not going back to the barn to train for Nationals. Ever.*

"I thought we could go trail riding. Just you and me. I'm sure Bantam and Dolly miss us. We haven't been to the stable in weeks."

Gigi stared at her in disbelief. When had her mother ever wanted to ride in the woods? Mom was all about drills, taking jumps, or doing dressage for hours at a time. Perfection, not fun.

"I don't know," Gigi hedged, searching for an excuse. "I still think it might be too hot."

"We could go to Bradley Palmer State Park, maybe swim in the river."

That was tempting. Gigi did miss Bantam, the black Morgan she'd shared with Dad since she turned thirteen. And she hadn't been to the river since she'd gone with Dad last year. She had a sudden, blindingly painful memory of Dad on the rope swing, yodeling as he swung out over the lazy green water.

"I can't go back there," she said, closing her eyes.

There was a small silence; then Gigi felt her mother's hand on hers. "I know you and your dad loved going to the river together. I don't know if I can take being there without him, either. But I think we should try. Dad would want us to."

Gigi opened her eyes and saw that her mother's cheeks were splotchy and red now, her gray eyes damp. "I don't know, Mom," she whispered. "I don't even know if I can ride again."

"You won't know until you try. It's hot. The horses would love the river. Let's just go together and get it over with, and we can always turn around if it's too awful."

She couldn't disappoint her mother, not when for once Mom was the one trying to be brave. Gigi nodded. "Give me a minute to change. I'll be right down."

The barn was empty, thank God. There was no riding camp on Sunday and most people were probably at their summerhouses for the weekend. They tacked up the horses and set off at a lazy trot. They talked a little, Mom mostly asking questions about Gigi's pottery and the band, their dialogue interspersed with an occasional horse snort.

Finally, Mom asked where Gigi had been all day yesterday, and Gigi had to tell her. She couldn't lie; if she did, Mom might question Ava, and Gigi didn't want Ava to get into trouble.

Mom listened quietly until Gigi got to the part about Finley not knowing what happened to Peter, and how Gigi had been trying to help Ava on the computer. Then Mom said, "This sounds like it's pretty important to you. Why?"

Gigi was in the lead on the trail; she swiveled in the saddle to look at her mother. Mom's head was bowed, the brim of her black velvet riding helmet shielding her expression. "Because if Peter's alive, I need to tell him what Dad said. I promised I would. Plus, Peter's a part of Dad, isn't he?"

Her mom raised her head a little and smiled. "Yes, he is," she agreed. "I think it's good you're looking for him. Your dad would be pleased."

It was like a blessing, Gigi realized, to have her mother know what she was doing and approve of it. She felt some of the tension ease from her shoulders.

They had worn about a gallon of bug spray, but an occasional mosquito still whined around Gigi's ears. Still, she'd forgotten how liberating it was to feel the power of a horse beneath you as you set off into a forest, away from cars and houses and everything else that made you so pathetically human. Here, deep in the woods, Gigi felt like she was part of the horse, bigger and better than her own small self. Her back relaxed and she let Bantam have his head, breaking into an easy canter ahead of her mother.

The river was surprisingly deserted for a summer Sunday. There were just a few kids on the rope swing, and a couple of families that had come by canoe from a place that rented them upriver. Gigi could still see her dad here, grinning like a monkey on that swing—a huge soft-bellied gorilla of a guy—but now the memory made her smile instead of cry. He had loved this place and taught her to love it, too. He would want her to be here.

To her surprise, her mother stripped off her jodhpurs and boots, revealing a blue tankini, and took her place in the line of kids. Mom looked very serious, unlike the laughing, whooping teenagers, and suddenly Gigi couldn't stand seeing her standing there alone, trying to be brave about the swing. She knew her mother had never been on the swing. Dad had tried to get her on it, but she was afraid of heights.

Gigi hadn't worn a suit, but she had on black underwear; she stripped off her jeans and boots and stood behind her mother in her underwear and T-shirt without saying a word.

When it was Mom's turn, she swung off the platform and over the river with a startled look, as if she hadn't really expected the rope to hold her. She forgot to let go until Gigi shouted, "Jump, Mom! Jump!"

She did, with a whoop of laughter. Gigi started laughing, too, and took her own turn off the rope, making the kind of cannonball her dad loved, splashing everyone around her.

She came up out of the water and saw Mom treading water next to her, pale hair plastered to her head, her gray eyes smiling as she blew a stream of water between her teeth, hitting Gigi square on the forehead.

Mark was supposed to bring the boys back after dinner, but instead they were home by four o'clock. Mark looked sheepish; he didn't come in like he usually did, but hugged the boys in the doorway and then hovered on the step. Ava could see Sasha sitting in Mark's car, talking on her phone. Sasha waved but didn't get out.

"Everything okay?" she asked. Ava felt slightly responsible for whatever happened between Sasha and Mark. Sasha had been on Ava's tennis team two years ago, and Ava was the one who'd told Mark to call her after first discussing him with Sasha.

Sasha was divorced, a lawyer with a grown daughter and a nice house in West Newbury, an energetic brunette whose blistering tennis serve put opponents in their place. She was pretty in a no-nonsense way and extremely practical. Mark tended to be disorganized and forgetful. It seemed like the perfect fit.

"Oh, yeah," Mark said. "We spent the weekend at Sasha's house on the Cape. I'm just not sure it was much fun for the boys. You know. A little too much white carpet and table manners, that sort of thing."

Ava laughed. "Did they take their shoes off and use their napkins, I hope?"

"Sure. But their socks weren't much better than their shoes. And I don't think Sasha's had a lot of experience with boys. Anyway, I hope you don't mind me bringing them back early." Mark gave another anxious glance over his shoulder. "I thought I might take her to dinner."

And to bed, probably, Ava thought, because Sasha wouldn't have wanted to do anything with the boys in the house. She waved him off. "Have fun," she said. "Tell her I said hi."

She closed the door and went to see the boys, who had immediately retreated into their iPods and computers. "Everything okay this weekend?" she asked Sam.

He nodded. "Big glassy house. Good food. She's nice enough, I guess."

"Good. Need anything else to eat?"

Sam shook his head, his eyes on the computer screen, scrolling through Facebook. "Nope. I'm set."

Evan was similarly closemouthed and uninterested in food. All he said was "Sasha's fine. She asks so many questions my ears started bleeding, though."

Ava smothered a laugh and closed the door. She'd forgotten that about Sasha. Lawyers loved to ask questions.

Now that the boys were home but nobody seemed to want dinner, Ava was, at loose ends. She wandered out to the patio, into her studio, and back into the living room, wondering what to do with herself. So odd, this period in her life when the boys needed her to be around, but didn't really want her to do anything beyond filling the fridge and driving them places. It left her feeling nostalgic for the days when they were babies and she was a part of their lives nearly every minute they were awake.

She supposed it was a universal truth that mothers, after tearing out their hair and tacking their raw beating hearts to the outsides of their clothing for anyone to see, were given no warning that someday their baby-holding days would be over. When that day came, there was no clanging bell or siren, no banner flown across the sky to pinpoint that single precious moment when you rocked your child for the last time.

Ava reminded herself that she was lucky to have such good relationships with her teenagers and that she was happy for Mark, glad he'd found a woman whose company he enjoyed. Still, she felt a familiar stab of regret. Did she try hard enough? Could they have worked things out, if she'd only hung in there?

She should have seen the affair coming. They were living amicable but parallel lives. She cared for the kids during the day and took classes at night to earn her teaching certificate. She did pottery on the weekends. Mark was working long hours at his engineering firm in Andover and occasionally traveled overnight for work.

The years went by. Then, one night, Sam had been seized with a sudden pain, a stitch in his side that rapidly became so acute that he was doubled over and feverish, howling. He wasn't quite ten years old. Mark was on a business trip; Ava called the ambulance and then dialed Mark's cell. He didn't pick up.

The ambulance came and she followed it in the car with Evan, not wanting to leave him alone in the house. At the hospital, the doctors operated for a burst appendix. Mark still hadn't called her back. In desperation, she'd phoned Padma, his secretary, whose cell number she had because Padma occasionally house-sat for them when they went to visit Mark's mother in Florida. She thought Padma might know what hotel she could call to reach Mark.

Padma, distraught by the news, had handed her cell phone to

Mark. It was two o'clock in the morning and Mark's voice was blurry with sleep.

Ava hated remembering that night for all sorts of reasons, not least the fact that Padma had arrived with Mark at the hospital with an overcoat tossed over her pretty pink nightgown, her feet in white slippers, her hair a sleek dark curtain. She was young and beautiful. Ava was tired and frightened and betrayed.

She was also—though she had never admitted this to anyone—relieved. She had married Mark because he was sweet and good to her, the sort of courtly high school boyfriend who bought the right wrist corsage for the prom, helped her study for chemistry tests, and never lost his temper, even the time she rear-ended someone while driving his new Mustang. It was the opposite of the fractious relationship her own parents had, and Ava had taken that as a sign of true love.

They married right after freshman year of college, when Ava was only nineteen, not because she felt she couldn't live without Mark, but because she couldn't face ever living at home again. Mark was her escape. Her savior. She would always be grateful to him for that.

Then, when Sam and Evan were born, her passion for motherhood far outweighed any emotional or physical bond she'd ever felt with Mark. They had what Ava privately thought of as "good sport" sex around the edges of their busy domestic life; she sometimes counted the minutes and did whatever it took to satisfy her husband so she could get back to her book or go to sleep.

She had told herself she was content back then, excited by motherhood and by her new teaching career. Marriage wasn't supposed to be a lifelong honeymoon; she was determined to find solace in new interests rather than despair in the lack of emotional connection she felt with her husband. Mark was a good man and she never wanted to hurt him.

In a way, then, his affair, as short-lived and painful as it was for both of them, had been a gift. Now there was a "real" reason for a separation, a divorce, where there hadn't been one before. Ava was able to tell Mark how she had been feeling—well, not about the sex, she never told him that—and to absolve him of the betrayal. He, in turn, understood her, as he always had.

Remembering this led her to recall that first awful Christmas alone. She'd had the boys for Thanksgiving, so Mark, per their agreement, had taken them on Christmas. They'd gone to ski in Vermont, so Ava was alone on Beach Plum Island. She and the boys would celebrate Christmas the following weekend.

She was determined to put up a tree, and she had, but while unraveling the Christmas lights she'd suddenly fallen apart: there was no end to the tangled wires. She had put the Christmas tree outside instead, and made cranberry and popcorn strings to wind around its brittle branches, an offering to the cardinals and blue jays that fluttered like patriotic scarves on the snowy beach.

Ava shook her head. She had survived, and so had the boys. They were happy. Mark was doing well. They were still a family with lots of love between them. That was more than most people had.

And now, perhaps, she was about to add to their family. She had registered with the International Soundex Reunion Registry this afternoon, as she'd promised Gigi. The process hadn't been difficult, exactly, but it had been emotionally taxing. She was having mixed feelings now about the search. Or maybe she was just tired. Either way, her energy seemed to have drained away.

"Do I really want to know the truth?" she said aloud, staring at the little one-eyed stuffed dog she'd taken from Finley's house and put next to her computer in the kitchen.

She had run the dog through the washing machine; now its fur was white and fluffy instead of dingy and matted down, but that one eye still glared at her accusingly. It was a common enough glass eye; she wondered if the fabric store at the mall would have one to match it.

"Hey," she yelled up the stairs, "do either of you guys want to go to the mall?"

"No!" the boys answered in unison, so she tucked the little dog into her purse and headed out to buy an eye.

This, at least, was one thing she could fix right now.

As it turned out, however, she was wrong, at least about the "right now" bit. Ava stared in frustration at the CLOSED sign on the fabric store. She had forgotten the mall closed at five o'clock on Sundays. She had even forgotten it was Sunday. Now what? She was hungry, but she hated eating alone in restaurants.

She sat in her car, tapping her fingers on the steering wheel and feeling lonely. She finally phoned Elaine, but Elaine's phone went to voice mail. So did Caroline's. Olivia answered, but she was out with a friend. There was nothing for her to do but turn around and go home to scrounge dinner.

Then, almost as if she'd willed it to, her cell phone rang as she was tucking it back into her purse. She hit the button without recognizing the number, her heart beating hard. What if the registry had already found Peter?

"Hello?"

"Ava?"

"Yes?" She didn't recognize the man's voice.

"It's Simon. Simon Talbot."

As if she knew a hundred Simons. As if there was any Simon

who could unnerve her more than this one. "Oh. Hi," she said, grinning foolishly out her windshield at the nearly empty mall parking lot. "What's up?" She cringed, hearing herself. What was she, twelve years old?

"I know this is last-minute, but I was wondering if you might want to come to dinner at my place. I was just about to start the grill when the guy I invited to dinner bailed on me. Now I'm stuck with too much food and nobody to share it with, and I've been meaning to do something for you as a thank-you for being so nice to Gigi."

Ah. A charity call, then. "You don't have to do that," she said.

"I know," he said patiently. "But I want to. Will you come? The view here is spectacular. So is the service. I know it's a bit of a drive, but I promise to make the meal worth your time. Please say you'll join me."

She glanced down at her outfit: her usual tank top, but at least it was a clean one, and a decent denim skirt. She'd actually had a shower this afternoon before the boys came home. She was halfway to Boston already, Ava realized. It was Sunday night, so there would be no commuter traffic.

"I can probably be there in half an hour," she said. "I'm actually in Peabody right now."

"Peabody?" Simon sounded amused. "Why?"

"I was trying to buy an eye," she said, laughing. "I'll tell you all about it when I see you. What can I bring?"

"Just you," he said, in a way that made her hand tremble as she hung up the phone.

Simon's condominium was in one of the long wharf buildings overlooking Boston Harbor. She gave the car to a doorman, feeling like an impostor, then made her way into the lobby and walked up to his condo on the second floor.

He opened the door and kissed her lightly on the cheek before leading her into the kitchen. The condo was the sort photographed by architectural magazines. The living room had a soaring ceiling, an exposed brick wall, and massive wooden beams. No cautious beige or white walls, either, but bright gold. The furniture was black leather and the tables were made out of bamboo with glass tops. Waist-high statues of giraffes and elephants stood scattered about the hardwood floor at the edges of the deep red Oriental carpet.

"I feel like I'm on safari," Ava said.

Simon made a face. "The decorator got a little carried away. She was having so much fun that I didn't have the heart to stop her. I think she felt like she had to compete with the view."

He pointed and Ava turned around. The far wall of the living room was floor-to-ceiling windows overlooking the harbor. Tonight the water lay like a sequined cape fanned beneath the dusky sky.

"Wow. I see what you mean about vertigo."

"You get used to it after a while," Simon said, "but you still can't have more than two drinks, or you want to throw yourself into the water. How hungry are you?"

"As in portion size or timing?"

"Both."

"A lot, and soon. I've had an exciting weekend."

"How so?"

"The short version is that your niece, my sister, and I went on a hunt for our brother."

Simon raised an eyebrow, his blue eyes puzzled. "I didn't know you had a brother."

"Neither did we."

In the kitchen, Simon poured them each a glass of prosecco while Ava told him everything she knew and showed him the one-eyed dog, which Simon studied with the same deliberate attention he seemed to give to everything. "What are you feeling now that you have this information? What do you hope to find out?"

Ava frowned, turning the glass between her hands for a moment before answering. "Of course part of this is motivated by Dad dying," she said, swallowing hard as the grief welled in her chest. "And by Mom's death as well. This baby was part of their lives, so naturally he's a part of ours, too."

"What if he doesn't want to be?" Simon asked gently. "A lot of adopted kids aren't that keen on finding their birth parents."

"I know." Ava took a shaky breath. "But, even if that's the case, I thought if I were in his shoes, I'd want to know that people cared enough to look for me, no matter how my life was going. I'd want to know why my mother gave me up, and yes, I'd want to know if I had other family anywhere."

Simon nodded. "Fair enough. I think I'd feel the same way."

She looked up at him gratefully. "Thanks. That helps. Anyway, we might not ever know anything."

"But at least you'll know you tried."

"Yes. That's something." She smiled. "What smells so amazing in here?"

"Garlic roast potatoes. They're in the oven. I was going to grill the steaks and corn." He frowned. "Unless you're a vegetarian? I can scramble eggs if you'd prefer."

"Only if I can have steak on the side."

Simon smiled at her. "Have I told you yet how happy I am to see you?"

"You've told me that by cooking. No need to say more."

"All right. No more words, then." He reached out and pulled Ava to him. His kiss was swift and hard.

She returned the kiss instinctively. Simon felt bigger, broader than she'd thought he would; he was such a tall, slender-looking man. He smelled familiar to her somehow, his musky scent just right. Ava could have stayed locked in that position all night, her skin humming, but she forced herself to step out of his arms.

Simon looked chastened. "Sorry. Did you not want me to kiss you?"

A complicated question, Ava thought. "I can't imagine what your sister would say."

"Katy?" Now he laughed, surprised. "Katy would be fine about it, I think. She's afraid I'm going to die alone because I never date. And she says you're the one responsible for helping Gigi get through the summer without falling apart."

Ava was pleased by this. "Katy's a lot stronger than she knows."

"Oh yes. But I suppose that's true of all of us, isn't it?" Simon asked. "We blithely go along until some tree falls across the road in front of us and we have to suddenly figure out how to use a chain saw to keep going." He began removing the steaks from their packages. "So what is it, then? Not Katy. What else?"

"Elaine," she said simply.

"Ah. I see."

"I'm not sure you do. Elaine seems bitchy and spoiled, but she's not really, not on the inside. She's really generous and loving."

"You're right. I don't see her that way, so I'll have to take your word for it. I've only seen her act horrible in every possible circumstance involving the people I love."

This remark stung, but Ava knew it was true. "She's just having trouble grieving."

"She has a funny way of showing it."

Ava felt her scalp prickle with irritation. It was one thing for her to find fault with Elaine, but quite another matter when other people did. Her first impulse, upon hearing Elaine criticized, was to leap to her sister's defense. But Simon was only being honest. Ava clamped down on her temper.

"The truth is that everything is a slog right now, as we're trying to sort through our feelings about Dad and this other sibling of ours," she said. "My emotions are so volatile, it's better if I don't get involved with you." At Simon's pained look—God, this man's face was an open book—Ava quickly added, "It isn't that I don't like you. I like you a great deal. It's just that we, you know, can't . . . "

At that, Simon tipped his head back and laughed. "Can't what?"

"You know what I mean! Get involved!" Her face was on fire now. Ava gulped some of the prosecco, hoping it would help her cool off and calm down, but the fizz went up her nose and she began to choke, her eyes watering. Simon grabbed her glass, poured her a glass of water, and gave her a damp paper towel to wipe her face.

"You'd be a good nurse," Ava said crossly, as soon as she could speak again. "How do you always know what to do?"

"Single dad," he said sympathetically. "Now what do you mean by 'get involved'?"

"Have sex," she said at once, then wished she were still choking as Simon began to laugh again.

"What?" she demanded. "Is it really so hilarious, the idea of sex with me?"

"God, no!" He scrubbed at his face with both hands. "I can't think of anything more pleasurable than making love with you." Now it was Simon's turn to be embarrassed. His face had turned crimson. "Since the day we met at the service, I've been hoping you might feel about me the way I do about you." He shook his head and finished removing the steaks from their package and putting them on a plate. "But now you're making sex sound, I don't know . . . as if sex is the first and last thing you'd expect me to want from you. Is that really what you think of me? Or is there something I'm missing here?"

"No, you're not missing anything," Ava said glumly. "I was just telling you that we weren't going to have sex because I'm not ready."

He nodded and gave her a mock-serious look with his blue eyes. "All right. You can beg me for sex tonight all you want, and I promise not to give in. Are we still on for dinner, I hope?"

"I'm starving." She grinned. "See? There is something else I want from you besides your body."

He smiled back and gestured for her to follow him out to the balcony, where he'd already started the grill. "Great. We'll be sensible and well fed. Dissatisfied, maybe, but proud of our mature ability to defer gratification."

Simon grilled the steaks and corn while Ava tended to the potatoes and salad. She felt comfortable working with him in the kitchen, just as companionable as she'd felt walking with him on the beach. They ate dinner on the small kitchen table by the windows instead of in the dining room.

Afterward they went out on the deck. Ava sat on the teak lounge chair and he took the bench beside her, both of them facing the water as they finished the bottle of wine and continued talking. A lone boat motored up the harbor, a sleek white arrow on its black surface. Simon got up at one point and brought out a pair of striped cotton blankets to drape over their shoulders, but Ava still shivered in the breeze.

"Cold?" Simon opened his blanket wide around his shoulders. "If you sit over here, you'll be warmer."

Ava shook her head, though her eyes were drawn to his broad chest and strong thighs beneath his jeans. "Thanks, but I'm okay. I was just thinking about the time my parents took us on a ferry to Prince Edward Island to see some of Mom's relatives. They were French-Canadian. Most of her family stayed there; only her parents and Finley moved to Maine."

"Did you like the ferry?"

"Loved it. I wanted the ferry to keep right on going so I could watch the world pass by while we ate meals on trays."

"Next time, we'll go out on my boat and I'll serve your meal on a tray."

"I'd like that, actually. I've never sailed in Boston Harbor."

Simon offered her brandy or coffee. When she chose coffee, he made it in the kitchen and brought it out on a tray, setting it on her lap with a little bow and making Ava laugh. He sat down with his own coffee and, when he noticed her shivering again, opened his blanket. "Now are you cold? Say yes and come sit next to me!"

She laughed. "Stop that! You look like a flasher!"

He sighed, pretending to be wounded. "All right. I'll behave."

"About time," Ava said, but really what she felt was longing. She wanted him to kiss her again, to take her on his lap and wrap her in that blanket. They could make love and sleep out here on the balcony, watch the sun come up together.

If only she didn't have two boys at home. And if only this man weren't part of the family her own sister seemed determined to hate.

Ava sighed, finished her coffee, and stood up. "I'd better be going. Thank you for dinner. It really was wonderful. And your condo is lovely."

"Having you here makes me like it more." Simon stood up, too, again startling her with his height and the width of his shoulders, and walked her to the door. He reached to open the door for her just as she was putting her hand on the doorknob; the touch of his hand on hers was enough to make her draw a sharp, audible breath.

He heard her gasp, of course, and then she felt Simon pressing against her hips, lifting her hair and kissing her neck. Ava felt the rough shadow of his beard and the warmth of his soft lips along her neck and shoulders. Then he slipped his hand gently beneath her tank top and cupped her breast, his breath quickening to match her own, until at last she turned to him and kissed him full on the mouth, knowing there was no way she could leave, not yet.

Not without this.

Simon slid her clothes off so easily, it was as if the seams had come unstitched. She helped him out of his as well. Then the two of them stood there, naked and foolishly grinning for a minute, before Simon said, "I'm too old for wood floors, what about you?"

"Bed, please," she said.

He scooped her into his arms and carried her into the bedroom, where Ava felt paralyzed, self-conscious. The light was low in here, but it seemed as if every light were blazing. Would he want her, still desire her, when he saw what she looked like without the armor of her skirt and shirt, panties and bra, all those garments that kept her tender middle-aged flesh in place?

Simon refused to turn out the light when she asked. "I need to look at you," he said urgently. "I've been dreaming about this ever since the first time I held you."

"I can't believe how scared I am," she said. "My teeth are almost chattering."

"Why?" His voice was gentler now. "What are you afraid of?"

"Everything! Of doing or saying the wrong thing. Of having you see me without my clothes. Of feeling too much for you, too soon."

"Impossible," he said. "You're perfect. This moment is perfect." He led her to the bed, where they lay facing each other.

As Simon ran his hands over her body, Ava imagined herself as clay, being warmed and shaped and smoothed beneath his caresses.

Simon's chest hair was reddish gold against his tanned chest, his breathing faster now. He cupped her hips and moved her on top of him, centering her, groaning a little as he stared up at her swaying breasts.

Suddenly Ava didn't care how she looked, maybe because of the way Simon looked at her, never taking his eyes from her face, her body, as if she was worth savoring. She was trembling with desire, nearly feverish.

Afterward, as they lay together, she fell asleep to the rhythm of his heart.

# CHAPTER EIGHT

Elaine knew she should stay home—it was Sunday night, after all, a night when all conscientious professionals did laundry or curled up with a good book and refueled for the week to come—but she just couldn't do it. Despite the generous size of the rooms, the walls being so pristine white, and the carpet feeling so soft beneath her bare feet, the condo walls seemed to be closing in on her. The neighbor's television was too loud downstairs and she could hear every thump of that kid upstairs as he lifted weights or threw around his girlfriend or whatever he was doing. And the sirens wouldn't stop.

The noise was in her head, too. Her thoughts whirled. Tony was right. Gigi, poor thing, was just a kid who'd lost her father. And Ava had always been a good sister, generous to a fault with Elaine. Why wouldn't she be a good sister to Gigi?

*Want to borrow my bike? Want to wear my jeans? Want me to braid your hair?*

Whenever their mother was drinking or zonked on painkillers for some mysterious neck pain, Ava had taken over. For years, she had been there for Elaine, and Elaine had both loved and resented her for it. Ava deserved Gigi, a sister whose love for her would be uncomplicated, not mixed as Elaine's was with envy because everything came so easily to Ava: school, boyfriends, friends, art, their father's love.

*God, I am despicable,* Elaine thought.

Although she had promised herself she wouldn't, not tonight, she opened the refrigerator and took out the chardonnay, poured herself a generous glass, and carried it into the living room to watch television. Just one glass might help her quiet that self-berating voice buzzing in her head.

She surfed the channels with the sound on mute. After a while, she went back into the kitchen and brought the bottle back to the living room with her.

Unfortunately, this reminded Elaine of her own mother doing the same thing. At four o'clock every afternoon you could count on finding Mom at the kitchen table, no dinner on the stove, the television on. Mom always sat in the chair closest to the refrigerator so she could reach her box of white wine.

"Just another little glass and I'll get dinner started," she'd say.

Mom had given up real clothes by then, but wore beautiful bathrobes. Tea gowns, she called them. Her makeup was always impeccable, emphasizing the tilt of her dark eyes and her full mouth. She'd sit there while Ava made dinner and the girls did their homework at the table, keeping her company.

After Ava was gone, it was just Elaine doing homework at the table. She never attempted to make dinner; she ate cereal or toast and a piece of fruit. Her mother was quiet, mostly, watching the news, but occasionally she'd say something that only now, in retrospect, made sense to Elaine.

Once, for instance, they'd been following a news story about a woman who claimed she had been carjacked. The woman told the police the mugger had taken off with her child in the backseat of the car and driven it into a pond. The child had drowned. The next night, it was revealed that the woman herself had driven the car into the pond to drown her child.

"She was depressed," her mother said suddenly, making Elaine look up from her English homework. "That poor woman."

"'Poor woman'?" Elaine had said. "Mom, she killed her *baby*."

Her mother had turned on her then, baring her teeth like a cornered ferret. "Sometimes killing a baby is better than the alternative!" she'd shrieked. "At least she knows where her baby *is*!"

Then her mother had fled the room. Elaine was in sixth grade then; she'd just sighed over her mother being nuts and gone back to finishing her English essay.

Dad usually ate something on his way home from the bank, knowing there would be nothing at home. He might have a glass of whiskey at the kitchen table with them; then he'd head for his study "to catch up on paperwork."

His study was his sanctuary. Elaine had avoided her father whenever possible. Hated him for never dealing with their crazy mother and making things better. Only after seeing Aunt Finley had she realized Dad must have been broken, too, because he knew damn well why Mom was sad, but he couldn't fix it.

Her face was damp. Elaine wiped her eyes. Damn it. She wasn't a crier! She was a *doer*. She refused to sit here being maudlin and wet because of things she couldn't change.

Elaine tossed back the rest of the wine and hurriedly changed into a slinky green wrap jersey dress and gold wedge sandals. She did a quick job on her hair and makeup and was out the door in less than fifteen minutes.

Unfortunately, because it was a summer Sunday, there was less action than she'd hoped in the Cambridge clubs around MIT. She checked three of her favorite spots and then drove back across the bridge to Boston, thinking at least there would be tourists in the bars on Boylston and Tremont.

Elaine found a free spot by a meter on Berkeley Street—she always had great parking karma—and walked to Boylston Street, feeling invigorated. One of the hotels near the convention center had a decent bar.

Tonight it was crowded with businessmen, some kind of sales convention. More men than women, all of them fairly young and definitely single, or acting like it, some guys even dancing together on the tiny floor under the flashing lights. Good. The rooms were probably upscale. She could get what she wanted and go home, finally fall asleep, and give her brain a rest.

Elaine ordered a glass of wine and took a seat at the bar, feigning nonchalance, chatting with the woman bartender. She always felt more comfortable when the bartender was a woman. This one looked like she'd been at it a while, a curvy blonde in her forties with white eye shadow painted beneath her brows and in the corners of her eyes. Someone at the makeup counter in Macy's probably told her white eye shadow made her look less tired. It didn't.

Several men approached her. Elaine didn't like the looks of them. She could afford to be picky here; there were so many men. She told all of them she was waiting for someone. Finally, once she'd ordered her fourth glass of wine, she began feeling relaxed, her limbs fluid. The room took on a sweet glow with all the colored lights and clinking bottles.

Maybe that eye shadow trick did work, Elaine was thinking, as a new man took the empty stool beside her and introduced himself as Kevin O'Toole. He was a redhead. She didn't usually do gingers, as a rule, but this guy had that Kennedy style, big white teeth and a long face. Freckles.

She told Kevin her first name only, sticking to her rules. Kevin paid for her next glass of wine and right away ordered her another. They talked about work, naturally—that was always the first topic, as if your work defined you—and Kevin told her he'd just finished his MBA.

"I'm on a management track with the company," he said, his blue eyes shining with the pride of a guy who still thinks the world is his to claim.

On closer inspection, Kevin was even younger than she'd first thought, probably midtwenties. God, she was really doing the cougar thing. Wait until she told Tony! But this guy was out of college and working, or at least that's what he said. Everybody lied in these places.

Kevin had a pleasant face, despite the freckles and red hair, and nice hands. Long fingers that played nervously with the cocktail straw and napkins. Elaine thought about her nephews, and about how this kid was probably only ten years older than Sam. She couldn't imagine Sam, with his delicate features and blond hair, his twin passions for guitar and lacrosse, ending up in a hotel bar chatting up a cougar. She hoped that never happened. She loved her nephews. God, she really did.

Elaine's face was damp again. Kevin was looking alarmed. "You okay?" he asked. "You look upset."

She flashed him her brightest smile. "I'm upset we're not dancing!" She tossed her head back and laughed.

"I'm not much of a dancer," he said.

"Oh, come on. Who cares? We don't know anybody here. It'll be fun!" She took his hand and led him to the dance floor.

He was right: Kevin wasn't much of a dancer. More like a dog on hind legs, eager to please and get his treat. Elaine wanted to pat his little red head and tell him he'd done a good job.

"Are you staying in this hotel?" she asked. She had to lean forward to shout.

His blue eyes widened. "Sure. I have a great room. Why?"

"I thought we might be able to talk better if we go someplace quieter. Let's just finish this song," she said, wanting to keep him eager despite the swirling lights making her feel sick, and the memory of her mother, her poor broken mother, kneeling on the bathroom floor. Where had that image come from?

Elaine banished it, literally waving her hands crazily in the air as she danced, as if she could sweep away every lousy memory. Kevin, delighted, imitated her, his big hands making figure eights over his head.

She started to laugh, watching him, and then she was sick to her stomach. "Sorry. I've changed my mind," she said, and raced out of the bar, out of the hotel, out into the smoggy summer air, clutching her handbag and willing herself not to vomit.

Elaine hiked up Boylston Street to Tremont, trying to remember where the hell she'd left the car. Her head spun and her shoes hurt; the night was warm and sticky but she shivered in the dark, aware of Boston Common across the street.

Despite the lights along the sidewalks, Boston Common wasn't a place a single woman in heels should go alone at night. It loomed like a black lake, infinitely deep, full of danger. Elaine walked with her shoulder nearly pressing against the storefronts to put as much distance between herself and the Common as possible. Where did she leave the damn car? She needed to get home and lie down.

The danger, when it came, surprised her. She was on a brightly lit corner and had just passed a squad car coasting down Tremont when a trio of teenagers in hoodies approached her. Two black boys, one white. Probably Emerson College kids, she told herself. Nothing to worry about. Everyone wears hoodies.

But the three kids surrounded her, hulking beasts, their jeans low on their hips and ragged around their ankles, and demanded her purse. "Just give it to us without screaming and nobody gets hurt," the tallest one, the white kid, said. His voice wasn't menacing but his eyes meant business, and he had his hands jammed in his pockets in a way that suggested a weapon.

Furiously, Elaine said, "You can't just take my purse!"

The boys looked at one another and burst out laughing, like this was all some big prank and there was a camera on them. Then the tall white kid said, "Um, yeah we can. And we need it right now." He reached for her bag.

"Wait!" Elaine stopped him. "At least let me have my phone. I need it to get home, and the cops will track you if you take it."

The boy scowled. "Okay. Grab the phone and go before we change our minds."

She took the phone out and handed him her bag. The boys skulked off into an alley beside her that she hadn't even noticed. Elaine turned and ran for the spot where the cop had been, but of course he was gone.

There was nobody, even, to tell about the mugging. If that's what it was. Was it a mugging, if you just gave people your purse? Maybe those boys hadn't even had a weapon. Why, oh why, hadn't she taken a class in self-defense?

The adrenaline that had kicked in a few minutes ago was rapidly fading. Elaine suddenly felt dizzy again. Unable to take another step. And now it didn't matter if she found her car, because the boys had her keys. She couldn't even take a subway or a taxi, because she had no money and no way of getting inside her condo.

Whom could she call? She stood in the glare of a streetlamp, feeling stupidly conspicuous but not wanting to venture anywhere darker, her head swimming with wine and shame. She couldn't call

Ava. She lived too far away; Ava would take ages to get here. She couldn't call anyone at work. Not even Tony, who would scold her and maybe, just maybe, start to wonder if his vice president was losing her wits.

Like her mother. She was losing her mind, just like her mother.

Elaine was crying now, her eyes and nose running. An older couple dressed for the theater, their arms around each other, actually crossed the street to avoid passing by her. She must look a fright, a crackhead in two-hundred-dollar heels. Who the hell could she call?

She had nobody, Elaine realized. Nobody who would miss her if she wasn't in her bed tonight.

Then she remembered Gabe and his offer to rescue her. Okay. That was somebody to call, someone whose opinion she didn't hold so dear. She could get over the humiliation of having him see her like this. She shuddered at the thought of what else she had *almost* done with that sweet boy, Kevin. Though maybe that would have been better for her, it wouldn't have been great for Kevin, having some drunk cougar in his bed, weeping over her wreck of a family life or throwing up on his shoes.

She had a good signal on her phone and found Gabe's number easily online. He was the only Gabriel Blaustein listed. God, he had a landline. Who had a landline anymore? His address surprised her, too. It wasn't far from here, a street in the South End. She would have pegged him as a guy with an apartment in Jamaica Plain or one of those other ex-student ghettos.

Elaine dialed the number before she could chicken out. It was midnight; Gabe would most likely be asleep. Maybe he had someone with him. That hadn't occurred to her before; the thought nearly made her hang up. Oh, so what. She could crash on his couch and figure out what to do in the morning. It wasn't like she was interested in him. She just needed a ride and a safe haven.

Gabe answered on the third ring, sounding surprisingly awake and suspicious. "Yes?"

Well, of course he would wonder who was calling. Elaine had blocking on her phone. "Hi. This is Elaine Barrett, the woman you—"

"I remember. Where are you? What can I do?" He sounded even more alert now.

How humiliating! Gabe had obviously guessed that she had called because she needed him, not for any other reason. Well, there was nothing for it. "Tremont Street. I've been mugged. They took my purse and keys."

A sharp intake of breath. "Are you all right? You're not hurt?"

"No, no. I'm fine. I just need a place to crash tonight because I can't get into my condo. Do you have a couch?"

"Better than that. A spare guest room," he said. "I'll be right there. Go to the lobby of the Emerson dorm. The glass doors are always open and they have a security guard. You'll be safe."

She wanted to ask how he knew this, but Gabe hung up before she could. Elaine took off her shoes and walked barefoot the two blocks to Emerson College, feeling horrified that she'd just made that call. She might as well have been walking around Boston in torn underwear, that's how achingly vulnerable she felt.


On Monday, Gigi went to Ava's at the usual time. Sam had gone to work, but Evan was there, looking sleepy in pajama pants and a T-shirt. She could tell he wasn't ready to talk, so she said hello and then went out to help Ava unload the kiln from the last bisque firing.

When they were finished, Ava said, "Ready to make some calls?"

Gigi drew on a sketch pad at the kitchen table, where she could overhear Ava talking to various people at the adoption agencies. It took her only three calls before Ava found the right place, but then it was a disappointment. Ava nearly banged the phone down.

"They say they can't tell me anything without my mother's consent," Ava said, her face pinched and tired looking. "The records are sealed."

"Maybe the reunion registry will contact us," Gigi said. "You filled in the papers, right? And Peter might be looking for us, too, remember."

"Maybe," Ava said, but didn't sound convinced. She opened the patio doors and stepped outside, rubbing her hands up and down her arms even though it was already hot. "I'll be back soon," she said. "I need to take a walk." She set off without turning around, and Gigi knew not to follow her.

Evan had been lurking around the refrigerator. Now he sat down across the table with a bowl of cereal. "Mom was out really late," he said. "I was up gaming and heard her come in at, like, three in the morning. Was she at your house?"

Gigi shook her head. No wonder Ava looked exhausted. "Maybe she was with Elaine."

"I guess." He tipped the bowl to drink the milk. When he set it down, he had a milk mustache. Definitely the King of Cool, Evan.

"Hey. I need to do something and I don't want to do it alone," Gigi said. "Would you come with me?"

"Of course."

Gigi smiled at the way Evan agreed without even asking her what she needed to do. It was nice to have a friend like that. A friend who was also her family.

What she needed to do was go to the stables and get her riding helmet. She'd left it there yesterday, she explained to Evan as they set off on their bikes. "Mom won't let me leave it at the stables because it's expensive."

"Sure," he said, pedaling easily beside her. "You can introduce me to your horse."

On the way to the barn, Evan told Gigi he remembered her father taking him to the barn a couple of years ago. "Grandpa got up on the saddle of this big black beast. I mean, I really thought that horse would start snorting flames out of his nose or something, he was so fierce looking."

"Bantam? Fierce?" Gigi laughed. "Bantam is my horse, actually, and he's a big baby. Spooks at his own shadow. Dad never had a horse of his own. He didn't really have time to ride much. When we went out together, he usually rode Bantam and I took my mom's horse, Dolly."

"Well, all I could think looking up at Grandpa was that he looked like a king about to lead a parade of knights on that horse," Evan said. "Like a king in *Game of Thrones*."

The riding instructor looked surprised to see Gigi but was too busy yelling at someone about the right way to change leads during the canter to say hello. Gigi led Evan over to Bantam and showed him how to hold his hand flat to give the horse a carrot nub while she scooted into the tack room, hoping to grab her helmet and get out again before seeing anyone she knew. Then it would be her lucky day.

It wasn't. Lydia was in the tack room, soaping a saddle, her blond hair pulled back in a ponytail. "Hey, quitter," she said.

Gigi wanted to say something rude but knew she'd better not. "Hey," she said, and took her helmet off the peg.

"I hear Justin and you hooked up before he left for school," Lydia said.

Gigi turned away, her face flaming hot, and willed herself to leave. "How did you hear that?"

"He put it on Facebook. I bet you didn't know that."

Gigi forced herself to shrug.

"He only did it with you because he felt sorry for you."

Gigi spun on her heel. "You don't know anything."

"I only know what's on Facebook," Lydia said sweetly.

"Then I feel sorry for you," Evan said. He was standing in the doorway, his arms folded, looking down at Lydia like she was a piece of dog crap. "You might not be old enough to use social media if you believe everything you read. Come on, Gigi. Let's get out of here. I can't stand the stink of manure in this place."

Gigi stared at him. Evan—geeky, sweet Evan—actually looked strong and even a little bit hot, standing in the doorway. She'd never realized how muscular his arms were. Then she laughed and tossed her head. "See you, Lydia. Have fun on Facebook."

She was gratified to see Lydia's mouth fall open as they left.

"Thank you," she said to Evan as they pedaled back to Beach Plum Island.

"Is it true about you and that kid hooking up?" He pulled up beside her, but kept his eyes on the road.

Gigi felt her eyes burn. "Yes. But I was sorry right after. I was sorry during, actually. He's a nice kid, but I don't like him in that way."

"So why did you do it, then?"

"I don't know. He really wanted to. I was sad after Dad died. I don't really have any friends. I guess it was just something to take my mind off things, you know?"

He glanced at her then, his dark eyes serious and kind. "I'm your friend."

"I know. But you weren't around then."

"I'm not judging you," Evan said. "I get why you'd do that."

"You do?"

"Yes. But I think that kid is shit for putting anything on Facebook."

"Maybe he didn't. Lydia could have just said that."

"Are you going to check?"

Gigi considered this a minute, then said, "No. I don't really want to know. If I don't pay any attention, it'll go away. Either that, or people will think I'm a slut, and that will just make me more popular, right?"

"I have no idea how these things work," Evan said. "High school is a mystery to me."

"Yeah. To me, too." Gigi sighed. "At least your school is really huge, though. It must be easy to disappear, or to find kids you like. At my school, everyone knows what everybody else is doing."

"That could definitely suck," he said sympathetically. "You know, you could go to my high school. You could transfer, if you don't like yours."

The thought was appealing. What if she did that? What if she just started over, and everybody she met knew nothing about her? "I like that idea," Gigi said.

"The classes are big," he warned her. "And it's pretty chaotic in the halls. But Sam and I have some cool friends, like those kids who come hear the band. And they have honors classes and a great art department. Plus, Sam and me, we'd have your back."

"You know, if you don't become a musician, you should go into marketing like Elaine," Gigi said. "You can make anything sound good."

They both laughed, then rode in silence the rest of the way to Ava's house. It wasn't until they were putting their bikes away that Gigi dared to ask. "Have you ever done it?"

Evan shook his head. "Kissing, that's about it. I've never even had a serious girlfriend. I liked this one girl last year, but so did Sam. You can probably guess how that turned out."

"Her loss. You're cute and smart. And so out-there talented."

He grinned at her. "And nerdy. So fucking nerdy. I need a girl who's into music, Magic cards, and gaming."

"And drawing ogres that look like trees. Don't forget that," Gigi said.

"Oh, no, that goes without saying," he said. Then they both cracked up and went inside.

Elaine called Ava at ten o'clock to ask if she had a key to her condo. Her voice was so hoarse and muffled, Ava didn't recognize it at first.

"Why are you whispering?" Ava asked. "I'm out on the beach and I can hardly hear you."

"I don't want to disturb anybody here. Do you have a key to my place?"

"Yes. Why? Did you lose yours?" Ava stopped in a sheltered place between the dunes and squinted into the sunlight, trying to understand what Elaine was saying about last night.

Her sister's story was so convoluted—a nightclub, a mugging in Boston, a midnight call for help, *Jesus*—that Ava told Elaine to wait and tell her about it in person. "God," she muttered, "I can't believe you think I have nothing better to do than bail you out. I'll be there as soon as I can get home, shower, and drive down. It could take a couple of hours. Can't you just go to work?"

There was a faint laugh. "No way," Elaine said. "I don't have any clothes except what I wore last night. I slept at a friend's. Can you pick me up here? And bring me some clothes, too?"

"Where are you? At Tony's?"

"No. Another friend's." Elaine gave her an address Ava didn't recognize. "It's in the South End. I'll text it to you. You'll come, right? As soon as possible?"

"I'll be there as soon as I can." Ava hung up, feeling irritable.

There went half her day. As much as she hated thinking about Elaine alone and vulnerable at night in Boston, she couldn't help but wish her sister had better sense. She was probably drunk, too, if she'd been at a club.

As she walked back to the house, Ava had a sudden memory of how, in fifth or sixth grade, Elaine had fallen while riding her bike home from school. She'd popped a tire and skidded into a metal guardrail; the fall had caused an inch-long rock shard to become embedded in her knee. Over the next few days, Elaine's knee had swollen to the size of a baseball and the skin had gone red, then purple, before Elaine was in enough pain to mention it to Ava.

Ava had taken one look at the knee and, rather than wake their mother, who was hopeless at this sort of thing, called their father at the bank. He met them at the ER. It took a massive course of antibiotics to treat the blood poisoning; the doctor said it was a wonder Elaine didn't lose her leg.

"Why didn't you tell me right when it happened?" Ava asked her once they were home from the hospital.

"I thought it would just go away," Elaine had said. "Plus I didn't want to bother you. You're always busy with Mark."

At least her sister was safe for the moment. Ava racewalked back to the house and arrived to find Gigi and Evan sitting on the patio, drawing. "I have to go to Boston," she said.

The kids lifted their heads. "What for?" Evan asked.

"Elaine needs me to do something." No point in saying more, when Ava hardly knew anything herself.

"What about the kiln?" Gigi asked.

Shoot. She'd forgotten that she'd started it earlier this morning. Thank God Gigi remembered. "Can you check the cones and make sure it doesn't get too hot? And see that it shuts off at the right time?"

"Sure," Gigi said. "I was planning to hang out here and practice with the band anyway."

"Great. Thanks. There's pizza in the freezer if anybody gets hungry. Evan, unload the dishwasher, okay?"

"Yep."

They bent their heads down to their sketch pads again, sharing an iPod, bare feet tapping. Gigi's hair was growing out fast; the roots were nearly the same color as Evan's.

Ava headed upstairs for a quick shower. She was stopped by another phone call on the landing. This time it was Simon. Ava took the phone into the bedroom and shut the door.

"What are you doing?" he asked.

"I'm about to take a shower."

He groaned. "Don't torture me like that."

She laughed, her skin tingling. "You're so easy."

"Because you're so lovely."

There was a brief silence. Ava wondered if Simon was remembering the night before, as she was. She had replayed their lovemaking over and over again, knowing it wouldn't, couldn't happen again. "It was torture to leave you last night," she said.

"Not as bad as having you leave," he said. "Can you come to Boston for lunch?"

Ava glanced at the clock. "I can, actually. I'm headed there right now."

"What?" He gave a delighted laugh. "Why? To see me?"

She sighed. "To bail out Elaine, actually. Well, not literally, not out of jail, but she's gotten herself into some kind of mess. She was mugged and they took her keys and wallet."

"Oh, no." Simon sounded genuinely sympathetic. "How horrible for her."

"Yes, well, we won't get into the question of why Elaine was wandering the streets of Boston by herself at night, probably in high heels and most likely drunk."

"It must be hard for her to be alone," Simon said, unexpectedly. "Especially now, with you so taken up with Gigi and finding your brother."

Now Ava felt irritated with Simon, too. Was he actually criticizing her for not spending more time with Elaine? Why did everyone always expect her to be so understanding? When would it be her turn to fall apart and stop having to act so damn adult all the time?

It was an effort to keep her voice level, but she somehow managed. "Where should I meet you?"

Simon gave her the address where his boat was docked. "We're going for a ferry ride," he said, making her smile again.

Elaine had called Ava when she heard Gabe turn on the shower, hoping he'd be at work by the time Ava arrived. Now she flopped back onto the puffy pillows of the guest room bed and closed her eyes. Her mouth tasted like bile. Bile mixed with whatever shame tasted like.

Gabe had surprised her by showing up in a taxi last night instead of a car. She slid into the backseat and said, "Sorry. I could have gotten a cab to your place. I didn't realize you don't own a car."

"Who says I don't have a car?" Gabe gave the driver his address, then turned to Elaine. "I'm just lazy about getting it out of the garage."

"Oh," she said, and then felt so dizzy that she had to press her head to the window, hoping the cold glass would at least help keep her vision in focus. "Thanks for coming."

"You're welcome. I'm glad you kept my card."

She didn't tell Gabe that she had tossed his card into the recycling bin without a moment's hesitation.

It was only a ten-minute drive to his apartment, but the stops and starts of the cab made Elaine want to hang her head out the window like a dog. Ridiculous. She'd only had, what? Three glasses of wine at her place, and three or four at the bar. She shouldn't feel this wretched! She had definitely been drunker than this before.

*Yeah, and then you passed out,* she reminded herself.

Gabe, thankfully, didn't live in a fifth-floor walk-up apartment, the sort of building she'd imagined he might occupy, with his do-gooder sandals and unkempt hair, but in a tidy brownstone in the South End. She couldn't see much in the dark other than the red door and handsome black lanterns on either side of it. Maybe the brownstone belonged to his parents, or he was subletting from a professor. Yes, that was probably it. You could get furnished sublets for a song in Boston over the summer.

Elaine had followed him, meek and shivering, into a darkened living room and down a hallway to a blissfully silent bedroom. The white sheets and gray coverlet were turned down, as if she'd arrived at a boutique hotel. There was even a dark green cotton bathrobe tossed across the end of the bed.

"I imagine you're tired. We'll talk in the morning," Gabe said before closing the door. "Bathroom's across the hall, and don't worry, you won't run into me. The master bedroom has its own en suite."

Now bright sun was trying to creep in around the drawn window shades as Elaine lay in bed wearing the bathrobe. She had abandoned her dress, heels, and obnoxious Spanx and underwire bra on the blue armchair in the corner. With her eyes still half-shut, she admired the color of the walls in Gabe's guest room—somewhere between gray and lavender—and thought about how she'd been a little disappointed that he had left her alone in this bedroom without even trying to talk to her. What if she'd had alcohol poisoning?

*Don't be an idiot,* she told herself. *He could see you were well enough to walk up his front stairs. Nobody with alcohol poisoning does that. Plus, you woke him at midnight. He was a prince to come rescue you. Admit it.*

Elaine squinted at the time on her phone, which was rapidly running out of battery since she hadn't been able to charge it last night. It was after ten o'clock on a Monday morning. What the hell kind of man took a shower in the middle of a Monday morning? She hoped he didn't have the day off.

In her best version of what happened next, Gabe would leave her a pot of coffee and a note on the kitchen counter, telling her to let herself out of the house and lock up, and asking her to give him a call sometime for lunch. In her worst version of the future, Gabe had the day off and was in the shower feeling optimistic that she might invite him into this admittedly luxurious bed with the five-hundred-count Egyptian cotton sheets.

She couldn't let that happen. Elaine decided the best defense would be her own shower. She could stay in the bathroom a long time, long enough for Ava to arrive with her key and some clothes. Elaine would then have to apologize to Gabe about leaving in such a hurry, but she couldn't keep her sister waiting around, could she? They'd have lunch later in the week. She'd promise him that.

Yes, that sounded like a plan. Elaine hopped out of bed, then realized it was a mistake to let her feet hit the floor so hard. It was as if a spike had been hammered straight up her spine and there were knives in her brain. Holy crap.

She hobbled over to the bathroom across the hall after first peering out the door to make sure the coast was clear. Gabe had laid out towels for her in the bathroom—thick white Turkish tow-els, freshly laundered—and the shower was well equipped with soap and shampoo. There was even a blow-dryer in the drawer of the vanity beneath the mirror.

Elaine stood in the shower until her fingers started to prune up, wondering who usually used this guest bath. Gabe's mother? The wealthy parents of whatever lucky professor or medical student owned the place?

She'd brought her phone into the bathroom with her; she made sure half an hour had gone by before she finished blow-drying her hair and wrapped herself back up in the robe. Surely Gabe was gone now. Or, if he wasn't, Ava would be here soon.

She sneaked out of the bathroom and saw Gabe coming toward her, grinning, his curls bobbing along so happily that she felt nause-ated all over again just watching them. It was like the man had springs for hair. And P.S.? The seventies were dead. Today he had on a T-shirt that was even worse than Habitat for Humanity: a white shirt with "www.savetibet.org" on it in small lettering.

"Oh, good, you're up," he said. "I was afraid I might miss you."

"My sister's coming in a few minutes." *Please, Ava, get here soon.*

"Great. I'm looking forward to meeting her." Gabe smiled down at her—she'd forgotten he was so tall, over six feet—his brown eyes doing that thing she loved at the corners. It was almost possible to overlook the funky black glasses when he smiled at her like that. But not the Save Tibet T-shirt. Oh no.

"I don't want to hold you up," Elaine said. "You should just go ahead and do whatever it is you usually do on Mondays."

He burst out laughing. "You don't have any idea what I do, right?"

"Um, I might have forgotten."

"So how did you get my phone number? You obviously didn't

have my card, since my title is on there." He was still smiling down at her. He wasn't trying to trick her, Elaine realized. He genuinely wanted to know.

"Internet," she mumbled. "I used my phone. You're the only Gabriel Blaustein in the Boston white pages." She lifted her head. "I can't believe you still have a landline."

"Lucky for you, right? Come on. I'll make some coffee."

She didn't want to sit with him over some pseudo-postcoital coffee, especially when Gabe would probably interrogate her about last night. But what choice did she have? And Elaine did want coffee. Oh, how she wanted coffee.

The kitchen was painted a soft spring green and copper pots hung from hooks on a Peg-Board. There was a huge spider plant in one window—she hadn't seen one of those since college—and an enormous ginger cat curled on one of the wooden kitchen chairs. Again, Elaine thought about how much Gabe and Ava would like each other. Gabe's kitchen felt like her sister's: a place where you could imagine spending entire lazy Sunday afternoons.

But not Mondays. This was all wrong, being here. Elaine had called work and left a voice mail for Tony, saying she was out sick today, but he would know. Tony always knew when she was on a bender. Tony used to go on benders, too. Then he'd given it up, said he didn't want to be an old man with a double chin and a map of red veins across his nose.

There was a phone app now that showed what your face would look like if you kept drinking; some of the younger account managers in the office had used it last week and were shrieking with laughter. Elaine hadn't dared try it.

Jesus, how had she reached this low point in her life?

Gabe went to the stove and Elaine sat down at the kitchen table, unable to stand any longer. The cat immediately left his chair and jumped onto her lap, making himself entirely too comfortable. She didn't dare dump him off. Everybody she knew with a cat acted like it was a child. A royal child at that. She noted a ceramic bowl on the floor with "Psycho Kitty" written across it. Not a good sign.

Gabe handed her coffee in what seemed like no time at all—really, those Starbucks kids needed to take some tips from this guy; it was like an entire pierced Prozac Nation working behind those counters—and then, damn it, he was scrambling eggs and making toast, zipping around on the other side of the counter like he expected her to eat something after the hellish night she'd had.

Admittedly, the food smelled good. Then Gabe was sitting across from her at the table and looking at her with those warm brown eyes again, telegraphing his need to see her eat. What choice was there but to pick up her fork?

"Tommy certainly is glad you're here."

"Tommy?"

Gabe gestured at the cat. "He doesn't usually trust visitors enough to sit on them right away."

"His voice has a hitch in it. He sounds like his purr is broken."

"Yeah, I don't know what that's about. Tommy was a rescue from the MSPCA. He eats funny, too, kind of tipping his head sideways." Gabe demonstrated with his own plate of eggs, something she really didn't need to see.

"Thank you again for looking after me," she said. "This is more than I deserve, after waking you in the middle of the night."

"You didn't wake me."

"No? What were you doing up at midnight on a Sunday?"

"Working."

"Oh. Is that why you have the day off today?"

"What do you mean?"

Elaine eyed his T-shirt. "Not exactly a business suit."

Gabe laughed. "No, thank God. I don't think I could survive a day in a suit and tie."

"Many men do."

"Ah. But I'm not many men."

No, Gabe was not like many men, Elaine thought, finishing her piece of toast and wishing she didn't want another. She'd never known a man like this one, so comfortable in his own skin that she felt like she could say or do almost anything she wanted around him.

Maybe she and this cat with the broken purr had more in common than she'd realized. She stroked his fur. The stroking calmed her, made her feel sleepy. And her headache seemed to have receded to a place where she knew it was still there, and could come roaring back out at any time it chose, but for the moment she'd beaten it.

The coffee was perfect. So was the food. Maybe the cat, too. She scratched Tommy under his chin and he flipped over on her lap, nearly sliding off it in the process and making her laugh.

Oops. There was the headache again. She pressed her fingers to her temple. "Do you have any ibuprofen?"

"Of course. Just a sec." Gabe got up and went to the kitchen cupboard over the sink, rummaged around, and returned with a bottle and a glass of water.

"Thank you." She skipped the water and swallowed the pills dry. Where the hell was her sister? Surely Ava should be here by now.

"Want to tell me about last night?" Gabe asked.

He sensed her restlessness. She'd have to be on guard around this man. Her emotions were as plain to Gabe as if she'd written them out on the tablecloth between them in black Sharpie.

"Not really."

He held up a hand. "Don't feel like you owe me an explanation."

"I don't," she said. "So don't feel like you can use any tricky reverse psychology."

"Fine with me. We'll just be honest with each other. I'll ask you what the hell happened last night, and you'll tell me."

She snorted. "All right. I started drinking at my house and decided it was a good idea to look for an easy hookup. I kept drinking at this bar I know in a hotel and met some guy. We danced, we almost went to his room, and I changed my mind. Then, for being such a good girl, I got mugged."

Gabe cocked his head at her. "Interesting that you equate being a good girl with not sleeping with somebody."

"My sister thinks it's a terrible habit."

"The sister I'm going to meet this morning?"

"I only have one sister." Elaine winced, feeling a sharp pain in her temple. Maybe she was going to be like Pinocchio now, feeling her face bulge every time she told a lie. "Actually, I also have a half sister. But she's much younger and we didn't grow up together."

"And that's a problem for you."

"I never said that!"

"No. But it's in your voice."

Elaine tried to stare him down, but the pain in her head and the truth in his eyes were both too much. She lowered her glance. "All right. Yes, it's a problem. I don't like her much. But I don't have to see her much, either, thank God." She raised her chin at him. "What the hell are you, a shrinky dink? I thought by now you'd be trying to sleep with me."

She'd said that last bit to shock him. She'd succeeded, judging by the way Gabe's face reddened and he shifted in his chair. "Guilty as charged. I do want to sleep with you. But I won't."

"Why not?"

"I don't think you really want me to answer that question," he said.

The doorbell rang, making them both jump. Gabe didn't look at her as he left the kitchen to answer it. Elaine stroked the cat without being able to stand up, trying to process what had just happened.

Ava entered the kitchen ahead of Gabe, her face set in a deep frown. "Sorry it took me so long to get down here," she said breathlessly, her eyes taking in Gabe's bathrobe on Elaine's shoulders, Elaine's face, her bare feet, assessing for scrapes and bruises. The irritation so evident earlier on the phone had disappeared, replaced by her usual concern. "What happened?"

And of course Ava would apologize, despite the fact that it was Elaine who had disrupted her schedule, her day, her life. *The good sister is here,* Elaine thought, *my savior,* but that thought, instead of comforting her, only made her furious. She stood up so fast the cat had to scramble to land on its feet. Poor Tommy, betrayed by yet another human.

"I'll tell you in the car." Elaine reached to take the bag of clothes from Ava.

"I bet you'd like a cup of coffee after that long drive," Gabe said. "Can you stay a minute?"

As Ava turned to answer him, Elaine was struck by two things: by how pretty her sister was, with her windblown blond hair and clear green eyes, and by how right she'd been about Ava and Gabe being perfect for each other. A pair of do-gooder optimists in sandals.

"I'll just go change," she said, knowing they'd be fine without her.

## CHAPTER NINE

Ava had just come in from the studio when her cell phone rang, startling her. It was midmorning and she was clammy with clay, sweaty, and hungry. At the sight of an unfamiliar number, she started to silence the noise without answering. She wouldn't be in a fit mood to speak with anyone until she'd had another cup of coffee and a snack.

Then she remembered the adoption registry. Heart racing, she pressed the talk button. "Hello. This is Ava Barrett."

The caller didn't introduce herself, only said she was with the International Soundex Reunion Registry. Then, "I'm sorry, Mrs. Barrett, but we haven't been able to find a match to your request," she said.

The woman had the sort of unhurried, melodious voice you seldom heard anymore. Midwestern, probably. Ava dropped onto one of the kitchen chairs with the knees of her muddy overalls drawn close to her chin, her chest constricted with disappointment. "Are you sure?"

"Oh yes. Our organization leaves no stones unturned, even tiny pebbles."

"I see. Well. Thank you."

"Don't be discouraged," the woman said in her silky tone. "There are other avenues."

Ava wiped a damp hand across her face, leaving her skin gritty with bits of clay. "Like what? I'm looking for my older brother. I don't have my mother's written consent and she's been dead for ten years. I'm only the adoptee's sister." She stumbled a little over the strange words: "adoptee's sister."

There was a brief silence on the other end of the phone, as if the woman was holding her breath. Then she said, "Let me call you back."

Ava hung up and stared at the phone, bewildered. It rang a few seconds later, a different number on the screen now. "Hello?"

"Sorry. I couldn't talk from the volunteer line in the office," the woman said. "They don't like us giving out additional information. But I had to do a search for my own son, so I know what it's like. It's a scary process and can get very involved."

"Yes," Ava said, her eyes brimming. "I'm really not sure what to do next."

"Well, that depends."

"On what?"

"On how determined you are," the woman said. "People say adoption records are hermetically sealed, but that's bureaucratic BS. You can always find somebody who'll let you have a peek. But first you need to gather as much information as you can. The most useful thing is the baby's birth date. Do you have that?"

"No," Ava admitted. "I spoke to another relative, but she could only guess at the year. She thinks he was born in 1971."

"Well, dearie, you won't get far without a better date than that. Over 1.5 million babies were relinquished between 1945 and 1973, so you're fishing in a big pond. I'd start with the town where your mother was living when she had the baby. The town clerk may have a copy of the long-form birth certificate on file."

"But wouldn't he have a new birth certificate on file, listing his adoptive parents on it?" Ava had discovered this bit of information while calling every adoption agency in Maine, searching for the one that had handled Peter's records.

"Yes, of course."

"So how would I know what name to ask for, since I don't have any way of finding out who adopted him?"

"Was the father's name listed on the original birth certificate?"

"No." Ava felt herself wincing on her father's behalf. "Only my mother's."

"Then I suggest going to the town clerk and asking for the birth certificate that way. You'll have to pray for a bit of luck, of course," the woman added, "but, in my experience, most small towns don't typically have enough staff to thoroughly clean out their files. The old birth certificate may still be on file even if a clerk filed a new one with the adoptive parents' names on it. If you can get the original, it'll at least tell you exactly what day your brother was born and where. You'll even find the name of the doctor who delivered him on that certificate. Then you can try to find him to ask if he had anything to do with the placement."

Ava doubted this, since Peter had gone to Aunt Finley first; on the other hand, the doctor may have had a hand in helping unwed mothers put their children up for adoption and could have acted as a family resource. The doctor might also remember whether Peter had any other disabilities beyond being born blind.

"But how will finding the birth date help if I still don't know my brother's new last name?" she asked.

"Even with just a birth date, a place of birth, and a first name, you can find a lot on Google," the woman said. "Do a death records search. Try high school yearbooks, too. Don't rely only on the birth date, though; even if your brother did enter his information into our registry, if his parents gave him an incorrect birth date, it wouldn't match up with what you gave us."

Ava bit her lip, thinking hard. This was all so confusing. "Why would his parents record the wrong birthday?"

"Oh, who knows why people do what they do?" The woman said this as dismissively as if she were talking about toddler misbehavior in a sandbox. "Maybe they wanted him to remember the day they adopted him as his special day. Maybe they wanted to ensure he'd never find his birth family. Or they could have done it just because." The woman sputtered to a stop.

"Just because what?" Ava asked, mystified.

"Many parents keep adoptions secret for social reasons. More so back then, of course, but even now, some people are ashamed not to be able to produce their own biological children. Or they're afraid the adopted child will feel bad about himself if he finds out his 'real' family gave him up. This doesn't make them bad people," the woman added hastily. "Just misguided."

"So Peter might not even know he's adopted?" This possibility made Ava feel better. Maybe her brother hadn't tried to find them, but perhaps he wasn't deliberately trying to avoid being found, either.

"That's right." Ava could hear the smile in the woman's voice. "Now let's see what else we have to work with here. On your form you said your brother has disabilities. What sort?"

"He was blind. My aunt thought maybe there were other things wrong with him, too, but I don't know what."

"All right, then. Now we're getting someplace." The woman's voice was brisk now. "How many blind babies are born in a year? Can't be many. That narrows your search right there. And your brother's adoptive family probably put him in school or a training program. That could have been stipulated as part of the surrender process with social services, for a family to provide that sort of thing."

"I suppose you're right." Ava cradled the phone against her shoulder and went to her laptop, still open on the kitchen counter, where she'd been scrolling through news headlines at breakfast. After hastily wiping her hands on her overalls, she started a Google search. "The American Printing House for the Blind estimates just under sixty thousand visually impaired children in the U.S., with schools for the blind enrolling about five thousand students," she read aloud to the caller. Her knees were trembling; she had to sit down on one of the kitchen chairs. There couldn't be many schools for the blind. This was an avenue she hadn't yet considered.

The woman's excitement matched hers. "Easy as A-B-C! If you find your brother's actual birth date, you'll have a good chance of tracking him down through one of those institutions."

"But would the schools give me any information? Wouldn't that be illegal?" Ava's hand had started to ache; she forced herself to relax her fingers. She'd been clutching the phone like a lifeline.

"There's always somebody who'll leave a file on a counter and walk away, pretending to be busy." The woman chuckled, but it was laughter without mirth. "Remember: more of us have given up babies than you'd think. Be patient and don't give up. Okay. Gotta go. My break's over." She hung up before Ava could thank her.

Ava sat for a few minutes, trying to slow down her frantic breathing as she imagined herself getting into the car one more time and driving north to Maine.

The flicker of memory had come to Gigi in the middle of the night: her father had a cousin.

Cousin Mildred was the only relative on Dad's side that she knew of. His parents and brother were already dead by the time Gigi was born; truthfully, she'd never given Dad's extended family any thought before he died.

Gigi sat up in bed, thinking how odd it was that, her whole life, she'd been the center of her own universe. Learning about Peter was forcing her to see Dad as a person apart from her for the first time, as a man who'd been a teenager, fallen in love, and made mistakes like anyone else.

Mom, too. Her mother had always seemed so perfect, blond and pretty and well dressed, plenty of money. But now Gigi could see Mom's glaring mistake, the one she'd made by getting involved with Dad, a married man with a damaged wife and two daughters. Mom had pulled the ultimate skanky move. Yet Gigi knew she was a good person, too.

The adults in her life were diminishing before her eyes. No, that was wrong. They weren't disappearing. It was more like these tall, sheltering adults around her suddenly appeared to have cracks in them, as if they, too, could shatter into a million pieces, their hearts and bodies and minds gone, just like that.

Terrified by her own tunneling thoughts, Gigi forced herself to think about Dad's cousin, Mildred. She lived in Portsmouth, New Hampshire, a small city half an hour north of Newburyport. Gigi had gone on a school field trip there in sixth grade, to some kind of boring living history museum. They'd toured a bunch of old houses and watched people dressed up in Colonial clothes do things like make candles and cook in blackened pots hanging over open fires.

Portsmouth would be easy to get to from Newburyport by bus. She could go on her own, ride her bike to the bus station, if Ava wouldn't take her. All she needed was Mildred's address.

Gigi snapped on her yellow table lamp, the one with the cutout stars in the shade she'd had all her life, and sat up against the pillow. Mildred was older than Dad, so she must know about the baby. What if she was the one who adopted him after Finley gave him up?

She climbed out of bed. It was still dark outside, not even four o'clock in the morning. But she couldn't wait. Gigi had to find that last birthday card. Mildred sent them every year, inappropriately flowery cards on lavender or yellow paper, always with the name of some charity stamped on the back.

Gigi had no actual memory of Mildred, other than a squinty vision of a white-haired woman as tall and rawboned as Dad. She hadn't visited since the summer Gigi turned ten. Gigi remembered because that year she had found a crisp ten-dollar bill in her birthday card—Mildred always sent a dollar amount corresponding to Gigi's age—and that summer they'd taken a vacation to California while Mildred stayed at the house and watered Mom's garden.

She slid open her closet door and started pulling out the big plastic boxes stored on the shelves along the back wall, shelves that had probably been meant for shoes or sweaters. Since Gigi always wore the same T-shirts and jeans, her mother kept all of Gigi's school papers, artwork, and birthday cards in here, sorted into these plastic containers by year.

She found last year's box and pried open the plastic lid with such force that she tore a fingernail. She ignored the burning sensation and began flipping through the papers, laying out the cards, still in their envelopes, in a neat grid until she spotted Mildred's purple envelope with the tight blue letters. Her address in Portsmouth was printed in the corner.

Now she just had to wait until morning.

Gigi couldn't go back to sleep. She drew in her sketch pad and read a graphic novel about zombies without absorbing the words.

Finally, at seven o'clock, she dressed and went downstairs, the envelope folded in half and tucked into the back pocket of her cutoffs. Mom was already in the kitchen, her hair pulled into a ponytail, and wearing her gardening clothes, those black Lycra shorts that showed off what Dad called her *Dancing with the Stars* legs.

From the back, standing at the stove and jouncing her toned butt to some Kiss 108 FM song, Mom looked like a teenager. Gigi hoped like hell her mother wasn't really listening to it; the lyrics were so sexed up.

"Hey. How did you sleep, honey?" Mom asked when she noticed Gigi in the doorway. Without waiting for an answer, she wrinkled her nose and said, "You know, it wouldn't hurt to wash those shorts. Look at the stains!"

"No point. I'm just going to the studio." There, Gigi thought: she'd managed to lie without flinching. She felt bad about that, but Mom would flip if she knew Gigi's actual plan. "What smells like heaven in here?" A quick diversionary move.

Mom laughed. This was such an unusual sound that it stopped both of them for a second. Mom's eyes were a faded denim blue in the bright light, wide and surprised. "Pancakes and bacon," she said. "I thought you might want to eat before you leave for a change."

Gigi didn't have the heart to admit that Ava left breakfast on the counter for her the same way she did for Evan and Sam: a stack of bowls, a row of glasses, a plate of muffins and boxes of cereal. Or, sometimes, a plate of pancakes or waffles for them to microwave.

She sat down at the counter. "Thanks. That's really nice of you, Mom."

Her mother folded her arms, the spatula still in one hand. "What is it? What aren't you telling me?"

Panicked, Gigi deliberately rolled her eyes. "I mean it! It's really cool that you're cooking me breakfast."

"For a change, you mean."

"I didn't say that! *God!* Don't be so freakin' annoying!" Gigi bounced up from the stool and went to the fridge, holding the door wide open to hide her expression as she took out the juice. "Will you eat with me?"

Her mother hesitated, probably still trying to figure things out, but Gigi was damned if she'd tell her some other mother had been cooking for her all summer. Especially when that other mother was Dad's daughter. It hadn't been an issue before, when Mom was taking those pills and sleeping all the time, but who knew? It might matter now.

She needed to distract her mother before she asked any more nosy questions or offered to drive her to Ava's. "Come on, Mom. I poured you some juice. Let's sit outside. Your flowers look really sick."

They did, too, a mega-riot of blooms in neon colors and supernatural sizes nodding their heavy heads over the stone walls. The grass was so green it looked enameled, and hummingbirds darted around the feeder of sugar water Mom always dyed pink. It was like being in a Disney cartoon; any minute now, the birds would start talking or the yard would fill with dancing bunnies.

Her mother, Gigi noticed, ate only a single pancake. Gigi wolfed down four to make up for it. Mom even poured her half a cup of coffee, though it was so diluted with milk, it was practically like drinking that sour-smelling shitty blue milk in little cartons they served at school. Nothing like the double-shot espressos Gigi bought for herself at Starbucks whenever she was with Gramma Dawn, who pretty much never said no to anything.

They talked about the pottery studio. Then Mom told her about sailing around Boston Harbor last week in Uncle Simon's boat, and said he wanted to take Gigi out on the boat, too, and maybe even invite Ava, Evan, and Sam.

"Would that be too weird for you?" Mom asked.

Gigi put her fork down. "I think it might be weirder for you," she said carefully.

Mom shrugged. "It would be fine. I like Ava."

"What about Elaine?"

"She doesn't bother me. Anyway, I doubt she'd come." Mom turned her head away, fiddled with the elastic of her ponytail. "Elaine has her reasons to dislike us, you know." Mom always said vague things like that, as if Gigi didn't know that Mom was a home wrecker.

"Mom, she can't hold that past stuff against us forever," Gigi said. "She needs to stop being such a total bitch."

"Honey, please don't swear."

"Seriously, Mom? I was being *nice*. Think how horrible Elaine was at Dad's service. She treats Ava and me like crap, too."

"And please don't use *that* word, either," Mom said. "Honestly, being in a band with those boys isn't doing your manners any good at all."

"Maybe not. But it's doing *me* good."

Startled, Mom gave Gigi a long look. "I'm glad," she said. "I know how much your music means to you."

*And being in a family with Ava, Evan, and Sam,* Gigi nearly said, but didn't. No need to rub that in. "You should come hear us play."

"I might sometime." Her mother smiled.

That smile gave Gigi the courage she needed to get going, knowing today was going to be a decent day for Mom. She cleared the table, trying not to rush or do anything to arouse her mother's suspicions. "We should have breakfast more often," she said. "I'll try to save you more pancakes next time. Unless, of course, you make the mistake of putting chocolate chips in them. Then I can't hold myself accountable for the consequences."

This made Mom giggle, and after that, Gigi went into the house, where she hastily loaded the dishwasher before grabbing her backpack. She stuck her head back out the patio door just before leaving, relieved to find her mother pulling on gardening gloves and frowning at some insane-looking bush with flowers like yellow bells. Mom could be out here for hours.

"See you tonight, usual time," Gigi called, then quickly let the door slam behind her and wheeled her bike out of the garage.

When she'd made it a safe distance from the house, she stopped to call Ava on her cell phone. "Pick up, pick up," she muttered, but Ava's voice mail kicked in. Shit. She'd hoped to do this with Ava.

On the other hand, she didn't want to wait. Plus it would be cool to do something on her own, proving to Elaine that Gigi was just as much a part of Dad's family as they were. She dropped her cell into her backpack and started biking to the bus station.

Elaine hadn't been able to avoid confessing the whole tiresome debacle of her nightclub outing and mugging to Tony. They were sitting on a shady bench in the courtyard of the building next to their own, avoiding everyone else from their office while they shared a take-out salad gritty with unwashed lettuce.

After hearing about her teen muggers, Tony made her swear on the spot to stay sober "like for the next two hundred years," he pleaded. "I'm worried about you. Promise you won't turn into your mother."

Elaine glanced around to make sure they were alone before she slapped him. Not across the face or anything, just a single stinging whack of her hand on the top of his knee. "That was a rotten thing to say! Take that back!"

"Ow! Why? You know I'm right." Tony rubbed his knee.

"Oh my God." Elaine allowed herself to sag on the bench. "Of course I know. I'm not in a coma."

"Then act like you're awake! I mean, it's not like you have to start going to AA meetings in one of those dreadful moldy church basements. But think about a little detox program in the country, maybe. Or, I don't know, at least start mixing water with your booze."

"Okay. I'll do something. I don't know what. But something."

Tony patted her hand. "That's my girl. Meanwhile, how are you going to thank that nice guy who rescued you?"

Elaine snorted. "I rescued myself, remember? I'm the one who got those little thugs to give back my phone. Anyway, why do you care whether I call Gabe or not?"

Tony's face grew serious. "You owe that guy. Not a blow job or anything, but at least lunch. And truthfully I'd say dinner. Ask yourself this: who *didn't* take advantage of you when you were swimming in vodka?"

"For the record, my nice Irish dance puppy didn't. And it was wine, not vodka," Elaine reminded him.

"Fine, whatever. But if *you* won't thank him, honey, give me his number and I'll do it. I owe that guy at least a Trader Joe's certificate for keeping my best friend alive."

"Oh, please! I wouldn't have *died*. You keep forgetting that the muggers had already taken what they wanted by the time Gabe rode in on his white charger. Or, to be more accurate, in his battered yellow taxi."

Tony's dark eyes darkened even more. "You've had too many close calls lately. Remember the conference last year in San Francisco?"

"I remember." Elaine had tried hard to forget that blurry episode entirely, but couldn't completely erase the image of herself falling off a cable car after they'd been dancing at one of the clubs in the Marina. Mostly she blamed her ridiculous shoes for that, but she also had to admit that martinis were involved. Like, buckets of martinis.

"It wouldn't have been so bad if I'd been wearing pants instead of that tight leather skirt you insisted on buying me," she grumbled, and made herself sit upright. Good posture always made you feel less like a loser. "I admit I've done stupid things. I'm also willing to acknowledge that I self-medicate. But please spare me the shrinky-dink session. You don't have to tell me why I'm behaving badly: I get that it's because I'm lonely. So what? Working that crisis hotline has taught me that everybody is lonely. Life is all about making it from one day to the next without mud in your eye. Or maybe even *with* mud in your eye and up your ass, too."

"Oh my." Tony put a forefinger to his head and pretended to pull the trigger. "Let's just off ourselves now and escape this tiresome hamster wheel of torture."

"Ha-ha."

Tony lowered his hand and plucked another lettuce leaf out of the plastic container. "Look, the fix is obvious," he said, chewing. "You just need somebody to come home to at night. You're smart, attractive, and funny when you're not being too snarky. There's somebody out there for you. A lid for every pot, yadda yadda. Stop wasting time by wading around in the kiddie pool. Jump in the deep end and look for a real man."

"I cannot believe that you, of all people, are trying to tell me that life is better as a couple. You've been shacked up, what, a whole three months? I do *not* need a man in my life. I can barely even water my plants."

Tony stared at her with pity in his long-lashed eyes. "Oh really? Then what *do* you need? A special six-foot invisible rabbit? A rescue dog? Whatever you need, honey, it's time to get real about finding it. Meanwhile, pay your dues. Call that guy."

Absurdly, Elaine thought of Tommy, Gabe's huge ginger cat with the broken halting purr, and longed to be holding him on her lap this minute. Maybe adopting a cat wasn't such a terrible idea. You didn't even have to walk a cat.

"Fine," she said. "I'll call Gabe and treat him to whatever if it'll get you off my back."

Tony held out his phone.

"What's that for?"

"I want you to make that call."

"What, now?"

"Yes, now!" Tony said. "Call the Angel Gabriel and invite him to a meal. Tonight."

"He's probably busy tonight."

"You never know until you ask. Besides, it's a Monday," Tony pointed out. "Nobody ever makes plans for Mondays."

"Sometimes, having your best friend also be your boss is a real problem," Elaine said with a sigh as she dug her phone out of her purse. "I can't even sue you for harassment or bullying or whatever."

Before leaving Gabe's apartment, Elaine had put his number into her contacts list at his insistence; she dialed it now while Tony kept his eyes fixed on her.

Gabe picked up on the first ring. "Hi!" he said brightly, as if he'd been expecting her to call at this exact appointed time.

"Hey. This is Elaine. Sorry to bother you." Again, she wondered what the man did for a living, that he was at home on Mondays.

"You're not bothering me. It's nice to hear your voice again so soon. I wasn't expecting that."

Elaine hesitated, wondering what Gabe had been expecting her to do. Drop off the face of the planet, probably. That was certainly her plan where he was concerned.

Tony was watching her closely; now he made a motion like he was tearing into a giant sandwich, nearly making her spit with laughter.

Elaine bit her lip to keep a straight face and said, "I know this is short notice—"

"No, it's not," Gabe said immediately. "It's perfect timing."

She rolled her eyes at Tony. "You don't even know what I'm going to ask."

This time, Tony acted out the entire dogs-sharing-spaghetti scene from *Lady and the Tramp*, making Elaine mime a gagging motion in return.

"Doesn't matter," said Gabe. "I'm sure I'll want to do it."

This guy made Pollyanna look like a nihilist. Elaine hoped to hell he didn't think she was calling because she was interested. Though, in reality, why would this man want a relationship with her? Gabe had only seen her at her absolute worst. She was lucky he even took her calls. Not that she cared, of course, but she hated giving someone a bad impression.

"I was going to suggest dinner tonight," she said. "But it's such short notice, I'm sure you have other plans."

"Absolutely not. I'd love to," Gabe said.

They arranged to meet in Harvard Square in front of the newsstand. Elaine hung up and tucked the phone back into her purse. "Satisfied?" she asked Tony.

"I will be if you keep that date," he said. "Why Harvard Square?" They started walking back to the office, back to an afternoon of brainstorming ideas for how to make a certain college client look good to prospective families despite the fact that its provost had just made national news for embezzling money from the alumni fund.

Elaine shrugged. "I thought he'd feel comfortable in Cambridge. Gabe's kind of a hippie. In fact, I've been thinking of fixing him up with Ava. He's definitely her type."

"I thought you said Ava's busy and probably seeing somebody."

"Yeah, well. Whoever he is, he couldn't be nicer than Gabe."

Tony patted her shoulder. "Then the person who needs Gabe is you."

## CHAPTER TEN

The bus to Portsmouth took half an hour and went straight north on Route 95 from Newburyport. Gigi felt self-conscious at first, being the only teenager on the bus, but the other passengers ignored her, their noses in iPads and phones and newspapers. Soon she settled back on the cushioned leather seat, enjoying the air-conditioning and exhilarated by the idea that nobody else had a clue where she was.

Her ecstasy rapidly faded, though, as she realized that the downside about being alone was the lack of distraction from your memories. Being on the bus reminded Gigi of the first time she'd ever ridden city buses. It was in San Francisco on that trip to California, their last family vacation before Dad had his first surgery, when Mildred came and stayed at the house.

They chose California because Dad had never been there. It always surprised Gigi that Mom had traveled so many more places than her father, since Dad was practically Gramma Dawn's age. On the other hand, Mom's family had money, while Dad had worked his way through college and already had two kids—no, make that three—by the time he graduated.

They'd flown from Boston to Los Angeles, where they'd taken a tour of Universal Studios and gone on all the rides. Dad had screamed like a little girl on that crazy Jurassic Park water ride, making Mom laugh. Dad had also made a huge deal out of getting his picture taken with any employee dressed like a movie character, even the guys on stilts with the Transformer costumes.

In Los Angeles, they'd also rented fat-tired bikes to ride on Venice Beach and seen the fossils at La Brea Tar Pits, where Gigi freaked at the sight of hundreds of wolf skulls lined up in a yellow case, imagining the sloths and mastodons trapped in the tar, terrified, as wolves circled them and started pulling flesh from bone. Then they'd driven north in a rented red convertible to see surfers and redwood trees in Santa Cruz. Dad kept acting like a little kid or maybe a demented old person, crawling into the caves beneath the redwood trunks and begging Mom to take his picture. He and Gigi agreed on how they definitely would have built houses in the trunks of those giant trees, if they'd been the original explorers mapping the land.

Dad would have been happy doing that, riding a horse with a rifle slung over his shoulder and nothing to eat but beef jerky or whatever. He should have been a rock musician or an adventurer, but he never got a chance to do what he really loved in life. "Don't spend your whole life waiting for someday to come," he'd told Gigi on that trip. "You never know when you're going to run out of time."

Gigi felt her eyes burn and pressed her face against the window. She hadn't known, until Dad died, that a human body could produce this many tears. Sometimes she tried to squeeze her eyelids shut to seal in the water, but it never worked.

She was beginning to think that the death of somebody you loved was like throwing rocks in a pond. Piles and piles of rocks: the ripples kept on spreading, disrupting the smooth surface of your life long after you'd lost track of where, exactly, the rocks went into the water.

At least today she felt like she was actually doing something that would have made Dad happy. Gigi climbed down the bus steps in Portsmouth, blinking in the bright sun and feeling the heat of it slap her face. She was having an adventure and keeping her promise to him.

There were other people her age at the bus station, teenagers in raggedy jeans and T-shirts and bandannas, one of them carrying a guitar. The bus station was right off the highway; the college kids offered her weed and, shrugging when she said no, showed her the trolley stop and helped her find a schedule.

It was a touristy sort of trolley, no glass in the windows and painted bright green. This, too, made her think of that trip to California, of how Dad had insisted on standing on the running board of the cable car in San Francisco and leaning as far back as he could while they clanged up and down the hills. Mom did it with him, too, leaning her head back so that her hair, longer then, flowed like water down her back.

"Mom! Dad! That's dangerous and the conductor said don't do it!" Gigi was glued to her seat and clinging to the trolley pole. "Sit down!"

"Sit? We can't sit! This has been on my bucket list since I was a kid!" Dad yelled back, grinning like he'd won the lottery or something.

Gigi hadn't known then what he meant by a "bucket list" and had pictured her father carrying an actual black rubber bucket sloshing water, like the buckets at the barn.

Now, as a group of hefty sunburned girls in UNH T-shirts boarded the trolley, Gigi remembered that her dad's cousin Mildred had taught at the University of New Hampshire. Dad had bragged about Mildred getting a master's degree in nutrition, saying Mildred was the only person in his family besides him to go to college. Dad hadn't gone straight through, of course. He'd paid for his degree himself, taking one or two evening classes a semester at a local college to finish his accounting degree.

Gigi couldn't imagine not going to college right after high school. Everybody she knew—okay, a ridiculously small sample size, her mom's family and the kids at her school, but still—went to college right after high school. Otherwise, what were your options? McDonald's, or building houses. Fixing cars, maybe. Or music, but even Gigi knew you probably couldn't count on music to pay your rent, no matter how good you were. You still needed a stupid job.

The Portsmouth trolley wheezed into the brick city center and stopped across from a white church that looked like a blown-up version of the one Mom always put in the Christmas village. There were outdoor cafés crowded with people and dogs, small shops, and sidewalks jammed with people. There were college kids and men in navy uniforms, and tourists puzzling over maps and their cell phones. Some of the tourists were sunbaked a shiny red; they looked like they'd fallen into the same pots of boiling water used to cook the lobsters they were probably fantasizing about eating for lunch. "Cockroaches of the sea," Dad called them.

The lobsters, not the tourists.

Gigi could smell the river from here and used that to orient herself with the map on her phone. A blue line showed her how to walk to Cousin Mildred's house on the river, just a few blocks south of downtown. It wasn't a long walk, maybe fifteen minutes, and it took her alongside a pretty park. The river beyond it lay like a flat slate ribbon, and was wide enough for navy ships to be docked along the opposite bank. There was a decent breeze.

Still, Gigi arrived at her destination drenched in sweat and doubt. Her underarms and thighs were sticky with sweat. Even her feet felt sunburned, despite her neon green sneakers.

Why hadn't she asked Mom or Ava to drive her here? What if Cousin Mildred had died since sending that birthday card, or had gone senile? She was older than Dad and people didn't live forever. Obviously.

She ignored the tears that started to dampen her face again—by now, the salty moisture felt like her second skin—and studied the house. This neighborhood looked like the kind where the moms played tennis and drank pretty umbrella drinks and the dads willingly coached soccer on weekends. Mildred's house was tall and narrow, reminding her of a doll's house with its fancy cream trim. Or a postcard of a house, the shrubs trimmed into neat round balls on either side of the door and a copper-capped varnished picket fence dripping with scarlet roses that would make Mom jealous the same way other people craved good hair.

Gigi unwrapped a piece of gum and chewed it hard, sucking down mint juices to calm her nerves, then spit the little gray wad into its square of chalky paper and tucked it into her pocket. She had taken out her nose and eyebrow rings before leaving home, not wanting to terrify Dad's cousin; now she wished she'd left them in. She felt vulnerable without her armor, tingling and nervous, as if a thousand bees had landed on her skin.

There was no doorbell and nobody came to the door when she rapped her knuckles against it. Gigi knocked a second time, putting serious muscle into flipping the brass ring hanging through the door knocker lion's nose. The wooden door was shiny, varnished a warm henna; it smelled like forest, hot and earthy.

She was about to give up, already tugging the wrinkled damp bus schedule out of her pocket to study it, when the door finally opened. Gigi was bathed in a whoosh of cool lemon-scented air that made her blink. An old woman stood in the doorway and squinted in Gigi's general direction. Her words rustled together like expensive wrapping paper. "Yes? May I help you?"

Gigi's memory of what Cousin Mildred had looked like so many years ago was vague, yet she experienced a sharp jolt of recognition. Mildred was skinny and bent like a twig, but otherwise looked exactly like Dad would have looked if he'd made it to seventy and been a scrawny woman instead of a bulky man. "I'm Gigi."

"Speak up, child. Nobody likes a mumbler."

"I'm Gigi, your cousin Bob's daughter." She had rehearsed this. Her words came out like she was a robot imitating human speech. "You send me birthday cards. I live in Newburyport."

Cousin Mildred folded her arms and stared as if she were memorizing Gigi's face for a test. She didn't say a word. Maybe the woman had gone mental. Gigi decided to stare back and wait her out.

Mildred's own face was long and ended in a square jaw with one of those butt dents in it. Her belly was soft and round above the elastic waistband of her white slacks. Her hair, like Dad's, had gone white and was surprisingly long for an old woman's, unraveling in a feathery fountain spray from the top of her head. Behind the wire-frame glasses worn low on her nose, Mildred's eyes, too, were Dad's, that same warm honey brown with gold sparks.

Finally Mildred said, "Speak up. You're not a Girl Scout, are you?" She glanced past Gigi as if there might be a whole troop of girls swarming the sidewalk behind her. "This is the wrong time of year for cookies."

How could anyone mistake her—with her kohl eyeliner and magenta-tipped hair—for a Girl Scout? Gigi wondered if Mildred was blind, too, like Peter. No. Mildred was squinting at her. You wouldn't squint in bright light if you were blind, would you?

"I'm Gigi," she repeated. "Your cousin once removed." She had worked this much out on the bus. "Your cousin Bob's youngest daughter. Remember? You send me birthday cards every year."

"Of course I do. I'm not senile, you know."

"No, I don't. How would I know?" Gigi snapped back, then was immediately sorry. You shouldn't lose it with old people. That was like a Golden Rule or something.

But Mildred seemed to take no offense. Her face remained as expressionless as before. "You are correct," she said. "I send you birthday cards with money and you send me thank-you notes, which shows that at the very least your parents have taught you some manners. Unlike some," she added. "But there is no way you could know anything about me."

Mildred didn't apologize for this lack of contact. She only peered more intently into Gigi's face. "You have your father's nose, so you must be who you say you are. Might as well come inside. I apologize for keeping you waiting, but you can't be too careful these days. It's a terrible world. Well, you understand that, I'm sure. You're in school. I'm sure you're aware that you could be gunned down right in your own classroom." She stepped back and gestured for Gigi to enter the door with a little bow, as if Mildred were her own butler.

"You do know my dad's dead, right?" said Gigi, trying to blink away images of black-clad gunmen prowling the halls of her school.

"Yes, I'd heard your father passed. Ava sent me a card. I have been remiss in not writing back."

That was it. Nothing like, "What a shame," or, "I was sorry to hear that," or even, "My prayers are with you and your family." Which, when you thought about it, weren't especially useful phrases, just what Gigi was used to hearing.

She hurried to keep up with the old lady, who was a good foot taller than she was and didn't seem inclined to wait for anyone. Gigi hadn't known what to expect of this visit, since her father's parents were long dead and she'd never met anyone else in his family except Ava and Elaine. But she certainly wasn't prepared for this weird combo of doom and gloom overlaid with the royal duchess act.

What was it about small towns in Maine, she wondered, that old women like Finley and Mildred never saw their families and believed the world was about to be overrun by zombies or Communists or masked gunmen? At least her father had escaped that place.

She racewalked behind Mildred along the dim hallway, Mildred's square-heeled shoes hammering on the wood floors, and through a kitchen with dark pine cabinets. Finley's house was a treasure trove of secrets with its stacks of magazines and papers, the photographs stuffed into drawers, the cluttered little kitchen, but Mildred's house was devoid of personality. The counters were clear and the floors gleamed. The only pictures on the walls were landscapes in uncertain pastels. There wasn't a family photograph in sight. The stark contrast between Finley's house and Mildred's made Gigi wonder if money and education led people to tuck their personal effects out of sight, the same way Mom always said that a properly dressed man tucks in his shirt, even when wearing jeans.

They continued out the back door to a screened porch with those wicker chairs that looked comfortable but never were. Beyond the porch lay the only indication that a real person lived here: a small square yard crowded with animal statues. Around one bed of red and white flowers, Gigi counted fifteen stone rabbits in varying sizes. The ghostly white statue of a deer peered at her from behind a bush with a puzzled expression.

A large jar of murky brown liquid sweated on a wicker side table; sticks and leaves were floating in it. Gigi stopped to peer into the jar, wondering if Mildred was raising tadpoles. She and her father had done that every summer for years.

"My own special sun tea recipe," Mildred said, watching Gigi. "You'll have to try it."

"No, thank you."

"Oh, but you must!" For the first time, Mildred's stony face became animated, her skinny silver eyebrows twitching like the threads that held them in place were coming loose. "My sun tea is famous. Everyone at UNH used to absolutely *beg* me to bring it to parties. The trick is to add lemongrass and mint straight from the garden." She pointed to the twigs and leaves. "Some say bacteria grows in sun tea, but I'm seventy years old this month and healthier than most ten-year-olds. You'll love it."

"I'm not really thirsty."

"Piffle. Look at you! Your face looks like a tomato and you're all sweaty, like you ran all the way here from Newburyport. It's important to rehydrate." Mildred ladled tea into a tall clear plastic glass. She handed it to Gigi on a small enamel tray with elephants on it. On the tray next to the glass was a silver bowl of brown sugar cubes with a tiny pair of tongs.

Gigi thought about protesting again, but what would be the point? Mildred was clearly not going to give up. She dropped a couple of sugar cubes into the tea and sat down on the wicker chair across the narrow porch from Mildred's wicker rocker. Mildred must have been sitting out here when Gigi knocked, reading the novel on the table. The book had a woman in a red velvet gown on the cover, her shoulders bare.

Mildred sat down in the rocker and watched as Gigi took a tentative sip. Gigi's nose filled at once with mint and her teeth ached from the sugar.

"It's not bad," Gigi said, surprised that a liquid resembling muddy pond water was drinkable.

Mildred looked satisfied. "Nothing gives you energy like my special sun tea."

Mildred asked Gigi about her trip and seemed only mildly surprised to hear that Gigi had found Mildred's address on the envelope, then used an app on her phone to get here. Maybe being a college professor had made Mildred more tech savvy than most adults. Most parents and teachers, including her own mom, acted like the devil created the Internet to lure unsuspecting children into unmarked vans and basements.

Gigi offered Mildred a compliment about the porch. She meant it—the porch was clean and carpeted in fake green grass, so it felt like being outside—but she did wonder why Mildred didn't have a ceiling fan out here. Her T-shirt was glued to her back and she kept having to blink sweat out of her eyes.

Mildred nodded. "Yes, I've always loved this porch. It's like I'm in Vermont. My late husband and I used to have a house in Middlebury when he taught at the college there. This feels just as remote, yet I'm only a few blocks from downtown Portsmouth. Well, you saw that for yourself, walking from the trolley stop. Once we bought this house, I never needed to go anywhere else. That's how much I love it here."

This remark ticked Gigi off. "Is that why you didn't come to Dad's funeral? Because your porch is so perfect?"

Mildred's brown eyes gleamed pebble-shiny. "I was unable to attend."

Gigi wondered how true this was. As the woman had already told her, she was healthier than most kids. And Portsmouth wasn't far. Maybe she didn't drive, but if Gigi could travel by bus, so could Mildred. Again, it irked her that Mildred didn't at least say she was sorry about Dad dying.

"Why *couldn't* you come?" Gigi asked. "Were you in the hospital or something? Traveling through Europe? I hope you had a pretty freakin' good reason."

"There is no need to take that fresh attitude with me," Mildred said sharply. "Especially when you're a guest in my home, enjoying my tea and hospitality."

*Your muddy water and sweaty-ass porch,* Gigi thought, but clamped her lips shut.

Mildred set her glass down on the table and folded her hands across the lap of her flowered cotton skirt. Her bare legs were boiled-egg white and her feet were securely encased in sandals with straps as wide as seat belts. "If you must know, funerals depress me. I make it a point to avoid them."

"Funerals depress everybody," Gigi argued. "You should go anyway. Think how sad my dad would have been, if he'd known you skipped out on him."

"He *didn't* know. That's the point. It doesn't matter to the one in the ground."

"But it matters to everyone else! Even my half sisters showed up, and Dad walked out on them."

"A painful chapter in their lives, I'm sure," Mildred said, bobbing her long face in a way that reminded Gigi of a horse hanging its head over the paddock fence. "Still. He was their father. It was mandatory for them to appear at his service. We were only cousins. And we weren't close."

"Why not?" Gigi set down her glass, her fingers numb from the cold. Meanwhile, the rest of her overheated body felt like it was puddling into the fake-grass carpet on the porch. "You were family and you lived in the same town."

"I was much older. Are you close to your cousins?" Mildred's tone was politely conversational rather than curious.

Gigi shrugged. "No, but that's because I don't have any nearby. I only have one uncle, and his son goes to a boarding school in a different state. I don't see him very much." She felt alone, as she always did, saying this. Then she remembered: "But I'm getting to know my nephews now."

Mildred frowned. "Nephews?" She said it like a foreign word.

"Ava's kids. Evan and Sam. *Your cousin's children,*" Gigi added, feeling mean-spirited. "I guess you make it a point to avoid them, too."

Again, Mildred didn't appear to react emotionally to this jab. Not even a twitch around her mouth. "Of course. I met the boys once, long ago, before your father met your mother." She sat up even straighter. "Not that it's any of your business, but I also send them birthday cards every year with a check enclosed. Unlike you, however, those boys don't know how to send a thank-you note."

Probably because Ava didn't hound them to do it the way her own mother did her, Gigi thought, glancing around the porch. There was no evidence of anyone living here other than Mildred. She couldn't understand why this woman, who didn't live far away and appeared sane, had wanted nothing to do with her father and his families. "Do you have kids?"

Mildred shifted in her chair. "We had a daughter, but she died of breast cancer fifteen years ago after a long struggle. She chose not to have a family. My son was killed in a car accident the day he graduated from high school." She lifted her square chin. "My husband was a good man. We were married for thirty-eight years when he died. Now there's just me, waiting to join them."

Gigi's stomach twisted at the sight of Mildred's face, where the weight of loss was pulling down the corners of the old woman's mouth and eyes, tightening her sagging skin to reveal the outline of her narrow skull. "I'm sorry."

"No need to feel sorry. It was all a long time ago." Mildred crossed and uncrossed her feet. They looked like they might hurt to walk on, those feet, the toes gnarled and round like acorn caps in her sandals. "Besides, I've had as much happiness as anyone deserves. A career I loved, good friends." She picked up her tea and stared into the swampy liquid without drinking it. "When you get to be my age, you realize that life is not about being happy."

Gigi shuddered a little. "I get why you don't like funerals."

Mildred smiled. "Thank you," she said briskly. "But enough of that. Tell me about you. You'd be what now, a sophomore?"

Reluctantly, Gigi told Cousin Mildred the usual boring things about school, making up friends and favorite subjects she didn't have. Adults loved to hear those things. "Right now I'm working at my sister Ava's pottery studio," she added. "I sing in a band with her kids, too." Admitting she was a singer—something Gigi rarely told anyone—felt risky even here on this hidden porch.

"That all sounds wonderful, dear," Mildred said. Her face had plumped up again, the sorrow tucked back into its rightful place under her tongue and rib cage, the skin as soft looking as those apple-head dolls the art teacher taught Gigi's class to make last fall. They had put the apples in a shoe box in the closet to wither, then pinched terrifyingly human features into the fragrant skin. "But I don't suppose you came here to talk about school. There must be another reason you made this long trip by yourself."

"Yes." Gigi bit her lip, wondering how to proceed. Best not to ask about the baby right away and put her off, she decided. "I wanted to know more about my dad when he was young," she said. "You say you weren't close, but did you see him a lot, growing up?"

Mildred nodded. "I occasionally babysat for him. Adorable boy. Sweet and well behaved."

"What about when he was a teenager?"

"I can't say." The old woman frowned, the lines deep grooves between her eyes. "I had moved away by the time your father was in high school. I went to college, got married. I only came home on holidays. From what I remember, though, your father was hard-working, always had at least one job as soon as he was old enough to shovel snow. His parents were so certain that he'd follow me to the university. It broke their hearts when he got married instead."

"What about Dad's first wife, Suzanne? Do you remember her, too?"

"Of course. Beautiful girl. Shy and well liked, I think, despite her father."

"What was wrong with Suzanne's father?"

Mildred plucked at a thread on the seam of her skirt, wriggled it out, snapped it between her fingernails. "Oh, you know. Thought he was better than God because he had more money than most. Owned the biggest house on the Common. They didn't want Suzanne near our kind. We were the wrong side of the tracks. Not that our family would have tolerated hers, either. Suzanne's parents had money, but that didn't make up for them being French-Canadians in the eyes of most people. The French were mostly shunned. Children were banned from speaking French in Maine and the Ku Klux Klan even held rallies against the French Catholics in the nineteen twenties. I know that must seem like forever ago to you. But the point is, neither family wanted anything to do with the other."

Gigi hadn't known any of this. Why would anyone care if somebody was French-Canadian, especially if both her dad's family and Suzanne's were Catholic?

It all sounded like that *Romeo and Juliet* play they'd read in freshman English class, except those kids had been stupid enough to off themselves. At least Dad and Suzanne had defied everybody and run away together in the end. Somehow, even knowing how things eventually turned out, this thought comforted her.

"Tell me what you really want to know," Mildred said. "I don't have all day. I've got a luncheon at the senior center. The food is subpar, green beans limp as noodles and meat like old shoes. A nutritionist's nightmare. Most of the people are deaf, too. But they expect me. Besides, I've paid ahead for the meal. No refunds, you know."

The sun was nearly straight overhead, casting slatted shadows through the blinds over the porch windows. Gigi's head had started to ache from the heat. "I want to know about Dad's baby," she said. "The one he had with Suzanne when they were teenagers."

Mildred twisted her crooked fingers against the fabric of her skirt. "Why would you ask about an ugly rumor like that?"

"It wasn't a rumor!" Gigi was mad enough to spit. Why did grown-ups always act like kids couldn't possibly know the truth about them? "My dad told me to my face."

The old woman's skin had paled to the same bleached white as her legs. "Still, there's no reason for you and me to discuss it. That was a private matter, a secret meant to be taken to the grave."

"Taken by who?"

"Whom," Mildred corrected automatically. "By both of them. Suzanne and your father."

"Suzanne, maybe," Gigi acknowledged. "But Dad was sick of keeping it a secret. That's why he told Mom and me. And Ava, too," she added. "He asked Ava and me to find the baby."

"Why would he do that?" Mildred sounded bewildered. "What would be the point? That baby would be a man now, if he's even still alive. Your father must have been addled, talking rubbish like that to you."

"My dad was not addled. Only sick and dying."

"Same thing," Mildred muttered.

"Screw you!" Gigi said, then put a hand to her mouth, as if there were some way to pick up the shards of those words and swallow them. "I'm sorry," she whispered. "But I hate how everybody always thinks my dad was nuts or hallucinating on drugs or something. Dad knew where he was. He knew who *we* were. And he also knew he was dying. That's why he didn't want any more secrets."

"I'm the one who should apologize." Mildred folded her napkin, then opened it and refolded it again, pressing the creases straight with her fingers. "I should not have spoken disrespectfully of your father. It's just that this is a painful subject for our family, and I haven't had to remember it in a long time."

"So Dad never talked to you about what happened?"

"Not until many years later. I wasn't living in town, you see. Bob and I saw each other only on holidays with our parents. Never alone. I was already married, working on my master's degree in New Hampshire, by the time Bob and Suzanne were dating. I didn't hear anything about the baby until I went home one Christmas several years after they were married. They'd already had the two girls before your father even knew about the boy's existence, according to my mother. Suzanne had kept it a secret from everyone. That's the way things were then." Mildred sighed. "Such a shame, really, two bright kids getting themselves into trouble like that in high school and ruining their lives. Bob and Suzanne should have known better."

"They were in love!"

"They still should have had sense enough to restrain themselves," Mildred said. "Love is like a drug. You have to just say no."

Gigi nearly laughed at the phrase she'd heard a zillion times about drugs. But then she thought about the one time she'd felt like she was in love with that guy who'd dropped out of UMass to work at the mini-mart. He was funny and kind, a stoner with bleached hair who told everyone he was saving money to go to California and surf.

She could barely breathe around him. Gigi wasn't brave like the other girls in town, coming up with excuses to lean over the counter to see his tattoos up close, tossing their hair and practically prancing in front of him like wild ponies. But she made up excuses to go to the corner store to get milk or eggs or whatever for Mom, just to stare at that boy's thick white hair and imagine how it would feel, silky as water in your fingers. She wasn't actually in love. She knew that much. But being around that guy made her imagine what love felt like: like someone else was controlling your body, jerking you around like a puppet on strings while your belly and thighs felt like they were on fire.

Mildred was still talking. "If only Suzanne hadn't gotten pregnant, they might have just gone to prom and broken up after a few years like they were supposed to."

Gigi flushed, imagining her father as a boy the same age as the one in the corner store, and Suzanne as a ponytailed girl with her dark tilted eyes laughing up at him. But this was the moment she had been waiting for, and she seized it. "What happened to the baby?"

"How should I know? Suzanne put it up for adoption, didn't she? I'd heard there were some issues with the baby's health, but I never saw the poor thing."

"The baby was born blind," Gigi said. "Peter. That was his name. Suzanne didn't want to give him up, but they made her do it. She gave him to her aunt Finley."

"Finley?" Mildred's eyes popped wide open. The whites around her brown eyes were yellow and streaked red. "Are you certain?"

"Yes. Ava and Elaine and I went up to see her. Why not Finley?"

Mildred shuddered a little. "She lived in a different town, but I saw Finley a few times early on, when our families were forced together during holiday dinners and such. Finley wasn't like most women. Never married, seldom socialized. She wore pants like a man, even flannel shirts and boots. I'm shocked to hear Suzanne thought that would be an appropriate home for a child, though I suppose she wasn't in any position to be choosy."

"Finley was trying to do what she could to help Suzanne, which is more than what most people did," Gigi said flatly, feeling suddenly defensive on Finley's behalf. "Anyway, Finley had to give the baby up, too, and then somebody else adopted him."

"Just as well," Mildred said. "I'm sorry to hear the child was bounced around, but what else could anyone expect? At least everything worked out in the end."

Gigi felt her scalp sting with fury. "How can you say it all 'worked out'? Nothing worked out! Dad was miserable! Suzanne practically killed herself! Nobody even knows where Peter is!"

Mildred drew her narrow torso up straighter in the chair and buttoned her sweater. "No need to yell. Yelling never helped anybody."

"I'm sorry." Gigi sighed. It seemed like she'd come here to do nothing but apologize. "I'm just upset. Dad really never talked to you about any of this?"

Mildred picked up her glass and sipped at the tea, then licked her lips as a shadow crossed her face. Her tongue was as pink and wet as a kitten's, the only part of her that still looked young. "Now that you're bringing all of this back to me, I do remember him mentioning it once. My first summer alone after my husband's death, your father invited me to your house in Newburyport. I suppose he felt sorry for me. Anyway, Bob and I sat alone out on the patio after your mother left to put you to bed. You were only ten years old, a chubby little thing. That's the one time we talked about the baby. Your father wanted to know if I had any information."

*Five years ago,* Gigi thought. That's how long her father had been searching. Why hadn't he told her sooner? She sat up straighter, feeling little wicker needles through her thin T-shirt. "Why didn't he look for my brother before?"

"Bob said he'd tried to forget about the baby, like everyone kept telling him to do. He thought it would be better for everyone, since they'd already started another family."

"What changed?"

"When he left Suzanne for your mother, Bob started thinking about it all again, he said, and worrying about that child being given away like a puppy nobody wanted. Those were your dad's exact words: 'like a puppy.' He about cried when he said that. Your father didn't know he was dying, not then. But he'd gotten his diagnosis and knew he might not have as much time left as he thought."

"That's so sad," Gigi said.

"It is. I remember how Bob pointed to the sky over the fence. The reason we couldn't see the stars, he said, is because there was too much atmospheric light. He told me that's what he felt his whole life was like, like something blurry with brighter things beneath it. I think that's why he was so intent on marrying your mother."

"What do you mean?"

Mildred gave her a long look, the kind of look that makes you think somebody is behind you. Gigi wouldn't let herself turn around. "When we were talking that night on the patio, your dad also told me why he got divorced," she said. "You have to understand that he and I came from a long line of devout Catholics. In our family, you didn't divorce. I suspect the same was true in Suzanne's family, despite being French-Canadians. Marriage was a pact you made with God and the Church."

Gigi thought of the small stone Episcopalian church she and her mother went to some Sundays, the building that smelled of lilies all year round. "What does this have to do with me?"

Mildred plucked at a yellow thread in the loose stitching along the front of her skirt. "Your father wanted me to understand why he'd chosen to divorce Suzanne and leave the Church. I suppose he was afraid I judged him harshly."

"So why did he get divorced? Because he loved my mom so much, right?" Again, Gigi wanted to cover her mouth, talking that way about her own parents.

"He couldn't bear the thought of losing another child. When your mother got pregnant, he saw no choice but to marry her and raise you."

Gigi felt her tongue like cotton catching on the roof of her mouth, choking her: so she was the reason Dad had left them all— Ava, Suzanne, Elaine. Even, to some extent, Evan and Sam. Mildred's face was still smooth and expressionless, her bloodless legs crossed tightly at the ankles. "I do apologize if that came as a shock. I was sure you'd worked all that out for yourself."

"How would I?" Gigi was embarrassed by how young her voice sounded.

The older woman shrugged. "You know. Birth certificates, wedding dates, Google. I was under the impression that you young people knew everything these days, thanks to the Internet. I'm sorry to have upset you. But that's what you came for, isn't it? The truth?"

Gigi nodded, her vision clouding. Her father, all his life, had tried to do the right thing and failed. It was so sad.

On the other hand, maybe that's what happened to everyone. Maybe, no matter what right thing you tried to do, your action would be the wrong thing for somebody else.

She owed her brother her very existence. Her mother might

have thought about abortion. Her family and her friends were already freaked-out about her being with some old married dude; they'd probably told her to get rid of "the problem."

Dad loved Mom—Gigi had never doubted that, watching them together—but he had married Mom to make sure she had the baby. The baby, Gigi. Mildred was right: he had most likely married her mother because he'd already lost one child and didn't want to lose another.

Gigi bent over, put her head between her knees. "I feel sick," she said.

"Well, it can't possibly be the tea," Mildred said briskly.

"Whatever." Gigi pushed her head lower between her knees despite the sour taste in the back of her throat. She imagined vomiting those little twigs from the tea onto the fake green grass carpet, the sticks catching in her throat, choking her.

"It must be the heat," Mildred was saying. "Come with me into the house where it's cooler."

"I don't think I can walk."

"Lie down here, then."

Gigi heard a rustling sound, then felt Mildred's knobby fingers clamp around her wrist and tug her out of the chair with a sudden and unexpectedly powerful jerk.

Mildred led her to a wicker couch on the shady side of the porch. Gigi hadn't noticed it before because it had been covered with a tarp; the tarp was the sound she'd heard. Now it lay in a shiny blue puddle of plastic on the floor.

"Thanks." Gigi lay down on the couch, curled with her knees pressed to her chest, her face against the musty cushions.

"Cramps?" Mildred suggested. "Is it that time of month?"

If only things were that easy, Gigi thought, remembering with a flash of envy her own innocent self two years ago, before Dad's cancer came back and he started another round of chemo. She'd gotten her period for the first time and been stupid enough to be excited about it.

Mom had taken her out to lunch to celebrate, and Gigi thought that her life was finally beginning. She had happily imagined how she would transform overnight from a pudgy middle schooler into a woman, a woman who was thin and blond and beautiful like her mother. She would grow movie star boobs and find a boyfriend. She would win blue ribbons and trophies at horse shows. She wouldn't be afraid of anything anymore.

Those were her pitiful concerns, her silly fantasies. Back then, Gigi had no way of knowing what she did now, that nobody escapes this sick feeling that comes with discovering, over and over again, that the people you love are not who you thought they were.

## CHAPTER ELEVEN

A va worked in the studio until late afternoon, then brewed a strong cup of tea and drank it while staring at the phone. Still no word from Elaine, despite Ava's repeated attempts to call and text to tell her about what the woman at the registry had told her, and to ask what she thought about going back to Maine to see if Peter's original birth certificate remained on file, under their mother's maiden name.

Why was she bothering? Elaine didn't want anything to do with this. To be honest, Elaine seemed to want little to do with *her* these days. All their lives, they had seen each other every week, talked on the phone nearly every day. Now Ava felt both relieved and resentful about this yawning silence between them. Elaine was high maintenance, exhausting. But who else, besides her children, did Ava love unconditionally? Knowing that she was doing things to cause Elaine to pull away made Ava feel slightly queasy.

Ava folded laundry and scrubbed the bathrooms, trying to kill her caffeine buzz before returning to the studio. She was soon breathing hard from the exertion, which made her wonder if she needed to lie down for a few minutes. She threw herself down on the bed, a pillow over her face, which of course only led her to think about Simon with the kind of longing that made her resent her own crowded life: her brother, Elaine, Katy, Gigi, and even her sons stood between what she wanted with Simon and what she couldn't have.

She had repeatedly explained the impossibility of their relationship to Simon, yet he had been calling and e-mailing daily, trying to change her mind. Three times, she'd left after dinner to meet him halfway between Beach Plum Island and Boston; they'd sat in his car and kissed until her mouth felt bruised. It had gotten to the point where even the boys, who noticed little about her life as long as she went through the motions of putting food in the kitchen and driving them here and there, had started asking where she was. She supposed mothers were like air: you only missed them when they were gone and left you gasping for oxygen.

Last night, for instance, she'd crept in at two o'clock in the morning, hoping the boys were asleep, but instead Sam and Evan were in the living room, watching some dreadful movie that sounded like the house was under attack.

"Whoa, Mom," Sam had said, looking up from the screen as she tried to sneak in through the back door unnoticed. "Where were you? You're keeping, like, zombie hours."

"Yeah, well, I've got to get out while the hunting's good," she'd said, never pausing in her ascent to the second floor, afraid the boys would notice her red face and rumpled clothing. "Otherwise all the warm bodies are gone."

She'd told Simon last night that they couldn't see each other again. Absolutely, positively, they had to stop. She felt sick about it, but what else could she do? She needed to feel things were on an even keel with the other people in her life before even daring to imagine a relationship with him. With anyone, for that matter.

Thinking about not seeing Simon and the various complications leading to that decision made her so tense, it felt like someone had slipped a dozen rubber bands over her head. She needed a walk to clear her thoughts. Ava stepped outside and slipped off her shoes, then walked fast toward the refuge beach, dodging a group of birders in their brimmed hats, telescopes set up in a line like artillery. The sky was a metallic blue dome over the sparkling water. Ava glanced down and spotted a sand dollar. The chalky white circle glowed against the sand and reminded her of taking walks with the boys when they first moved here after the divorce. Evan and Sam used to love dashing in and out of the water or climbing the rocky breakwater by the mouth of the Merrimack River to watch the fishing boats. She missed those easy days, that uncomplicated bond with her children before they became teenagers with secrets, men taller than she was.

Back at the house, her headache had eased enough that Ava went straight to the studio in her tank top and shorts, leaving the sweatshirt draped over one of the Adirondack chairs. She spent the next several hours using slab molds to create trays she fluted around the edges to match the teacups she'd made yesterday, with slight depressions to hold two or four cups, depending on the size of the tray.

They turned out just as she'd imagined—a rare thing in pottery. She couldn't wait to glaze them; the effect would be as beautiful as it was utilitarian. She thought she might try that iridescent sand color on the trays. And the cups? With their wide mouths and fluted edges, the cups would look just like seashells with handles if she used the pearly blue glaze she loved. If you set a pair of those cups on a tray, it would be like holding shells on a small piece of beach in your hands.

Ava was so absorbed in her work that she didn't hear anyone

approaching until she was startled by the slam of the screen door to the studio. She glanced up to find Simon standing across the table from her, staring at her with eyes a shade darker than the blue glaze she'd been imagining on the cups. She blinked hard, thinking maybe she'd imagined him, conjured Simon out of her own longing.

He must have come from his office in Boston. He was wearing a charcoal suit over a shirt so white that it gleamed, and an expensive-looking green tie patterned with silver leaves. He looked both like a stranger and like a man she'd known all her life.

"You shouldn't be here," Ava said, thinking, *I want you.*

"I couldn't help it," Simon said. "I was having lunch with a client and I couldn't make myself go back to the office without seeing you."

"Why?" Ava stared at him, her hands dripping cold sludge. She shouldn't see him. This was impossible. Yet, now that Simon was here, she wanted to hold him and never let him go.

"Why do you think?" Simon laughed, a rough sound as gritty as clay. "Ava, you're driving me crazy. I have to know the truth. Did you really mean what you said last night, that you can't see me anymore? That I shouldn't call you? Is that what you honestly need? Say the word, and I will leave you alone. But I need to hear it in broad daylight."

She sighed. "You know it's not what I want. But it's the best thing—the *only* thing—we can do right now. What would your sister think if she knew about us? Or Elaine? And I can't even imagine how confused Gigi would feel about us."

Simon's face had paled, but his eyes, slate blue and shining with pain, stayed on hers. "You're absolutely right," he said. "It would be hard on everyone."

"Then you should leave," Ava said.

He continued to stand on the opposite side of the table, his hands loose at his sides, looking at her. "The day we walked on the beach, that very first day?" he said. "I couldn't look at the ocean. I felt like I was drowning in your eyes. It scared me, that pull. And now that I know you better, I feel it even more. But all I want to do is keep drowning. I need to be with you, Ava. What do you need?"

Ava saw him then, really saw Simon in a way she never had before. Just as she sometimes stood on the beach in the fog, and the fog would suddenly lift enough for her to take in the sharper details of the landscape, she looked into Simon's face and became fully aware of him. He stood almost within reach, warm and solid and yearning. Yearning for her, just as she longed for him.

She felt a sharp pain beneath her rib cage. "Everything is too complicated. I don't know what I need."

"Yes, you do. You need me," Simon said. "Just a little." He began walking slowly around the table, coming toward her.

Ava held up her hands. "Don't touch me. You'll get clay on your suit."

He laughed. "That's the reason you don't want me to touch you? Hell, I'd gladly *wear* a clay suit if you'd let me hold you a minute, Ava." He closed the gap between them.

Ava let Simon pull her close, but kept her arms folded between them. Pressed against her breasts, her arms were a flesh-and-bone shield that served only to make her want him more.

"We can't do this," Ava said. "Not now. Maybe not ever."

"I know," he murmured into her hair, then tipped her head up and kissed her.

His mouth was warm on hers. For a moment, Ava forgot everything—the clay on her hands and arms, the studio around her, the sound of the surf beyond, her brother and sisters and sons—as she gave herself over to the feel of Simon's soft lips and muscular body pressed against her own, anchoring her, giving her a reason to be right here, right now, fully in the moment. Embraced, embracing.

"So where's your cause of the day?" Elaine asked when Gabe met her by the newsstand in Harvard Square. He was dressed in a black V-neck T-shirt and plaid shorts. Still in sandals, though at least he hadn't paired them with socks.

"Right here." Gabe turned around. On the back of his T-shirt was a shield with words in white cursive letters printed inside it: *A Cure Is Our Battle Cry.*

"What is it?" she asked, squinting to read the letters. "Cancer?"

He nodded.

"Well, that covers just about everybody," Elaine said as they began walking toward the sushi place above Staples. She could never remember the name of the restaurant, but it would be just the thing for tonight. The decor was casual, the prices were cheap, the sushi was decent, and they could be in and out in under an hour.

She had planned on stopping off at one of the pubs to grab a drink by herself once she and Gabe said good-bye, but seeing him brought back her memories of that Boston fiasco. Maybe this would be a good night to stick to tea and go home early. That way she could prove to Gabe—and to Tony—that she wasn't a complete head case.

The night was rapidly cooling; good thing she'd brought the black cardigan she kept in her office. She slipped the sweater on over her sleeveless white blouse. She was wearing black pants; in this outfit, she felt like a choir girl, sober and upright in black and white. Her only real concession to fashion was a pair of pink platform sandals with straps that wrapped around her ankles. She felt like a gladiator when she wore them, which made up for the choir girl top half.

They talked about the stores and restaurants in Harvard Square, some of them places they'd both first discovered as college students. Gabe had grown up in Washington, D.C., and graduated from Boston University two years before Elaine left Tufts to care for her mother, a fact she mentioned but glossed over.

It was amazing how much Harvard Square had changed yet remained the same, they agreed, with its mix of preppy undergrads, homeless people, pot smokers in wishful dreadlocks, and out-of-tune buskers with instruments that ranged from guitars to didgeridoos.

Her sandals weren't ideally suited to the hallowed, pitted sidewalks of Harvard Square. Twice Elaine pitched forward and had to grab Gabe's arm. He finally looped his arm around her waist. "How much pregame time did you do tonight?"

She jabbed him with an elbow. "Relax. I've had nothing to drink all day but coffee. These are just really dumb shoes."

"Ah." Gabe glanced down at her feet. "But they're pink. That must make up for them being so dumb." They had gotten on the escalator; at the top of it he stopped and stared at the restaurant window. "This place? Really?"

"What's wrong with sushi?" she demanded. Elaine had brought dates here before; in her experience, most men didn't care about dinner, only what might happen afterward. Dinner was merely foreplay.

"Sushi's not really a meal," Gabe said. "Three hours after having sushi, I want to eat again because I've had nothing but cold balls of rice and fish. I'm still hungry, but it's too late because I've already spent too much money."

"I'm paying," she pointed out. "You won't have spent any money at all."

He gave her a look. "That's hardly the point. Also, this particular sushi palace feels like a high school cafeteria. I'm too old to eat at an orange plastic table with green plastic chairs. If I wanted to do that, I'd work in a day care center."

Elaine stepped away from him and glared. "My, my. Somebody took his snarky pills today. Fine, Mr. Picky. Where do you want to go?"

"Just because I don't like a place doesn't mean I'm picky. Though I do admit to being something of a foodie," Gabe added. "Meals are more than just fuel for me. Dinner, especially, should count as a daily ritual, now that we've experienced the downfall of religion as a cornerstone of Western civilization."

"Good God. *Fine.* Just quit yammering and choose someplace else," Elaine said. She'd had only salad for lunch and didn't want to think about food as ritual. For her, food was mostly a temptation she battled every day, with every fiber of her being. The minute she caved and was forced into elastic-waist pants, the uniform of her generation, her life might as well be over. "Look, just to be clear, this is not a date," she added. "I only wanted to take you out to a nice dinner to say thank you for the other night," she said. "Sorry you're so insulted."

Gabe gave her arm a squeeze. "I'm not! I'm delighted that you called, despite being somewhat despondent that you don't see me as date potential. Even so, is a cheap college sushi bar really your idea of a nice thank-you? I mean, honestly?"

Honestly, Elaine was beginning to wish she could summon a cab, go home, take off these stupid shoes, and gorge on wine and cashews for dinner. But that would hardly pay off her debt to this man.

"Look, I just picked this place because I know it," she said. "I hardly ever come to Harvard Square anymore. So why don't you take us someplace else, but it'll still be my treat."

"What if it's too expensive?"

"I make good money! Probably more than you do, judging from your wardrobe. If you really wanted me to take you someplace decent, then you should have dressed accordingly!"

"What? This is my formal T-shirt!" Gabe tried to look wounded. This act might have been convincing—his brown eyes were sorrowful and long-lashed, like the eyes of those greyhounds PETA used in their commercials to shut down the Wonderland Dog Track—except then he started to laugh, a snorting that he tried to smother with one hand. In a few seconds he was doubled over, laughing so hard that he started to wheeze.

Then Elaine was laughing, too, wiping tears from her eyes and saying, "None of this is funny!" when, really, it was: the absurdity of his stupid save-the-world clothing and her stupid pink shoes, their mismatched ideas about food. She hadn't laughed this hard in forever.

They kept trying to catch a breath, then failing because the other was still laughing. Eventually, Elaine had to lean against the wall outside the sushi restaurant and swab the mascara out from under her eyes.

"Here, clown face, you missed a spot." Gabe helped her with a tissue, concentrating so hard that a frown line appeared above his glasses. Afterward, he led her to Henrietta's Table, a restaurant in the Charles Hotel with French bistro tables and locally grown food. "Simple, good meals," he promised.

He ordered a pork chop with mashed potatoes. Elaine was going to stick with spinach salad, but Gabe coerced her into ordering roast chicken and Elaine found herself savoring every mouthful. She even did serious damage to a side dish of risotto with mushrooms. She suddenly felt much happier, even relaxed.

"Yum. I'm such a barbarian," she said, gnawing on a chicken leg. "You bring out the worst in me. I swear I've never eaten two pieces of toast until breakfast at your place."

"Then you should eat breakfast at my house more often." Gabe signaled the waiter and ordered coffee and a slice of blueberry pie. "You obviously don't eat enough." He gestured at her figure.

She bristled. "What's wrong with the way I look? I'm very fit."

"I'm sure you are," Gabe said mildly. "But I can also see your ribs under that shirt. One strong wind and you'd be on the other side of Harvard Yard."

"I've always been thin. I can really put food away, in case you hadn't noticed." She gestured at the pile of bones on her plate, picked clean. "I love to eat."

Gabe patted his own belly. "Me, too."

"Yeah, I can see that." At the shadow of hurt in his eyes, she quickly added, "But you look good the way you are."

"Right, I'm sure you think so," he said, then busied himself with the coffee and pie.

"I mean it." Elaine touched his hand.

Gabe still didn't meet her eyes. "Thanks." He asked her about work then, and she talked about college marketing, something she seldom did. She tried to be honest about it, to make up for hurting his feelings with that stupid food remark. She admitted she'd never imagined herself in marketing, but was glad to be selling education, and proud to have created new identities for certain struggling but worthy colleges.

He continued to ask questions: about her childhood in Newburyport, her parents' divorce, her decision to live in Boston. Elaine even told him about her father's battle with cancer and her resentment, intense and irrational and totally petty as it was, toward Katy and Gigi.

One question seemed to naturally lead Gabe to ask another. It was flattering but unnerving to see how deftly he managed to turn the conversation back in her direction just as she was ready to ask him something in return.

Elaine kept her eyes on his face. Seated across the table from Gabe and being neither drunk nor hungover—he'd suggested they stick to water and tea rather than order wine, and she'd gritted her teeth but concluded it was probably a good idea to prove that she could do without alcohol—she enjoyed looking at him. At his eyes, mostly: they were so warm, the brown irises shot through with gold and green. Gabe's prominent nose was the right shape for his long face, too. She even admired the silver in his brown curls.

Gabe, unlike most of the younger men she'd gone home with in the past few years, looked like a man who had experienced regret as well as joy, taken risks and been sorry. He was kind, too, even to their clueless waiter, an elderly man who twice brought the wrong items to the table.

Perfect, she thought again, for Ava. "How did you like my sister?" she asked as he finished his pie.

"Ava? She's lovely. You're lucky. I wish I had siblings."

Elaine nodded. "We don't always see eye to eye, but Ava was like a second mother to me growing up. You should get to know her."

"I'd like that." Gabe picked up his coffee cup and sipped. "If you're trying to play Cupid, however, you're aiming at the wrong target. Missed by a mile."

"Why? She's smart, gorgeous, generous to a fault." Elaine made a deliberate show of lifting the tablecloth to look at Gabe's sandals. "You even shop at the same shoe store."

He tossed his napkin onto the table, signaling for the check. "Our shoes can date, then, but sorry. That's it."

Elaine felt defensive on Ava's behalf. "Why? You'd be good together."

Gabe gave her an impatient look, pulled a credit card out of his wallet, and handed it to the waiter before Elaine could reach for her purse. "Ava's a nice person, I'm sure, but I'm not equipped to take on two teenaged boys."

"Hey, this was supposed to be my treat," Elaine protested.

"Forget it. I chose the restaurant," Gabe said, waving a hand. "You can take me out next time."

As if there would be one, Elaine thought. "I wouldn't have expected you, of all people, to be child-averse," she said. "Why would Ava's kids put you off?"

"I know my limits." Gabe stood and offered his elbow to escort her out of the dining room. She ignored the gesture and walked ahead of him. Out on the sidewalk, though, he took her arm anyway and said, "What made you think I'd be gaga over kids?"

"You adopted a cat."

Gabe tipped his head back and howled. "That's it? I have a *cat*? That's proof of my potential parenting prowess?"

Elaine was trying not to laugh, but it was difficult. Gabe's laugh was a deep rumble, a little rough, and very infectious; she caught people smiling at them as they passed. "Not just any cat. A homeless cat," she said. "You're a natural caretaker. I can't believe you don't have a litter of your own kids already."

"How do you know I don't?"

They had stopped to cross the street, though Elaine had no idea where they were headed. "Oh," she said, startled. "I'm sorry. Do you? Were you married before? I never asked you that, did I?"

Gabe shook his head. "No. Never married. No kids. But never assume."

She was offended that he would think she was the sort of person who went around judging other people. Not because he was wrong, but because she hated that about herself. "And you're how old?"

"Thirty-nine," he said. "You?"

She stiffened. "Younger than you."

He patted her hand. "By what, a week?"

"Shut up!"

"No, seriously. How old are you?" The light turned but Gabe held her in place, his arm still linked through hers.

Elaine sighed. "Thirty-six."

"All right, so I was off by a couple of years."

Tears sprang to Elaine's eyes, unexpected and unwelcome. "Do I really look that old?"

"Don't be an idiot. I can't tell how old you are. I Googled you."

"Jesus. You're sick."

"No. Just careful about who I choose to see."

*Unlike you.* That was what Gabe wasn't saying, and it made Elaine furious.

The light changed again. This time Gabe led her across the street and toward the gates to Harvard Yard. The buildings were dark, the dorms unoccupied at the height of August, the ancient trees looming around them.

"I still don't understand," Elaine said. "Why wouldn't you date a woman with children?"

"You still don't know what I do for a living, do you?"

"No. So tell me already."

"You really want to know?"

God, this man's mind games were exhausting. "Not really, no," she said. "I hate defining people by their jobs, just like I hate being defined by mine. And, truthfully? I can already guess by looking at your sandals. And by your T-shirts, which shout their slogans and make me feel guilty for not saving the baby seals or whatever."

"Oh, I see. Clothes make the man. Or unmake me, in your eyes."

"That's not what I meant," she said, though it was.

"All right, so what do I do? Go ahead and guess."

This was too easy. "You're a social worker or a teacher."

Gabe led her to the steps of Widener Library, where they sat next to each other on the chilly stone. "Pretty good. I taught at an alternative high school right after graduating from college, and then I became a social worker. But I'm not doing that anymore."

Exasperated, Elaine wanted to slap Gabe's knee the way she had Tony's earlier today, which led her once again to think about how her best friend and this man had so many qualities in common, yet couldn't be more different.

She took a white tissue out of her purse and waved it in front of Gabe's face. "I give up! Uncle! Aunt! Grandmother! Whatever you want me to say, I concede! Just tell me. What the hell do you do for a living?"

"I'm a judge," Gabe said.

Elaine nearly fell off the step. "You are *not*." She stuffed the tissue back into her purse.

"I am! I *used* to be a social worker," he said. "I worked for the Department of Children and Families for a while after earning my MSW. When I got tired of that, I went to law school. I was named to the bench two years ago. Now, before you get all impressed and deferential . . ."

". . . which I would never," Elaine said.

Gabe smiled. "Which is why I like you. But let's put it out there:

I'm only a juvenile court judge. So forget about me fixing your parking tickets."

The weird thing was, despite suffering a brain cramp whenever she tried to picture Gabe in a black robe instead of a T-shirt, she could easily imagine him talking to kids about their mistakes, working with parents and social workers. He was a caretaker, yes, but one with authority. "Let's see your judge face," she said.

Gabe furrowed his brow and peered down at her over his glasses, tightening his mouth. "Do you have anything to say on your behalf, young lady?"

"Ouch!" she said. "I think you just burned a hole in my forehead."

"Yes, well, now you'll be more accountable for your actions, won't you?"

"I will," she promised, smiling. Then she thought of something. "Wait. But why were you at home on that Monday morning I was at your apartment? And again when I called today?"

He shrugged. "I never take vacations, but I have to use up the days before the end of December. So I take most Mondays off. And that's when I try to do volunteer work for the causes I believe in." He pointed at the back of his own T-shirt.

"You're one of the good guys," Elaine summarized. "Not a capitalist barfly like me. See, that's why you'd be perfect for Ava. She's a teacher and an artist, and she loves saving people like my wayward half sister. My nephews are really wonderful, you know," she added loyally.

"I'm sure they're great. But, even if I were interested in Ava—which I'm not, lovely as she is—I have zero interest in being a replacement father, especially to teen boys."

"Ouch. That sounds pretty harsh." Elaine stood up; the stone step was chilly on her bare legs and it was getting late.

"Just being honest."

"I know. It's fine. Really. Ava's probably too busy to date now anyway, because she's trying to find our brother."

Gabe linked his arm through hers again as they walked back toward the Harvard Square T stop. "What do you mean? What brother?"

"Exactly what I said." Elaine filled him in as they crossed the street and began threading their way through the crowds outside the Harvard Coop.

"Sounds like your heart's not in the search," Gabe said once she'd finished. By now, they were standing by the frozen yogurt place near the subway entrance. A group of teen girls jostled around them, squealing as they passed a phone around and took pictures of themselves.

"It's not," Elaine admitted. "I hope we never find him, actually."

She had expected Gabe to be critical, but again he surprised her. "I don't blame you," he said.

"You don't?"

He shook his head. "You've just lost your father. You're an orphan now. That's a mind-blowing event. It means there's one less layer between us and whatever we think the hereafter has waiting for us. We all grieve that enormous rift in our own ways. Ava's way might be to reach out and collect whatever new pieces of your dad she can find, while you guard yourself against fresh emotional onslaughts."

"Thank you," Elaine said.

"For what?"

"For helping me feel normal. I don't always feel normal around Ava. She's so much better at coping with life than I am."

"That's probably an illusion," Gabe said. "We all have our soft underbellies. Ava just might not show hers as often as you do yours."

Elaine looked up at him and was startled again by the warmth in his eyes. "Funny. I would have said my soft underbelly is completely crusted over by now."

"*There's* a lovely image," Gabe said, making her laugh.

She smiled, but wondered if he was right. Was she going soft? It was true that she'd felt more vulnerable lately. Before her father died, she had been living her life as if she'd figured everything out—work, family, friendships, even hot sex. Now everything felt precarious, even her relationship with Ava—always her true north.

"Hey." Gabe nudged her. "Why the glum face?" He pushed the subway turnstile for her and led the way to the inbound tracks. The air was immediately thick, hot, and rank.

"I was wondering if I'd regret not helping Ava and Gigi with their search," Elaine said, "and worrying about what will happen if they do find Peter and tell him I was against it."

"You're worrying about things that haven't even happened yet. I'm sure you'll handle everything fine if you just take it slowly. Especially if you stay sober."

Gabe might as well have slapped her. Elaine felt her face burn and stopped walking so abruptly that he nearly ran into her. "Is that what this whole night was about?" she demanded. "A chance to issue some tired platitudes about the dangers of alcohol? Look, I'm not one of your juvies. Just because you get to play God on the bench doesn't mean you can do it on a date."

"I'm sorry. That wasn't my intent." Gabe held up both hands. "And I thought this wasn't a date, only a thank-you dinner."

"It was! But you didn't even give me the courtesy of accepting!" Elaine wobbled on her sandals but pulled away from Gabe and stepped out of reach. "You paid for dinner, so now you think you can tell me how to live my life. Sorry. It doesn't work that way. I don't owe you a thing."

"I know you don't." Gabe's voice dropped in pitch and become deliberately soothing, the way Ava's voice used to dip when she had to calm her boys in the middle of tantrums. "Look, Elaine, I'm certainly not telling you how to live your life. I've just seen you get into trouble because you drink too much, so I worry."

Elaine was infuriated by Gabe's tone—how dare he condescend to her?—and about what amounted to a blanket judgment on her lifestyle. Sure, she was having a little trouble staying grounded now, maybe, but that was temporary.

"What is it you worry about?" she asked sweetly. "About me being an alcoholic and a sex addict besides?"

Gabe's mouth twitched. "Come on. Did I say anything about sex? Has there been a single word uttered about sex this entire evening?"

"No, and that's my point," Elaine declared. "I thought you liked me. Clearly, I was wrong."

"You don't know anything about what I feel because you don't *ask*," Gabe said.

"You didn't give me a chance! You were in trial attorney mode, grilling me all night!" Elaine said. "You think I'm on guard to protect my underbelly? Have you examined your own behavior lately, Judge Blaustein?" She was shouting now. People on the subway platform had turned to stare. Good. Maybe the judge's photograph would be in tomorrow's *Boston Globe*. That would teach him to patronize her.

Gabe was still trying to reason with her when the train rattled into the station, the cars too brightly lit, the passengers inside them looking as waxy as mannequins on the molded plastic seats. They stepped into the car together, but just as the doors started to slide shut, Elaine slipped back onto the platform.

She waved at Gabe's startled face as the train left the station. If she needed a lecture, she'd rather get one from her sister. At least Ava loved her. Most of the time, anyway.

There were a couple of new kids at band practice. The boy looked slightly familiar and the girl was totally crushing on Sam. *Good luck with that,* Gigi thought. Sam didn't seem to care about anything except his guitar and lacrosse.

She took a break after singing "Highway to Hell," a song that felt amazing to belt but always made her throat hurt like she'd swallowed toothpicks. She went into the kitchen for a drink of water and a slice of pizza. Gigi had no clue how much boys ate until hanging with Evan and Sam. By now, she'd learned to grab a slice of pizza early, before the boys inhaled the entire box.

Tonight she was surprised to come into the kitchen and see Ava on the patio, talking to Les's mother, who wore funky green eyeglasses and a sundress but otherwise looked exactly like Les, dumpy and short, with rabbity teeth.

Gigi took a slice of pizza and watched Ava wave good-bye to Les's mom. Then Ava disappeared, shoving her hands into her pockets as she headed for the studio. Gigi resisted the urge to follow her. She had asked Ava earlier today whether she'd heard from the adoption registry. Ava said they hadn't found a match; Gigi wasn't exactly surprised, but she was definitely disappointed.

"So what are we going to do now?" she'd asked Ava as they loaded the kiln together this afternoon.

"I don't know. Maybe nothing," Ava had said.

A completely unacceptable answer, in Gigi's opinion, but still, she'd kept the visit to Cousin Mildred to herself. Even her mother hadn't figured out she'd gone to Portsmouth. What would be the point of telling them what she knew, that Dad had married Mom because she was pregnant? That she was the real reason Elaine had been stuck taking care of Suzanne, and Evan and Sam's time with their grandfather had been shortchanged? The boys didn't seem resentful of this—they always acted like it was no biggie that their grandfather had run off with Katy—but Gigi thought maybe that was because boys just didn't obsess about relationships the way girls did. What if Evan and Sam knew the truth, though, that their grandparents might have stayed together if it hadn't been for her? The idea of having them angry with her made Gigi dizzy with fear.

She went over the day in her mind again as she wiggled another pizza slice out of the box on Ava's kitchen counter. She had done her jobs the way she usually did in the studio. The band had practiced as usual. Nothing was different.

Nothing, that is, except Ava, who kept looking distracted and shut herself in her bedroom at odd times to talk on the phone, something she had never done until a few weeks ago. Who was she talking to, that she had to keep their conversations so private?

Maybe Ava had a secret boyfriend. Gigi hoped he wasn't secret because he was married or something weird like that.

*Ava's a grown-up,* she reminded herself. Adults did things for weird reasons that had nothing to do with their children. Kids orbited adult fields of gravity, being pulled along through the confusing adult universe without having any control over the direction or speed of the changes in their lives.

This led Gigi to wonder what her own mom did when she was alone, and whether she'd find a boyfriend, too, after a few years. She hoped so. Mom needed more people around, since Gigi definitely planned on moving to New York or Denver or Hollywood, somewhere with a cool music scene. She hated the idea of Mom being lonely and sad without her.

The patio was empty now, the breeze off the ocean sticky and fishy smelling. Must be low tide. Gigi was drawn outside by the soothing sound of the surf to sit on one of the Adirondack chairs, hoping the air would clear her muddled thoughts. Her ears were ringing from the music. Maybe she should wear earplugs when she sang, like everybody said. But then it was so hard to really *feel* the music.

The beach was empty, the light compressed to a silver arrow along the horizon, the last flinty bit of heat in the sky before night swallowed the ocean. Gigi thought she'd never loved anywhere as much as she loved Beach Plum Island. She wished Dad could be here right now, to see this sky.

Dad used to always wake her up in the middle of the night if there was a comet or a meteor shower, or sometimes just because it was a clear night. They'd lie on the ground even in winter to watch the sparks shooting across the sky. Her dad's deep voice rumbled as he pointed out the constellations, Venus glowing like a diamond chip, Mars a foggy red, shooting stars, the Milky Way. The two of them would lie shoulder to shoulder under the big afghan from the living room couch, like they were trapped beneath a sparkling glass bowl.

"We're swimming in the night soup," Dad always said.

Gigi's eyes welled. *Shit.* She couldn't stop missing him, because she didn't know how to fill all the holes in her life he had left behind.

Someone cleared his throat behind her. Gigi whipped her head around.

It was that boy who'd come in halfway through the first set with Sarah, the girl being so obvious about wanting to hook up with Sam. He and Sarah must be brother and sister; they had the same angular faces, beaky noses and sharp chins, like their faces had been chiseled out of rock.

Sarah wore her light brown hair wound in a complicated braid halfway down her back. This kid's hair was darker, but almost as long as his sister's and twisted into dreadlocks. He'd tamed it with a red bandanna and wore a blue earring shaped like a crescent moon in one ear.

"Wow. Sick spot." The boy was holding a slice of pizza in one hand, a glass of lemonade in the other. "You surf out there?" He gestured with his chin.

"I can barely swim out there," she admitted.

"Yeah, I hear you. The island's got a gnarly undertow. I usually take my board to Salisbury."

The boy perched on the back step of Ava's house. Instead of looking at each other, they both stared out at the surf. They could hear the water but couldn't see it, other than an occasional white flutter, as if someone were running and pulling a long white ribbon across the sand.

"I'm Neal, by the way," the boy said. "Sarah's brother. My mom made me drive her over here so she could hear your band."

"That was nice of you."

Neal turned his head toward Gigi. "I didn't want to do it. I'm not that nice, usually, at least not to my sister, but I'm glad I did. You were really rockin' up there. Smoking-hot voice. I'm seriously not kidding."

She laughed. "Why would I think you were?"

"Hey. Guys say whatever they think other people want to hear sometimes, right? Especially girls. But I'm not into that." Neal ate the pizza slice in three bites, never taking his eyes off her face. Then he said, "I know you. Just not your name."

"You do? I'm Gigi. My sister is Sam's mom, Ava." Gigi wiped her hands on the napkin and balled it up, tossed it into Ava's fire pit. Saying Ava was her sister sounded a lot less weird than saying Sam and Evan were her nephews. Let people work that out for themselves.

"Yeah, I know you from the barn. You're that girl who's really good with horses."

"No, I'm not," Gigi said, startled. "You're probably mixing me up with somebody else. I'm the girl who quit summer camp and can hardly even ride after five years of torturing myself with lessons." She steeled herself, waiting for Neal to say something about Lydia or Justin, but he didn't.

"No, you're definitely the one," Neal said. "I've seen the horses talk to you."

Gigi got up off the chair and joined him on the step to see Neal's face better in the fading light. She had always thought the horses talked to her, too, but she never would have admitted it. "When?" she asked, narrowing her eyes so Neal would know he couldn't prank her.

"Dude, I work at the barn. You and your friends just don't notice me."

Her *friends*? Ha! She didn't have any friends at the barn. In fact, Gigi had only had one real friend before Evan and Sam: Kirsten, and she was camping with her family in New Hampshire practically all summer.

Suddenly, studying the boy's face, she did remember Neal. He looked different with that bandanna over his head; usually he pulled his dreads into a ponytail at the stables and wore a weird brimmed hat with a feather. "You're the guy who mucks out the stalls and tacks up horses for lessons, right?"

Neal smiled, his teeth as white and square as Chiclets. "One of them, yeah. Sometimes I exercise horses for people who are away, too. My parents don't belong to the club, but Jessica gives me enough hours to pay for lessons."

"You mean Jessica the Robot?" The words were out before Gigi could stop herself.

Neal tipped his head back and laughed. "Yeah, that's her. She's my cousin. That's why she hired me. She's pretty nice, actually. She only acts like such a be-atch because the girls at the club are so friggin' full of themselves, you know?" He spread his hands. "The moms are even worse."

Gigi supposed he was right. The women at the club were a tough crowd. Still, after being around Ava, Gigi wasn't so sure you had to be nasty to put people in their places. She'd seen Ava turn Sam's rowdiest lacrosse friends to stone with one sideways look.

"So do you compete?" she asked.

Neal rolled his eyes. "As if. I can barely stay in the saddle. I mainly like to ride the trails. Hey, we should go together sometime. I could borrow a horse. Lots of peeps are away this month and want some flunky to exercise their beasts."

"Sure, I guess," Gigi said, thinking how odd it was to have a boy look at her like this, like she was actually worth paying attention to.

"Cool." Neal's smile, nice enough before, widened now. "Ready to get back in there?" He stood up and offered his hand to her with his palm open, as if he were going to catch raindrops or snowflakes in it.

Gigi hesitated, then put her hand in his and let Neal pull her to her feet.

## CHAPTER TWELVE

Despite Gigi's help, she'd still fallen behind on her gallery deadlines. Ava worked through the night and into the early morning, trimming, glazing, and finally loading the kiln.

It was often daunting to look at the bisqued pots on her shelves, knowing she still had to mix the glazes and dip the pots into them or pour on the glaze. Glazing was exhausting because it required her to be on her feet so much, and the studio floor was cement. For once, though, she was grateful for the hours of labor, for the way it cleansed her mind.

Each kiln load held nearly five thousand dollars' worth of pots, she'd calculated once. Ava imagined it was even more now that her work had been reviewed in several magazines and commanded higher prices. In any case, it typically took her half a week to glaze a full kiln load, but this time she managed to finish it in a single long day. Afterward, she turned on the kiln and made up the futon in the studio.

It was hot with the kiln going. She slept in her underwear, wrapped only in a sheet, and set the alarm to wake her every two hours to check the pyrometer and temperature cones. She stayed in the studio until the firing was complete, then shut off the kiln and went outside.

She had lost all track of time. It was just after sunrise, but what day?

Ava wandered a little way down the beach, where the air was raw and damp and fishy. Fog lay over the shoreline. She imagined it as a gray shawl tossed over Beach Plum Island as she walked a little more, wondering where Elaine had spent the night, then returned to the house.

She had intended to clean today, but the house defeated her before she began. Dust bunnies had morphed into dust buffaloes roaming the floor. Dishes cluttered every horizontal surface, and the floors were gritty with sand. She had always hated this never-ending stream of chores, even knowing it helped define her as a mother, and had helped justify her existence through the years whenever she felt doubts about her art, her teaching, herself.

Furiously, Ava made coffee and poured cereal into a chipped blue bowl she should have thrown away, slamming cupboard doors. She wanted to wake Sam and Evan to yell at them to clean up after themselves. At the same time, she wanted the kitchen to herself.

The boys slept through the noise like coma victims. She never would have predicted this, given that both boys were cranky infants and toddlers who thought five a.m. was a fine time to wake up, but then teen hormones kicked in and drugged them. Left to their own devices, her sons would stay up until four a.m. and sleep until noon. It was like living with vampires.

Ava sighed. She really couldn't keep letting them trash the house with their friends. Elaine was right: she had enabled her sons by being too kind, too forgiving, instead of instilling the sort of army barracks discipline that would make them grow up tough and independent.

What was the phrase Elaine used? The boys suffered from "learned helplessness." That was it.

"Think of their poor wives," Elaine always said. "You've got to train Evan and Sam right, Ava, or they'll be divorced before they're thirty because nobody will want to live with them."

Hearing Elaine criticize her—even in her own mind—made Ava even angrier. As if Elaine knew one thing about motherhood!

And where was her sister, anyway? Ava wondered, searching for her car keys under the piles of newspapers and magazines drifting across the kitchen table. She hadn't heard a thing from her in days. She hoped Elaine wasn't drinking or off screwing some stranger who'd slit her throat in the middle of the night.

Self-absorbed and spoiled, that's what her sister was, no better than Evan and Sam. Elaine had no idea how her behavior impacted other people, or what it was like to put somebody else first.

*Except Mom,* a tiny voice trumpeted inside Ava's left temple, giving her a sharp headache. *Elaine took care of Mom, not you.*

Finally, car keys located, Ava headed for the grocery store, intent on leaving the mess in the kitchen behind along with her worries about her children and her sister. Once on the road, all she wanted to do was keep driving south—to Boston, to Simon, to a life other than the one she was living right now, where memories of her parents kept rising up with the power to literally knock her legs out from under her.

Yesterday she'd seen an older man, tall and broad and silver-haired like her father, wearing the same khaki shorts Dad wore on weekends, and she'd felt her knees turn to jelly. And everyone, it seemed, had adopted her mother's lavender-scented hand cream. "You can always tell a woman's age by her hands," Mom used to say.

Why hadn't she spent more time with either of them?

Ava stared at her own strong, callused hands on the steering wheel. Anyone who noticed her hands would think she was a hundred years old. She *felt* a hundred years old. She couldn't cope with this grief, much less with the energy it was taking to locate her brother, this chronic anxiety about what might happen if they found him, or the deep sadness and irrational fury she felt toward Elaine for shutting her out.

Maybe it was time for her to just corner her sister in Boston, to insist that Elaine have dinner with her.

Ava had pulled into the parking lot of the grocery store when her cell phone rang. She unrolled the window—there was still a cool breeze, despite the heat promised for later today—and picked up the phone, answering only because she saw it was Mark.

There was a time, soon after the divorce, when she and Mark had talked on the phone almost daily, making arrangements for the boys and catching up on each other's lives. But he called so rarely now, preferring instead to communicate directly with the boys by texting them, that Ava knew he must have something important to tell her.

"Hey," he said. "Hope I'm not interrupting a masterpiece in progress."

Ava bit her lip to keep her temper in check. To Mark, a busy civil engineer whose paychecks had been doled out by the same big corporation for nearly twenty years, her decision to go back to school after the kids were born to earn her teaching degree had been a rational one. Yet he still couldn't wrap his mind around the idea that, besides being a teacher, she was a potter with her own studio and gallery shows. Mark was apt to start a conversation by saying, "So, are you still playing with clay?" as if pottery were a passing phase in her life instead of a lifelong passion.

On the other hand, one reason their divorce had been amicable was that both of them managed to sidestep small irritations and focus on the boys. She took a minute to remind herself that Mark was a good person and a loving father. She didn't have to try, anymore, to convince him that artwork *is* work.

"Nope, no masterpieces," she said. "Not unless you call my grocery list a novel, which it nearly is these days. The boys are eating anything not nailed down."

Mark chuckled, but his laughter sounded forced. "Listen, I won't keep you. I was just calling to arrange to talk to you in person about something."

Ava's mouth went dry. Mark never asked to see her. "What about?"

"I'd rather discuss it face-to-face."

"All right." Ava's mind raced, sorting through possibilities, none of them good: Mark had cancer; he'd lost his job; his mother was dying; one of the boys was in trouble but hadn't told her yet. "Can you give me a hint, at least? How worried should I be?"

There was a brief silence; then Mark sighed. "God. I'm sorry. I should have known better than to do this by phone. No, it's nothing terrible, Ava. I'll just come out with it, and then if you want, we can discuss it later. Or not."

By now, Ava was shivering with nerves in the hot car. "Okay. Tell me."

"I'm thinking of asking Sasha to move in with me."

Ava nearly laughed; she was so relieved that Mark's news didn't include any of the catastrophes she'd imagined. Almost immediately, though, she felt the wind go out of her, as if someone had suddenly tightened the seat belt. She unbuckled it with fumbling fingers.

If Mark was telling her this now, he had probably already asked Sasha to marry him; he was never the sort of man to take relationships lightly. "Have you asked her yet?" Ava purposefully left the question vague.

"Not exactly."

She could tell by the strain in his voice that Mark was lying. He had asked and Sasha had said yes. He just hadn't wanted to spring it on her. Fair enough. Ava didn't like the idea that he might be lying; at the same time, she reminded herself that Mark didn't owe it to her to share his personal life and he was a good man who deserved to be with a woman who loved him more than she had.

So why did she feel this knot in her stomach?

"Ava?" Mark's voice was gentle. "You okay?"

"I'm fine," she said. "It's a surprise, but I'm glad for you. I really am. Sasha is a wonderful person. I hope you'll be happy together."

She could hear his sigh—relief? Then Mark said, "Listen, I haven't told the boys. Do you think we should tell them together?"

This request, too, was being made out of respect to her, Ava knew, and perhaps with Sasha—ever the lawyer—coaxing him to tread lightly. Sasha had seen the worst of the worst among broken families in divorce court.

"No," Ava said. "The boys will be fine. Tell them whenever you're ready. I'll let you know if there's any fallout at home."

"Okay. Thanks. I'll probably tell them next weekend. We'll talk before then."

They hung up. Ava wanted to turn on the engine and drive—drive anywhere from here, maybe straight to Simon's office or his sailboat. She longed to do something unexpected, unlike her usual practical self, in response to Mark's call. Having him live with Sasha would inevitably alter how easy things had always been between them. This was definitely shaky new territory.

In the grocery store, she squinted beneath the unforgiving buzz of fluorescent lights at the plastic-wrapped vegetables and artfully bewildering array of cans and boxes. She was in such a daze that she nearly collided with another shopper, a woman with two runny-nosed kids trapped and wailing in the metal cage of a shopping cart.

It was like running into a mirror of herself as a single mother long ago: Resentment clung to that young woman like a favorite threadbare sweater. Ava imagined her flipping the pages of her calendar at home in despair, thinking, *Maybe I'll try that other recipe for chicken breasts,* already knowing she wouldn't have the energy to be creative once she actually got the kids dressed, went to the store, came home to unload the groceries, fed the children, put them down for naps, and muscled the next load of laundry into the wash before starting dinner. In the end, they would all have cereal, maybe a banana.

So exhausting, the whole business of motherhood. It *was* a business, too, complete with compromises and disappointing returns for your investments, with budgets and schedules and task lists and surly underlings. As a single mother, Ava had resorted to locking the boys in their bedroom at night, fearing for their lives as much as for her own sanity. Otherwise Sam—the ringleader—would get up and start his little experiments, pulling out the kitchen drawers to use as steps to reach the high cupboards and pretending to cook, encouraging Evan to help.

Once, Sam had even turned on the stove, lighting the pilot with a match before climbing onto the stove to reach the flour in the cupboard above it. He'd burned his hand and was in a cast for weeks, often bloodying his own nose with the cast in sleep, which meant washing the sheets over and over again until Ava finally gave up and made him go to bed in an old sleeping bag. Afterward she'd just thrown the sleeping bag away. Sometimes Ava marveled that she'd managed to keep her kids from killing themselves.

"Alive at twenty-five." That was Olivia's motto with kids. "All you gotta do is keep 'em alive 'til then. At twenty-five, they finally get their brains handed to them on their birthdays and you can re-lax a little."

Ava had been horrified when Olivia said this to her the first time, but now she repeated this mantra often.

Mark's phone call had made her realize again that now it was nearly over, everything she had once considered her life: her marriage, motherhood, the rhythm she'd established in her life between work and pottery and family. Her life as a daughter had ended, too, with her father's death, and Elaine was slipping farther and farther away.

Soon the boys would be adults, out of the house and living their own adventures. Would they even come home on holidays, once they were entrenched in college, off to jobs, families of their own? Was a home with a single mother in a shabby beach cottage enough of a home to make the trip worth it? Maybe Evan and Sam would prefer being with Mark and Sasha, in a nice house with two parents ready to greet them.

*That's it. Stop the pity party. Blow out the candles and leave yourself alone!* Ava wanted to rap her own knuckles the way her piano teacher, an ancient barrel of a woman smelling of eucalyptus cough drops, used to do.

By the time she finished food shopping—she hardly bought any-thing but the usual staples, the things like bread and milk they seemed to need every hour with boys this size, yet spent over a hun-dred dollars—the pavement of the grocery store parking lot had al-ready softened in the heat, even though it was only eight o'clock in the morning. Ava had left her phone in the car where she'd tossed it onto the passenger seat after that distressing call from Mark. She glanced at the screen and saw a new text message from Olivia, ask-ing if she wanted to play tennis. Ava decided she did, even though it meant driving back across the bridge to the island to drop off her groceries, then collecting Olivia and returning to Newburyport to see if they could snag one of the shady courts at Atkinson Common.

Olivia had turned fifty last year. Today she wore spandex shorts and a T-shirt, but her usual outfit, even in summer, consisted of jeans, cowboy boots in various colors, and formfitting T-shirts. With her sleek curtain of waist-length dark hair streaked shamelessly gray, she looked like a woman who'd reached the right age at last and was enjoying every minute of it. She was tall and angular, graceful whether she was running after tennis balls or commanding a gallery show in her cowboy boots.

She was the one who had inspired Ava to pursue her career as an artist rather than just dabble outside of her teaching hours. Once an artist's model, Olivia had left art school to marry a Spanish painter who "drank and fucked around like Hemingway," she'd told Ava, "but never had the guts to shoot himself." She had three children with him, all grown and out of the house. She had left Spain, and the husband, when he took on a younger woman as a model and installed her in his studio nights as well as days.

Now Olivia did that rarest of things: managed to support herself as an artist. She had begun her career as an oil painter while she was an impoverished single mother, doing meticulously detailed miniature landscapes requiring only postcard-sized bits of canvas because that was all she could afford.

The miniatures were a hit with tourists. Olivia still did them to keep her income stream steady, but she'd graduated to larger paintings. Now her work was shown in dozens of New England galleries.

The tennis courts were empty. Olivia won the first set because of her aggressive net work and initial bursts of speed. Half an hour into the match, Ava had to wrap a bandanna around her forehead to keep her eyes free of the perspiration raining down her forehead.

Happily, playing tennis forced Ava's mind to be still. Dad had taught her to keep her eye on the ball by trying to read the letters on it. Soon there was nothing but the ball and her own breathing, her staccato pulse, because she knew if she lost her concentration, Olivia would come in for a kill, slamming an overhead.

Once she focused, Ava was able to take the next two sets by consistently lobbing over Olivia's head when her friend rushed the net and by aiming her returns at Olivia's weaker backhand. Afterward, they picked up bagels and coffee in Newburyport and drove back to the island.

Ava wasn't ready to face the mess at home. She drove instead to the lighthouse at the northern tip of the island. They parked and took the sandy path by the playground to the beach. Fishing boats and pleasure craft traveled through this channel from upriver, from the marinas in Newburyport and from as far away as Lowell, into the open sea.

On the opposite side of the river, they could see the crowded campground at Salisbury Beach. Cormorants ducked their gleaming black snake necks into the water or stood on buoys with wings outspread to dry. Ava spotted a lone seal drifting in the current.

Along the beach there were a few sunbathers and shell pickers, but hardly anyone swam here. The currents were too unpredictable. Every year, a few kayakers or fishermen were swept away by riptides or rogue waves and drowned.

They had left their sneakers in the car; Ava and Olivia ran gasping across the scorching soft yellow sand to the cooler plum-colored river's edge. They followed the river toward the breakwater. It had been a brutal year for erosion. Two spring hurricanes had damaged several houses at this end of the island severely enough that the buildings capsized like badly stacked children's blocks, toppling off their foundations and onto their sides. The police had cordoned off the area for weeks to keep looters and curious onlookers out of the abandoned properties. Now only rubble remained.

Residents of the island were searching for a sustainable solution to the erosion. Recent plans discussed at town hall meetings had included beach mining—scooping up sand at low tide and dumping it near the high-tide mark to rebuild the dunes—or using a system that relied on planting rows of thin cedar shims that might mimic the native beach vegetation by collecting and stabilizing windblown sand. Ava and Olivia talked about these ideas as they walked, dismissing both as improbable solutions. There would always be another, more powerful storm, they agreed.

"Seems crazy that anybody would build a house this close to the water after that last hurricane," Ava said.

"I know. I feel lucky to be on the basin side of the island," Olivia said. "And you're lucky your cottage is so high up on the beach and protected by dunes."

"Maybe it'll just wash away with me in it when I'm an old woman," Ava suggested. "Sometimes during those bad storms that's what I imagine, me in that ancient cottage, bobbing on the waves like it's a little gray boat."

"Worse ways to go, I suppose."

Ava followed her up the rocks to the flat part of the breakers, thinking about Beach Plum Island as a barrier island. The original settlers along this part of the Massachusetts North Shore had counted on the island to protect them from storms.

Now, four hundred years later, it seemed that Beach Plum Island was doomed to wash away. Oddly, this made Ava feel more connected to this small bit of land than ever. "I've never felt more like I belong on this island than right now," she told Olivia, wincing as they climbed the breakwater and the sharp edges of the rocks bit into her bare feet. "I'm old and eroded. Beaten up. All of my edges are changing shape."

She'd meant to joke, but Olivia knew her better than that. "What are you complaining about?" Olivia said. "You're hardly old and you're in great shape. You've got work you love, two sons who adore you, and an ex-husband who's less of a prick than most. Count yourself lucky."

"I do, mostly. But lately my life feels out of control," Ava said. "Everything is changing so fast, it's like I'm losing the ability to protect everybody I love from seismic shifts in our lives."

They settled with their bagels and coffees on a flat, sun-warmed rock midway down the breakwater. "What changes?" Olivia asked. "You mean the boys getting older and leaving home?"

"Partly. Evan and Sam drive me crazy, but I hate the idea of them leaving."

"They'll be back," Olivia said. "With laundry and empty bellies and cars that need fixing, I might add. Then you'll resent them for intruding on your new freedom."

"Maybe. But I still feel dismal about it all. It seems like the end of an era. The end of me feeling useful."

"And really, really tired," Olivia reminded her. "Don't forget that."

Ava laughed. "How could I? I hardly have the energy to match my own shoes in the morning."

She chewed her bagel for a minute, thinking about Simon and the conversation with Mark. Even with Olivia, she didn't dare talk about Simon. She couldn't risk Elaine finding out. Or Gigi.

"Mark called me this morning," she said. "He's going to move in with Sasha. Which, knowing him, means they're probably already engaged."

"Well, he lasted on his own longer than most men," Olivia said.

"And he's always been a good father, unlike some I won't name. *Enrique*." She jabbed her finger in the general direction of Spain across the Atlantic.

"I know. Mark is a genuinely nice guy, right? Maybe that's why the news hit me hard." Ava shook her head. "So weird. I've never had regrets about the divorce, so why do I mind this change so much?"

"Because it's a permanent separation," Olivia said. "You and Mark stayed so close after the divorce, it's like you were still married, just living in separate houses. I always admired that about you, but I did wonder how you kept yourself emotionally separate when your lives were so entangled."

"I don't know," Ava said. "It was such a relief when we started living apart that I wonder if I ever really loved Mark at all. Maybe Elaine was right, and I only married him to escape my parents."

"Well, so what? At least you were happy for a while. And now you're mourning him being with another woman. That must tell you something about your feelings for him."

"I know. It's just that, with everything that's happened since Dad died, I haven't quite trusted my emotions. They're all over the map. Like, I've been realizing how alone Elaine must have felt when I married Mark. And now, by hanging out with Gigi and looking for Peter, I don't know. It feels like I'm abandoning Elaine all over again."

"What makes you think she feels abandoned?"

"Elaine's on this self-destructive path lately, drinking and hooking up with guys. Her behavior reminds me of Mom's, with her bouts of drinking and depression."

"That's out of your control. Elaine's a big girl. How she behaves doesn't mean you should stop seeing Gigi or give up on looking for your brother. Elaine is probably just scared about having someone else in her life to care for, since things didn't go so well with your mom. But Elaine's not you."

"I'm scared, too," Ava said.

"You'd be stupid not to be scared. But you've always been stronger than Elaine. I know you'll be fine, no matter what."

Ava crumpled up her napkin and stuffed it into the empty coffee cup, then lay back on the rock, shielding her face from the sun with one arm. "I'm tired of being strong," she muttered. "All my life, I've been the good sister, the responsible one with a house and kids, the one who gives the holiday dinners and tells Elaine what to get the boys for their birthdays so they'll think she's cool. What the hell. I feel like I'm always tiptoeing around her delicate little feelings."

"So stop."

"I'm not sure I can," Ava said glumly. "Even though I'm lying here and telling you how much I resent my sister, I'm also constantly worrying about her. I wish I knew how to feel close to her again, but all of my actions lately are pushing her away." *Not to mention what Elaine would do if she found out about my feelings for Simon,* Ava thought. "I feel guilty because if I'm going to really lay myself bare, I have to admit that Elaine was the one who stuck it out and took care of Mom while I ran off and did my own thing. She must resent me for that even though she hasn't ever said so. Who was the irresponsible one then?"

"Jesus, you make the top of my head feel like it's going to fly right off, going in circles like that," Olivia said. "Cut it out! You and Elaine are both high-functioning, productive people. Neither of you has anything to feel guilty about."

Ava sat up again and took a deep breath. She stared out across the river at the Salisbury Beach campground, where the puffy roofs of the oversized RVs gleamed like frozen marshmallows. A family with three small children was walking along the opposite shore with a black dog. A pair of mute swans floated in the reeds.

*How fragile everything is,* she thought. One of those children could drown; the dog could get hit by a car; the dog could kill one of the swans; the camper vans could be upended by a hurricane. Meanwhile, Beach Plum Island was being washed away beneath them, one grain of sand at a time, even as they sat here, oblivious to the loss.

No matter how much sand people might want to dump along its shores to build back this island, there was no guarantee the sand would stay put. The shoreline would continue to be carved away; the endangered piping plovers nesting in the dunes really could disappear forever from the face of the planet. Her beloved cottage might wash out to sea with her in it. Her own children were in danger every day just by existing. You couldn't completely protect anything or anyone, least of all yourself.

Yet she couldn't help it. She had to try, even with Olivia, to keep some boundaries intact. She couldn't tell anyone about Simon. She couldn't *be* with Simon again.

"Lately I've been thinking I should stop looking for Peter, at least for a little while," she said. "Until things are better between Elaine and me."

"But I thought you *wanted* to find your brother."

"My *dad* wanted me to find him," Ava said. "I was mainly doing it for him." She stood up suddenly, brushing off her shorts. "Sorry. I don't know what the hell is wrong with me. I should get back to the studio and focus on work. At least that's something I can control."

"Unless the kiln blows up."

"Gee, thanks."

They started picking their way down the rocks. When they reached the beach, though, Olivia wrapped one arm around Ava's waist, forcing her to match her strides to Olivia's own longer ones. "You can't go back to work today," Olivia said.

"Why not? I've got a million deadlines."

"Yes, but you have something more important to do first. You need to go to Maine and look for that birth certificate."

Ava shook her head. "Not until I talk with Elaine about it."

"This isn't about Elaine! You're the one your dad asked to do this, and you won't be happy until you do it. This is a crazy time in your life, I know, but you can't let fear hold you back. You have to keep moving forward." Olivia gave Ava's waist a squeeze, made her stop walking. "Turn around," she commanded.

Ava did, laughing a little at the intense expression on Olivia's face. "Okay. Now what?"

"What do you see?"

"The beach. Rocks. A few boats. Some shells."

"And?" Olivia pointed down at the sand.

"Our footprints. I never realized how much your feet turn in and mine turn out. I walk like a duck," Ava added.

"You do, but it doesn't matter," Olivia said. "Because in a little while, guess what? The tide will come in and there won't be any more footprints. It's like our lives, right? Whatever we do before this moment in time, we can't do over. We have no choice in life but to keep moving ahead."

"Moving ahead to *what*?" Ava said.

"To a future where you have answered important questions about your life so that you can feel less guilty," Olivia suggested. "Those answers about your parents and your brother will help define who you are as a woman apart from being a sister, a mother, and a daughter. And don't Evan and Sam deserve to have a mother who works as hard to make herself happy as she does for everyone else? You don't want them feeling as guilty as you do when *they're* adults."

Ava sighed and leaned her head on Olivia's bony shoulder. "You're a good friend," she said.

"I'm only telling you what you already know," Olivia answered, and kissed the top of her head.

Somehow, they had pulled it off: they'd created an ad campaign for a dying South Carolina university that made it sound like the best possible place to earn your degree and get job skills at the same time. The copy made the university sound friendly but worldly, using the requisite points about personal attention, a relevant curriculum, and a global perspective without actually invoking those cobwebbed catchphrases. The university's admissions people were over the moon about it, Tony had said when he called from their campus earlier today.

Joan Toledo had written the copy, Elaine was pleased to see. Joan had become their top copywriter in just a few short weeks, stripping the fat out of Web copy and going for an emotional impact with creative, energetic, even muscular headlines. This last campaign was pure genius.

Elaine stopped by Joan's cubicle to tell her about Tony's call and congratulate her. Joan was looking sleeker and better dressed these days, more up to speed in stylish peep-toe shoes and a knee-length blue cap-sleeve dress that flattered her round figure and set off her silvery hair nicely. She looked adorable and Elaine told her so.

Joan flushed and produced a lipstick out of her bag. "You were right about war paint," she said. "Makes a big difference. Hey, I was just going for lunch. Want to join me?"

It was an impulsive invitation, Elaine knew. She also knew better than to accept; after all, she was the vice president and what was Joan? A disposable copywriter. She was amazed Joan had the balls to invite her.

Elaine—deliberately—had never eaten lunch with anyone from the office other than Tony, wanting to keep boundaries clear. Not that Tony did; he sometimes invited the younger employees out for lunch and even drinks after work, saying it built company morale. Maybe it did. What did she know about morale, with her own self-esteem in the ditch lately?

"Sure," Elaine heard herself say, and knew the voice had sprung from some deep need of her own, a loneliness she seldom acknowledged.

At Joan's suggestion, they went to a new Thai place on Mass Ave. The restaurant was packed but quiet enough that they could talk once they got their meals—noodle soup for Joan, Thai chicken salad for Elaine.

Naturally, they discussed work at first. They were in the process of creating an online magazine for a university in Connecticut. The university had asked Elaine if she had any writers who could handle the feature stories; Joan would be perfect for that. Luckily, when Elaine mentioned it, Joan was all over the project. She could check that off her task list.

Eventually the conversation turned personal, which was the reason Elaine avoided having lunch with employees. Lately, hearing other people talk about their families made her feel inadequate. It seemed like everyone around her had a partner and kids whose bad art and toothless photos were tacked onto cubicle walls. The only single employees were under thirty. Of course, that was partly the nature of their work; Tony liked hiring younger people, figuring they were closer to understanding what kind of branding appealed to prospective college students.

Not that it mattered where you went to college. Despite her lofty career in marketing institutions of higher education, as far as Elaine could tell, what it said on your degree didn't matter nearly as much these days as what you did while you were in school. One case in point: their best account manager graduated from some podunk Catholic college in Connecticut she'd never heard of before hiring him; he had earned his chops by writing for Web sites senior year to make beer money.

Joan was talking about her husband now, who apparently was a police officer on disability and learning to cook. She hadn't pictured Joan married to a cop, certainly, but apparently they'd known each other since high school. What would that be like, Elaine wondered, having someone who knew you, really *got* you, and stayed with you through mortgages and hair loss, toddler tantrums and college bills, hospital stays and retirement plans?

It would be boring, she reminded herself. There would be days when your spouse would drone on about the plumbing and nag you about groceries and dry cleaning. The kids—as she'd seen with Ava's boys—would forget to do their chores and expect food on the table, night after night, without noticing how much you did for them. You wouldn't be alone. That was the upside of domestic life. But you wouldn't ever be alone, and that was the downside, too.

"Listen to me, droning on," Joan said happily, pushing away her empty bowl. "What about you? Do you have a family?"

Elaine gave her the obligatory glossy version of her sister, and of her sister's kids being like her own, wanting to slide out of sight beneath the booth because of how big a lie that was. She had a family, sure. But she wasn't part of it.

Joan must have understood, though, because Elaine could see a flicker of pity in the other woman's round brown eyes, even as she said, "I always envy you single women your freedom," and offered to treat Elaine to lunch, which of course Elaine had to refuse.

"This was lovely," Elaine said, knowing she wouldn't make this mistake again.

Back at the office, she dove eagerly into e-mail mode, sorting priorities, then made up a calendar of work assignments to present at the staff meeting on Friday. She was just finishing that when her phone rang.

It was the receptionist, Carl. "Your sister is here to see you," he said.

Elaine felt a flutter of alarm in her throat. Ava had only been to the office a few times, and always at Elaine's invitation to lunch or a company event. If she was here, it must be something important.

"Send her in," she said with a smile so forced it actually hurt. "What a nice surprise." No need for gossipy Carl to know anything was odd about Ava visiting the office.

Elaine straightened the pens on her desk that were already regimented into lines by color and type, then folded her hands on top of a stack of papers. That felt wrong, though, so she turned back to her computer, opened a document, and stared at the screen without seeing it.

It was only a few minutes, but it seemed like an eternity before Carl ushered Ava into the office. Carl Rossi was greyhound lean, and usually dressed in black shirts and black pants that were somehow miraculously lint free. He had a convict's haircut and, except for the turquoise jewelry, looked like an undertaker. But he had a killer smile, never forgot a name, and handled their baffling phone system with the techie grace of a professional computer gamer.

Carl had given Ava a cup of coffee in one of the office mugs with the company logo that turned colors depending on the temperature of your beverage. Ava set it down on Elaine's desk, carefully centering the mug on the cork coaster before sitting down in one of the leather chairs angled in front of the desk.

"What are you doing here?" Elaine asked. No point in pretending this was normal, when both of them knew it wasn't.

"I wanted to see you." Ava's face contorted into what might pass for a smile with anyone but Elaine. She wore a yellow summer dress— something totally out of character—and looked tan and muscular, attractive and confident. Elaine felt suddenly self-conscious in her tight black skirt, ruched red top, and red open-toed heels, like a little girl caught playing dress-up by a cool teenager.

"Obviously, you wanted to see me, or you wouldn't be here," Elaine said. "What's up?" She picked up a pen, forced herself to put it down again.

"I had to run some errands and thought I might take you to lunch."

"Errands? In *Boston*?"

Ava looked sheepish. "Okay, only in Danvers. But since I was that far south, I figured I might as well drive the rest of the way. Apparently you don't have time to return my calls. Can you spare a few minutes to grab a bite to eat?"

"I've already eaten. I went out with another woman from the office."

"Oh!" Ava's green eyes widened in surprise. She knew Elaine's lunch habit was typically salad at her desk. "Too bad."

"It's already one o'clock," Elaine pointed out. "You should have called to let me know you were coming."

"I didn't know I was coming until I was on my way. Besides, I was pretty sure you'd find an excuse not to see me."

Elaine didn't want to admit how true this was. "I've been busy, as you can see." She gestured to the folders on her desk, the computer. "Look, text me some good days for you next week and I'll check my calendar after our Friday staff meeting. How are the boys?" she asked suddenly, because seeing Ava in front of her made her realize how much she'd missed seeing Evan and Sam.

"Fine. Working less than they should, gaming more than they're sleeping. Growing an inch an hour. The usual." Ava pulled her chair closer to the desk and reached for the coffee, made an appreciative noise as she drank. "Wow. You should definitely keep that guy out front."

"If only to look at him."

For a minute, the women smiled at each other. Then Ava frowned and said, "Why are you avoiding me?"

Elaine hadn't expected an actual confrontation. That wasn't something Ava did. "I'm not!"

Ava's green eyes were fixed on her face like twin suns. "Don't bullshit me. You don't answer my calls or texts. We haven't spoken in over a week. We don't *do* that, Elaine. That's not who we are as sisters. I want to know what's going on."

Ava was right, of course. They'd been angry at each other, hurt, irritated, impatient, in the past. They'd been a lot of things, as sisters. But never, ever silent.

"You know why." Elaine felt suddenly, wearyingly tearful.

Ava didn't look away. "I know you don't like Gigi being around, but that's getting a little old. Grow up."

"She isn't just *around*! She's practically living at your house!" Elaine said fiercely, surprising them both with her vehemence, then bit her lip, ashamed. "I don't *want* to hate her. I know she's just a kid. But I can't help it. I hate everything she represents."

"Honey, you can't keep holding Dad's decision to leave against her. For that matter, it wasn't Dad's fault that Mom died. Or yours. You keep acting like she killed herself, but she didn't. Mom had a heart attack. Yes, she might have lived if she'd gotten help in time, but whose choice was it for her to live the way she did? Not yours! It was never your choice, Elaine, not any of it," Ava said. "Let it go."

Elaine bolted out of her chair so fast that she bumped the desk, making Ava's coffee spill over the sides of the mug. So much for a cork coaster. "I don't know *how to let it go*," she said. "Every time I look at Gigi, I think about it. And then this whole brother thing?

Why would Dad tell you and Gigi about that, but not me? *Why?*" Elaine spun in a circle and, trapped in her corner, folded her arms and leaned against the big windows overlooking Boylston Street.

"You couldn't have saved Mom," Ava said quietly. "The more we find out about what happened, the more sure I am of that."

"I know," Elaine said miserably, "but it doesn't mean I'm ready to make nice with people who make me remember everything bad that happened."

"What about me? Am I somebody you have to avoid now, because I make you remember the bad times, too? What about all of the *good* things between us? Can't you focus on that?"

Elaine couldn't breathe. It was as if the air in the room had been sucked out onto Boylston Street through the big windows behind her. "No. Not right now," she said, staring down at her ridiculous too-red shoes.

Ava's eyes glistened with tears. "*Look* at me," she hissed. "Pick up your head and *look* at me. Don't you think I feel guilty and angry, too, for not being there to help you cope with Mom? I *left* you. I don't feel great about that. But we all have things that happen that are beyond our control. We just have to figure out how to live with the chaos."

"Maybe you do. Not me. I've never liked chaos." Elaine lifted her eyes just as far as the desk, where she focused on the neat stacks of papers and folders and the line of pens in every color. What she needed, more than anything, was a drink. "I'm sorry. But could you leave now, please? I've got work to do."

Neal texted early in the morning to ask if Gigi wanted to ride. She called Ava just to make sure it was all right if she skipped a morning in the studio, then texted Neal back to say yes.

She'd been riding with her mother a few times since that first time they went out, but it still felt weird to return to the stables. Especially pedaling her bike up the road to meet Neal, who'd been at the barns since early morning, turning horses out into the paddocks so he could muck out the stalls. He greeted her with a big grin, though, putting her at ease, accompanied by a goofy-looking dog she'd seen around the stables without realizing that Neal and the dog belonged together.

"Meet Beast," Neal said. "Beast, meet Gigi."

The dog looked like a bear, black with short ears that stood straight up. It had almost no tail at all, but wagged its hind end and made a big show of jumping around Gigi like she was a long-lost friend.

Neal had an easy way with horses, gentling them with his deep voice and slow hands. He swung up onto LazyBoy, a young Thoroughbred just brought in from the track by a woman "with more money than sense," Neal said, who was determined to turn the colt into a hunter-jumper. Not many people wanted to ride that horse because nobody trusted him.

Gigi could see why. LazyBoy was one big nerve, a glossy red chestnut with a strung-out way of tossing his head and prancing in place. Gigi prayed no car alarm would go off; she knew the horse would race toward an invisible finish line at any sound remotely like a bell.

Soon, though, Neal had LazyBoy trotting along on the trails, only occasionally shying away from shadows, swinging his big hind end around as he eyeballed a chickadee or squirrel in terror, making Gigi laugh. Oddly, instead of making the horse more nervous, Beast seemed to calm it down, trotting right next to LazyBoy's legs as if he were just one more horse on the trail.

The only other guy Gigi had ever been riding with was her father. Neal, she noticed, had the same unschooled but graceful way of relaxing in the saddle, paying little attention to whether his heels were up or down in the stirrups but easily commanding the horse with the pressure of his long legs. This was how she imagined cowboys would ride.

They talked in little snatches, depending on whether they were trotting or walking, and whether they were on a single track or cart road. She found out that Neal was seventeen, starting his senior year at the same public high school Evan and Sam went to; he was interested in pretty much the opposite of everything Gigi liked. For instance, he was in AP calculus and she could barely manage algebraic equations. She loved English, but Neal said he'd rather slit his wrists than ever write another paper.

"Especially one with friggin' footnotes," he muttered. "What's the point of that, when you can Google everything? Get with the program, people."

Gigi, he said, was lucky to go to a private school, since the public school was a "sit-down-and-shut-up sort of place," where the teachers acted like drill sergeants and he'd been in trouble pretty much all of his first two years of high school. "Been honor roll since then," he added with a shy glance over his shoulder. "And my robotics team took first in the state."

They rode to one of the bridges over the Ipswich River, where they tied the horses in the shade and jumped off the bridge into the brackish water, giving some poor old dude in a kayak a heart attack because he thought they were trying to capsize him. Neal apologized and helped the guy mop water off the inside of his boat, which Gigi thought was cool.

Afterward they took the horses to a sandy spot on the riverbank. Neal had thought to bring lead lines and halters; they tied the horses to a tree and let them graze while Gigi and Neal lay on a rock to dry, not quite touching. Gigi was aware of Neal's muscular long arms and legs, of his chest rising and falling beside her own. He smelled like sweet hay and river water. She felt a warmth in her stomach and was having trouble swallowing. He was older than she was; had he ever had sex? She wasn't sure she was ready to think about sex again, not after the thing with Justin.

Again, Beast put her at ease, dunking himself in the river and then coming to shake on them, wriggling between them like some annoying little brother until Gigi and Neal were both bent over, laughing. Then it was time to head back to the barns so Neal could do the afternoon feeding. He hadn't even tried to kiss her, and Gigi was disappointed but relieved, too. Maybe Neal really had just wanted a friend to ride with and nothing more.

There were two barns; Neal led LazyBoy to the bigger one by the paddocks while Gigi took Bantam to the small barn near the indoor arena. She slipped off the saddle and bridle, curried her horse until he stretched his neck and curled his upper lip in pleasure, and cleaned his hooves. Then she led Bantam into his stall, kissed his soft muzzle good-bye, and carried the saddle and bridle into the tack room.

Lydia was in there, of course, ready to ruin her day. She seemed to be everywhere; occasionally Gigi imagined this girl must be lying in wait for her. Lydia wore bright yellow jodhpurs that showed off her tight butt. She shook her long blond hair out of her black velvet riding helmet and grinned at the sight of Gigi in her T-shirt and stained jeans, still damp from the river.

"Nice hair," Lydia said.

Involuntarily, Gigi put her hand up to touch it; her hair had grown out, the pink tips mostly faded, the rest of her hair nearly back to its natural blond. It had gotten wet in the river and now she felt it standing in stiff spikes. She probably looked like a pissed-off chicken. No wonder Neal hadn't kissed her.

"I was swimming," Gigi said, furious that Lydia tried to keep lording it over her. What was this girl's problem?

"Sure you were. Good times," Lydia said.

"It was fun," Gigi said, exhausted already. "How about you? How are your lessons going?"

Lydia rested her perfect butt against one of the saddle racks. "Good. I'm getting ready for dressage at the Nationals."

"That's cool," Gigi said, though privately she thought dressage was about the most useless thing imaginable. What kind of deviant human mind would think of putting horses through those intricate steps? A horse was born to graze and run and buck out of sheer joy. "Good luck."

Apparently, Lydia wasn't ready to play nice. "Heard from Justin?"

Gigi shook her head. "He's spending the summer on the Cape."

"He's back in town," Lydia said. "His parents have a wicked big boat docked in Newburyport. I saw Justin two nights ago at this awesome party Sheila had."

Lydia would know, of course, that Gigi hadn't been invited to one of Sheila's parties. "That's cool," Gigi repeated. She turned to leave.

"He was asking about you."

Gigi kept moving toward the door. "Yeah? Tell him I said hello."

"We hooked up," Lydia said. "He's going to show me around Amherst."

Gigi thought of Justin panting in her ear like a dying dog, of him shoving her jeans down around her ankles, and suddenly felt sorrier for Lydia than she'd ever felt for anybody. "Good for you," she said, just as Beast charged into the tack room, grinning, tongue lolling, as if he'd been hunting for her for days. Gigi put a hand on the dog's big warm head, thinking she'd never been happier to see anything in her life.

Except, maybe, Neal, who was striding toward her across the paddock, lanky in his low-slung blue jeans and grinning like he'd been searching for her, too.

## CHAPTER THIRTEEN

Her brother was born exactly two years, one month, and one day before she was. Ava knew that much now. She also knew the name of the doctor who delivered him.

The woman at the reunion registry had been right: there was still a copy of the original birth certificate on file at the town clerk's office in her mother's hometown. When Ava said she was doing genealogy research for a family history, the clerk had happily pulled out a copy of the certificate and let her write down the pertinent information. Ava didn't bring up the possibility that her brother might have another birth certificate on file. She wouldn't have known what name to ask for anyway.

She had left the house at six a.m. to drive to Maine. With no one to talk to, and in her poky Honda instead of Elaine's BMW, the three-hour trek to her mother's hometown up Route 95 through a corridor of thick pines and tractor-trailer trucks belching fumes was so monotonous that Ava had to play one of Sam's CDs to keep herself awake. Mumford & Sons: she loved the banjo and knew enough of the lyrics to sing along with it. Singing made her feel guilty about Gigi, though, and she had to stop. She should have called to ask her to come, but she'd wanted to do this alone. She didn't quite know why; maybe because it made her feel less like she was betraying Elaine.

Thinking about that last conversation with her sister made Ava so angry. Olivia was right. She owed it to her father, and to herself, to see this through, no matter what Elaine wanted. Otherwise, Ava would always feel like she'd let her parents down, because this secret had defined who they were as husband and wife, as parents, as people.

After leaving the town clerk's office in town, Ava walked to the tiny brick library her parents must have frequented growing up. After finding what she wanted on the computers, she sat outside on one of the stone benches in front and tried to picture her parents here as they'd been in high school. She hoped they'd laughed and held hands.

Ava ate the granola bar and apple she'd stashed in her purse, then retrieved her cell phone to call the doctor whose name was on her brother's certificate, using the phone number she'd found online in the library and hoping he wasn't dead or living in some Florida retirement community. She didn't know how many more of these Nancy Drew sleuthing trips to Maine she could stomach.

Astoundingly, Dr. Mansfield answered the phone himself on the second ring. When Ava told him she was doing a family history and thought he might have delivered her brother over forty years ago, he asked no questions and freely admitted to being a widower eager for company.

"Sure, come visit," he said. "Always nice to have company. Don't get much these days."

It was another hour's drive northeast to Bangor. Dr. Mansfield's house was a small yellow Victorian in the historic district, a few blocks uphill from the brick downtown area and the Penobscot

River. As the doctor made coffee and laid out a tray with a sugar bowl and a small pitcher of milk, Ava told him the real reason she'd come.

"I hope you don't mind." She held her breath, half expecting him to turn her away.

But he shrugged his bony shoulders. "Water under the bridge now," Dr. Mansfield said, "especially since I'm no longer practicing medicine. I'll be dead long before anybody could sue me for breaching those damn privacy laws. Come out to the porch. I'll tell you what I know, which probably isn't much."

The elderly man wore a brown cardigan over a red plaid shirt buttoned to the neck despite the August heat. They sat in a pair of green metal camp chairs on his front porch. By the way Dr. Mansfield heartily greeted the few people walking by, Ava suspected this was his morning ritual. She felt like she'd somehow stumbled into a Norman Rockwell painting.

They drank their coffee and made small talk about Bangor and Dr. Mansfield's wife, who'd worked alongside him as a nurse and office receptionist until her death. Finally, the doctor said, "So let's get down to business, now you've got my curiosity aroused and I've had a good dose of caffeine to keep me awake."

Ava smiled. "All right. You signed the birth certificate for my brother. Here's what was on it." She had copied the information from the birth certificate into a notebook at the town clerk's. She slid the open notebook to him across the metal café table. "My brother was born August 28, 1971, at Notre Dame Hospital. I know from my aunt that my mother was sent to a Catholic home for unwed mothers. She didn't know the name, but I think it must have been St. Margaret's, since that's close to the hospital and the only Catholic-run home for girls I could find online."

Dr. Mansfield scanned the paper. "Yes, that would be right. For a while, the Good Shepherd Sisters had a maternity ward right inside St. Margaret's. It was a big brick house with white pillars. Looked respectable enough on the outside, but it was a pile of rubble and down at the heels. Never enough money to fix it up properly. The sisters liked to tell me God always put them last on the grocery list, figuring he had to get his milk and eggs first. Anyway, once the hospital was built, the girls delivered there instead. I saw the girls both at St. Margaret's for prenatal care and again at the hospital when it was their time."

"It must have been tough on my mom. She was only fifteen."

"I'm sure, but she wasn't the youngest I saw. Not by a long stretch." Dr. Mansfield's pale gray eyes were watering, though whether from age or sympathy, Ava couldn't be sure. His hand trembled, the paper rustling between his fingers. "I saw maybe fifty of those poor girls through the years before I moved on to private practice. Most doctors wouldn't deliver their infants. Too high-and-mighty with their moral principles. Plus, there was no money in it. People didn't pay big bucks to adopt like they do now."

"Nobody profited when the girls gave up their babies?" Ava found this difficult to believe; she'd had many friends struggle to adopt, paying thousands of dollars for an infant whether the baby was born in the United States or adopted internationally.

"No. The sisters took care of the necessary paperwork and placements when the girls surrendered their infants. Donations were made to the Church by grateful families, of course, but that had nothing to do with me."

That word, "surrendered," gave Ava chills. It made it sound as if the girls were in battle. Which, in a way, they were. "Why do you say 'poor girls'? Were they mistreated?"

"Not to my knowledge. The nuns were strict, of course, but not unduly harsh. Merely disciplined. They required the girls to conform to certain rules and do chores around the house. Around 1965 or so the younger Sisters even started high school classes so girls could keep up their schoolwork. That was a blessing for many. I doubt any high school in Maine would have knowingly allowed a pregnant girl to take classes back then."

"Like pregnancy might be catching or something," Ava said, thinking again of her mother's humiliation.

"I believe they were mainly concerned about parents believing the administration condoned wayward behavior," Dr. Mansfield said. "In any case, the nuns truly believed they were saving the souls of these girls. This was a time when there weren't many other options for young women, Catholic or otherwise, you understand."

Ava nodded. Birth control pills were on the market but probably not widely used by high school girls the way they were now. Abortion was still illegal and it would have been next to impossible to find a doctor willing to perform one in Maine, even if her mother's Catholic family would have given permission. "Did a lot of girls want to keep their babies?"

Dr. Mansfield furrowed his brow. His scalp gleamed, pale and waxy, through the thin strands of his silver hair. "Oh, a few. But most knew they didn't have the resources to do so." He passed the notebook back to her and stared up at the pale blue wooden ceiling of the porch. "Despite the difficult circumstances, some girls were actually happy there. At least they had each other. A few even asked if they could stay in Bangor after the birth rather than go home. My wife and I actually took in two of those girls and helped raise their babies."

Ava smiled. "That must have been nice for them."

"For us, too." He sighed. "We had a son who died at childbirth and couldn't have more children. My wife understood the grief of losing a child, perhaps better than I did. Certainly better than the nuns." Dr. Mansfield set his coffee cup down on the table, the cup rattling in its saucer as his hand suffered a small tremor. "I wish I could tell you more, but I saw so many girls. Is there anything that would have made your mother stand out?"

Ava was silent for a minute, wondering what she could tell this man about her mother that would jar his memory. Her mother's dark eyes, with that unusual feline tilt to them, like Elaine's, were probably her most unique feature. But this doctor wouldn't remember a girl's eyes. He'd seen too many lovely girls scared out of their wits over the years to remember how they all looked.

"I guess the only thing different about her was that Mom refused to let the nuns take her baby," Ava said. "She ran away instead and gave him to my aunt to raise."

Dr. Mansfield raised his silver eyebrows in surprise. "Your aunt took him in? Then why are you looking for him?"

"He's not with our family anymore. My aunt found him too difficult to care for, so when my brother was about four or five, she gave him up to social services. The child was eventually adopted by another family."

"Ah." Dr. Mansfield studied the porch ceiling. "Dark hair?"

"What?"

"Your mother. Did she have dark hair?" He shot her a sharply appraising glance. "You don't look much like her, if it's the girl I'm thinking of. Very young, on the small side. Pretty little thing."

"Yes. She was beautiful, actually. Everyone said so. My sister looks like her. I look more like our father. Mom had dark hair down to her waist. Very straight hair, and very thick."

Ava had a sudden memory of her mother, despairing over hot rollers she'd been so excited to buy, only to find they left her hair in strange misshapen lumps instead of the curls she wanted. "It looks like I've got snails crawling all over my head," she'd said, then tossed the rollers into the trash. Mom never set her hair again, just kept it long and sleek, a curtain she could hide behind. In the 1970s, when Ava was young, everyone had made a fuss over her mother's hair. It was what every woman wanted.

"I think I remember her."

"You do?" Ava realized belatedly that she should have brought a photograph of her mother.

"Yes, now that you tell me she left with the baby," Dr. Mansfield said. "Only one girl did that during my tenure. Your mother left the hospital the day of delivery. Escaped in the middle of the night. The nuns were so worried. They woke me up out of a sound sleep. It was summer, one of the hottest on record."

That fit with her brother's late August birthday. "How did she leave the hospital? Did someone pick her up?" Ava wanted to imagine her father rushing to the hospital in the big blue Chevy he drove during high school, a car he'd inherited when his only brother was killed in an accident at the paper mill. But that was impossible if, as Finley believed, her mother hadn't told him about the pregnancy until after she and Elaine were born.

"No," Dr. Mansfield said. "She called a cab, bold as brass. I don't know where she got the money. The girls weren't allowed to bring purses to the hospital for fear of that very thing happening. I have no idea how she paid the cab. Your mother must have been very determined, running off like that."

"Do you remember anything else about her baby?" Ava asked. "I called the hospital, but they don't have a record of my brother's birth. None of their old paper files were transferred onto their computer system."

Dr. Mansfield pursed his lips. "What kind of record? You have the birth certificate."

"His medical records. We'd like to know whether the baby was born with any disabilities. Other than being blind, I mean."

The doctor frowned. "I should think that would be enough for anyone."

"Yes, of course. But if my brother was born blind, but with a normal IQ and no other physical handicaps, he might have been educated instead of institutionalized," Ava said. "It's also more likely that he's still alive."

Dr. Mansfield gave her a sympathetic look. "Well, young lady, then I can set your mind at ease. I'm remembering this particular baby now, too, because of that rigamarole about your mother. As I recall, he was quite healthy."

As they said good-bye a few minutes later, Ava thanked him with a hug.

She arrived home by late afternoon. Gigi had already left. The band didn't practice on Thursdays, which was why Ava had felt comfortable leaving the house for as long as she did. By the time she returned, however, Sam was hunkered down on the living room couch with his new girlfriend, Sarah or Sally or Shawn—he had introduced her, but Ava couldn't remember the girl's name—and Ava saw only the tops of their heads as she passed by. She cleared her throat noisily as she continued down the hall and took the stairs two at a time, making a thunderous noise and feeling flustered.

As she passed Evan's room, Ava could hear the sounds of gunfire behind his closed door. She poked her head in, said hello, and was rewarded with a grunted "You made me die, Mom!"

She sat down at the desk in her own bedroom and opened her laptop, Googling "schools for the blind and visually impaired." It took all of a minute to find the site she'd discovered the day she spoke with the woman from the adoption registry. There were only forty-five schools listed in the entire country. She could start by contacting those that were geographically closest and gradually widen her search.

The tricky part would be figuring out Peter's last name. If he'd been adopted at seven or eight, say, after spending a few years in foster families, Peter's new family surely would have kept his first name but changed his surname. To do otherwise would have been cruel. Anyway, she had to start someplace. It was the best she could do.

Ava began scanning the list of schools. There were only a handful in New York, plus one each in New Jersey and Massachusetts. If the baby was adopted in Maine, the Thompson School for the Blind in Boston would have been the closest residential school. If, that is, Peter's family had spent the money on tuition at an academic school and not sent him to a vocational training center.

So many ifs.

Ava glanced at her watch. It was after five o'clock already. She could call Thompson, but the administrative offices would be closed. Besides, her experiences over the past few days had taught her that she'd find out more if she went to the school in person. That would have to wait until tomorrow; they seemed to have summer programs, according to the Web site, but like any school, probably the official personnel dispersed well before five o'clock and the offices would be locked by the time she got down there.

She'd go tomorrow, Ava decided, and get a good night's sleep first.

Ava probably would have sneaked off without her again if Gigi hadn't arrived at the studio earlier than usual to glaze her own pots. She pedaled up the driveway on her bike, head down against the stiff sea breeze, just as Ava was getting into her car. "Hey. Where are you going?"

"Boston." Ava had one hand on the car door, already open. Her

big orange canvas purse lay on the passenger seat. She wasn't wearing her usual jeans and T-shirt, but a short black dress, tan sandals,
gold hoop earrings, and clunky wooden beads painted in bright colors. Her hair was fancier than usual, too, smoothed down and
pinned up in a complicated way, exposing her long neck.

Gigi always thought Ava looked nice, the way your favorite
teachers look nice: kind face, clear eyes, nothing skanky. But today
Gigi realized that Ava was beautiful, maybe even prettier than her
own mom because she was different looking. This gave Gigi more
hope for herself. Still, why was Ava so decked out? It had to be a
guy. This thought, too, was exciting, since the whole way here Gigi
had been fantasizing about kissing Neal.

Ava was still talking, giving Gigi instructions about studio work.
"When you're done glazing your own pots, you can do the two shelves
of bisqued pots near the door."

She meant the newest racks of vases and bowls. Gigi was excited; she loved glazing, that mysterious process where you painted
on chalky pale colors, the glaze cold to the touch, and somehow the
heat of the kiln turned that chalky liquid into glass in the most
beautiful deep jewel tones and browns and golds. She was pleased,
too, that Ava trusted her to do it without supervision.

Still, her curiosity was too big to contain. "So what are you doing in Boston?"

"Just a few errands."

That evasive answer confirmed Gigi's suspicions. It also pissed
her off. Why would Ava run errands in Boston?

Suddenly, Gigi knew the answer. She folded her arms. Her torso
felt hot and foreign beneath them. "Are you going to that school for
blind kids? Thompson or whatever it's called?" Gigi knew exactly
what it was called; she had been on the school's Web site just last
night, trying to find lists of past graduates.

Ava slammed the car door and gave her an exasperated look. Gigi hadn't realized that the keys were in the ignition until the door was shut and the pinging sound stopped. "Yikes," Ava said. "You're like Sherlock Holmes or something. How did you know?"

"I've been using a computer practically since I was born," Gigi reminded her. "Seems like a pretty logical step to check schools for blind kids. That's the only one in New England."

To her relief, Ava smiled, her green eyes narrowing against the sun. "Wow. Impressive. Somebody else had to help me think of checking schools."

"I probably thought of it because I'm still *in* school," Gigi said. "Unfortunately."

"You don't really hate your school that much, do you?"

Gigi sighed. "Don't even go there. Of course I hate my school. It totally sucks. But quit trying to change the subject. What's your plan?"

Ava shrugged. "I thought I'd go to the admissions office and ask around, see if anybody there will show me school records from back when Peter could have been there."

This didn't sound like much of a plan to Gigi. "They'll show you the school records, just like that?"

"Probably not. That's why I wasn't going to bring you. I didn't want you to be disappointed."

Gigi stared at her in disbelief. "Me? But what about you? I thought you cared about finding Peter even more than I do."

"I'm having mixed feelings about it now, actually," Ava said. "But I still want to go down there. I'm guessing you'd rather come with me to the city than stay here and glaze pots."

Now that the offer was there, Gigi felt uncertain. Ava was in her city clothes and Gigi wore her usual ripped cutoffs and faded Green Day T-shirt. Did Ava really want her company? Ava was always so nice it was hard to tell. Besides, going to Boston meant giving up a day here on Beach Plum Island, with her pottery and practicing with Evan and Sam, and maybe with the chance of Neal coming by to go to the beach with her later.

She'd go insane waiting around to hear what Ava found out, though, and they should do this together. Gigi parked her bike in the shade and got into the front seat of the car. "Maybe if I'm with you, the people at the school will be less suspicious," she said.

"Maybe," Ava agreed.

Gigi went to Boston several times a year, usually for special dates with her grandmother, but the sight of the city was still pretty cool. Boston was such a small city that, in a single drive, like today, you actually passed the things they put on postcards of Boston: the Fleet Center, where she'd seen a few concerts with Dad; the Charles River with its sailboats and Hatch Shell; the Kenmore Square Citgo sign.

Once they were downtown, she and Ava had to stop talking so the GPS lady could give them directions in her annoying know-it-all voice, directing them west into a section of Boston Gigi had never seen. Here, the street they were on was wide and the buildings were mostly brick, and there was a strip down the middle of the avenue for the rattling green trolley cars.

Then they turned left into a neighborhood of mostly grand, serious-looking houses. The houses had broad porches and shade trees that made every lawn look like a park. They drove up a hill, where Ava said the bell tower was part of the school. In a few minutes, they were turning into a driveway through wrought iron gates.

Gigi had been expecting the school to look like a hospital. Instead, Thompson looked like any fancy private school or college, and it was nearly deserted.

They parked near a brand-new technology center with floor-to-ceiling glass windows and followed a path between brick dormitories with funky arched windows. The pond in the center of campus was protected by a tall fence; Gigi supposed that was to keep blind kids from tumbling into the water.

At last they reached what must have been the original heart of the school, a castle of a brick building with the bell tower Gigi had seen from the car. It looked like the Hogwarts school in the Harry Potter movies, she thought; it had gargoyle statues, a huge clock, and low brick wings fanning out from its center with classrooms and offices.

"Here we go," Ava said, pointing to a sign that said LIBRARY. Under that, of course, were Braille letters; in fact, every room they passed had Braille. There were classrooms in here, and a cafeteria, and somewhere there must be an auditorium because Gigi could hear kids singing to a piano.

In one of the rooms Gigi saw a girl about her own age, a black girl with long braids whose eyes were sapphire blue. She couldn't see out of those eyes, Gigi reminded herself—they were just contacts or something—but still they looked cool.

"I thought we were going to Admissions. Why are we going to the library?" Gigi asked, hurrying to catch up. Even in sandals, their footsteps sounded like noisy hammer blows on the shiny flagstone floor.

"It occurred to me that they must have student yearbooks in their archives," Ava said.

Now Gigi got it. "Since we don't have Peter's real name, you're thinking it'll be easier to find him if we look at pictures of students instead of asking for names in the Admissions Office. That's brilliant!"

In her excitement, she took Ava's hand and held it the rest of the way to the library. Ava didn't seem to mind, and Gigi liked how Ava's hand was stronger and bigger than her own. With her mother, Gigi always felt like she had to protect her.

With its tall shelves of books, soft carpeting, and long tables, the Thompson library looked like it could be in any high school in the world, other than having signs in Braille everywhere. Gigi supposed the books must be in Braille as well.

The librarian's office was a glassed-in room so cluttered with books and papers that it took a minute for Gigi to realize an actual person was in there. She had been afraid the librarian would be blind—well, why not, it would make sense that this place would hire blind people—but the woman blinked at them behind big round glasses, looking more like a cartoon owl than a person as Ava asked if it would be possible to see the yearbooks from 1986 to 1989.

"I suppose so," the librarian said, sounding uncertain. "Are you looking for something in particular?"

"Our brother," Ava said. "He was adopted out of our family and we're trying to find him. We think he might have gone to school here."

Gigi held her breath as the librarian considered their request with pursed lips. She was afraid Ava had done the wrong thing by telling the truth, and that the librarian might kick them out because they didn't belong. But no, the woman was nodding, now, saying, "Please wait here. I have to go downstairs to get the yearbooks you need from the archives."

They sat in the matching leather chairs outside the librarian's glass office. Looking at it, Gigi thought of a terrarium she'd made years ago out of an old glass kitchen bowl. She'd kept a garden toad in it until her mother made her set it free.

It took the librarian fifteen minutes to return. She carried an armload of navy blue hardbound books with white lettering, ten in all, each from a different year. "I thought you might want to look at the whole decade," she explained. "Not every student appears in every yearbook. We don't have the resources for individual photos, just group graduation pictures. But there are some candid shots. You might get lucky with those."

Gigi saw Ava frown a little as she considered the task, and knew she was probably thinking the same thing Gigi was: this was going to be a lot harder without individual student photos labeled by name. But Ava took a deep breath as they followed the librarian to a long wooden worktable in the far corner, near a trio of tall arched windows, and suggested they divide the books.

"Remember, we're looking for any photograph of a boy whose first name is Peter," Ava said. "Then we can compare all of those photos with the one we got from Aunt Finley. He probably changed a lot as he grew up, so it might not be easy."

Ava gently placed the photograph they'd gotten from Aunt Finley between them. Gigi tried to memorize her brother's face so she could compare it to the yearbook photos: Peter's dark eyes; his hair, darker and straighter than hers. His eyes were what made him look like their family, Gigi thought.

After a while, she didn't bother looking at the pictures, only the names, skimming photo captions for boys playing sports—how did they run a cross-country course, she marveled, if they were blind?— and doing science experiments and having barbecues. It seemed like a normal enough high school experience, but maybe the school was selective about what pictures it chose to use: nothing showing students weeping or getting lost or falling down, no photographs of kids tripping over their canes or running into walls.

Gigi flipped slowly through three books, four, five. Then, in the sixth yearbook she opened, she found a photograph of boys dressed like sailors, singing on a stage under the headline "Students Set Sail in *South Pacific.*" *Those are wicked lame costumes,* Gigi thought, *good thing those kids are blind and can't see how they look.*

Then she'd immediately felt bad about thinking that and skimmed the caption. She spotted "Peter" in the list of names and went back to look at the photographs more closely.

What she saw—a handsome dark-haired teenager whose eyes were identical to Elaine's—made her gasp. Ava immediately dropped the yearbook she'd been holding and circled around to Gigi's side of the table.

"Oh my God," Ava said, for she'd seen it at once, too, of course. She touched her brother's face with a trembling finger. "He was really here."

Gigi put her finger next to the photo caption. Now both of their hands were on the page. If only Peter could know his sisters were here, acting as if one touch could free him from the page and bring him to life, he would have to know he was loved. "Peter Winslow," she whispered. "That's our brother's name."

It had been another frenzied day at work. At least she'd made it to spin class early this morning so she wouldn't have to stop at the gym between leaving the office and going to her shift at the suicide hotline. Elaine picked up a salad—God, how many leaves of lettuce had she eaten in her pitiful life? Entire fields full, probably—and ate it while driving to the help center's office.

Never a good idea to eat anything with blue cheese dressing in the car, but nobody at the crisis center would care. Or even notice, probably. Mostly Elaine took shifts with four other women who were at least ten years older than she was, all of them undereducated, overweight, and motherly. Elaine could arrive with a head of lettuce jammed between her front teeth and wash her hair in blue cheese dressing, and not one of them would criticize her.

In the year she'd been volunteering, Elaine had learned that each woman she worked with had a story that had led her here. The stories were all mind-blowingly tragic, involving parents, children, or siblings who'd found ways to off themselves. The most spectacular— if that was the right word—death involved the daughter of one of these women who drove herself off a cliff somewhere in California after her first attempt, a wrist-cutting episode, had failed.

Elaine had managed to snag a bottle of vodka and a bottle of cranberry juice at that cute new shop on Boylston Street to help ease her frantic brain. So convenient, a block from their building. She'd mixed the two together in the car in the stainless steel water bottle she took to spin class. The nice thing about vodka was that nobody could smell it, and cranberry juice was a guarantee against bladder infections. She'd been restrained, drinking only one bottle of the mixture before coming to the hotline. She'd save the rest for the ride home.

Not that she didn't deserve the whole thing now, Jesus, Elaine thought as she searched for a parking space. As if that free-for-all with Ava the other day wasn't enough, this morning Ava had called her even before Elaine left for spin class, saying she planned to go on some wild-goose chase at a school for the blind in Boston to ask questions about Peter.

"I wanted you to know, just in case you want to change your mind and come with me," Ava had said. Her voice sounded stiff, formal.

Elaine was proud of herself for not flying off the handle, considering she hadn't yet had her coffee and her sister was springing this on her. "That's considerate of you, but I meant what I said before. Even if I could take time out of the office—which I can't, we've got a slew of tight deadlines at the moment—I don't have the energy to do this. Or the interest. Sorry. Good luck. Let me know how it turns out."

She'd sounded mature. Thoughtful. And then Elaine had thrown the phone across the room after pressing the button to end the call. Fortunately, her iPhone bounced off the wall and landed on the white carpet, unharmed.

Elaine fielded seven calls during her two-hour shift. Only one was bad. It came from a woman who told Elaine she was standing on the Tobin Bridge, staring down at the water and thinking about jumping. From the sound of traffic on the woman's cell phone, Elaine knew the caller was probably telling the truth. She wrote a note and passed it to the supervisor, who dialed 911 to report the potential jumper to the police.

*Keep them talking*: that was Rule #1. If a suicidal person was talking to you, she couldn't be killing herself. Elaine asked the woman's name—Liza—and what had brought her to the bridge, why this bridge and not somewhere else, and was there anyone she could call to be with her right now.

"That's the whole point," Liza wailed. "I've got nobody since my boyfriend left me. That bastard even took my *dog*!"

That did seem pretty low, Elaine had to agree, if only to herself. Then she had a sudden inspiration. "What if he wanted to give the dog back?" she said, repeating her question so Liza could hear her over the traffic.

"What do you mean? He's not going to want to do that. He's a lying sick bastard!"

"I'm sure you're right," Elaine said soothingly. "But let's say your boyfriend suddenly changed his mind about the dog and wanted to give it back. Where would the dog live, if you weren't around to take care of it?"

"He'd probably shoot it," Liza muttered.

"Maybe he would," Elaine said, trying to sound positive. "On the other hand, if you were there, he might give the dog back. That would be less hassle for him than finding another home for it or killing it or whatever, so it would be better if you were around, right? Just in case that happened?"

"That's never going to happen."

"Maybe not. On the other hand, he sounds lazy."

"You got that right," Liza said.

"And think about your dog," Elaine said. "You still love that dog, right?"

Liza had to admit she did, then said, "Gotta go. I have another call."

Elaine replaced the receiver with a sigh.

"You did good on that one," Marcia said. Marcia's husband had committed suicide by shutting himself in the garage with the engine running in the family's SUV.

"I don't know," Elaine said. "It might not have been enough."

"We never know if it's enough," Marcia reminded her. "All we can do is give them a few minutes of connection. You're not going to cure anybody in one phone call. They've got to do that themselves. We'll just hope the patrol car gets to the bridge on time. Now put it out of your head."

After finishing her shift, Elaine sat in her car and refilled the steel water bottle with vodka and cranberry. There was still a little salad left, but the lettuce was now limp with dressing. Elaine put the take-out container on the backseat and sat there, sipping her warm cocktail and wondering what to do. She hadn't brought any clothes for a club, but maybe there was a place she could go for a nightcap where it wouldn't matter how she looked. She didn't want a hookup anyway, just one drink with other people so she didn't feel like such a social pariah.

She pulled cautiously away from the curb, the bottle in one hand, making sure to use her turn signal and driving slowly up one street and down another. She couldn't risk having a cop stop her with booze. Even if he didn't give her a ticket—which a Boston cop sure as shit would—she'd never live down the humiliation of Tony finding out. Or the Angel Gabriel. Man, the look on Gabe's face when she'd jumped out of the subway car in Harvard Square was priceless!

She hadn't heard from Gabe since. Well, it was his own stupid fault. They'd had a fun time and then he'd climbed on his soapbox. Still, she was sorry. If nothing else, she'd miss that cat of his.

The alcohol was making her fuzzy-headed and maudlin. Vodka did that to her. She should have stuck with wine. Or gin. A gin martini was the right thing to set you on your feet.

Elaine spotted a club that looked better than most, a decent-looking Irish pub. She thought of the little Irish salesman she'd danced with the night she was mugged and smiled for a minute, remembering how thrilled he'd looked while she was dancing with him, as if somebody had finally given him that pony he wanted for Christmas.

Then she remembered how Gabe had rescued her and the smile faded. Gabe the judge. Gabe the *judgmental*, ha! Like that guy with his broken cat was any role model for living happily ever after. He wouldn't even date her sister!

*You didn't want him to date Ava*, Elaine reminded herself. She'd been aware of this before, but for the first time, she was expressing this thought in a cogent way.

Well, almost cogent. She'd drunk the entire bottle of vodka by now. That, combined with having only salad for lunch and more salad for dinner, left her definitely feeling too out of it to drive. She'd have one martini and then switch to coffee. Irish coffee! The hair of the dog, then home for a good night's sleep, so she could hit the gym earlier for a double workout, undo the calories she drank tonight.

Elaine pulled over to park across the street from the pub and was nearly sideswiped. She must have forgotten her turn signal. Well, screw 'em if they couldn't take a joke. This was Boston. There was a hydrant there, but so what, with city budgets so tight these days, no cops would be out ticketing.

She carefully locked her purse inside the car, taking only her driver's license and a twenty-dollar bill. That would limit any chance of buying more than two martinis and eliminate the possibility of a mugger taking more than whatever few dollars she had left after visiting this friendly neighborhood pub for a nightcap.

The pub was underground. Elaine held on to the metal railing, surprisingly cold, and wobbled down the cement steps in her red heels. Inside, the place was done up to look more Irish than the Blarney Stone, with a low ceiling, thick wooden beams, and white stucco walls decorated with Irish sports teams' flags and haying implements. At least she supposed that's what those big rusty tools were.

The place was packed, this being a Friday night in Boston. Elaine managed to squeeze herself over to a barstool between a pair of guys in leather jackets and, Jesus God, those tweed caps they must wear in Ireland to look like characters in a Danny Boyle film. "Heya," one of the guys said with a nod. "Looks like this stool's got your name on it, sweetheart." His accent was thick, South Boston: *sweethot*. He doffed his cap and gestured for her to sit.

The guy was forty if he was a day, but he had a kind red face and friendly blue eyes, so Elaine hauled herself up onto the wooden stool, leaving her poor red shoes behind because it was too hard to climb like a monkey in heels and a tight skirt, both. One of them had to go, and she wasn't planning on losing her skirt. Not yet. She nearly giggled but managed a straight face as she ordered a dry martini, straight up.

Right away, the guys started chatting her up. Well, they would, wouldn't they? Too late, Elaine realized she was the only woman at the bar, other than some blowsy redhead practically giving her boy toy a blow job on his ear at the other end of the bar. How did a woman like that get a guy so hot? If Elaine hadn't already downed a bottle of vodka, she might have been inclined to give that girl some competition, but tonight she was going to be sensible. One martini, then out of here.

The only problem was that the twins in tweed caps had other ideas. They really were twins, they said, and she had to believe them because they had identical faces, except one was a little puffier than the other's.

"I'm seeing double," she complained, making them laugh like they'd never heard *that* one before.

Her new friends kept magically making the martinis appear, and the drinks were so crisp, so cold, that she kept downing them. This kind of low-key social evening was just what she needed to forget about today, about this string of wretched weeks since Dad died.

The guys told her jokes, mostly bawdy ones she imagined were told in every pub in Boston, and they talked sports until her ears were throbbing like she was too deep underwater. Suddenly one of them said something about the Red Sox, and there it was, the day she'd gone to a Red Sox game with Dad. Only her, because Ava was off with Mark someplace. How thrilled Elaine had been to sit there in the bleachers with her father when she was maybe eleven years old. They'd done the seventh-inning stretch and eaten hot dogs together and cheered themselves hoarse.

At the end of the game, a fight erupted—not surprising; they were playing the Yankees—and Dad had scooped her up in his arms like Elaine weighed nothing. He carried her right out of Fenway Park, singing "Walk Like an Egyptian." Singing to her, and making her laugh when he set her down by doing the dance, too.

"You okay?" Dad said once they'd danced their way down the sidewalk and were far from the noise and crowds. "Not scared?"

She took his hand. "I'm never scared with you, Daddy."

"So right, too," he said with a nod. "That's what families do, darlin'. We look out for each other. Never forget that and you'll have a happy life." He stopped suddenly and got on one knee, looked her in the eye. "Honey, I mean what I say. Don't forget your family. I did that once, and I've been paying for it ever since." Then he stood up again and started singing, urging her to keep dancing with him all the way to the car.

He had tried to tell her. Elaine stared into her martini and wished she could dive into the drink, forget that memory and everything else that had brought her here to this lousy pub, this low point in her life.

Her father had told her, but she had turned her back on him. On her family.

Elaine understood, finally, that phrase "drowning my sorrows." If she stayed here, she might do just that and never go home again. But what, then, would have been the point of her father protecting her, singing to her, loving her? What would have been the point of taking care of Mom, if she was not going to take care of herself? And what was her life when she and Ava were on the outs, with nothing in it but herself?

Her life would be nothing. *She* would be nothing.

"Hey, you okay, girlie?" one of the tweed caps asked, his voice suddenly fatherly, his blue eyes still watering with drink but kind, very kind.

"I think I'm going to be sick," she said.

She left her shoes at the bar but made it to the ladies' room, where she shut herself in one of the cubicles and threw up, retching until there was nothing more. Then she passed out for a bit, kneeling on the bathroom floor, her head cradled in her arms above the toilet seat.

When she came to, Elaine washed her face with cold water and stared at her own pale crooked reflection in the mirror. Above it there was a bumper sticker: "Need help? Call 1-800-Alcohol." What a joke. She knew how those help lines worked, didn't she? What kinds of pathetic slobs doled out nonsense platitudes to desperate people?

Then her vision began clouding up and she was retching again, this time into the sink. When she'd finished, she dialed the number just before she blacked out again.

On Monday morning, Gigi worked with Ava, cleaning the studio and wedging clay as Ava furiously produced cup after cup, bowl after bowl, and stacks of plates on the wheel. She was obviously upset. Finally Gigi worked up the courage to ask why.

"Everything is changing," Ava said.

Gigi blinked. "Everything always changes," she said.

Ava gave a weak laugh. "Yes, I suppose you're right. You found that out too early when Dad died. I'm sorry. I'm just in an odd mood."

"I can see that," Gigi said. "But why?" For some reason, even though Ava was older than her own mother, it seemed okay to ask Ava questions like that because she was her sister.

"Elaine called yesterday," Ava said, and right there Gigi's stomach dropped. Nothing related to Elaine was ever good.

Ava must have seen this thought on Gigi's face, because she smiled. "No, it's actually a good thing, something I've hoped for," she said.

"What is it?"

Gigi could tell by Ava's expression that she was wondering whether Gigi was old enough to hear whatever it was she was about to say. Finally, Ava gave a little nod. "This isn't something you can repeat to anyone else," she said. "Not to your mother or the boys."

"Okay."

"Elaine has a drinking problem."

"The boys already know that," Gigi said. "My mom probably does, too."

Ava tightened her mouth and stood up from the wheel, swiped clay off her face with the back of one arm. "That obvious, huh? Well, anyway, Elaine called to say she was taken to a hospital on Friday night for alcohol poisoning and a concussion. Now she's decided to get sober."

"Wow." Gigi remembered a party she'd been to last year where an ambulance had to come get a girl with alcohol poisoning; that girl had practically been in a coma and vomited all over herself. Not a pretty sight. "Who took her to the hospital?"

"I have no idea. She didn't want to talk much on the phone. She just apologized and said I was right about a lot of things, and she wanted to say she loved me." Ava's voice caught and she brushed her arm against her face again, though there was no clay on her cheeks.

"So that's good news, right?"

"It is, yes." Ava bit her lip. "The thing is, I didn't tell her we'd found Peter in the yearbook. I didn't want to upset her and, I don't know, make her relapse or anything."

Gigi thought about this. What Ava was really saying was that she wasn't sure they should keep looking for Peter, not right now, with this happening to Elaine. Gigi got that. But she wasn't about to stop. Ava could take a break, sure, but now that they had a last name and a birth date, Gigi had been Googling the shit out of everything, trying to track down her brother. So far, nothing had popped up. But it would. She was sure of that.

"I'm going to keep looking for him," Gigi said. "But I understand why you might need to quit."

"I'm not going to quit," Ava said. "I'm just taking a break. For Elaine's sake."

Gigi nodded. "I know," she said, and then they went back to work and didn't talk about it anymore.

Ava went to play tennis with Olivia after lunch. Evan and Sam had gone to their dad's for the weekend, but they were back at the house by the time Gigi went up to try a new song on her guitar. The boys were sitting together on the couch, and the weird thing was that the Xbox wasn't on and neither was the TV. They were just sitting there like zombies, Sam with his legs stretched out and Evan in his geek yoga pose.

"You look like your dog just died," she said.

"Hey," Evan said. Sam just grunted.

Gigi decided to hang around instead of taking off to see if Neal was at the barn. She'd been riding with him most afternoons, and once he'd come to her house and listened to music. He still hadn't kissed her, but she was beginning to think he wanted to. This was a good feeling; it was the first time ever that she'd felt like a boy was more nervous around her than she was around him. Plus it was great to see Lydia looking all bug-eyed when she and Neal were together.

Gigi picked up her guitar and started working out some chords. Pretty soon, Sam and Evan joined her and they worked out a couple of Cure songs. Then Gigi put down her guitar and said, "Seriously, guys. What's up? You can tell me. I'm your auntie."

This made Sam snort. Evan relaxed back against the sofa with his bass cradled between his knees. "Dad's getting married," he said.

"Dude! We're not supposed to tell anybody!" Sam said.

"We're not supposed to tell *Mom*," Evan corrected. "Those were Dad's exact words. He wants to tell her himself."

"I won't tell her," Gigi promised, though she suspected Ava would probably guess on her own. "You didn't see this coming?"

"No, man, Dad's dated before, but nobody ever lasted more than a few months," Sam said. "Dad's just not the marrying type."

"He married your mother," Gigi said.

"Yeah, but that was, like, a million years ago," Sam said.

"Does his girlfriend have kids?" Gigi asked.

"One. She's already married, though. We won't have to live with her, at least."

"She could be nice," Gigi suggested. "Maybe your stepmom is nice, too."

"Yeah, but the point is, we like staying with our dad on weekends because we're *bachelors*," Sam said. "We can be slobs and leave things lying around and whatever. This woman, Sasha, she's like a drill sergeant. Napkins on the lap, chores, the whole bit!"

Evan was nodding. "Yeah, she even makes us make our *beds*."

Gigi thought about how the boys lived with Ava, like wolf cubs or something, keeping their own hours, eating and drinking whatever. Personally, she couldn't stand the mess they made. "That will be different," she said. "On the other hand, if you guys grow up to have, like, jobs, you'll probably have to learn to put your napkins on your laps at company lunches or whatever. And if you ever get married, your wives will run you over with their cars if you don't pick up your dirty clothes. I know I would."

The boys stared at her. "Dude, I thought you'd be on our side," Sam said.

Gigi sighed. "I am," she said. "I have your backs, whatever happens. But the thing is, how long will you live with your dad, realistically? We're all going to college, right? And you don't want him to be alone forever."

"Too true," Evan said.

"So be glad he found somebody, and that she's not a psycho."

"We don't know that," Sam grumbled. "She seems like the kind of chick who'd go postal if you made a mistake."

"Better not make any, then," Gigi suggested. "Meanwhile, I need your help." She had made copies of the yearbook picture and the only photograph they had of Peter. Now she showed these to the boys and told them the whole story.

"This sucks," Evan said. "We have an uncle and Mom didn't tell us?"

"It's complicated," Gigi said, and told them about Elaine. As she'd suspected, they knew about Elaine's bouts with alcohol and understood she might have put pressure on their mother not to look for Peter. Gigi loved how Sam and Evan were immediately ready to defend Ava, to go to battle for her whether it was to find a lost brother or put a surly aunt in her place. She wished, not for the first time, that her dad could have known them better.

This thought made her shadow of guilt return, knowing that she was the real reason her father had left this family for her own. But, as she'd told Sam and Evan, sometimes all you could do was accept what happened and find the good in it.

It was Sam who found Peter Winslow online. Gigi had tried every social media site she could think of except the obvious: the online white pages for Maine and Massachusetts. There were two Peter Winslows in Maine and four in Massachusetts; only one of the six names matched the age they'd estimated her brother to be. Unfortunately, that address was unlisted.

"No worries," Sam said with a grin, and typed in a credit card number to access a full report. There he was: Peter Winslow, age forty-three, with a home address in Cambridge. Next, Sam typed her brother's name into LinkedIn. There were thirteen professionals listed with that name, but only one was in Massachusetts. Dr. Peter Winslow was a clinical psychologist with an office in Cambridge.

Sam printed out the information. "Wow," Gigi said, staring at the paper in her hand. "You scare me. Want to take a field trip?"

They left a note for Ava, saying only that they'd gone out for the afternoon and would be back by dinner. Sam had a license but no car; they rode their bikes to the train station in Newburyport and took the commuter rail into the city.

They had decided to stake out Peter's office in Cambridge. From North Station, they took the green line to Park Street, then changed to the red line to Central Square. This wasn't an area Gigi had been to before, but Sam and Evan had been to a used-guitar store here with Les, so they weren't intimidated by the traffic or the homeless guys holding out cups or squatting on blankets in doorways, some with trembling, sad-faced little dogs. Most had cardboard signs saying things like WILL WORK FOR FOOD. Gigi gave away most of her money before Sam stopped her, saying they were probably just going to buy booze with it.

Peter's office was upstairs from a busy coffee shop with college students parked at outdoor tables and along a counter just inside the window, most with their laptops open and headphones dangling from their ears. The three of them bought coffees and took up positions around a metal table on the sidewalk with a sweet view of the doorway to Peter's office. The simple gold plaque on the door read PETER WINSLOW, PHD, CLINICAL PSYCHOLOGIST, along with three other names of psychologists who must all be in the same practice. By the Braille letters beneath it, Gigi knew they had to be in the right place.

Sam and Evan seemed as nervous as she was, checking the time on their phones about every five minutes and jittering their knees under the table. Most of the customers looked like students; the guys wore skinny jeans and black glasses, the girls Daisy Dukes or flowing colorful skirts, tank tops, and sandals. Evan and Sam fit right in, but Gigi felt suddenly awkward in her cutoffs and T-shirt. At least she'd put the rings back in her nose and eyebrow.

Nobody came and went through the doorway next door, which made Gigi worry that maybe Dr. Peter Winslow didn't see clients on Mondays. Then, around three o'clock, a woman went inside, and every hour after that, another client appeared. She and the boys continued to sit there—nobody in the café seemed to mind, or even notice—and eventually Gigi bought them sandwiches to help pay for their time at the table. The boys gobbled the food down in three bites, but Gigi was too nervous to eat.

Just after seven o'clock, Peter came downstairs. It was so unexpected a sighting after so many tedious hours that Gigi didn't know whether to believe it was him, until Evan nudged her sharply in the ribs.

"Hey," Evan hissed. "That's our guy."

Gigi's mouth went dry. Peter was walking toward them, tapping a white cane on the sidewalk. His hair was dark, almost black, with a few gray streaks. His face was lined but otherwise the same as the face in the yearbook. His brown eyes were so familiar that Sam said, "Wow. He looks just like Aunt Elaine."

"And Grandpa," Evan said. "Weird." He turned to Gigi. "Think he'd recognize you?"

Sam snorted. "He's blind, you douche bag."

"Shut up!" Gigi hissed, because Peter was coming closer.

He walked right past them, a handsome man whose only flaw was that his brown eyes jittered a little from side to side with the motion of his walk. He had a square jaw and high cheekbones. He looked like a perfect blend of Ava, with her sharp cheekbones and strong build, and Elaine, with her exotic features and pale skin. Nothing but the cane and those eyes would have clued anybody in to his inability to see.

"What now?" Sam asked once Peter was inside the café.

"We should totally ambush him," Evan suggested. "Surround him and start talking."

"What if he doesn't believe me?" Gigi said, suddenly panicking.

"He's going to believe you, dude," Sam said, rolling his eyes. "Nobody could make up a story like this."

"Yeah, but what if he doesn't even know he's adopted?" Gigi whispered back. "This might ruin his life."

"He's got to know," Evan said. "He was already in school by then, right?"

"Right," Gigi said.

"Do you want to call our mom? Maybe come here another day with her to talk to him?" Evan said. He was thinking hard about the consequences of their actions, Gigi could tell. Evan was like that.

"No," Gigi said. "I'm going for it." She stood up, brushed off her clothes. She was tired of waiting, of thinking *What if?* Her first priority was to do what Dad wanted. "I don't think I should do it here, though. I should go up to his office, where it's more private."

"Dude, he might think you're a psycho stalker if you corner him," Sam said. "Besides, we should be with you."

"No, she's right," Evan said. "No guy wants to get all emo on a street corner. And he won't freak if she goes in alone."

"What if he's the psycho, and we let her go in alone?" Sam demanded.

Evan arched an eyebrow. "I'm pretty sure she could defend herself against a blind man," he said. "Besides, we'll be right out here with our phones. We'll give her fifteen minutes, max, to call us and say she's all right."

Peter came out again after a few minutes, carrying a cup of coffee. He tapped his cane past them and went back through the doorway to his office, walking like a man who wasn't in a hurry.

"Go," Evan said, nudging her. "We'll be right here."

"Yeah, I can drink coffee all night long," Sam said. "And if the café kicks us out, we'll pretend we're homeless and camp out on the corner."

"Okay," Gigi said. "But, before I go, can I just say I love you guys?"

"Only if you want to make me gag," Sam said, but he ducked his head and grinned.

Evan gave her a one-armed hug. "We love you, too. Now go in there and get 'er done."

It was a modest entryway, a pale gold hallway tiled in black and white. Peter's office was on the second floor; Gigi climbed the stairs with her chest hurting, knowing her feet were falling where her brother's had been just minutes before.

She hadn't expected a receptionist, but an Asian woman with delicate features and a punk haircut sat at a desk in the common waiting room shared by the suite of offices. The waiting room was empty, the magazines too neatly arranged, a basket of children's toys gathered neatly in one corner. They must have seen their last patient of the day, Gigi guessed. Good.

"Hello. May I help you?" the woman asked.

"I'm here to see Dr. Winslow," Gigi said.

"Do you have an appointment?"

She should have thought to make one, Gigi realized. "No. I'm just a friend stopping by to say hello."

"A friend?"

The receptionist clearly didn't believe her. It was a pretty lame thing to say. Well, there was always the truth.

But, before Gigi could say more, the receptionist was picking up the phone and dialing. Peter must have answered the phone, for the woman said, "Dr. Winslow? There's a young woman here to see you. She says she's a friend of yours." She looked up at Gigi. "What's your name, please?"

"Gigi." Gigi didn't use her last name, suddenly afraid that Peter might have looked for them after all, maybe discovered who his parents were and didn't want to have anything to do with them. He might recognize their father's name.

Except that Peter had been given his mother's name. Did he even know who his father was?

Nearly dizzy now with fear, Gigi perched on the edge of the puffy white sofa across from the receptionist's desk. After what seemed like an hour but was probably just a few minutes, the receptionist told Gigi to head down the hallway.

"Dr. Winslow's office is the last door on the left," she said.

The hallway was carpeted in bright teal and the walls were painted a soothing plum. Gigi supposed this was meant to make people feel more at peace; in art class, she'd learned something about the impact colors have on moods. She wondered if blind people could feel colors, or could at least feel the moods of the people around them as they reacted to color.

Peter's door was a deeper plum color with his nameplate screwed onto it. She knocked, and when he said, "Come in," she slowly pushed the door open.

"Yes?" he said.

Gigi opened her mouth but no sound emerged. She was face-to-face with her brother. There was no doubt in her mind, and even less in her heart. Peter had the same solemn expression he'd worn for the photograph taken of him as a little boy on Aunt Finley's couch. His hands were folded on the desk, too, the same way that little boy's hands had been folded for the camera, as if he were holding himself in place.

She cleared her throat. "I'm not really your friend," she said. "We've never met before."

Peter's lip twitched, but he didn't smile. He cocked his head at the sound of her voice. "Is this one of those situations where I'm going to need to call security to remove you from my office?"

"No!" It took Gigi a minute to realize he was teasing her. She tried to laugh but didn't succeed. Every sound stuck in her throat like a burr. "I need to sit down," she said.

Peter came around the desk, not using his cane. He must know where his furniture was, Gigi realized, as he took her elbow and guided her to a couch against the opposite wall. It was the twin of the couch in the waiting area, puffy and white, an unexpected color for an office, Gigi would think, but then, white went with everything.

"I'm sorry," she said, "but this is scary, seeing you."

Peter didn't return to the desk, but sat next to her on the couch and patted her hand. "I can hear how upset you are."

Her brother must be a great therapist, Gigi thought, and then she couldn't help it: his voice was so much like Dad's that she started crying. Her eyes and nose and even her mouth began gushing water, like she was one of those fountain statues that had sprung leaks in unexpected places.

Peter must have been used to situations like this, because he calmly gathered tissues and pressed them into her hands, murmuring soothing words she mostly didn't care about but needed to hear anyway, like "Let it out" and "It'll all get better with time."

"Maybe for me it'll be better, but not for you," Gigi mumbled miserably into one of the tissues when she'd finally dried out enough to speak. "You might be sorry you didn't throw me out."

"You're not here to take care of me," Peter said. "That's my job, to care for people."

She looked up at his brown eyes, seeing herself mirrored there, wondering what it would be like, knowing people only by their voices and footsteps and smells. Maybe, she thought, you could understand people better, see more into their hearts, if you didn't have to first get past how people looked.

"I know," she said. "It must be an interesting job."

"Especially when strange girls show up claiming to be my friends."

This made her laugh, finally, and Peter smiled, too. "Now," he said. "Why are you here?"

When Ava had seen the note from Gigi and the boys, her first thought was to wonder where they were, of course, but knowing they were together made her worry less. They would take care of one another.

That left her free to worry again about Elaine, who had called to say she was home from the hospital and "determined to dry out." Ava hoped it was true. She wished Elaine would let her come down to the condo, to take her to dinner at least, but Elaine had gently but firmly refused. "Let's wait to see if I've really pulled myself together," she said. "I'm sorry."

At loose ends, Ava called Simon to tell him what was going on. He stopped her midway through her tangled explanations of going to Thompson with Gigi, finding Peter's picture in the yearbook, and hearing that Elaine had been hospitalized for alcohol poisoning. "Come to Boston," he said.

"What? I can't do that!"

"Sure you can," Simon said. "Just jump in the car and come down. I'll take you to dinner if you don't feel comfortable coming to my place. Besides, I have something to tell you. Something good."

Nervously, Ava glanced around her empty but messy house, as if someone else were here, eavesdropping. She could use some good news right now. And what the hell. Elaine had pushed her away, and probably for good reason: Elaine needed to find her own way in the world, without Ava's help. If Elaine became more responsible, and Ava slightly less, wouldn't it make sense that someday they might find common ground?

"I'll be there in an hour," she told Simon.

He took her to a small Italian wine bar on Newbury Street, a place with copper-topped tables and sleek waiters dressed in black who glided around the patio. They lingered over tiramisu and thimble-sized glasses of port after dinner. It was still early, not quite seven o'clock, and Newbury Street was crowded. They sat side by side facing the street and watching the crowd, thighs touching, until Ava couldn't stand it any longer. "How long would it take us to get to your condo from here?" she whispered.

Then they were there, miraculously together in a bed, Simon's bed, her legs wrapped around his waist, his hand in her tangled hair. They made love twice in an hour. Afterward, Ava felt as though someone had pulled out her bones; to stand, she had to grip the back of a chair, and even then she was swaying a little, drunk with lovemaking, with love.

Simon made espresso and they took the gilded white porcelain cups out to the narrow balcony overlooking the harbor. It was only eight thirty, but it felt like a month had passed. Ava had never felt more transported out of her life, her mind. She wasn't sure she liked it, but there it was, the truth: this was who she was, too, not just a mother and high school teacher and potter and decent tennis player and lousy housekeeper. She was Simon's lover. She was in love with Simon.

"What was it you wanted to tell me?" she asked, realizing that was how he'd lured her down here in the first place, as if she'd needed more bait than her own desire. "The good news?"

"I told Katy about us." Simon's hand was trembling a little as it held the tiny cup; he had to set it down on the table between them. "She had guessed anyway."

"How?" Ava's mouth had gone dry.

"I guess I was maybe less subtle than I'd thought," Simon said sheepishly. "Katy said she could tell by the way I talked about you, any time your name came up, that something was going on. The good news is that she's okay with it. She really likes you, Ava. She wants us to be happy."

He said this last in a rush, as if he was afraid she'd be upset, or disbelieving. Maybe she was a little bit. But she was also relieved. "I'm glad," she said, just as her cell phone rang in the other room.

"Don't answer it," Simon said, covering her hand with his own. "Just be with me."

She shook her head. "I can't. The kids," she said, and went in search of her phone.

It was Sam, sounding excited but otherwise okay. "Mom, we need you to come to Boston."

"What?" Ava stared out the windows at the terrace and the glittering lights of Boston Harbor beyond it, as if Sam were standing out there. Impossible. "Where are you? What are you doing in Boston?" Immediately, her maternal panic button was pushed. She concocted scenarios, most involving friends who shouldn't be driving and illegal substances.

"It's okay, Mom. We're safe."

"Where are you, and who's 'we'?" she said. "Are you still with Gigi and Evan?"

"Yeah, they're here." She could hear Gigi in the background, sounding excited. "Gigi says to tell you we're all fine and we haven't done anything stupid. We just need you to come get us. We have something important to show you."

Then it dawned on Ava: Gigi must have found Peter's house. She had said she was going to keep looking. At least the girl would have the sense not to try and meet him alone.

Wouldn't she?

"Hang on. I'll be right there."

Then she realized they didn't know where she was, either. They'd be expecting her to take an hour to drive down. Well, they'd just have to think she drove like hell.

"I'm going with you," Simon said when she told him her suspicions.

"No you're not." Ava pulled on her jeans and T-shirt. "Sorry, but this is something I have to do alone."

He grabbed both her hands, pulled her to him. "You won't be alone. The kids will be there. Gigi is my niece. I need to be there for her, as well as for you. This is a really big deal. I should drive you, at least, even if I don't come inside."

He was right, she supposed. And besides, she might be too shaky to drive. "All right. But could we just act like friends?"

Simon kissed her. "We *are* friends."

They took Simon's Mercedes and followed the GPS directions to the address in Cambridge that Ava had gotten from Sam. It took them all of fifteen minutes to pull up to a modest bungalow, painted brick red with a yellow door, in one of the funky student neighborhoods off Mass Ave between Harvard and MIT. This particular street seemed mostly upscale, a mix of tidy brick apartment buildings, two-family homes, and small bungalows like this one, suggesting it was where students moved after they'd kicked their professional lives in gear.

Ava peered at the neat yard with its picket fence. There were rocking chairs on the porch like the ones you saw all over Maine, painted white. Children's toys cluttered the yard.

She checked the address against the one Sam had texted her to be sure it was the right place. "Where are they?"

"Probably inside."

"You think they convinced Peter to let them inside? Two teen-aged boys and a girl? What was he thinking? My brother's blind!"

Simon gave her an amused look. "That doesn't make him stupid."

Ashamed, Ava got out of the car and slammed the door hard enough to make the car rattle. Simon climbed out, too, pocketed the keys, and offered her his arm. She took it and they crossed the street together.

Of all of the possible reunions she'd imagined for herself and Peter, this wasn't one of them: on a poorly lit street in Cambridge, on the porch of a bungalow after having just made love with her stepmother's brother, hoping her sons and half sister were inside. Ava felt faint with the sheer craziness of her misshapen family life.

"Are you going to ring the bell, or should we just wait until he comes out to get the morning paper?" Simon asked.

She punched his arm and knocked on the door.

A woman opened it. She was in her forties, small but curvy, streaked short hair. She smiled. "You must be Ava," she said. "Come in. I'm Charley Winslow, Peter's wife." She stuck out her hand.

"I," Ava began, but couldn't say anything else, because Peter appeared in the hallway, Gigi at his side, and behind them Evan and Sam.

"Surprise!" Sam said. "Hey, who's that with you? And how did you get here so fast? Way to go, Mom!"

"Uncle Simon?" Gigi said.

"Oh!" Ava said, staring at Peter, at a face so like her father's and Elaine's, so like her own and Gigi's, that she burst into tears.

Charley and Simon led her like an invalid to the futon sofa in the snug living room. Charley brought her a cup of mint tea and sat cross-legged in front of Peter, who sat in a mission-style chair across from Ava. She stared at him while the kids told her about their detective work, and how Peter had let Gigi in his office. Meanwhile, Ava's mind buzzed with questions she couldn't ask yet: Had Peter looked for them? Had he been happy and loved as a child? Did he know, now, that he wasn't ever forgotten, no matter how many people tried to erase the past?

"How did Gigi convince you that she was really your sister?" Ava asked once she'd collected herself enough to speak.

"Gigi didn't need to work too hard," Peter said, his voice gentle. "I wasn't adopted until I was eight. I knew I had another family."

"Where did you go?" Ava asked when she could trust her voice. "After Finley, I mean. Do you remember her? Aunt Finley, our mother's sister? Mom wanted her to raise you."

Peter nodded. "I have a couple of memories of that house. Mostly of being kept in one room and wanting so much to go outside. I used to think of ways to escape." A smile flashed across his handsome face. "Once, I even made it out the window and down the street before she caught me."

He told Ava then about the cause of his blindness—his optic nerves hadn't developed, "just one of those things, nobody's fault"— his foster homes, a series of them in Maine, and about the family in Portland that finally adopted him because his adoptive mother's own brother had been blinded in Vietnam. "She was on a mission to adopt a blind child, and I got lucky," Peter said simply. "She and her husband were good to me, and I had two sisters who didn't seem to mind a little brother tagging along. My uncle was a big role model for me, too, showing me that being blind doesn't have to define or limit who you are."

Charley reached up from where she was sitting to take his hand. "I always wanted him to find his birth mother," she said, "but Peter didn't want to hurt the family he had by making them think they weren't enough for him."

"Your family sent you to Thompson?" Ava asked. "I'm sure Gigi told you that's how we found you, through the yearbooks."

"My family couldn't have afforded a school like that. Luckily, I was in middle school in Portland, in a special program, and I got a scholarship. That changed my life and meant I could go to college, live on my own." Peter laughed. "I can't believe you found me because of *South Pacific*. Man, did I love to sing when I was in school."

"Me, too," Gigi said. "Evan and Sam and I have a band with another guy, a drummer, and I'm the singer."

"Dad loved to sing," Ava said.

Peter cocked his head at her. "A family thing, then. And you, Ava?"

"Can't carry a tune."

"Are there any more of us?" Peter asked.

Ava thought he must be asking about other people in the room, since he couldn't see them. Then she realized he meant family. "We have another sister," she said.

Peter glanced around the room as if he could, indeed, count heads. "Where is she?"

"She lives in Boston," Ava said. "Her name is Elaine."

"A half sister or full?"

"Full. She's five years younger than I am," Ava said. Then, after a minute, she felt compelled to add, "Elaine knows we were looking for you, but she's not sure she's ready to meet you yet."

"I understand," Peter said, and Ava thought, from the grave expression on his face, that Peter was probably used to hearing people say they weren't ready for changes in their life. It's what he did for a living, after all.

"She's a good person," Ava said. "She's just going through a hard time since Dad died."

"Are the three of you close, now that our dad is gone?" Peter asked.

Gigi met Ava's eyes, giving her permission to speak the truth. But what was the truth? "We're family," Ava said finally. "We look out for each other. That's why we're here. Dad wanted us to find you and tell you he made a mistake by not looking for you once Mom told him about the pregnancy. If things had been left up to him, he never would have given you up in the first place. He always regretted losing you."

Peter lowered his head. "That's nice of you to say."

"It's true," Ava said.

"And even if it weren't for Dad, we'd feel like that," Gigi added. "We hope you're glad we found you, too."

Peter turned his head in Gigi's direction. "I am," he said. "Unbelievably glad."

# CHAPTER FOURTEEN

Six days sober now. Five days, so far, of wretched AA meetings. Elaine had called in sick with the flu even though it was August, the entire city was shut down, and she was owed about three weeks of vacation.

Now it was Sunday. Tony had returned from his golf trip to North Carolina and he'd be back in the office on Monday; she had to tell him the truth before then. Alcoholics Anonymous was all about asking for help, getting on your knees, telling the truth, making amends, staying sober one day at a time, etc. Great advice if you could follow it. Which she totally could. Maybe.

Her AA sponsor, Greta, said it was probably too soon to try making amends, since that was step eight and she'd just started her *personal journey*—Christ, the worst phrase ever, one she'd banned from college admissions materials the first week she started with Tony's company—but Elaine was in no mood to wait. She'd take her sobriety vows seriously, but some things she had to do on her own terms, her own schedule.

Elaine called Tony early to see if he was going to the usual spin class; when he said he was, she said she'd meet him there. Then she asked if he'd go with her to the pool at the North End. She'd chosen that spot because it was one of her happiest memories of the summer.

"You're so pale," Tony said when they emerged from their respective bathhouses in their swimsuits and met on the concrete walkway around the pool. "Are you sure you feel well enough to be here?"

Elaine had caked on concealer and makeup to cover the black eye. She'd hit her head hard on something when she fell in the pub bathroom, fracturing her skull. The bruising on her head had caused blood to pool down her face and gather around her eye until she looked like a battered wife. The weird thing was that nobody asked what happened to her, not in restaurants, coffee shops, or gas stations. No wonder women didn't like to admit being victims of domestic violence: they felt invisible. The bruising had gone from green to blue to deep plum and then violet and yellow, which is what it was now beneath the makeup.

"I'm sober," she said.

Tony laughed. "Yeah, you should be, sweetie, after that killer workout this morning. Sweated every drop of alcohol right out of you, I bet." Then he saw her expression and reached for her hand. "Tell me," he said.

Elaine related everything that had happened while he was away: the failed date with Gabe, Ava getting even closer to Gigi as the two of them looked for their brother, and Elaine's own irrational rage and sorrow. And drinking. Drinking more than she ever had in her life, even during their party years at Tufts.

"I screwed up," she said. "Big-time."

Elaine told him about drinking vodka and cranberry juice in the car—not the first time—and about her night at the pub drinking martinis with the twin Irishmen, which had led to her being sick in the bathroom and falling. She'd made the call and been taken to the hospital by the woman who came to her rescue, Greta, who was now her AA sponsor.

"And yes, before you ask me, the ugly rumors are true: those meetings really are held in awful church basements," she said.

"I know," Tony said quietly.

"*What?* Who told you about me?"

"Nobody, you ninny." They were sitting on the edge of the pool, their legs dangling in the lukewarm water.

"How did you know I'd joined AA, then?" she asked.

"I didn't," Tony said. "It's not like anything you did made Fox News or caused people in the office to say you were a falling-down drunk. I just know about the church basements because George is in AA. He's been sober for ten years." Tony said this with pride.

Elaine was stunned. "George? Your George, who loves to cook four-course meals and wear Armani? Why didn't you tell me?"

Tony shrugged. "Not my dirty laundry to air, honey. But I'm sure George would be okay with you knowing this, given the circumstances." He smiled and feathered his fingers across her cheekbone, just below her black eye. "You're very brave, both of you."

Elaine wanted to cry; she was so grateful that Tony hadn't made her feel like more of a loser than she already was. Instead she kissed him and pulled him into the water. After their swim, they ate ice cream at the snack bar, moaning about the hour of spin class they'd have to do tomorrow to work it off.

They had brought separate cars to the pool because Elaine had one more thing to do today. She drove to Gabe's house in the South End and parked down the street from his brownstone, admiring the flowers blooming in the tidy postage stamp lawns in front of the buildings.

Outside his door, though, she began to lose her resolve. Maybe

Greta was right and it was too soon to make amends with everyone on her list. Another, cynical voice inside her head demanded why she even cared what this guy thought of her. It wasn't like she planned to date him.

Plus—and this was the smallest, most insignificant concern, but couldn't be ignored—did she really want anyone other than Tony or hospital orderlies seeing her without makeup, especially with a black eye? She'd come straight from the pool and had barely combed her hair, which still hung straight and wet and cold on her shoulders.

In the window, there was a movement behind the curtain. Elaine nearly jumped out of her skin, thinking it was Gabe watching her spy on his house. Then she realized it was the psycho kitty, Tommy, parting the curtains with his big round head. He looked like the Cheshire cat, sitting like that between the curtains with just his head showing. She imagined his grin and nearly waved to him.

Then the door opened and Gabe stepped outside. He wore the same cotton bathrobe she'd borrowed the night of the mugging and he was blinking at her in the bright sunlight. It took her a minute to realize he wasn't wearing his glasses, which must be why he was squinting like that.

"Oh!" he said. "I thought you were the woman who delivers the *Times*. I called them to say the paper hadn't arrived."

"I didn't steal it. I promise."

Gabe came down the steps and padded toward her on the sidewalk on bare feet. He fished his black glasses out of one pocket of the robe and put them on. "Wow." He peered at her eye. "What did you do to yourself?"

"You should see the other guy," Elaine said, hating the wobble in her voice.

Gabe didn't laugh. "You'd better come in. Looks like you could use a cup of coffee."

Coffee was just what she needed, even if Gabe had probably suggested it because he'd jumped to the conclusion that she'd been out carousing last night. Elaine followed him meekly up the sidewalk. She had gone through spin class and swimming at the pool on nothing more than a peach yogurt and that ice cream sandwich. Her head felt stuffed with cotton and her pores were oozing chlorine at a time of day when they should have been oozing caffeine.

"I'm sorry to barge in on you like this," she said as they made their way down the cool dim hallway to the kitchen.

"Who's barging? I invited you in," Gabe said with a waggle of his fingers over one shoulder. "I'm barely out of bed. Looks like you've been running or something."

"Spin class, then swimming." Again, she heard the unspoken accusation and felt the questions he wasn't asking, saw them written in the tension across his shoulders. "Gabe, I was home and in bed at nine o'clock last night. And all I had to drink was water."

He went to the cupboard, took out a pair of mugs without looking at her. "Why? Who died?"

"That's not funny," she said.

"No? Well, neither are you." He turned around, and for the first time Elaine saw how angry Gabe was. His brown eyes were fierce, sparking gold behind the thick frames of his glasses, and his shoulders were squared, his bare feet centered beneath him. He looked like he could pick up the refrigerator next to him and toss it out a window.

"I'm so, so sorry," she whispered, and sank into one of the kitchen chairs, her head in her hands. "I never meant to hurt you."

"You pissed me off, that's what you did," Gabe said. "I didn't realize how much until I saw you just now. I thought I'd written you off as one more crazy I can't save, like pretty much every damaged woman I dated in high school and college. That's me, the sappy Jew, always attracted to girls who need saving. Not your fault, me and my do-gooder habits. I expect to get my heart stomped on, that's my MO, and, well, somebody's gotta be the schmuck in every relationship. But for some reason—silly me—I really thought we were developing a friendship. And then you turned on me because I was *honest*. Because I was trying to *help* you. Well, screw you!"

Elaine lifted her head and stared at him. "Whoa," she said, genuinely impressed. "Nice rant. Maybe you're way less nice than I thought. Good job. I really feel like crap now."

For a minute, she thought Gabe might hurl the coffeepot at the wall. Instead, he glowered at her but set the coffee down carefully on the counter. Then he brought the mugs to the table and put those down, too.

He pulled out the chair next to hers with one foot and sat down, wrapping the robe around his legs. He was staring at her the whole time, his dark eyes gradually lightening to warm hazel, and then he was smiling and rubbing his eyes under the glasses, shaking his head. "Jesus," he said. "What the hell are you doing here, Elaine?"

"I came to apologize." She reached over and touched his hand to make him look at her. "I came to say you were right. I was drinking and it was screwing up my life. I ended up at Mass General last weekend with alcohol poisoning."

He took a sharp breath. "Why didn't you call me? I put my number in your phone for a reason."

Elaine shrugged. "I had to call somebody else. Somebody disconnected from me and my family. Now I'm in AA. End of story." She smiled. "Or the beginning, I hope."

"Just tell me who gave this to you." Gabe touched her face, his finger cool on her warm cheek.

She shivered a little but didn't pull away. "I did," she said. "I blacked out and fell. I had a lump on my head the size of an orange. This is the residual bleeding under the skin, apparently. I didn't even hit my face."

"You were lucky you weren't concussed."

"It would have been hard to tell if I was, the condition I was in," Elaine said. "It scared me, though, so it was a good thing it happened."

"I wish it hadn't come to that."

"Me, too. But things go the way they do, right? And all we can do is get back up again." Elaine sipped her coffee. "Got any toast?"

He laughed and stood up to make some. The cat came in and jumped onto her lap, purring in his broken way, and Elaine stroked him until his fur crackled. She ate two pieces of wheat toast with strawberry jam, and then Gabe made cheese omelets and she ate one of those, too, and had two more cups of coffee. She told him about Ava leaving a phone message for her last night, saying they had news about Peter.

"I couldn't tell from her voice whether it was good news or bad," Elaine said. She loaded their dishes into the dishwasher and began scrubbing the egg pan.

"What are you hoping for?"

Gabe reached above her to put away the glasses she'd washed, and she smelled his skin, spicy and warm. It was a comforting scent; Elaine wanted to lean her head back against his chest and rest there, smelling him.

"I hope he had a happy life," she said slowly. "I feel sorry for the guy. But I hope he's so happy that he only wants minimal contact with us. You know, like occasional holidays. That would be enough for me, and it would make Ava and Gigi happy."

"You sound very mature."

Elaine could hear a smile in Gabe's voice. He was still behind her, rustling around in a closet now, it sounded like. She finished washing the pan and did the spatula, then wiped the counters clean. "I'm trying to be less of a spoiled drunken dimwit," she said.

"Sounds like a reasonable plan. Think you'll succeed?"

He was standing very close to her now, doing nothing. Elaine laid the sponge down and slowly turned around to face him. Gabe was only a foot away, holding a bag of cat food in one hand, his dark corkscrew curls in a tangle.

"I don't know. Do you?" she asked.

"I hope so." Slowly, Gabe stepped toward her. He cupped her chin in one hand and tipped her face up to the light, peering at her eye. "Have you put ice on that?"

"It's too late now," she said.

"It's never too late to try again," he said, and kissed her.

It should have been an awkward kiss, with him in his robe and bare feet and holding the bag of cat food, and her smelling of swimming pool and ice cream and coffee. It should have been the kind of tame, passing-ships kiss that married people have, a kiss that acknowledges imperfection as well as passion, the kind of kiss that happens long after two people have disappointed each other and then forgiven each other, too, so many times that they feel safe.

It was a kiss in a kitchen, for one thing, a kiss with a hungry cat meowing in the background, a kiss taken and given without makeup or showering or combing, a kiss that lasted, Elaine would think later, much longer than it should have, but not nearly long enough. Because she had never been kissed like that before, and she would never get tired of it. That much she knew.

.  .  .

Sarah had come to band practice and now she was sitting at Ava's kitchen table, her head resting on her arms. Something must have happened between her and Sam.

Gigi wanted to ignore her—she barely knew Sarah—but here they were, the only two in the kitchen, and the only girls in the house other than Ava, who mostly stayed upstairs or out in her studio while the band was playing, "giving them space," as she always said, when really Gigi knew Ava was in and out of the house enough to spot anything skeezy going down.

Neal hadn't come tonight. He'd taken a job as a busboy at Panera, working there as well as the barn now so he could put away money for college. He and Sarah had a single mom who worked ten-hour shifts at the hospital as a nurse, so they were on their own a lot. Gigi couldn't imagine this; she'd always had so many adults in her life.

And now Peter, too, who she was getting to know through e-mail, mostly. He told her he had a speech recognition program for his computer and he could also type in Braille, which she thought was cool. He was coming to Beach Plum Island this weekend; Gigi and Ava were planning a birthday party for him with Charley's help. They had a baby girl; Gigi would get to meet her this weekend, too. The baby was asleep that night they'd found Peter.

Gigi took a slice of pizza out of one of the boxes on the counter— that's what she'd come into the kitchen for—and ate it standing by the fridge. Sarah was still snuffling. The guys were in the other room arguing about *Doctor Who*, a TV show that only guys seemed to get. Guys didn't seem to care that the special effects on that show looked like they'd been made by fifth graders. Evan told her that was the point.

Apparently Sarah either didn't know Gigi was in the room, didn't care, or was waiting for someone to ask her what happened.

Most girls were a mystery to Gigi. Why didn't they just say what they wanted?

"What's wrong?" Gigi finally asked.

"You wouldn't understand," Sarah muttered.

"I'd understand better if you picked your head up and talked so I could hear you."

This was mean, something a mother would say, but it did the trick. Sarah sat up and wiped her eyes with her hand. She looked so much like Neal it was freaky, really: that long brown hair, the sharp features. She and Neal even had matching clover tattoos on the backs of their necks. "Sorry," Sarah said.

"It's fine." Gigi handed her a napkin for her to blow her nose, then sat down at the table. Maybe it was because Sarah did look so much like her brother, or maybe it was because, for about the first time ever, Gigi felt like she could talk to a girl her own age without being self-conscious about it, but she found herself wanting to help. "Did you and Sam break up or something?"

Sarah shook her head. Her eyes were nearly swollen shut; they were so puffy and red from crying. "We can't really do that, since we're not going out, right?" She sighed and lifted her shoulders in a shrug. "He says he likes me, but he doesn't like me enough for us to commit."

"That sounds like Sam," Gigi said. "He doesn't commit to much. I mean, except to music and lacrosse. Those are his two big loves."

"So you're saying I'm wasting my time."

"I don't know," Gigi said, trying to be as honest as possible, because otherwise what was the point of a conversation like this? "In the movies, they always show people waiting, like, their whole lives for that one person they love. Sometimes the endings are happy, and sometimes it's all a big ironic tragedy or whatever. But how can you know if somebody will love you if you don't wait around? And then there's another way to look at it, too, which is what else would you be doing if you weren't being with this person? I mean, do you like Sam enough to hang out with him while he's making up his mind, or are you always feeling disappointed and sad like you are tonight? If most of the time it's good when you're together, then it's probably worth sticking it out. Otherwise, you should walk."

Sarah smiled. "I can see why my brother likes you so much," she said. "You're really wise about love."

Gigi laughed. "No, I'm not," she said, then thought of Neal, of the way she had finally kissed him at the barn, with the rain falling like a thousand soft kisses on the cobblestones outside the tack room. She'd tried to make her lips as soft as the rain, and she could tell by the way he kissed her back that Neal liked it. "I only know love is out there."

They practiced until about eleven; Gigi was happy to see that Sarah stayed and even danced with another kid during a couple of the songs toward the end. She hoped this would make Sam jealous, but who knew what went through Sam's mind? He always acted so cool in front of his friends even though Gigi knew that he was as geeky as Evan on the inside. She didn't envy Sarah.

Afterward, Gigi made Sam and Evan help her clean up. She'd suggested they'd better start doing this, or Ava might say they couldn't use the cottage as a practice space anymore. She was startled to see Uncle Simon show up at the back door. At first she thought he must have come to pick her up instead of Gramma Dawn, but then she saw the overnight bag in his hand and everything clicked into place.

"Ooh la la," she said.

"Don't tell your grandmother," Uncle Simon begged, looking sheepish. He put the bag down and gave her a hug. "How was practice?"

"Decent. We've got two new songs. I think we'll be ready for the show. We're going to play for Peter's party as a sort of dress rehearsal."

"That's great. I can't wait to hear you guys," he said.

Then Gramma Dawn was blowing her horn—she never got out of the car, so Uncle Simon's secret was safe unless she noticed his car on the street in front—and Gigi kissed him good night. "See you in the morning," she said. "I'm coming over to help Ava load the kiln."

It was weird, thinking about him with Ava, but it was good, too, Gigi thought as Ava came in from the studio, her smile lighting the whole room when she saw Uncle Simon. Gigi liked thinking about so many of her favorite people—Evan and Sam, Simon and Ava—all in one house together for her to visit whenever she wanted. Her family.

Elaine hadn't been planning to drive to Beach Plum Island on Monday. But Tony had called last night to insist that she take another week of vacation and really commit to her new life, and it was such a gorgeous day that the first thing she thought of when she looked out the window of her condo was Ava's cottage and how long it had been since she'd seen her and the boys.

She would surprise Ava, Elaine decided, and come up with those pecan rolls she loved so much from the Blue Heron bakery as a peace offering. She would listen to whatever news Ava wanted to tell her about Peter, the thing Ava had hinted at in her message the other day. Maybe she could even try to reach out to Gigi. She might not ever love Gigi, but she could be kind to her. Everyone deserved kindness.

Elaine knew she felt generous in part because Tony and Gabe

had both been so generous with her. She hadn't stayed at Gabe's long after that knee-quaking kiss in the kitchen, but she knew now that she would go back and try it again.

Elaine made the drive to Beach Plum Island in record time, keeping the windows open and listening to whatever was on Pandora. She hadn't even texted Ava, though she'd been tempted, especially after getting a text from Ava asking her to call. *We need to talk,* the text had said.

"You got that right," Elaine said aloud, smiling as one of her favorite Pink songs came on. This gave her a good excuse to shake her hair and howl into the wind, thinking of Dad. A happy memory, this time, of him holding her hand and Ava's, too, one day at the beach, and running into surf so cold that they had all come up out of the water shrieking, Dad making his voice a girly scream. He knew how to have fun, her father. And maybe that's what was making the pain of losing him less, lately: she was able to conjure some of the happier memories as well as the bitter ones.

Elaine drove fast, as she always did, taking the bridge at sixty instead of the posted twenty-five. It was fine. It was Monday, after all, not a heavy beach traffic day, and she loved imagining how surprised, how pleased, Ava would be to see her, to hear what she had to say.

Elaine parked the car a little way down the street from Ava's cottage, risking a ticket in order to surprise her sister. She crept around the studio side of the house and approached from the back along the beach. She could make out Ava's fair head over the fence; she must be sitting outside with the newspaper.

Good. This was their morning ritual, hers and Ava's, something they'd done almost every time Elaine had spent the night up here, starting back when her sister first got divorced and moved to the beach with the boys. Elaine used to spend entire weekends helping

Ava with Evan and Sam when they were little. God, she loved those kids. Why hadn't she seen more of them?

Well, that was about to change, too. She still had time before they left for college. Maybe she could even take Sam on college tours. She certainly knew enough admissions officers.

Elaine drew closer to the fence and saw Ava clearly now, sitting in one of the Adirondack chairs with the newspaper spread on the table beside her. She was laughing, tipping her head back and laughing. She must have seen something funny in the paper, something she'd share with Elaine in a minute.

Then the picture shifted, as surely as if someone had cut up the scene with scissors in front of Elaine's eyes: a man stepped out of Ava's sliding doors onto the patio, a handsome bare-chested blond man in pajama bottoms carrying two mugs. He handed one of the cups to Ava and bent down to kiss her.

Ava put her arms around the man's neck and pulled him to her. As the man turned his head to put his own cup down on the table next to Ava's, Elaine at last saw his face and realized the man was somebody she'd seen before. Someone she'd never liked, simply because he was Katy's brother. Simon! Ava was with Simon!

The screech in her head was so unbearable that Elaine was afraid it might have escaped her like a siren. But no, Ava was still laughing, and Simon was kissing her neck now, lowering himself to his knees in front of Ava's chair, pressing himself between her legs, lifting up her shirt and putting his mouth on her breasts.

Elaine fled. She ran so fast that she fell once and dropped the bag of pastries. She left the bag there—the seagulls would make short work of that—and kept running, losing a shoe and picking it up but not bothering to put it on again.

Ava with Simon! How had that happened? How long had it been going on? Clearly, a long time. Ava *never* brought men home. She'd never shown any interest in *any* man since Mark, except, briefly, that architect who tried to talk her into moving to California. Ava had made it clear then—had always made it clear—that she lived for her children, not for herself. And certainly not for any man.

So how had this happened? And when? Was this the news Ava had been saving for her?

The shrieking in Elaine's head was duller but still painful, drowning out her rational thoughts as the questions cascaded, the hurt and betrayal like someone sticking pins in her sides, a prickling of pain all over her body.

She slid behind the wheel of her car, her red baby, her sanctuary with the white leather seats, and gunned the engine, spinning the tires in the sand as she turned around and drove down Ava's street, back past the center of the tiny town and toward Newburyport, building speed on the Beach Plum Island Turnpike. Such a grand name for such a little road. She didn't care. Elaine treated the road like a turnpike: she hit fifty, sixty miles an hour, no music on the radio, just the screeching in her head as she took the bridge as fast as she always did, maybe faster, trying to leave the scene behind her in the dark blur of the past. Ava with Simon, Katy's brother! His lips on her sister's neck and breasts!

Elaine's chest heaved. She thought she might be sick. She turned her head toward the window for an instant just in case.

An instant was all it took: suddenly she was driving in the middle of the bridge instead of on her side of the road. A cyclist was headed toward her, pedaling fast, a slim girl in jeans and a bright yellow T-shirt.

It was the T-shirt that saved her, saved them both, as Elaine caught the color out of the corner of her eye. She overcorrected, yanking the wheel to the right, wanting to close her eyes but knowing she shouldn't.

There was a sickening crunch of metal and she was afraid she'd killed her, killed that poor girl, until the car slammed to a stop and she realized the smashing sound was her car, her sweet car, on the metal guardrail of the bridge. She'd been wearing her seat belt, thank Christ, but she was immobilized now, pinned against the seat by the air bag. How the hell did you get out of one of these? Nobody every taught you that.

Furiously, Elaine punched at the air bag until she ran out of energy. Then she realized she could put the seat back and did, which gave her enough room to slide out. Her legs were trembling so violently that she almost collapsed on the pavement.

The entire front end of the car was totaled, folded like an accordion, the grille steaming in the sunlight. Her beautiful baby, ruined! But at least she hadn't hit the girl. Or had she, after all?

Terrified, Elaine limped the rest of the way across the bridge and glanced wildly about for the bicycle and the girl. Nobody. Nothing. What the hell? Was it an illusion? Had she imagined that cyclist? Was this what happened when you went cold turkey and gave up booze? Wouldn't that be her luck? All this, and Ava with Simon, too.

Now the screech did come out of her head and out of her mouth, a wailing Elaine had never heard come out of a human being, certainly not out of her.

"Are you okay?" The voice was soft, tentative, and someone was touching her shoulder.

Elaine shut her mouth and nodded, still trying not to vomit. She glanced out of the corner of her eye without looking up. It was the girl on the bike, in her yellow T-shirt and black helmet. Not a scratch on her, thank God.

"I didn't kill you," Elaine whispered.

"No, but I think you killed your car." The girl sat down beside her. "I'm sorry."

"*You're* sorry? I almost hit you!"

"It's a skinny bridge. I should have been farther over."

Elaine snorted. "Me, too." Then she looked at the girl again, this time in horror as the girl pulled off the helmet and her face came into focus. "Oh, God," Elaine moaned. "Gigi?"

Gigi nodded. "For a minute I thought you didn't know who I was."

"Shit," Elaine said. "I almost killed you! My own sister!"

"I bet most sisters want to kill each other sometimes."

"Yeah, but I bet they don't literally nearly run them over with cars," Elaine said glumly. She glanced over her shoulder at the car. Yep, still totaled.

"You didn't," Gigi insisted. "I could have made it by you. I think you just took your eyes off the road for a minute and then panicked when you saw me in front of you."

"I panicked, all right. But I was already panicked."

"Why?"

Elaine didn't want to tell Gigi. But maybe Gigi already knew? She shook her head. "I was at Ava's," she said. "I was going to surprise her. But I'm the one who got surprised."

Gigi's eyes widened. "Oh," she said. "Uncle Simon was still there?"

"You knew," Elaine said flatly.

"She didn't tell me. I only figured it out a couple of days ago," Gigi said. "But I think they've been seeing each other a while. They were probably just afraid to tell us because they thought it would be awkward."

"It *is* awkward," Elaine said sourly, rubbing her stiffening neck.

Still, Ava had looked so *happy*. She'd never, ever seen Ava that happy with a man, not since high school with Mark, laughing and looking up at the guy like he was her own personal God. She turned to Gigi. "You don't mind that Ava's seeing your uncle?"

Gigi looked surprised. "Well, it's a little weird, I guess. But why would I mind? Uncle Simon is one of my favorite people and so is Ava. And it's not like it's incest or anything like that."

"Ew," Elaine said.

"I think it's kind of cool," Gigi said. "You should be happy for Ava. Simon's really a nice guy even if he is superrich."

"I don't actually mind the superrich part," Elaine said. "Don't forget that I'm the corporate sister. You two are the artsy tofu eaters."

"Whatever. But I'm glad Ava found somebody, especially since Sam's applying to colleges this fall and Mark's getting married."

"Mark's getting married?" Elaine had started to stand; the shock of this news made her legs nearly buckle again. "When did *that* happen?"

"Boy, you really have been out of it, I guess."

It should have been an insult, but Gigi hadn't said it that way, so Elaine decided to just agree and try to stand up again before her whole aching body stiffened into this crouched position on the curb.

"Here. Let me help you." Gigi stood first and reached her hand down to Elaine.

Elaine hesitated, then took it. What else could she do? "I'm really sorry," she said again.

"It wasn't your fault," Gigi said. "I told you that."

"Not just for the crash."

"Oh. That's okay." They stood by the side of the road, looking at each other for a minute, then Gigi grinned. It was Dad's grin, wide and flawless, with that dimple in the left cheek. "You might want to call somebody for your car."

"Then what?" Elaine said helplessly, turning to look at the wreck.

"They'll tow it and we'll go have breakfast with Ava and Simon," Gigi said.

"I'm not ready to do that."

"I guess you could get a cab to the bus station and go home," Gigi said. "Beach Plum Island doesn't have a cab service, but there's Port Taxi in Newburyport. Is that what you really want, though? To turn around without seeing Ava? You came all the way up here. Might as well get 'er done."

Where had she heard that phrase? Evan, Elaine realized. "I didn't come up here expecting all this," she said, gesturing at the car, at Gigi. "This was more than I bargained for."

"Yeah, well, that's life, right?" Gigi said, and pulled the cell phone out of her pocket. "You're noodling along and then you're flat on your face. Come on. I'll wait with you while they tow your car. Then we'll walk to Ava's. It's only a mile."

It would be the longest mile of her life, Elaine thought, but maybe the most important journey. A great blue heron flew low across the marsh in front of them, its long legs dangling, the wings magnificent, glinting silver as it glided over the water. A bird that looked too primitive to survive, yet it did.

## CHAPTER FIFTEEN

He wanted to see her alone, Peter had said. "Come to Cambridge and we'll have dinner. Just the two of us. I'll get takeout and we can sit on my porch. Charley took the baby over to her mother's."

The boys had spent Wednesday night at their father's, so Ava was planning to spend the night with Simon at his condo. She drove to Cambridge on the way, weaving through the warren of streets around Tufts University to Porter Square.

Then her GPS led her even deeper through these oddly mixed neighborhoods of transitional housing, student ghettos, and young professionals, with the grander Victorians near Mass Ave occupied by professors, she imagined, or the business owners of the shops and bars and restaurants around the universities. It was like driving in one of those horrible Grand Theft Auto games the boys loved to play, with people jumping out in front of her in cop cars, on motorcycles, on foot, on skateboards, bikes, even a unicycle. She was shaking a little by the time she turned onto Peter's street.

He was waiting for her on the porch, sitting on one of the rockers. Ava couldn't get over the shock of recognition as she walked up the flagstone path, some kind of internal compass that must make you gravitate toward people who looked and felt familiar. Maybe it was the same innate sense animals had that drove them into herds or flocks; even sheep could recognize faces.

Whatever the reason, Peter was unmistakably family, just like Gigi and Elaine. They were connected by something other than pieces of paper, and that blood connection couldn't be completely severed by distance or years apart.

Peter heard her footsteps and stood up, called a greeting. He was dressed in a faded red T-shirt that suited his complexion, long plaid shorts, and sandals: a Cambridge professional's weekend uniform. He didn't use the cane to come down the steps to greet her; she supposed he must know his own home and yard well enough that it wasn't necessary.

As Ava approached him, she thought of his school, Thompson, and the years it must have taken those teachers and Peter's family to undo the nearly feral upbringing he'd had with Aunt Finley. She felt sorry about that, but happy that somebody had turned him into a loving man with an open heart.

They sat together on the creaky rocking chairs—Peter made a joke about how he liked furniture to make noise so he could find it—and peppered each other with questions. Ava told him everything she knew about their parents, how they'd met and what kept them apart, about their mother trying to keep him, running away from the nuns with him despite being only fifteen and frightened. About their father's frustration at having his name omitted from the birth certificate and his determination to find Peter, a mission he'd passed on to his daughters.

"I couldn't have found you without Gigi," Ava said. "She was pretty determined."

"Gigi's pretty amazing," Peter said happily.

He told her more about his own upbringing. He'd been taken from Aunt Finley's and placed in a foster home on a dairy farm. "My most lingering memory of that place is of how warm the milk was, when the other kids taught me how to drink it straight from an udder. Oh yeah, and how this one time a hissing goose chased me."

He had no idea what kind of beast was after him, Peter admitted with a laugh. "I only knew I was terrified. The goose chased me right into a pigsty because I couldn't see where I was going. They had to spray me down with the hose in the cow barns afterward. That farmer had no problem letting me run wild in the farmyard with the other kids, which I suppose is why social services took me out of there. But that was the first place I remember being truly happy, because I was treated just like everybody else."

There had been three foster homes in four years, and Peter gave up thinking he'd ever be placed in a permanent home. Then, when he was eight years old, he was adopted. He'd spent the rest of his childhood in Eliot, Maine, in a classic New England Cape on the water, with two older sisters and a golden retriever. "It was everything a kid could hope to have," he said simply. "People who love you, a dog to play with, and the smell of the sea."

His mother had encouraged him to apply for the Thompson School scholarship after his father died of a stroke; Peter hadn't wanted to do it because he didn't want to leave home. His uncle, the one blinded during his tour in Vietnam, had been adamant that he take it when the school called to say Peter had won the scholarship.

"He told me I could live in a corner of the world, like I was doing now, and think I was happy, or I could live in the whole world and know where I belonged," Peter said. After that, it had been easy to get into college, to pursue his dream of helping other people the way he'd been helped by others. "I specialize in working with families," he said. "I've been trying to put families together my whole life, because I felt so lucky to find one of my own."

"Were you ever angry at our parents for giving you up?" Ava asked. "I would have been."

Peter shrugged. "Maybe. Probably. But that was all so long ago, and I was very busy being happy, after spending those first few years of my life in the dark. Quite literally, in the dark."

"So you do remember Aunt Finley's house, where she kept you in that back bedroom."

"Not every minute," he said. "She let me into the kitchen for meals, and sometimes I sat in the living room with her and listened to the television. She had this little harness and leash contraption. My wife says she's seen other people use them with toddlers, so I suppose it wasn't all that barbaric. It just seemed so to me at the time. All I wanted to do was run around outside, even if it meant falling down."

"Finley was sad about how everything ended up."

"Huh," Peter said, his face clouding. "If you say so."

Ava reached into her bag and pulled out the little stuffed dog she'd taken from Peter's bedroom and mended. "Hold out your hands," she said. When he did, laughing a little, she placed the dog between them. "This is from your room at Aunt Finley's. She'd kept it, all those years, right on your bed."

Peter's face was open, naked with vulnerability despite the shadow of a beard on his strong jaw. He closed his eyes and concentrated on moving his hands over the dog. "It can't be mine," he said softly. "Mine had only one eye."

Ava swallowed hard. So he did remember. "I fixed it," she said.

His eyes flew open, the irises dark. He reached for her with one hand; it crept up her arm, her shoulder, her face. Ava held her breath

as Peter moved his fingers lightly over her mouth, her nose, her eyes
and hair. "Why?" he whispered.

"Because I knew we'd find you. I wanted to give it to you so
you'd know that your family never forgot about you," she said, and
leaned into him then, gathering her brother into her arms.

Elaine had just gotten home from work when the doorbell rang. Had
to be a mistake. Nobody ever rang her doorbell after work, unless
she'd ordered takeout or convinced Gabe to come over. They'd taken
it slow, seeing each other only once last week and again at the beginning of this week, both times for just a few hours. Nothing she did
or said had convinced Gabe to sleep with her, which was frustrating,
but in a way also exhilarating. And maybe, too, a relief. He wasn't
with her just to sleep with her. Gabe was with *her*. And kissing him
made the waiting sweeter.

Last week, Gabe had helped her sort through finding another
car in a hurry, convincing her that a Toyota Prius was just the thing
for the city. She'd resisted. "Not my style," she'd said. "That's a total
do-gooder's car. Next thing you know, I'd be wearing T-shirts with
slogans."

"Who's the one working the suicide prevention hotline?" Gabe
had argued. "Besides, wouldn't a smart businesswoman want a car
that's less likely to be broken into than a BMW, more fuel efficient,
and easy to park, especially if she's trekking up to Beach Plum Island every weekend?"

"Not every weekend," Elaine said. "Not unless you come with
me."

He hadn't, yet. But Gabe had promised that he would come
with her to Ava's tomorrow, to hear Gigi sing at a birthday party for
Peter. It would be an ordeal. Elaine still couldn't wrap her mind

around the idea of Ava being with Simon, of all people, despite the fact that Simon had been so gracious, dealing with the police after the car accident and then leaving her alone with Ava to apologize and cry and, well, to basically leak all over the place while Evan and Sam crept around the house like visitors at a zoo where some exotic animal was dying. Or giving birth.

Okay, yes, that was a better metaphor: last weekend, she'd given birth to yet another Elaine, a different, better sister to Ava and Gigi, she hoped. Someone who could make amends and accept what came her way with more grace and less fury. Jesus, it was hard, though. She still wasn't sure she was ready for this big meet-and-greet birthday party tomorrow. The idea of it made her feel nauseous with fear. By now, Elaine had heard the stories Ava and Gigi had told about how they'd tracked down Peter, gone to his office, his house. The guy would have to know that she was the one hold-out, the family member who hadn't wanted to look for him.

The door buzzed again. Some people had no manners. Elaine stomped over to the intercom, pressed the button, and shouted, "What!" into the speaker.

There was a brief—and she imagined panicked—silence. Then a man's gentle voice. "I'm sorry to bother you, Miss Barrett, but I'm here to collect for the Seva Foundation. I was told you might want to make a donation."

"You were told wrong," Elaine said icily, her thumb firmly pressed on the button. "Who gave you this address? Don't you know soliciting is prohibited in this neighborhood?"

"Oh. My apologies." The man sounded genuinely contrite. "I was given this address by a Miss Ava Barrett. She seemed sure you might have something for our organization. We provide eye care services to people in need. I can come back another time if this isn't convenient."

Ava! That figured. Ava was probably going to pour her money—what little she had—into charities for blind people to make up for whatever had happened to Peter in his pitiful life. Well, Elaine supposed she could do this much for her sister. Then she could tell the guy to go away and put her on their "do not call" list with a clear conscience.

"All right. Just a minute. I'll be right down," Elaine said.

She slipped her feet into moccasins, threw a sweater on over her tank top, then grabbed a handful of dollar bills out of her purse and went downstairs. She peered through the spy hole first, of course—God, all she needed was another mugging—and saw that the caller was, indeed, a handsome guy with a cane and dark glasses, which immediately made her feel contrite.

How the hell did a blind guy have the nerve and ability to navigate strange streets at night and ring other people's doorbells?

Wait, scratch that: it wouldn't matter to a blind guy if it was day or night. Duh. But shouldn't he at least have a companion, the way the Jehovah's Witnesses always did, in case things turned ugly?

Elaine opened the door, expecting to see an envelope or a folder in the man's hand for the money, but he wasn't carrying anything. "I'm here," she said, then realized this was unnecessary. Of course he must have heard the door open.

The man removed his glasses. "Hello, Elaine."

She stumbled back into the doorway, literally blown backward by the shock of seeing her own tilted brown eyes and Ava's broad cheekbones melded together in the face of this handsome dark-haired man on her front step.

"Peter," she whispered.

He grinned, and the smile transformed his face so that she no longer saw the separate features or the ghosts of family members, but just the face of a good-looking man in his forties with deep smile lines and a strong jaw. A man who was dressed like an academic, in a tweed jacket over a black T-shirt and khakis, but who stood like a soldier, straight and square.

"If I didn't think you'd fall off that step, I'd hit you," she said. "Jesus, what the hell kind of stupid stunt is this to pull?"

Peter laughed. "A stunt that worked, thank God. I didn't think you'd see me otherwise."

That word, "see," had a whole other meaning here, Elaine supposed, but she was too muzzy-headed with shock to contemplate the enormity of the moment, only the small things: a car driving slowly down her street, the sound of a dog barking in the distance, the hissing light rain that had started to fall, and the frantic flutter of her own heartbeat trapped behind her rib cage.

"I'm getting wet," Peter said mildly. "Mind if I come in?"

"Can you do stairs?" Elaine asked, and could have kicked herself. He wasn't crippled. Her brother had a PhD, for God's sake. In psychology! He was a therapist of some kind and had probably already read her emotions like an open book.

But Peter didn't seem to think the question was stupid. He simply asked, "Do you have a railing? Otherwise, you can just tell me what floor you're on and how many stairs."

"No railing. Second floor, twenty-one stairs," Elaine answered automatically, because she had counted them back when she was still drinking and trying to make it upstairs without falling. "Is it better for you to go ahead of me or behind me?"

"Well, if you go ahead of me, I can hear your footsteps and know when you've reached the landing," Peter said. "But the obvious advantage of going ahead of you is that if I fall, you get to catch me."

The joke took her by surprise. She laughed, snorted, really, and said, "I think I'll precede you, then, thank you," and turned around to lead the way up the stairs, listening closely to make sure he wasn't fumbling or falling behind her.

She was glad she'd had the cleaning team into her apartment this week. Of course Peter couldn't see dust, but she imagined he must be sensitive to whatever was underfoot, and to smells as well. She'd microwaved leftover Chinese for dinner; the kitchen smelled of ginger, though, so that wasn't too bad.

Once they were upstairs, Elaine realized she should guide Peter to a chair, because otherwise how would he know where they were? Before she could speak, though, he was tapping with his cane, delicate pecking motions. He reminded her of the great blue herons on Beach Plum Island, with his height, his thin strong frame, and the determined jut of his chin on his neck.

In seconds Peter had settled into her most comfortable chair, a tall flowered armchair with a matching hassock that had been her mother's favorite place to read to Elaine when she was little and their family still lived in the Newburyport house. Before everything fell apart, it was their nightly ritual, Elaine cradled in her mother's arms, sometimes not even looking at whatever picture book her mother held but drawing on a pad of paper Mom always kept on the table next to the chair.

Elaine hadn't been able to stand the thought of leaving the chair in the house for Katy; she'd taken it to the cabin in Maine when they left, then brought it back to Boston after Mom died. Such pointless anger, that rage against Katy and Gigi. Now it was mixed with sorrow: her mother had never held Peter and read to him. He had never known her at all.

"Nice place," Peter said, glancing around as if he could see it.

Maybe if you were blind from birth, you found other ways of appreciating spaces, Elaine decided: the feeling of a rug underfoot, the furniture, the smell from an open window. Her front windows were open despite the traffic sounds because she loved the sweet fragrance of the huge white flowering bushes that flanked the condo building like snowdrifts.

"Thank you," Elaine said. "Can I get you something? Tea? Water?"

"Do you have any beer?"

Elaine shook her head, then realized he couldn't see that. Such a learning curve here. "No, sorry. I don't drink."

He raised an eyebrow, but didn't comment on this. Only said, "Water would be great. Thanks."

"Flat or sparkling? Ice or no ice?"

He steepled his fingers, rested his chin on them, considering. "Sparkling on ice. More festive that way."

Peter was trying to lighten this moment, and Elaine appreciated that. She wasn't sure if she could reciprocate. Right now, she felt as if her skin were cracking and about to split in various places, to peel right off her and expose the nerves beneath.

She brought him the glass, then sat on the couch across from him. He had relaxed against the chair, the cane resting against one side of it, and he'd put a foot up on the hassock.

"You sure know how to make yourself at home," she said. She'd meant it as a compliment, but as a shadow crossed her brother's face, she could see how the remark could be taken the wrong way. "Sorry. I didn't mean . . . "

"No, it's fine," he said, waving a hand. "I'm used to getting around on my own because most people don't know what the hell to do when a blind person comes to visit. They're afraid of being too helpful, and some people are. Other people are oblivious. One of the most important things we learned at Thompson—that's where I went to high school—is how to navigate situations independently, and also how to accept the idea that other people don't know what we can do for ourselves unless they ask us, which most are too scared to do."

Elaine had never thought about this before. Now she felt terrible about never asking people with disabilities whether they needed help. She'd always been afraid of insulting them.

"Why are you here?" she said. "I was planning to go to your party at Ava's tomorrow. You didn't need to come all the way here."

That eyebrow again. "All the way here? You mean, like ten minutes in a cab to cross the river from Cambridge? We're practically neighbors."

Elaine thought about her date with Gabe in Harvard Square. She didn't have good memories of Cambridge. But maybe that would change now. "Still," she said, "what's the point?"

He laughed. He had a deep laugh, deeper than she would have expected, given his thin build. "I love it that you're not groveling and apologetic for not coming to see me with Ava and Gigi that first night they found me."

"I didn't know they were doing that," Elaine said. "But you're probably right that I wouldn't have gone with them. I wasn't ready. I was working on some other things at the time. My own issues. Grief. Anger." She took a deep breath, then added, "And I'm an alcoholic."

Peter whistled. "Wow. I wish all my clients had your backbone. You just zero in on the problems and meet them head-on, don't you?"

"I'm not sure what you mean." Elaine was trembling so hard she had to put down her glass of sparkling water, not even bothering with finding a coaster in the drawer of the coffee table.

She still couldn't believe this was her brother, or that she had a blind man sitting in her living room, or that she was an alcoholic and, furthermore, had just admitted it to a man who was both a total stranger and, with Ava, her closest blood relative.

Peter leaned forward, his face in shadows now, hawkish with that long nose. "I meant that as a compliment," he said. "It's a gift, being so clear-sighted about your feelings."

"I'm not."

"Oh, I think you are. You know who you are, Elaine. You've just been peeling away the layers, one by one, and discovering there's more underneath. You should be proud of yourself. It wouldn't have made sense for you to want me in your life until you knew what your life *was*."

"Right," she snorted. "Thanks for the psychobabble. If I wanted a shrink, I'd pay for one."

Peter shrugged, sat back in the chair. "Anyway, in answer to your earlier question, I came here tonight for a few reasons. The first one is that I was pretty sure, after hearing about you from Ava, that you might find a way to duck out of the party tomorrow."

Elaine made a sputtering noise of protest, though of course that thought had crossed her mind.

Her brother held up a hand to stop her. "The other reason is that you were close to our mother. I wanted to know what she was like, especially at the end. Ava doesn't seem to know much about that."

"You don't want to know, either." Elaine felt a chill go through her. "Trust me. It wasn't good."

"I gathered that." He sighed, sipped his drink. His fingers were long and thin on the glass, like her own. Like their mother's. "Do you feel comfortable talking about her? Not the bitter end, maybe, but something? What kind of music did she like?"

"Rock and roll," Elaine said at once, making him laugh. "Seriously. She and Dad were hard-core rockers when they were teenagers. She had the hots for Mick Jagger."

"Wow," Peter said, still smiling. "That, I wouldn't have guessed. What else?"

Elaine closed her eyes. "Mom loved to read. She never went to college, but she seemed like she did. She was so smart and well-spoken. She was in a book club in Newburyport and took the readings seriously, making notes, looking things up about authors. She read us lots of stories when we were kids. She'd really get into it, acting out the voices. I used to hate sitting still, but she figured out early on that I'd listen to her read me a story if I could draw or color while she did it. Later, when it was just Mom and me in Maine, I used to read to her while she drew. I guess we went full circle. I never thought about that before."

Elaine was quiet for a minute. She'd forgotten about those contented times with her mother. She still had some of the drawings Mom had made in the last months of her life. She liked to work with colored pencils and used vivid colors, bold strokes. For the first time, Elaine realized that must be where Ava had gotten her eye for color.

There was one particular drawing her mother had done that Elaine had always loved, a picture of purple lupine in a field, a red-roofed barn in the background. That had hung on the refrigerator for a long time; Elaine had put up her mother's drawings that last year together in the same way her mother used to hang up school papers for Elaine and Ava.

She swallowed hard. Maybe in a way she had taken good care of her mother, giving her those moments of peace. That was something to hang on to.

"Mom wasn't ever a truly happy person," Elaine said. "She tried to hide her depression. She functioned pretty well for a lot of years, but then, I don't know, when Ava left home, Mom left, too, emotionally. She retreated into herself and it took a lot to bring her back. Aunt Finley thinks it's because Mom never forgave herself for giving you up."

"She was young," Peter said. "How could she have kept me? Girls didn't, back then, unless their families helped."

"You must have thought about this a lot over the years."

Peter nodded. "I have, but it's good to hear the real story. It's too easy to have monsters living in your head unless you find the truth and put those babies to bed."

"I keep tucking my monsters into bed, but they keep getting up again."

"Naughty things, those mind monsters," Peter said, and they laughed.

"I'm glad you came," Elaine said. "Thank you."

He shrugged. "I was feeling guilty, letting your sisters do all the work."

"So what happens now?"

Peter stood up, leaned on his cane. "Now I go home to my wife and daughter, who I hope you'll meet tomorrow at the party. But if you don't feel like coming, Elaine, if it's too much for you, it's okay for you to stay home."

She stood up, too. "I see. Is this your therapist self giving me permission?"

"No. This is your big brother, being supportive."

Elaine couldn't move, paralyzed by emotions too powerful and complicated to name. Peter came to her, feeling his way until the cane hit her bare foot.

"Ow," she whispered.

"Sorry," he said, and put his arms around her. "I promise it'll hurt less with time."

Okay, it did feel weird at first, Gigi had to admit, setting up with the band in the middle of a Sunday afternoon instead of playing after dark. She wasn't sure how she felt about facing the big glass windows overlooking the rippling surf while she sang. For one thing, it made her squint, and she'd spent a lot of time getting her makeup on right. Her hair, too. It was all blond, now, with just one hot pink streak Neal had put in for her, saying it would look cool.

He wasn't even here today. They'd decided to make this a family birthday party for Peter, and that's why they were playing in the afternoon, so Peter could bring his wife and baby. Everyone had teased Gigi about how the baby, Emma, had punked-out hair like hers and would probably grow up to be a rocker.

It was true: Emma had a thatch of bright red hair that stood almost straight up, giving her "one badass attitude," Sam had declared, jouncing the baby on his knee, making Ava reprimand him for swearing and making Peter tip his head back and laugh.

"You got that right," Peter said. "My daughter is all about attitude."

Then Gigi had held the baby for the first time, and Emma had fastened her dark eyes on Gigi's face and smiled in that toothless damp way babies had that made you want to do anything in the world to keep them smiling.

"Hey," she whispered close to the baby's ear, though not close enough for those fat fingers to grab her earring. "I'm your auntie. It's time we had another girl in this family. Welcome."

"Give her back," Sam said. "You don't want to corrupt her with some feminist crap."

"Right," Evan said. "She needs to learn all about real stuff, like computer games."

"God help her," Ava said, rolling her eyes, while Charley, clearly comfortable in a big crowd, passed around the cake she'd made for Peter's birthday and laughed.

They'd played a full set after the cake and ice cream, surprising Peter with his favorite Springsteen song, communicated via text message from Charley when Ava asked her last week. He'd gotten up and danced, looking about as goofy as a blind guy dancing could look, but when he stood at the microphone with Gigi to sing the chorus, his voice blended pretty well with hers, making it hard for her to keep going because all she could hear was how much he sounded like Dad, singing with her.

Luckily everybody else was dancing by then, even Elaine and her friend Gabe, whose curls seemed to be doing a dance of their own on top of his head, separate from his pillowy body. He definitely wasn't the sort of guy Gigi would have expected Elaine to choose, but Gabe was cool. He even picked up the drumsticks at one point and played decently enough.

After that, they took a break. Some of them drifted to the kitchen for cold drinks. Simon and Gabe went out to buy more ice and a cooler, too, since of course today of all days, Ava's freezer had quit. At the last minute, Katy had decided to go with them, saying she wanted avocado for the salad she'd brought and the guys wouldn't know how to choose a ripe one. Gigi thought this might have been an excuse; her mom and Elaine were being polite but still having trouble making any conversation that didn't sound scripted. Still, it was a start.

Gigi grabbed a glass of lemonade and went outside where Ava was watering her tomato plants on the patio with a tall metal can that glinted in the sun. Ava glanced over at Gigi and smiled. "If I don't do this now, I might forget, and it isn't supposed to rain again until the end of the week. The poor things are parched."

The tomato plants were tall and thick with ripe tomatoes; Gigi picked one and bit into it like an apple. It was almost that sweet. She wiped the juice from her chin with one hand and said, "Do you think Peter likes his party?"

Ava put down the watering can and came over to drape an arm around her shoulders. "How could he not, with the best live music in town?"

"You really think we sound okay?" Sometimes Gigi couldn't hear herself sing with the noise of the band around her; it was like she was inside the music.

"Definitely. All those hours of practicing have paid off. Too bad you have to go back to school soon."

Gigi rolled her eyes. "Don't remind me," she said.

She didn't really mean it. Her mother had agreed, after she and Sam and Evan had spent an entire night convincing her, that it would be all right for Gigi to try her sophomore year at the public school, if Gigi signed up for honors classes and joined the chorus and did theater after school. She wouldn't have to see Lydia, and instead she could look forward to seeing Evan and Sam and Sarah and Neal in the lunchroom, at least, and Sarah might even be in some of her classes.

"Hey, can I crash your party?" Elaine said from behind them. She came forward tentatively, carrying her own glass of lemonade. Her black eye had faded to a pale purple bruise. "You killed that Springsteen song for Peter. Nice job."

Gigi felt her face flush with pleasure. She hadn't really seen Elaine since the accident. "Thanks."

"Hey," Elaine said to Ava, setting her glass down on the table. "I have something for you in Gabe's car. I almost forgot. Wait here a sec."

A few minutes later, Sam and Evan came through the gate from the driveway, carrying two more Adirondack chairs painted to match Ava's. They set the chairs down on either side of the pair by the door and retreated back into the house, complaining about being abused for their muscles.

"Oh my God," Ava said, putting her hands to her face. "Thank you! They're perfect."

Elaine grinned and sat down in one, patted the arms. "Yeah,

well. I figured two chairs might not be enough for your patio any-more," she said. "It's kind of a birthday present for Peter, too."

Ava leaned down to hug her, then sat down in one of the old chairs, leaving a chair empty between her own and Elaine's. "I be-lieve this is yours," she said to Gigi, pointing.

Gigi sat down, too, tipping her face to the sun and resting her arms on the broad smooth wooden armrests, hearing her brother laughing in the kitchen behind her, a song playing in her head. It was a song she wanted to write, a song about this island, the dunes and the herons and the sharp sting of salt in the air.

Music for her family, sad and sweet at the same time.

# ACKNOWLEDGMENTS

I truly do believe it takes a village to raise a child. When it comes to writing novels, it takes several villages.

In my home village, my husband, Dan, is my biggest emotional supporter, cheerleader, and bringer-of-meals. I would be eating tuna out of a can every day without you, honey. I am also lucky to be graced by the presence of my mother, Sally Robinson, who imbued me with a love of books and is a keen first reader. My children—Drew, Blaise, Taylor, Maya, and Aidan—are always and forever supporting me as well, and inspiring me with their own adventures. My life would be hollow without them. My brother Donald makes his pride clear and wows me with his tales of travel and forging iron (literally), while my brother Philip keeps making music.

Farther afield, I have wonderful in-laws, David and Christine, who not only take time to read what I write, but then pen thoughtful notes to me about the books. My father's family in Ohio makes me feel like a celebrity, and I am especially grateful to Jeff and Barbara, who gave me a sanctuary in their amazing garden at a time when I needed it most.

In my publishing village, I thank my stars every day for leading me to my agent, Richard Parks. He continues to be the nicest man in New York, never failing to pick up the phone when I call for hand-holding or editorial suggestions. He is, by now, family to me as well.

I am also blessed to have found an incredibly savvy, thoughtful, empathic editor in Tracy Bernstein, who I hope will let me crown her "My Editor for Life." New American Library publisher Kara Welsh has my heartfelt gratitude for supporting my career. *Beach Plum Island* is a better book because of all of your faith and hard work.

In my village of writers, I want to thank Toby Neal, who found the perfect sanctuary for our writing retreat in Mendocino, California, as I started *Beach Plum Island*, and Emily Ferrara, who accompanied me to Boothbay Harbor, Maine, while I finished the book—with a black eye and a concussion, just like Elaine (though not from drinking, thank God). Susan Straight, my friend and mentor for so many years, provided wonderful companionship during the middle of the book as we spent a glorious two weeks writing on Prince Edward Island.

Other writers have been instrumental not only in helping me with tricky bits of the manuscript, but with keeping my sanity intact, especially Melanie Wold, who gave me her Boothbay Harbor house as a retreat; and Elisabeth Brink, Maddie Dawson, Diane Debrovner, Lorraine Glennon, Terri Giuliano Long, Kate Kelly, Cathleen Medwick, Amy Sue Nathan, Carla Panciera, Sandi Kahn Shelton, Ginnie Smith, and Jane Ward, who all made me believe I really am a novelist.

How lucky am I to be a member of such villages? The luckiest.

**Holly Robinson** is a ghostwriter and journalist whose work appears regularly in national venues such as *Better Homes and Gardens*, Huffington Post, *Ladies' Home Journal*, *More*, Open Salon, and *Parents*. She is the author of *The Gerbil Farmer's Daughter: A Memoir* and *The Wishing Hill*, her first NAL Accent novel. She holds a BA in biology from Clark University and an MFA in creative writing from the University of Massachusetts, Amherst.

CONNECT ONLINE

authorhollyrobinson.com

# BEACH PLUM ISLAND

## HOLLY ROBINSON

*This Conversation Guide is intended to enrich the
individual reading experience, as well as encourage us
to explore these topics together—because books,
and life, are meant for sharing.*

# A CONVERSATION WITH HOLLY ROBINSON

*Q. What gave you the original story idea for* Beach Plum Island?

A. Every writer's mind is a bit like a junk drawer. Just as I stash odd rubber bands, bits of string, coins, bottle caps, and mystery objects in my kitchen drawer, I keep interesting stories, scenery, and characters in some dark, cluttered compartment of my mind. When I need an idea, I pull out the drawer and marvel at what tumbles out. In this case, what tumbled out was a story my mom told me years ago about babysitting for a local family in her small Maine town. She was twelve years old when she went to this neighbor's house and was told, "The kids are asleep, so you won't have much to do. All we ask is that you don't go into the back bedroom." Soon after the parents went out for the evening, my mother heard a strange sound behind that bedroom door and opened it to find a blind little boy, who came running out and tried to climb on everything— and clung to my mom. That story kernel blossomed into this complex, emotional novel.

*Q. You published your first novel,* The Wishing Hill, *in July 2013. Was the process of writing this novel different from writing that one?*

A. Absolutely! I wrote *The Wishing Hill* organically—that is, by the seat of my pants, floundering around until the story evolved. When my wonderful editor, Tracy Bernstein, asked me for a synopsis describing the second novel, I was horrified. A synopsis is odiously hard to write, plus I was worried that I might lose interest in the book if I knew how it ended. Instead, the opposite happened: Writing a synopsis provided me with a blueprint for *Beach Plum Island*, which ended up making the writing go faster. I still had plenty of room to play around and the characters continuously surprised me. I am now a firm believer in writing a synopsis when plotting out a novel.

*Q. At one point in* Beach Plum Island, *Ava reflects that motherhood is a "business, complete with compromises and disappointing returns for your investments, with budgets and schedules and task lists and surly underlings." On balance, do you feel like being a mother has helped or hurt your career as a writer?*

A. Like most working mothers, I feel a combination of frustration and joy on most days as I juggle family, household, and work responsibilities. It's probably true that I would have started publishing novels sooner if I hadn't had children. However, I feel, as Ava does, that motherhood has helped define not only who I am as a person, but who I am as a writer, in a profound way. I feel incredibly blessed to have both my family and work that I love. Who cares if the vacuuming doesn't get done?

*Q. A lot of the tensions in this novel arise because a father leaves one family to create another. Do you have any experience with blended families?*

A. I do. I married my second husband when our children—a boy and a girl from each side—were six, seven, eight, and nine years old. We then added another child of our own two years later, which gave us the "yours, mine, and ours" sort of blended family. It has been a happy experience for us, overall, but not without struggles along the way, due to challenges unique to navigating two distinct family cultures. I love writing about blended families because I think it gives readers hope that these families can be just as happy as so-called "normal" biological ones.

Q. *There are a lot of surprising facts in this book, such as those about the adoption process, horseback riding, pottery, and schools for the visually impaired. Did you do a lot of research as you were writing?*

A. I did. I love doing research for my novels, because I always learn surprising things. For instance, as I was writing this book, I took pottery lessons at a local studio. In any subject, though, after I've gathered as much information as I can, I try to use as little of it as possible. I hate reading novels where the writer does an "information dump" in the middle of a crucial scene, so that you're suddenly aware you're reading a book and not living the story anymore.

Q. *Are you working on another novel now?*

A. Yes, I've just started a novel called *Lake Utopia*. This is another powerfully emotional novel based on a family story my mother told me about the mysterious drowning of a child. Like *The Wishing Hill* and *Beach Plum Island*, it unfolds like a tensely paced mystery, with new secrets unveiled in every chapter.

# QUESTIONS FOR DISCUSSION

1. Elaine chooses to live with her mother during her last year of life, while Ava steers clear of her mother's mental health issues and concentrates on her own family. Did these women make the right choices?

2. Why is it so much easier for Ava to acknowledge that Gigi is their sister than it is for Elaine, and how do their attitudes toward their father's second family help determine the events in the novel?

3. Gigi and Elaine both have unsatisfactory sexual encounters in *Beach Plum Island*. What propels them into these relationships? Do you think their behavior is realistic or not?

4. Ava tells Simon that we each "carry landscapes inside us." What does she mean by this? If you had to describe a landscape to represent your own life, what would that landscape look like?

5. At one point, Ava says to Gigi, "Nobody outside a marriage can really know what's happening on the inside of it." How is this true for the married couples in this book? In your own life?

6. Ava compares raising a child to making a piece of art. Do you think parenting is more of an art or a science?

7. Do you agree with Elaine's assessment early in the novel that Ava has "no idea what it was like to live in the real world"? Or is Elaine deluding herself by thinking she's more worldly than her sister?

8. Ava and Elaine both fall in love with men who they think are "wrong" for them. Why do they think that, and what makes these relationships work, contrary to their own expectations?

9. What role do sibling relationships play in this novel? How have your own sibling relationships helped shape your life?

10. At some point, Elaine thinks, "Why are we here? Why do one thing and not another? Why love one person and not someone else, or anyone at all, if everyone's story ends the same way?" Do you think she answers these questions by the end of *Beach Plum Island*? Have you answered them in your own life?

11. Many women gave Peter up when he was a child: Suzanne, Marie, and Finley. What were the societal and cultural reasons each woman did what she did? How might things have gone differently if Peter had been born now instead of in the nineteen seventies?